finding Jim

Two friends on a Worldwide Search for the Lizard King

Rebecca J. Johnston

For information regarding permission, please write to:
info@barringerpublishing.com
Barringer Publishing, Naples, Florida
www.barringerpublishing.com

Cover and Layout by Linda S. Duider
Cape Coral, Florida

ISBN: 978-1-954396-90-6
Library of Congress Cataloging-in-Publication Data
Finding Jim: Two Friends on a Worldwide Search for the Lizard King
Rebecca J. Johnston

Printed in U.S.A.

To BJ, my favorite person to road trip and shenanigan with.

"Blessings be with them, and eternal praise,
Who gave us nobler loves, and nobler cares!
The Poets, who on earth have made us heirs
Of truth and pure delight by heavenly lays"

—WORDSWORTH

"The music is your special friend"

—MORRISON

Contents

Author's Note

Dear readers,

Thank you for taking the time to pick up my book. It represents three years of hard work, editing, tears, and laughter that have resulted in what appears to be ridiculousness and absolutely nothing serious. It balanced my overly serious doctoral work and for that I will always be thankful to Tabby and Charlie.

Speaking of thanks, I will also be forever grateful to the Key West Literary Seminar for the opportunity to serve as a Writer-in-Residence—your encouragement and hospitality sustained this book's creation.

As a warning, as with my previous book, *Not to Keep*, which one reviewer warned readers should "be aware" contains "foul language", this book contains "foul language", and possibly some fowl language. *Finding Jim* has been reviewed as being "full of snark" and having "hefty doses of sarcasm." If this novel had been written a few hundred years ago, I may have been burned as a witch at the stake. So, for those of you willing to charge ahead with a few "foul" words and a whole lot of snark, I wish you well.

One last note of thanks to everyone who has every road tripped with me. While Tabby and Charlie do not represent two people in my life, they are a bit of an amalgamation of many trips and many people I have had the good fortune to know. I have enjoyed every trip, real and imaginary.

Rebecca J Johnston

CHAPTER ONE

Women Seem Wicked[1]

Tabby and Charlie sat on the wet sand letting the coolness soak through their pants. It was too cold for swimming, so they accepted this as the best connection they would get to the portion of the Atlantic that touches South Africa. They missed their home beach.[2] The warm caress of white sand and the soothing blue waters of the Gulf of Mexico always brought them comfort and hope. They'd followed that sense of hope around the world, and so far, they hadn't found the fruition of those hopes and dreams, so they sat and stared into the dark abyss, listening to the sounds of the waves on the shore, and letting their thoughts run away with them.[3] In the morning they would continue looking for Jim, but for now, they would let the sand hold them until the cold drove them to bed. However, to follow their journey, we have to go back to where it began . . . in the long-forgotten halls of Florida State University's Panama City campus. . . .

---

1. Morrison, Jim. "People are Strange." *Strange Days*. Elektra Records, 1967.
2. All Florida girls have home beaches
3. Mostly, their thoughts were wondering if penguins live on all beaches in South Africa or just specific beaches

CHAPTER TWO

Twenty-First Century Foxes[4]

Panama City Beach—a paradise on earth. The white sand beaches seem endless, and if the beach shells don't satisfy, the barrier island across the water will serve up more shells than seems humanly possible.[5] The turquoise water, hedged in by white sand beaches, is filled with people kayaking, dolphin spotting, and driving those weird boats with slides off the back for drunk tourists to play in the waters of Panama City Beach.[6]

If you keep going inland, past the glorious white sand beaches, past the long and terrifying bridge, there, on the left you will see the bay side of Panama City, and right on the shores of the bay, commanding a view of the entire area, is Florida State University's Panama City campus. Long ago, universities realized that they could make more money if they put campuses closer to people who have no education. So, here it sits—a glorious three-story brick building with a park-like lawn and frisbee course looking out over the brackish waters of the bay. If you keep going past the broad,

---

4. Krieger, Robby and Jim Morrison. "Twentieth Century Fox." *The Doors*. Elektra Records, 1967
5. It's not humanly possible as humans do not make shells, but it is possible on Shell Island, and thus the name—Shell Island
6. Beach going tourists are 63% more likely to overindulge than mountain going vacationers.

accessible glass doors, you will find employees, like bees in a hive, running around getting the campus ready for the students about to bust from their cars and dorm rooms into this hall of learning. This is where we find our brown-haired heroines: Tabitha Divine and Charlie Eliot. Like 89% of college professors, Tabitha and Charlie are adjuncts.[7;8] As with most part-time jobs, when the full-time employees need hours, part-time hours get cut. Unlike many career fields, when professors are full-time and seasoned, they often retreat to the bare minimum of work, since they can no longer be fired (without a sex scandal or something of that nature), so there is no need to work.

That is not the case for Charlie and Tabitha, or Tabby, as she prefers.[9] Tabby and Charlie have a corner office in the basement. They usually leave off the basement part when they describe their office to family and friends. To all who ask, they're distinct professors with a corner office. Charlie even won a professor of distinction award, well, adjunct of distinction, and the girls are leading a study abroad trip to Ireland this coming year, so they feel pretty distinguished. In fact, Charlie was how Tabby was awarded the right to lead a trip next summer, and she was also how they landed a college funded professional development trip to Ireland during the fall semester, so that they could prepare for their study abroad. While the college understood a history professor such as Charlie taking students to Ireland, given Ireland's vast history and connections with the United States, Tabby would be the first math professor to lead a study abroad trip anywhere. Turns out

---

7. "Survey of College Professorships." Journal of Modern Colleges and Universities. South Dakota University Press. 3 March 2019. P. 864-66
8. Adjuncts are professors who are just as smart as full professors, but they are stuck on the hamster wheel of broken promises that is academia. They teach almost as many college classes per semester as full-time professors but are paid half as much with the motivating carrot in front of them that if they work hard enough, maybe they will get a full-time job offer one day.
9. Tabby's parents were religious and didn't think about the lifelong consequences of having a name like Tabitha.

administration also does not understand numbers and sees no need for traveling numbers.[10] Charlie and Tabby pulled out all stops and used high academic jargon and some Latin[11] to get Tabby leading the trip the following summer, and the college thought it so odd that math could indeed do study abroad that they decided to send both girls for professional development ahead of the trip.

The trip is why Tabby and Charlie could be found sitting in their corner office planning the semester—their classes felt safe given their upcoming study abroad trip. Classes were starting tomorrow, and they were prepping over Publix turkey subs, or emotional support subs as Charlie likes to call them. Their office was humming with the possibilities of the coming semester, or is that the humming of the constantly running hot water kettle?[12] On the door leading into their office hang signs with both of their names—Dr. Tabby and Dr. Charlie, as they like to be called, along with charts that state their availability[13] and ways to reach them. More importantly, above their names is the sign that defines them and their goals for life and the passion that bonds the two doctors:

If **The doors** *of perception were cleansed, everything would appear to man as it is: infinite.*

—WILLIAM BLAKE

To the full-timers, who rarely venture down to basement offices, the sign appeared to be philosophical in nature, and if we're being

---

10. Studies show that 94.8% of society does not like numbers
11. Hic novus libellus plenus nugarum, which Life has taught means Latin makes everything more believable
12. The girls prefer tea
13. As with most adjuncts, availability means 24/7 availability via classrooms, zoom links, email, phones, Google voice, office hours, and Batman style signs in the sky.

honest, they don't understand it.[14] But to the student who enters in desperate search of help with math, because students rarely need help with the humanities,[15] the sign takes on a new meaning. The sex symbol that is Jim Morrison lives on every wall of Charlie and Tabby's office. Posters of his shirtless wonder hang from every angle, and his eyes gaze down on Charlie and Tabby as they work. Album covers stand on their desks like a kitchen backsplash, and a record player takes up what should've been a desk for their fellow adjunct;[16] music plays throughout their office hours, and on the highest shelf is Tabby's personal favorite—a Jim Morrison bobble head to remind them of their trip to the Rock and Roll Hall of Fame—where Jim Morrison bobble heads have consistently outsold Mick Jagger bobble heads since bobble head appearance in the Hall of Fame in 1994.

Unfortunately, on this day, Tabby and Charlie's dreams of a stable income, stemming from years of education and college debt, are about to be crushed. The bad news comes not from a call, which would allow the receiver to immediately voice a complaint, but from an email. Charlie reads her email first:

> Dear Charlie,
>
> I regret to inform you that due to low enrollment, your schedule has been adjusted to reflect department needs. We look forward to working with you again in the Spring semester.
>
> Dr. Mira Hanson
> Chair of the History Department

---

14. To save themselves from possible embarrassment, professors do not ask questions and are masters at hiding their own confusion.
15. 99.5% of college students need help with math while only .8% of students seek tutoring in the humanities, according to a new study out by the University of Key Largo
16. Who needs Colonel Bob in the office anyway

Change is the end result of all true learning.
~ LEO BUSCAGLIA

Attached to the email was a PDF showing an empty course schedule. Charlie slumped in her chair as she read the email.

"Bullshit. Tabby, I just lost all my classes."

Tabby, ever supportive, rolled her chair over, which is no small feat on 1980s carpet that has never been cleaned.[17]

"All your classes? No, that can't be."

"It can be, but I don't think enrollment is down that much. Mel just emailed an enrollment report that said the opposite. Those full-timers just can't keep their classes full. Trash *Rate My Professor* scores are keeping kids out of their classes."

As Charlie stared at her email, the ding of a new email broke from Tabby's office computer, and she was forced to wheel back to her own desk:

> Dear Tabitha,
>
> I regret to inform you that due to low enrollment your schedule has been adjusted to reflect department needs. We look forward to working with you again in the Spring semester.
>
> Dr. Ron Watson
> Chair of the Math Department

———

Math—the only subject that counts.

---

17. The Journal of American Cleaning Companies reported in 2021 that college campuses are rarely cleaned in their entirety, but in this instance, Facilities has in fact forgotten the building has a basement.

The girls sat in disbelief as their new reality sank in: they had no income for the fall semester, and as roommates, that meant no one would be able to pay rent.

Tabby and Charlie have been teaching together since their graduation and living together even longer. While math and history don't often mingle, due to the insane nature of all that is math, the girls had met at a local trivia night at Panama City's favorite pizza place: Panama Pizzeria. Trivia night was held every Thursday, unbeknownst to the girls who both came with friends, of which they had few. Happy to be out, they took the night as it came and played the game.

When the categories rolled around to 1960s rock, the room silenced.[18] And the questions were all Doors related:

"Which city was Jim Morrison born in?"

"*Melbourne!*" rang out Tabby and Charlie simultaneously.

"In which city was Jim Morrison convicted and sentenced to jail time?"

"*Miami!!*"

"Which band member wrote 'Break on Through to the Other Side'?"

"*Jim Morrison!!*"

"Who was the only rock star to ever be arrested on stage during a performance?"

"*Jim Morrison!*"

And so the night went as Charlie and Tabby put all the other patrons to shame with their vast knowledge of the Doors. They knew they had to meet, and it didn't take long for them to bond over their shared passion for Jim Morrison.[19] Within a month they

---

18. College students in the 90s were too busy making mixed tapes to study old music
19. Who they both believe is still alive

were moving in together, and they've stayed together ever since.[20] Now as they sit in their office that has become their tiny kingdom of control, reality sets in: adjuncts don't get paid over the summer, and as they've been paid so close to the poverty level, savings have always been a dream and never an option. Charlie and Tabby will be homeless before the next semester starts.

"Will there even be a next semester?" moaned Tabby, ever the realist.

"They already funded our study abroad. Our names are all over the campus advertising the trip."

"Well, they did spell our names wrong on the posters."

"That they did," said Charlie with a sigh.

There's only one logical step for the girls—they have to call HR. Truth be told, no one likes HR. The name implies they are a resource to the humans employed by the company, but in reality, they are the overlords who control the resource of human life for any employer.

The college had made the mistake of naming all buildings with letters with the idea that campus would be easier to navigate for freshman if each building had a giant letter on it like something out of *Sesame Street*. The downside to this plan was the letter F. Eventually, it had to be used, and the wise, all-knowing administration had placed the giant F on the side of the administration building, dedicating it forever to be known as "F" building, despite an attempt to change the name to the only non-lettered building after a few years of snickering comments from employees. This was one of the reasons why, after many years working at FSU Panama City, Charlie had no faith in the system represented by HR. Calling Mel at HR seemed like an exercise in futility. Charlie had seen the girl

---

20. Given their obsession with the Lizard King, Jim Morrison, they have stayed single. They do not understand this singleness but believe the right guy will share their obsessions.

at meetings—always wearing a tight skirt that somehow shaped her ample body into curves. Charlie suspected some financially out of reach shape wear, but what adjuncts can and cannot afford doesn't concern Mel.[21]

The girls decided to make the call anyway. To their surprise, Mel answered and was aware of their situation. She offered Charlie no hope for the semester and a reassurance that a full-timer could fill in for their spring trip to Ireland if their classes should all be cut, so no need to worry about the trip. Their tickets to Ireland in the fall were bought in their names, and the professional development trip is safe, thanks to the magnanimous nature of the department and the college as a whole.

"Did she give any hope?" Tabby asked when Charlie hung up the phone.

"No. She ended with some metaphor about hiring being like waves, and that the college is on a part of the wave that means they're cutting and not hiring, or something like that."

"Well, that sounds like bullshit."

"Indeed," said Charlie as she hung her head.

Aware that there was no need for them to come to the office for the remainder of the semester, the girls packed their decorations, records, and bobblehead into boxes from the recycling bin and headed out to their cars.[22] Given their low rate of pay, the girls don't live in the best neighborhood in Panama City; in fact, they don't even live in Panama City. They live outside of the city that is outside of Panama City to the east. While they can't afford to live on the water, they do work at FSU. Their goal was to teach at a school

---

21. HR employees are too busy trying to pick up coworkers to do actual work (ref. The Office)

22. US colleges are notorious for not emptying the recycling bins, in fact, often the decomposition process is in mid cycle by the time someone remembers to take out the bin

Jim had attended,[23] and while he never attended FSU's Panama City campus, he did attend FSU. Close enough. The campus is right on the water with views of the bay from nearly every window, other than basement windows. When leaving campus if you turn to the right, you go over one of the world's longest bridges and past the coolest Navy base.[24] However, that is not the direction the girls live in. No, their apartment is to the left in the small town of Callaway. Well, if we're being honest here, it isn't really Callaway, either. It's the swampy wooded area to the east of Callaway that Bay County likes to forget exists.

Today, though—today has been rough, so the girls decided to brave the bridge and head out. Today deserves a drink, so they headed to their favorite bar.[25] Some might favor the seedy bar side of Panama City, or the college frat side, but not Charlie and Tabby. Years ago, someone built a giant wood pirate boat on the bay. It's not really in the water. It's a building next to the water that gives the illusion of being a boat. Much like the famous song says, this is the place where everybody knows their names.[26] Well, not everyone, but Alec does. Tabby and Charlie have been teaching in Panama City for so long, they now have grown students in places all over this small city. Alec's dad is some kind of antiquities importer, but when he moved to this small Southern town with his mysterious accent and his even more mysterious ability to buy an island, everyone decided he was a mob boss. Tabby and Charlie, however, are open to all kinds of students and don't care what their parents do or don't do for a living. Alec was one of the admitted portions of society that needs math tutoring, and as such, he spent a lot of time listening to

---

23. Given Jim's track record, this gave them several options
24. There is no factual basis for these stated opinions
25. All professors have a favorite bar. It's how they survive working with students.
26. Portnoy, Gary and Judy Hart-Angelo. "Where Everybody Knows Your Name." Applause, 1982.

music in the girls' office while supposedly getting tutoring. Now he manages his father's bar/restaurant/pirate ship, and he always has a table for Tabby and Charlie.

The inside of the pirate ship is much like the outside—red Cedar beams and tables, and faux silver and gold chandeliers hanging from the ceiling, giving the appearance of waterside luxury. The girls walked in past the hostess and took the empty table by the window overlooking the water, which is the table they always sit at. The view is what brings customers in—both locals and tourists. The hostess watched their claim of the best table in the room, but before she could express outrage,[27] Alec walked to their table to personally take their order. They are, after all, his all-time favorite professors, and on the day of his graduation he promised them a seat in any bar he ran.

"What can I get for you two?" Alec asked with his sly grin that masked his true kind nature.

"Tito's with vodka," said Charlie without looking away from her ocean view.

"Cosmo," echoed Tabby, also without looking at Alec.

Alec understood something greater to be at work,[28] so he went and personally prepared the drinks he knew the girls wanted and immediately came back with an order of onion rings[29] that had been slated for another table.

"I don't usually see the two of you in here on your lunch break," Alec said as he took a seat. The girls started mindlessly eating the onion rings without registering the gift of food not ordered.

"We were let go for the semester," responded Charlie between bites.

---

27. Hostesses often feel outrage when a guest challenges their reign over the restaurant kingdom.
28. Bar tenders always see when something more is going on, but they rarely care
29. According to the National Society of Onion Growers, onion rings are best paired with Cosmos

"What? No way. You're the best they have. No way they let you go."

"Indeed, they did," said Tabby with a sigh.

"Want me to have my dad call and raise some hell? Or maybe slash some tires? Make someone disappear?" he said with the raise of an eyebrow and a wink of the eye.

While the image of sweet revenge was momentarily, fleetingly soothing, both girls shook their heads and finished off their first round of drinks. Alec signaled for refills.

"What will you do?"[30]

"No idea. Rent is due and we're both unemployed," Tabby said, giving personal information to a former student that she normally wouldn't give.

"Do you guys want a job? We're always hiring waiters and kitchen staff. Maybe that could tide you over?"

"Maybe," said Charlie. "It probably would pay more, but it's hard to think about such a big change."

"We were planning classes an hour ago. My PPTs are already made," Tabby sighed as the next round of drinks arrived.

"Well, I'll tell you what. My dad still has his place in Key West," Alec said, taking out his phone. "Do you still have the same Google Voice numbers?" the girls nodded as they sipped their drinks and watched the birds playing above the water.

"Great. Listen, my parents are taking care of business in Milan for the rest of the year. The house is empty. I'm texting you the address and key code. Feel free to stay all semester while you sort out your next steps," Alec said as he tapped the table and headed back to work.

---

30. Bar tenders know better than to try to solve the problems of drunk middle-aged women, but Alec is briefly trying

CHAPTER THREE

Unhappy Girls[31]

"Back at the shack," as the girls liked to call their house, well, to be accurate, their trailer,[32] they sat in silence on their lusty, green velvet couch, which had somehow survived from the seventies era in which it was mistakenly created, and thought about life. This was certainly not the twist they thought their lives would take when they spent countless hours working all night to complete three degrees. Fortunately, they had a good spot to think. While the trailer didn't look like much from the outside with its decades old metal siding and original single pane aluminum windows, inside they had created a veritable palace, well, a verdant palace.

They'd had no control over the furniture, as the trailer came furnished with the furniture the original tenant (the landlord's dead mother-in-law) had left behind, so they'd filled any empty space with plants. They'd rented the trailer as soon as they'd accepted jobs at FSU. At the time, they were grateful for any kind of furniture. Newly graduated doctors, of the variety that are mostly useless

---

31. Inspired by Morrison, Jim. "Unhappy Girl." Strange Days. Elektra Records, 1967.
32. While many in and out of Florida feel hurricanes and tornados are drawn to trailers, actually, it is the high percentage of trailer parks in Florida that makes them being hit by said weather more likely. Trailer parks are hidden from tourists by the state of Florida through massive amounts of annual construction.

and cannot actually save lives, have no money for furniture. The landlords (unfortunately named the Bunderoffs) had only changed the furniture in the bedroom by adding a second single bed when they'd developed the hope that their adult children would visit them.[33] They had a son and a daughter, and when the mother-in-law had died, leaving them the trailer paid in full, saving it for their children seemed the right thing to do, but after it sat vacant a few months, they'd put it up for rent and rented it to the first people who stopped by—Tabby and Charlie.

The Bunderoffs were now in their eighties, and they had more friends than they had teeth. They often dropped by to say hello with questionable homemade candy in an attempt to fill the gaps their children left with these women who were happy sharing a one-bedroom trailer.[34] In all honesty, it was the plants that kept Mrs. Bunderoff coming. She loved plants; they brought her joy, they never talked back, and they filled the void her adult children left in her life. When the girls were at work she regularly snuck over with her key and cared for the plants. The "Wall of African Violets," as she called them, she'd helped the girls propagate from one plant years ago. Now they filled the spaces between Charlie's history books on the shelf that took up an entire wall. Tabby owned almost no books but liked the look of the books and even more so loved the violets that multiplied.[35] While the girls thought their occasional magnanimous gift of water for the plants was enough to keep them going, it was actually the secret hours Mrs. Bunderoff spent pruning, feeding, and watering that kept them going.

---

33. A hope that is often fruitless for parents
34. The Bunderoffs had no judgement for Tabby and Charlie. Due to the copious amounts of pot they had smoked in the seventies, they were permanently relaxed and accepted all people
35. Mathematicians love multiplication but do not need books

The girls knew none of this as they sat staring at the nearly life-sized cloth poster of Morrison that hung where many would've put a television;[36] it didn't take long for them to come to the obvious conclusion:

They would take the free space in Key West. Maybe while in Key West they could explore the possibility of working at the community college[37] or the local library. While the high school would be a clear choice for some, they'd visited a high school once for an event a neighbor put on for the graduating seniors that year and realized the jungle that is public school was no place for them. In fact, many in their position feel the same, which is why colleges and universities have an influx of people willing to teach and Florida public schools are now hiring people to teach who don't have college degrees.

Once the plan was formed, there seemed to be no reason to delay. They had an invitation from Alec for the semester. They had keys to the castle, so to speak, and no way to pay the rent that was already late for the month of August. In actuality, Mrs. Bunderoff had been waiting for them to move out. While the girls were unaware of her philanthropic plant actions, they were aware she wanted them out. Mr. Bunderoff had taken to lounging around his trailer in his underwear all day since his retirement ten years ago, not long after the girls moved in next door. He broke up the monotony of his day with long naps bathed in deep snoring sessions. While the sight of Mr. Bunderoff in his "tighty-whities" wasn't new to Mrs. Bunderoff, his new involuntary habit of snoring was a shock, and one she could not get used to. Ever since Mrs. Dean down the road had gotten a "She Shed" for her plants and knitting, Mrs. Bunderoff had been eyeing the girls' trailer. It was hers, after all, and the Bunderoff's

---

36. Living in the twenty-first century, they preferred watching shows separately on their respective tablets
37. Unbeknownst to the girls, the College of the Florida Keys, the southernmost school in the continental US, is nearly entirely staffed by retired professors who work as adjuncts

meager pensions would cover the taxes on both trailers, which had been paid in full for some time. Like many Floridians, they planned to ride out any hurricanes that came. That was how they planned to meet their maker, so there was no need for home insurance costs—of this the girls were aware. Looking around, they realized they could pack suitcases of clothes, a favorite book or two,[38] and the necessary Jim Morrison memorabilia. They would leave the wall hanging for Mrs. Bunderoff, who shared in their love of staring at shirtless Jim,[39] forever stuck in his sexy twenties, keep the box they'd packed from the office, and immediately start packing for Key West—the land of tourism that all Floridians hope to reach one day.

The girls dutifully packed their clothes, leaving behind all the "skinny clothes" they were holding on to, as many do, because they'd collectively decided this wouldn't be a skinny trip. After all, they did essentially just get fired. They might as well enjoy food while they had the money to pay for it. They left behind the skinny clothes but packed their work clothes in case they could cinch up some Fall B classes in Key West.[40] They packed their suitcases, which were relics bought used by Charlie's dad, who may've been led to believe they were full professors at FSU; they laid their suitcases out in front of the poster of Jim like it was an altar they hoped would bless their trip, and they went to sleep, leaving last minute packing for the morning. They'd lost their jobs and decided to leave their home of so many years all in one afternoon. They were tired.

---

38. Whenever a professor says "a book or two", they mean at least ten
39. Named the 7th sexiest artist by VH1 in 2002, behind Elvis, Mick Jagger and Prince, he was always #1 in their hearts
40. Fall B classes, like all half semester classes, were the college's way of getting full price for half the time, with full knowledge students would be ignorant of the unlikely chance they would have at passing a course that crammed a full semester of work in eight weeks, because essentially, colleges are out for money.

Morning came as it usually does—earlier than expected. The girls woke in their twin beds[41] with their eye masks on in an attempt to block the sub tropical sun from their eyes. The attempts, however, were in vain. The girls, like many in their late thirties, were up on time every morning, regardless of whether or not they had to go to work, which they did not. They rose with a newfound hope that often comes on the morning of an adventure.

"Tabby," Charlie said while they sat staring over their cereal bowls to the vine growing up and over the window, once again surprised at how well it grew instinctively and perfectly around the window.

"Ya, what's up," Tabby said, her nose engrossed in a game of solitaire on her phone.

"I've been thinking. Key West is really far for a one-day drive."

"Yep. About thirteen hours, eleven if we want to take I-75, which we do not," said Tabby, always with the math and the logic.

"Well, what if we didn't rush down there. What if we went on the Jim Trail we always talked about?"

And with those words, a plan was born. The girls, ever the academics, had always planned on driving Jim's route from Tally to his grandparents' house in Clearwater, stopping in places where he may've stopped, documenting as they went, and applying for state funded plaques to commemorate Jim's existence in Florida. Now was the time. They'd never been able to justify the expense, but now they had an excuse and could even venture over to the house in Melbourne that boasts of being his birth home. From there, they could also hit the sights in Miami, the sights being the courthouse where Jim was convicted and the spot where his infamous performance went down, of course. It wouldn't be the

---

41. The fact that they do not share a bed was unknown to all neighbors, except for the Bunderoffs, who kept that information to themselves

most practical route, but it would be the most fulfilling, and the girls were ready to throw caution to the wind.

"Wait—What did you say the address is for Alec's compound?" Charlie asked, interrupting Tabby's thoughts.

"Hmmm something Love Lane?"

"Love Lane, are you sure it's Love Lane?" Charlie said, excitedly getting to her feet.

"Ya, why?" asked Tabby, never too surprised at Charlie's antics.

"Love Lane—the common wife and Jim's first home together was on a street known as Love Street—it's a sign."[42]

"We have to do this. We are meant to go to Clearwater, and Melbourne, and Miami and then we can sit in the sun in Key West until professional development in Ireland, or maybe we find jobs in Key West and just stay and fight for Jim plaques to be put up all over the state like we've always wanted to."

With the plans set, the girls loaded their chargers and toiletries into their bags and grabbed some snacks for the road from the kitchen. Charlie elected herself to walk over and notify the Bunderoffs, leaving Tabby to load the car. Mrs. Bunderoff attempted to hide her joy at the news she was finally getting her "She Shed"/trailer, and she waved goodbye, insisting on sending them off with some hard candy and stale cookies. She yelled something to the effect of "Have fun storming the castle" as Charlie ran back to the car[43] just in time to see Tabby close the trunk on the fully loaded suitcases and boxes.

While the girls had gone as cheap as possible when it came to housing, they didn't cheap out on their car. Well, it was technically Charlie's car. Turns out that listening to Tabby's advice about

---

42. For academics, the girls bought into a lot of signs and wonders.
43. Mrs. Bunderoff, like the students in the girls' classes, was not actually listening to the details of what was being said

numbers helped with credit, so Charlie was able to get a loan for her dream car—a 2019 maroon Dodge Challenger SRT. She wisely waited until December when she knew car dealers would be anxious to clear out 2019 stock in favor of the incoming 2020 stock. At the time, both parties were unaware of the oncoming plague that would bring sky rocketing car prices in its wake.

The loan was Charlie's, but the girls shared the payments evenly, and they shared in their constant care and attention of the car they affectionately named Baby.[44] Care of Baby included, but was not limited to, baths of the exterior, polishing and vacuuming of the interior, maintenance, and, perhaps most important, careful parking. Owning a muscle car enters one into an elite group of people who would rather walk from the ends of the earth[45] than rashly park their cars in those close spots where people in a hurry often leave their cars, rushing in and out without caring if their car doors scratch or ding the cars around them. On campus this translated into parking in student parking spots. While one would think faculty parking would be safer, Tabby and Charlie quickly learned that most professors were too absent minded to avoid dinging the neighboring faculty car in any given spot. Students, on the other hand, were in awe of Baby and showed her the respect a car of her caliber deserved.

With the car packed, they were off. Tabby drove first, as she always did. Tabby is the practical one of the two, and Charlie would prefer to watch the scenery as it goes by. Charlie contributed to the trip by mapping out the most likely Jim route. They'd already taken day trips through FSU's campus to see Jim related spots, such as places he roomed and where the FSU commercial featuring Jim was filmed, and since they were just fired, they decided Jim would

---

44. This was in fact the only baby either of the girls would ever have
45. In this case, the farthest spots in any given parking lot

support leaving FSU behind. Instead of taking the practical route, they decided to follow the old route through Florida—route 19/98. The old road was the path spring breakers and tourists alike would have taken through Florida "back in the day," and the girls preferred it anyways as it kept them off the beaten path.

It wasn't long before they reached Mexico Beach, which had been so badly damaged by Hurricane Michael. Similar to the west side of Tally on I 10, trees could still be seen beaten down in odd groupings where Michael had torn his path. There were still some blue tarps on houses in poorer neighborhoods where perhaps no insurance was had or insurance money was pocketed. People make choices to survive. Mexico Beach and its neighboring city of Port St. Joe were favorites for Tabby and Charlie. Last year they came down to Port St. Joe and rented a cabin at the state park. The cabins had been rebuilt since Michael and the girls were fortunate to have the inside scoop from a former student who'd become a park ranger, so they were sitting online the night the cabins finally opened for reservations, and they snagged one immediately. The cabins sit at the end of a long, skinny peninsula, and each one has its own small bit of beach.

The cabins weren't fancy, but Tabby and Charlie aren't fancy girls. The cabins had two bedrooms, albeit one was a loft, and they'd had their own beach during horseshoe crab mating season. The location gave them the ability to walk past the neighboring cabins to the long and desolate stretch of beach that was only open to cabin renters. The gulf side of the peninsula was gorgeous, with clear water crashing down at their feet and white sandy beaches that seemed to stretch on for miles. They were always wanting to go back, but today was for Jim, and so they made a goal of getting to Carrabelle[46] before lunch. They couldn't be certain where Jim would have stopped on his regular route from Tally to Clearwater. Since he hitchhiked, there was no telling where he got in and out of cars on his way. As mostly practical girls, they'd packed a lunch and planned on stopping at the public beach picnic spot at Carrabelle. The concrete tables and benches, along with the structure holding up the wing-like roof, were painted a turquoise color suggesting the clear waters found in the Keys, while the water itself stretched out beyond the horizon in a deeper shade of blue. The white sands and occasional tuft of sea grass were a welcome site to Tabby and Charlie.

"Great job finding this spot," said Tabby, eager to stretch her legs a bit. "How'd you find it?"

"Well, let me explain. This is really close to Camp Gordon Johnston where US troops came to practice amphibious landings before shipping overseas," Charlie began as she went into the very depths of her knowledge of the intersections of Florida history and the Second World War. Tabby inwardly rolled her eyes but sat and got out the sandwiches and waters.

The girls were looking forward to cold drinks in the Keys, but for the drive, they had caffeinated canned water, something they found hilarious and delicious, paired with peanut butter and honey sandwiches. After all, they were out of work, gas was expensive, and Baby was a thirsty girl. As they sat and ate, and Charlie continued to explain the importance of Florida in training for WWII, she stood to emphasize her point, waving her PB and H as she spoke, flowing into full professor mode. As if perfectly on cue, a seagull swooped in under the roof of the pavilion, grabbing Charlie's sandwich as he went on his way off into the sand, followed by his peers who were

---

46. On road trips they liked to keep their goals small and manageable

eager for a bite of his stolen lunch. Charlie stood, frozen in surprise, while Tabby fell on her side on the bench laughing at her friend whose long speech had finally been interrupted by nature.

"Not cool, Mr. Seagull, not cool," Charlie pouted.

"No worries, I brought the loaf of bread and supplies. We can make another," laughed Tabby. Charlie continued pouting but moved into a more silent mode while she made another sandwich and carefully ate it, now that she was fully aware her lunch was in danger.

The rest of their brief lunch break was spent laughing at the shore birds and looking for shells along the water like children. Before getting back into Baby, they religiously rinsed their feet at the public shower along the beach and dried their legs using the towels Tabby had carefully made accessible in the trunk and used the old Florida trick of baby powder to get the rest of the sand off. Baby was a Florida girl, but not a sandy girl. Before long, they were back on the road.

"Where to next?" asked Tabby, who was committed to driving while Charlie was committed to navigating.

"Well, since we're wanting to enjoy the drive and not to get there quickly, I thought we could make a quick stop at another state park."

"Why?" asked Tabby, who sensed a historical theme to Charlie's plans.

"Well, there's this book. It's called *Walk the World's Rim*. It tells the story of a Spanish ship that landed there, and everyone died except Escobar, the enslaved man, his enslaver, and some other guy. The four of them survived the diseases, the mosquitos, and the natives, who weren't happy about being invaded. They actually walk all the way to Mexico, and the enslaver would've died if not for his enslaved man, so there was hope that he would see the light and grant freedom, but spoiler alert—he did not. You know why?" Charlie asked rhetorically, "because people who enslave other people are assholes who don't make good choices."

"Well, there you go. No need to stop. You told me the whole story."

"What? But hearing the story is supposed to make you want to stop," Charlie argued as the girls made their way south on 19/98, enjoying every glimpse of the beautiful coastline to their right when it came along, before heading into the part of Florida that is dominated by trailers and swamps.

"Nope. We did one historical stop, and that was a bit sneaky if I do say so myself. This is a Jim trip. Any other history stop will be met with a math stop."

"There's no such thing."

"I will find a way."

Charlie felt she could call Tabby's bluff but instead decided to wait and make another history stop more covertly next time, maybe even keeping the history to herself, which wouldn't be easy. After all, she'd sought out a career that allowed her to speak her mind whenever she wanted, unless it was honestly telling a student what she thought of their research paper.

"Ok. I have a stop planned just for you. Now, I don't actually know the history of the shop, so I can't say if Jim stopped in this exact spot, but, Perry is a nice halfway marker, and a bigger city for the area, so it seems likely to be a spot he could've gotten a ride to. If he did, the historic downtown is where he would've gotten out and worked on another ride. So, right in the middle of the historic district is the world's best donut shop."

"Now you're talkin'."

"Seriously. These donuts are homemade, and they're like a dollar each."

"How'd you find it?"

"I went there years ago with my grandmother. They played my grandma's favorite—Sinatra—"

"Her favorite and Jim's, so we can take that as a sign. Let me know when to pull off the road," said Tabby, who was always ready for an excuse to stop for donuts. And with that, they drove on in silence, Earle Bailey blessedly discussing Rock and Roll history on the radio, waiting for the inevitable moment when he would play the Lizard King. And so, the miles passed, they sang along, discussed music, and eventually made it to Perry, the city in Florida that you smell before you see.

"What is that god awful smell,"[47] asked Tabby gagging.

"That is a paper mill. It was out of commission for a long while, but recently came back, to the joy of everyone who has to drive through the area."

"No kidding."

"Ok, now we're going to come up to a light here with a Kentucky Fried Chicken and a Hardees. Deny the fast food and turn left."

"No problem there," laughed Tabby, who had no interest in eating at either location.

"Ok, we drive maybe a mile, and it'll be on the right—the most glorious donut spot in all of Florida."

"Way to set the bar of expectations high."

"Oh, Johnson's will rise to meet those expectations," laughed Charlie as the girls parked in front of the rather unassuming storefront and walked into the small restaurant, only to be greeted

---

47. No one is actually sure what makes a smell god awful. Is it cursed by God to be awful?

with a wave of deliciousness that suggested they shouldn't worry about calories, this was indeed a calorie free zone.[48]

"Good afternoon, how can we help you?" asked the teenage girl working behind the counter, which was full of every kind of donut one could possibly imagine and then some. Voodoo Donuts has nothing on this place, hidden deeply in the heart of Florida, away from the prying eyes of tourists on their way to Disney, but blessedly on the "Route of Jim."

"My goodness this place is amazing."

"Thank you, ma'am, we try."

"Can we get two cake donuts and two teas," asked Charlie, already aware of what they'd want to eat.[49] The girls sat in blissful, sugary joy, eating every blessed bite of their donuts. As Charlie ate her last bite and sipped her tea she asked, "Do you know the history of donuts?"

"Really? I'm eating."

"Exactly. You're eating a donut, which has its roots in the First World War when American women serving along the front lines, not in the front lines, mind you, because women weren't allowed in the military at that point—"

"Or African Americans, unless in segregated units," said Tabby, at this point accepting her fate as someone stuck listening to history and egging Charlie on.

"That's too long of a discussion for today, unless you want to talk about the segregation of the US military on the drive—"

"I don't."

"Ok, then back to the donuts. Now, while the donut has a history beyond the First World War, they really came into their own in the

---

48. As in a zone where no one cares about calories, not a zone where there are no calories
49. When traveling, the girls prefer to eat the same thing so their experiences align, and they can discuss the foods more thoroughly

First World War when women brought them into the trenches to serve American soldiers, who naturally came home craving more doughnuts—"[50]

"And alcohol during the start of prohibition."

"You've been listening."

"You gave me no option."

With donuts discussed and eaten, they hit the road again, with the next stop planned in Dixie County, the Wild Wild West of Florida, or the West Virginia of Florida, depending on who you ask. The county where the local government built a road to no where in the sixties just to fly drugs in. Where else would Jim stop aside from a county where lawlessness could be accepted as part of the culture, depending on who you are and what your last name is. The girls drove on through the monotonous Florida landscape of swamps, pine trees, and farmland. Without Earle Bailey's[51] voice to keep them going, they may have fallen asleep, well Charlie at least.

The highlights of the trip are always the stops, and for Charlie and Tabby another stop wouldn't come until they hit the Cypress Inn, in Dixie County's Cross City. The inn harkened more of an hourly rate sort of place, if one was considering it an actual inn. Charlie and Tabby weren't sure if it served as an inn anymore, but it was certainly one of the older standing but still functioning places to eat in Dixie County, and so it seemed a very likely spot for Jim to have stopped on his hitchhiked route from Tally to his grandparents' house in Clearwater. The name of the place made more sense when they walked inside and saw all the walls and ceiling were lined with Cypress.

---

50. For more information on the ever glorious history of donuts: https://www.smithsonianmag.com/history/the-history-of-the- doughnut-150405177
51. The very best of radio DJ's

"You see, this area was known for its mills, so it would've had access to lots of wood for building," explained Charlie as the girls took a seat and waited for their waitress to come over.

"Morning, ladies," said the waitress, "now where are ya'll from, cuz I know ya ain't from around here," she asked with a laugh.

"We're driving from Panama City down to Clearwater in search of the route Jim Morrison would have taken back in the day."

"Is that right?" asked the waitress who was too young to know Jim's name off hand.[52] "What can I get for y'all?"

"Two unsweet teas."

"Anything to eat? We've got some great pies," she asked, struggling to hide the judgement she felt for these women whose drink order clearly designated them as Yankees.

"No, just the drinks."

"Actually, I think I'll get some pie. Do you have any peach pie?"

"Yes, ma'am, but I'll be honest with y'all. Those peach pies are frozen. Peak season ended a bit early this year, you know, but I could get you a fresh apple pie."

"Dutch?" asked Tabby

"Yes, ma'am."

"We'll take two," said Charlie.

The waitress returned with the girls' second dessert for the day and stood to talk with them for a bit about their trip. Once she realized who Jim was,[53] she offered up more local knowledge. Across the road a bit was the Putnam Lodge where Al Capone had stayed back in the day. He'd stayed often enough that he had an escape route out the backside of the place and a car waiting for him to run.

"Too bad we can't stay the night," commented Charlie once the waitress left.

---

52. There is no hope for this generation
53. Often Gen Z knows the songs, but not the music gods and goddesses

"Well, it's not really a Jim stop, but I imagine if he heard Al Capone stayed there, he might've gone for a drink. I think we could justify popping our heads in." The girls settled with the waitress and drove over to the Putnam Lodge, which was on the other side of the four-lane highway, so it was a bit of driving difficulty, but nothing Baby couldn't handle, as she is quite a pro at U turns (both of the legal and illegal varieties).

The lodge was impressive at first sight. The brick lined driveway welcomed guests to the white historic mansion with a wooden carport for important guests to leave their cars under.[54] They approached the hostess stand inside the wooden doorway and asked if it was possible to walk around and see the place. As it was a slow day, one of the waiters overheard and offered to give them a tour of the grounds, but they wouldn't be able to see Al Capone's room as it was currently occupied. The waiter explained that it was their most popular room. Tabby and Charlie nodded, glad to confirm the truth behind the rumor, but also doubting the veracity of the young boy whose wire rim glasses kept slipping down his long, bony nose. He led them around speaking of the glory days of the restaurant and the artist who'd painted murals on the walls in the main rooms.[55] He walked them onto the grounds, which were impressive in nature with their clear wedding venue goals, pool, and carefully sculpted gardens.

"This is a beautiful location, there must be a lot of history here," asked Charlie.

"Oh, are you interested in history?" asked the waiter, perking up.

"A bit," said Charlie as Tabby snorted quietly.

---

54. In today's day and age, important guests are usually local kids coming for prom
55. The girls were not interested in art today

"Well, let me show you something that isn't normally on the tour,"[56] the waiter said, leading them further into the woods behind the lodge. As he led them into the coolness of the shade, the girls felt a chill as they approached one of the biggest oak trees they'd ever seen.

"This is a beautiful tree," commented Tabby, whose mind was on measurements.

"Oh my," said Charlie, sensing a connection with Florida's darker history.

"This was the hanging tree," said the waiter with a nod that didn't appear to be embarrassed about his county's dark history.

"And it's still standing," said Charlie.

"Ma'am, this tree is a part of history. My granddaddy used to tell me stories about it," said the boy.

"I bet he did," said Charlie, realizing the cold chill wasn't in her mind, and it was time to get back on the road. "Well, thank you for this, uhm, tour. We best get back on the road," said Charlie, falling back into her own Southern drawl. Tabby handed the boy some cash and they both bee-lined for the safety Dodge.

"Dang," said Tabby. "Right here near the road."

"And he wasn't even embarrassed by it."

"Well, my granddaddy was a racist alcoholic, and I don't feel the need to hide the ugly side of my family's history, but I certainly wouldn't be out there parading it around for random tourists."

"Let's get back on the road. No more stops in Dixie." With that agreed on, the girls continued south on 19, wondering what Jim would've thought of the place.

"I hesitate to ask after that last experience, but is there another stop before Clearwater?" asked Tabby. The girls saw road trips not

---

56. At the mention of a tour, the girls realized they would have to tip the boy

as a way to get from point A to point B, but as a way to explore things between point A and point B.

"You know me too well. Let's stop along the Suwannee River. Surely Jim would've been curious about the Suwannee. Since he loved dogs so much, I think he would've stopped at Dogland at least once," said Charlie.

"What, pray tell, is Dogland?"

"Was. Dogland was a roadside tourist attraction that had a giant wooden sign in the shape of a dog. It was owned by a family who was local at the time[57] and opened in 1960. They had 113 dog breeds on display, all pure bred except for one, who was named Pirate."

"How appropriate. Are there any dogs left there?"

"Well, no, it closed in the seventies."

"I see, then maybe we should just drive by and keep on going?"

"I suppose, but we should at least slow down."

Tabby agreed and they made their way over the bridge that takes cars across the Suwannee River, before turning onto what was known as Old Fanning Road, the road Charlie swore Jim would've taken down towards Clearwater. The road was barely a two-lane road, and it was one of those roads the county had forgotten to maintain, which made Tabby a bit too eager to get through, and soon they were seeing blue lights in their rearview.

"Great" said Tabby, pulling over to the side of the road and waiting for the officer to approach. Fortunately, he was good-looking, so at least they would have a nice view while he wrote them a ticket.

The tall, broad, and built Black man leaned into the window, his sunglasses sliding down his nose as he asked, "Do you ladies know how fast you were going?"

---

57. Various counties in Florida have different definitions for the term 'local', and in North Central Florida that was a designation that could take generations to achieve

"No, officer, I'm sorry. I wasn't paying attention."

"I don't see a sign; what is the speed limit here?" asked Charlie, leaning over towards the driver side window to get a closer look at this man with his gorgeous hazel eyes.

"The speed limit is 35 through this section."

"You're kidding."

"I am not, and I got you girls at 65. Now, where are you headed in that kind of a hurry?" asked the officer, unaware, or perhaps very aware, of the effect he had on women. The girls quickly stumbled over themselves to explain their quest to visit all spots connected to Jim Morrison in the state.

"Is that so? You know, my daddy had a good friend who roomed with Jim in college at FSU."

"Really?"

"Really. Said he was a pain in the ass," the officer said with a laugh, "but I don't believe that. That's jealousy speaking. I like to think he's still alive out there somewhere. His death seems suspicious to me, and that's coming from a police officer," he said, laughing again. The girls laughed too, glad to find a kindred spirit in such an unlikely place.

"Now, you girls move along down towards Tampa, and keep an eye on your speed in my county," he said as he tapped the roof of Baby and went back to his car. With that narrow escape, the girls decided to drive carefully on down to Clearwater.

CHAPTER FOUR

Queens of the Highway[58]

The issue is that Clearwater is actually nowhere near the main road. You drive down the highway thinking Clearwater is right there, but there is so much further to go once you get to Tampa, and the traffic in and around the mass of land that is Tampa[59] doesn't help. The girls had to keep the Doors on repeat and practice slow breathing to get themselves over the bridges into Clearwater. While the location of the grandparents' home was before the bridges heading over to the portion of Clearwater they hoped to stay at due to better beaches, they also knew the home had been torn down by progress.[60]

When they arrived over what appeared to be the final bridge to Clearwater, they pulled into the first hotel on the right—the Sheraton Sand Key Resort. While the label "resort" made them hesitant, they hoped to make this the only hotel they would need for the trip, and they planned to share a room to save costs. They parked Baby in the most reasonable spot possible—one very far from the hotel

---

58. Inspired by Morrison, Jim. "Queen of the Highway." Morrison Hotel/Hard Rock Cafe. Elektra Records, 1970
59. While Tampa is facing urban sprawl, it does not get the designation of nation's largest city land mass wise, JAX does
60. Actually, by Scientologists and not by progress

and next to a cement barrier that made it more likely no one would speed through and accidentally hit Baby. The walk to the front door wasn't as long as they expected, but the hotel was deceptive. Having been built in the seventies, it was designed to mislead newcomers into thinking they were entering an important front door, when in all actuality, they were entering a side door to the Twilight Zone in which they would have to walk through long hallways of now empty banquet rooms used by corporate America to hold expensive conferences in which their employees learned nothing, drank too much, and came to like their employer even less. They walked what felt like a half mile inside the hallway, which was lined with art that would be expected in a beach hotel, to finally make their way, dragging their suitcases behind them, into the large lobby with check-in desks and closer doors leading to a side parking lot they'd not seen when entering the front parking lot.

"Ah, so we could've parked closer," said Charlie, grateful there was at least AC.

"Yes, but we wouldn't have, for Baby's sake."

"Of course not."

"And knowing that there's a better, closer parking lot only makes me feel more confident in where we left her."

"True, true. Let's get checked in," Charlie said, walking up to the desk.

"One room or two?" the tired hotel manager asked, clearly eyeing the clock as it clicked closer towards midnight.

"One," said Tabby, noticing the eyebrow raise on the manager's face as he made assumptions.

"No problem. This is our slow season, so I can offer you an ocean view at the rate of a normal parking lot facing room."

"That sounds great," said Tabby as she began to pay and the girls both dreamt of bed and a shower, with no thoughts of the view. After they made their way past the restaurants and gift shops that all resorts hook patrons with and made it to the elevator, they found their room on the second floor to be larger than expected, and the balcony at the end was the length of the room with doors that could be opened to let a warm ocean breeze in. While the girls couldn't see the ocean in the dark, they could just barely hear it since the hotel courtyard below was empty and quiet in the evening.

"Well, you know we're leaving that open," said Tabby.

"Just a little, though, for the salt air smell. We have to run the AC."

"Of course." And with that the girls fell onto their beds and collapsed. Sleep came fast as they dreamt of finding Jim and assumed that things would work out, as things often do.

As the girls had fallen asleep without the showers they knew they needed, and without their eye masks, they woke to the sun piercing into the room through the open curtains on the balcony door, but the sound of the waves crashing in the distance lulled away any resentment they may have felt for the sun otherwise. They both wandered out onto the balcony and sat mesmerized by the far-off sight of the waves past the long length of white sand beaches. While they'd lived and worked near the beach for years, they never tired of seeing it, especially from new vantage points.[61]

"Should we head down?"

"Ya. It's only seven, so let's hop in the water real quick and then head back for showers and breakfast."

---

61. Indeed, the beach never becomes a dull view in any weather

"Now that's a plan," said Tabby as both girls headed to suitcases to unpack bikinis and make their way down to the water.

The trip to the first floor and out to the pool area was uneventful, and they soon walked past the pool and hot tub and hit the beach, but unlike Panama City beach, once they hit the sand, they still couldn't see the water. However, as they could hear the waves and feel the sand beneath their toes, they were certain they were headed in the right direction. While the walk from the parking lot entrance to the lobby of the hotel felt like a half mile, this walk through the sand to the water most certainly was a half mile or more. When they finally reached the water, they were greeted by the sights and sounds of Florida beaches, red tide included. The shoreline was littered with fish that had met the fate of many fish who accidentally make their way into the red tide bloom. The girls coughed as the algae was turned up into the air by the crashing of the waves. They looked around to see only a handful of people sitting on blankets on the long stretch of sand along the shoreline and even fewer getting into the water.

"See, this is why it is America's favorite beach, but Floridians never talk about vacationing here," said Charlie.

"Clearly. Let's go back to the pool."

The girls made their way back through the Sahara Desert of Florida until their tired, sandy toes finally reached the tile surrounding the pool area, and they were able to begin the Florida ritual of hot tub, pool, hot tub, far enough away from the water to escape the memory and the smell of the red tide and its victims. The water refreshed them, and they were soon ready to change, pack, and head down to one of the three restaurant options the resort offered.

The restaurant of their choosing harkened back to the 1970s with mirrored walls in the back and a raised floor for those who wanted to sit next to the mirrors. On the opposite side of the room was a buffet hiding behind a partition for those unfortunate enough to sit near the buffet. The girls were quickly seated, with their luggage stowed beside them, and they ordered fruit-topped pancakes and tea, which were promptly brought out, giving the girls plenty of time to relax in the multi-tiered, mirror-lined restaurant that spoke of opulence in past decades. The tea wasn't Twining's, their favorite brand, but it did the job, and the girls were soon ready to finish the long walk back out of the resort and head over to Jim's grandparents' house. Tabby, always the bold one, called over the waitress to ask for the check.

They had arrived so hungry, they hadn't even noticed the kind woman in her mid-sixties who was more than happy to bring them their check. When she came back to the table with their check, she asked where they were visiting from and where they were headed. They explained their plan to find Jim's grandparents' house, and she smiled.

"Jim. You know, I don't think he actually died," said the waitress with a wink. "It's a shame, though, that corporation buying the house, selling off the doors of the home, and promising a plaque, but you know what? No plaque. It's been years. That's how it goes. Developers tearing up Florida and forgetting to remember the history they've buried."

"Amen," said Charlie.

"What's it look like?"

"Not much. You have to drive by, of course. It's always surprising to see how close they lived to the water, but you know where you need to go is the Francis Wilson Playhouse, St. Cecelia Church, and

St Petersburg Jr. College." Grateful for the intel and the conversation with a mutual fan, the girls paid their bill and headed out, excited to take on the day.

The drive over the first bridge was a spectacle the girls hadn't expected after crossing in the dark the night before. The water surrounded them in a welcoming way that was both familiar and different from their home bridge in Panama City Beach. They fought the traffic and the tourists walking in the road and made their way back off the island to head to 314 N. Osceola Ave, or what would've been about 314 N. Osceola. The waitress had been right, the water really was only a block or so from the street, which made the girls realize Jim, like them, had loved Florida and the water. They knew he was an avid swimmer, so the reminder came as no surprise.

They wondered aloud if he would've had a view of the beach, which was hard to tell sixty years later with the growth of Clearwater. They parked and walked on the street to breathe the air in the space where Jim once walked, wondering if the grandparents were surprised that he made his way back to them so often.

"She must have been something else, his grandmother, to keep him coming back."

"Maybe she just accepted him."

"True. That is what most college students want. That and food and free laundry. I read he had his own door in and out of the house, so he could come and go as he liked."

"So, they probably accepted him—bisexuality and all."

"Really something for that era. Well, until he trashed their car."

"Ya, that would be the last straw for me, too."[62]

They made their way back to the car, determined to find the spots the waitress had recommended before heading over to Melbourne,

---

62. The girls preferred to ignore all aspects of Jim they didn't approve of, thinking of the one Bible verse Tabby's parents taught her before leaving church all together—Love covers a multitude of sins.

Miami, and finally Key West. However, as they continued to fight traffic to get from one location to the next, finding a few they already had in mind torn down and left vacant or replaced with a Pizza Hut, they decided only to see St. Cecelia's, where they were sure to get inside. They parked and went in, wondering how similar it was to the time when Jim went there. As they sat in the back of the cold, dark sanctuary, looking at candles flickering on the table to the left of the altar, they thought about their future, and what would've brought their party idol, Jim, into the church, which was easier to think about than their own future.

"Do you think he had some inner core of morality?"

"I think he had his own sense of morals."

"And wanted some sense of comfort maybe?"

"Maybe."

"I imagine the abuse from his father left him with a lot of questions and not a lot of answers. I suppose we'll never know. We should get back on the road. We've got a long drive." And so, they left behind the versions of Clearwater and St. Petersburg that were clearly not the cities that Jim had lived in and hit the road determined to be in Key West before sundown.

The drive from Tampa across the middle of Florida is an experience in progress, or the evil remnants of progress. The roads surrounding Tampa are a vast maze of stress where more lanes than had previously seemed possible wind together and confuse tourists who've mistakenly fallen into their trap.[63] The stress began to lessen when the girls finally made their way through the traffic laden roads that wind through cow fields north of Tampa and turned right to

---

63. This is why Floridians not from the Tampa or Orlando area choose Orlando airport and not Tampa airport

head out on Florida's "Less Stress" highway to get through Orlando. Using their favorite Jim biography, they were able to decide there wasn't a significant Jim location in Orlando, and they could make their way past the mouse that was the draw for explorers from around the world and continue towards Melbourne—the birthplace of greatness.

But before the greatness in Florida comes miles, and miles, and miles of Villages. The Villages have become the last bastion of hope and sex-fueled parties for the Boomers who'd hoped their years of psychedelic exploration would help to preserve their bodies for longer, but apparently, that theory had no scientific value, so they were hiding their aging with loofa color coded sex parties in the town built just for them that now spanned the state and reportedly could be seen from outer space. The girls did not stop, did not slow down, and did not roll down the windows.[64]

After the Villages, Orlando passed by and soon the girls needed to stop for gas. Baby is a thirsty girl who will abandon her charges if neglected, so they stopped at what they thought might be the last stop for gas situated between the east and west bound lanes before they headed into the last stand of farm lands, rednecks, and garbage dumps before reaching the sprawling urban realms of Fort Lauderdale and Melbourne.

The issue with middle of the highway gas stations is that lanes coming from both directions are attempting to collide on an island of gas without colliding with each other. In order to help lessen the chance of collisions, the state provided signs in the most confusing way possible, hoping not that the signs would reduce damage, but that the signs would protect from what the state really feared most—lawsuits. They made their way through the minivans of

---

64. The Villages have been noted for being the STD capital of the nation, so indeed there was reason to worry what could be in the water or the air

envious fathers driving their children to and fro across the state who all wished they too could drive a Challenger and eventually backed into the perfect spot. Well, at least one they could pull the extensive gas hose across the low car and fuel on the opposite side before heading in for bottled water and a bathroom break.

The inside of the large building providing rest, AC, greasy chicken and stale donuts wasn't tempting to stay in, so the girls quickly returned to the safety of Baby and got back on the long road where time seems to stop as the landscape's only variance would be the garbage dump[65] and the odd large black pipes that seem to connect farmers' fields with the worrisome roadside water that comes suspiciously close to both the garbage hill and the highway. They couldn't welcome the signs of the Merritt Island and Titusville exits more, although they themselves would avoid those distractions and keep going to what they longed to see: 2100 Vernon Place, Melbourne—the Birthplace of Greatness. The exit off I-95 came like a beacon of hope, and they turned left quickly towards the long stretch past Best Buy, Home Depot, and Target wondering what this road was like when Jim lived here. They only needed four turns to get to the palace of Jim's birth. The house was a block from Crane Creek and a few more blocks from Indian River, which was only a sliver away from the ocean itself. Jim was born in the most Florida-like home—a house off of an alligator invested creek, near a river filled with alligators, and close enough to get to the ocean whenever he wanted to, while also being in real danger of a hurricane, more so by the closeness of multiple sources of water.

Vernon Place was an older street, by Florida standards. The road consisted of two lanes with room for parallel parking[66] on both sides. The homes all seemed to have been built around the

---

65. Voted Florida's largest hill five years in a row, but also voted worst hill for a picnic
66. A dying art

boom of military men moving their families to Florida in the years surrounding WWII. Jim's house was one that someone could easily pass by, but Charlie and Tabby would make no such mistake. They pulled miraculously into a parallel space, which is no easy feat in a wide bodied[67] car, and came to a stop, pausing only briefly to catch their breath before getting out on the sidewalk to adore the home that was built in the same fashion, and likely by the same builder, as many of the homes on the street. The house had been recently painted red with a cream trim. The wide front door was welcoming and blended well into the neighborhood of wealthy homes. What made it stand out was the giant Jim Morrison pictures in windows on both sides of the door. There was no doubt—this was it. The girls sat on the sidewalk and gazed at the house, imagining Jim walking up those very steps. However, they were realists, and since Jim moved out of the house before his first birthday, they knew that he never walked up those steps. The "Birthplace of Greatness" seemed a great place to start their own new beginnings, and so they sat and vowed to make the upcoming months the best they'd ever had, and to take the trip as it came—which is a great ambition to have in mind when heading into Miami traffic.

The drive to Miami fought the built-up ambition and solace they'd found at Jim's house. The mass of roads intertwining and occasionally veering off into lanes only for those in groups did what they were built to do—confuse the driver of the vehicle. Tabby had volunteered to drive but was certainly regretting her decision. To make matters worse, the rain was falling in the way that it only falls in Florida—blindingly. Like all good Floridians, they kept going despite their inability to see the cars in front of them. They hoped

---

67. While technically not a wide-bodied car, the girls felt Baby's girth whenever they parked her.

that they'd be able to stop for food soon, since they hadn't eaten since they left Clearwater.

As they made their way south, the rain slowed, and they decided to brave an exit for food. Being the educated women that they were, they wanted to try a local place instead of a fast food chain restaurant.[68] The girls parked in the most reasonable location and got out to walk around the trendy outdoor shopping plaza to look for food. While the outdoor plaza provided more opportunities for walking in the fresh air, the purpose was really to allow the plaza owners to easily plow over buildings of stores that went under and then rebuild with a new trendier store. Fortunately, there were several food options, and the girls were so hungry they didn't care about the business practices of plaza owners.

"Looks like we have a Panda Express, Pizza Hut, and some Thai place."

"Some Thai place it is," said Tabby. The girls walked in the front door and were greeted by an older man in a collared shirt that was tucked around his growing belly and into his pants in a way that seemed to help his back support his forward growth.

"Table for two?" the man asked and led the girls to a table after they nodded consent.

The girls were seated at a table to the left of the bar, which was lit up with soccer games and bright red and cobalt blue ceiling lights, none of which screamed Thai to the girls. However, the menu had their favorite—Shrimp Pad Thai—and before the waiter left for their drinks, they'd ordered chicken egg rolls, as well. The drinks came in record time, and the girls settled in for some relaxation and time away from the road, letting their Thai tea wash the road stress from their minds. As they sat, a middle-aged couple was seated behind

---

68. The local place was of course built into a giant shopping center, still pouring money from the hands of the family-run business into the hands of the massively rich shop owners

them and ordered their food, something that only became noticeable as the clock continued to tick and the girls still waited for their food as the new couple received theirs. The couple, unknowingly rubbing in the fastidious nature of their order by ordering multiple appetizers, continued happily eating delivery after delivery of food to their table while the middle-aged manager continued walking by the girls' table with a smile and a nod.

"It's been 45 minutes."

"Are you sure?" asked Tabby.

"I'm sure. I sent Alec a text about the house in Key West when we got here. Time stamp shows it's been 45 minutes."

"And no appetizers."

"And no food," added Charlie.

The girls sat in silence as the resentment for the happy couple grew with the level of their hunger. As the one-hour mark approached, the girls finally had a delivery of vegetable spring rolls followed closely by cold Chicken Pad Thai. In their hunger, they decided to eat in silence and express their outrage by leaving a 20% tip instead of a 25% tip.[69] Finally, they were able to walk to the solace of Baby and head out on the highway for Miami.

"Do we still have time to find the courthouse?" asked Charlie.

"That depends on what time you want to get in. We left early enough that with our added stops we could still get in before dark, but that food slowed us down."

"But we're not stopping again, right?"

"Well, the courthouse, if we do that."

"Ok, let's get gas and do a drive by of the Dade County Courthouse."

"You mean the Miami-Dade County Courthouse."

---

69. As former waitresses themselves, they could not find it in themselves to stiff a waiter no matter how terrible the service

"No, I do not. They charged Jim there, and they do not get an updated name," said Charlie.

"Surely they've done some good to recompense in the last fifty years."

"Doesn't matter. No forgiveness for businesses."

"Courts aren't businesses," said Tabby as she loaded the directions into the GPS and started to back out of the parking spot and head for the highway.

"Doesn't matter," said Charlie, and Tabby let her be as they headed south towards whatever the future held for them.

CHAPTER FIVE

I See the Bathroom is Clear[70]

The girls fell into the mindless routine of following GPS directions. Although they'd been raised on *Terminator*, they found it easy to follow the directions of a machine without question. They thought of the GPS as an extension of Baby, who would never do them wrong, and they wove in and out of traffic, feeling the exhilaration of the purr[71] of their engine and the knowledge that they can always pass any cars in front of them.[72] Eventually, the joy of passing lulled to the hesitant Miami driving of following endless streams of twelve lanes of traffic. Charlie stared out the window, feeling a bit ill from the cold Pad Thai and anxious to get out of the car.

"Do you want some Benadryl to help you sleep?" Tabby asked, always aware of where her friend was at, despite her apparent gruff exterior.

"No, I mean, it's not that far, right?"

"Map says twenty minutes," Tabby answered.

---

70. Morrison, Jim. "Hyacinth House." L.A. Woman. Elektra Records, 1971.
71. In this case the purr is more like the purr of a tiger and not that of a house cat, which would be the purr of a Prius.
72. They want to pass anyone except for the black and tan Challengers that roam the highway often unseen

Charlie went back to her thoughts of life when she had a job and somewhat of a financial plan and life now that she was broke and homeless. The traffic eventually led over bridges surrounded by turquoise water filled with yachts that were larger than any apartment or trailer the girls had ever lived in. It didn't escape them that they taught future generations who would go on to afford yachts and lives that they would, as educators who enabled growth and learning, never be able to afford. As the car came to an intersection, the girls decided it was time to park and get out to walk and look for the courthouse. The decision to park is never an easy one given the likelihood of someone hitting Baby.[73] However, as they turned onto a side street, they found an open parallel spot right across from a police station and surrounded by police cars. Leaving Baby surrounded by armed guards seemed like a good idea, so they parked and got out to fumble with the paid parking app.

"So, how far is the courthouse?" asked Charlie, who was starting to realize she was hungry again as she hadn't eaten her fill of cold lunch.

"Oh, sorry, I turned off the GPS out of habit when I got out of the car," said Tabby, getting her phone back out and punching in Miami Dade Courthouse. "Dude. We are no where near it."

"What? I mean you put it in at lunchtime, right?" asked Charlie, looking at the phone as Tabby pulled up her last GPS search.

"Dade County Pizza. I got us to Dade County Pizza," said Tabby in frustration.

"What," said Charlie with a bit of a laugh as it was normally Charlie who led them off on rabbit trails and misdirections.

---

73. Door slammers who hit other parked cars with their car doors are ten times more likely to ding the door of a parked Challenger than the car door of a Prius, according to Dodge Challenger Weekly.

"I think I was so focused on the argument over Dade County Courthouse or Miami Dade, that I just typed in Dade County and hit the first suggestion without paying attention."

"Wow."

"I know," said Tabby with her head down.

"No, I mean wow," said Charlie with a laugh. "Sorry, I have to enjoy this. It's always me that does this sort of thing."

"Right? Soak it up," said Tabby.

"Well, let's go there."

"Where?"

"Dade County Pizza. I'm hungry."

"Chicken Pad Thai didn't do it for you?"

"I'm not even sure that was chicken. Seemed like one of those vegan places that quietly lets you know it's not real chicken, so you eat it anyways."

"Or in your case, you don't eat it."

"Exactly."

"Ok, so pizza and no courthouse?"

"I mean, he's not in the courthouse, and the last few stops for Jim didn't really turn a lot up."

"Pizza it is." So, the girls walked down Miami Beach, passing college students who should've been in classes and definitely should've been wearing more pants.[74]

As they followed the GPS directions, this time aware of where they were headed, they walked past the Wolfsonian, an oddly structured building that seemed inspired by a child who was building with Duplo and hadn't yet progressed to building with actual Lego. Charlie regaled Tabby with stories of how the rich and famous had used the building as storage for their furs and jewels, protecting

---

74. Surveys show 68% of girls walking down Miami Beach are not in fact covering their assets

them from Miami's less than finest, along with protecting them from mold and mildew. The building now houses artistic treasures connected to a local university that likely also serves mostly the wealthy who will go on to own yachts and furs.

As they passed buildings and Charlie talked to no one in particular, the phone eventually led them to a store corner with windows on both sides, a pizza bar, and one row of bar stools on which customers could sit and eat pizza. It was exactly the sort of dive that would have the best pizza in town. The girls walked in, and Tabby ordered pizza from the slight Hispanic woman working behind the counter. Charlie followed suite, and once they'd ordered, the woman turned and said "Ven a ca," and being the educated women they are, they followed her the length of the counter to the register. The woman jumped a bit when she turned and saw Tabby and Charlie standing behind her.

"Oh, sorry, I'll get to you in a second," she said waving to the Hispanic man behind them to come and pay.

"She didn't know we understood."

"Yep."

While they waited, Tabby went to find the bathroom, which was back past the cash register, and she got to use one of her few lines of Spanish she felt comfortable speaking,[75] only to find the bathroom was occupied. They wandered back to the front and found some seats by the window to wait. The pizza was quickly put into a brick fire oven to cook and in no time they were eating the best pizza they'd had in years on a paper plate, burning the roofs of their mouths as it was really too good to wait for the glorious cheese to cool down. "The bathroom is clear," came a shout from the back,

---

75. Donde esta el baño

which brought Tabby out of her seat to go find the bathroom. She returned almost as quickly as she left.

"It is, in fact, not clear."

"Not clear or not clean?"

"So not clean that it isn't clear."

"Ah."

The silent decision to stop along the drive somewhere was made. The girls had lived in Florida long enough to know that there is a Publix on nearly every corner, and that Publix will almost always have a clean bathroom and no one paying attention to women who come in and use the bathroom without shopping.

As they sat eating in silence, enjoying every bite, two white men wearing matching polo shirts that were trimmed a bit too tight on the arms, giving the false appearance of muscles, came in and asked for pizza. As the woman behind the counter asked them how she could help, they responded with a yell, "speak English, we're in America."

"Wonderful," said Tabby as she finished her last bite.

"Wasn't she speaking English?"

"Yes. Yes, she was," and as the vibe began to shift, the girls got up and left, glad for food that had warmed them and glad for a kind welcome in a strange city. They worked their way back to Baby with no discussion. With any luck, they would be halfway to Key West by the time the sun set and maybe they could watch the sun make her dive into the ocean from one of the long bridges on the drive.

The stress from driving to, through, and near Miami lessened as the girls began the slow descent down the long hodgepodge of bridges that connect the upper keys with the lower keys. Each side of the road was surrounded by water that was impossibly clear.[76] The girls could see why so many choose to live in an area that would clearly be destroyed by a hurricane should one hit head on. The beauty and peace of the ocean welcomed them to come and stay like a siren expressing their permanent safety in her arms. To the right, the girls could see the old bridge that non-Floridians were surprised by, but Charlie had been raised and bred with the knowledge of. The bridge had declined severely decades ago, and the state was left with not only the need to build a better and safer bridge to their money making market of the Keys, but also the problem of what to do with a massive amount of concrete left to rot and slowly tumble into the ocean. In true governmental style, they decided for the most part to do nothing. Charlie's father, Tom, had told her about his father driving them down that bridge as kids. The traffic on what had been built as railroad trusses was stop and go with the ability to stop and lean out the window to see the ocean through a hole in the road below them. The state built a slightly larger, but not large enough, stretch of bridges to bring tourists to the Keys, and cut out a few sections of the old bridge to be sure no one would drive down the old bridge.[77]

Only the Florida State Park system made real use of the old bridge by allowing tourists and locals to walk out and fish from specific sections. The rest of the bridge was left to rot with no access to the public and no intention of removal. As is often the case, nature began working to reclaim the bridge. At some point, likely a bird planted a tree, several, in fact, along the bridge. Birds aren't always seen as tree planters, but the little shits actually drop seeds by being exactly who they are, and the combination of bird fertilizer

---

76. The girls felt that Jim, who always struggled with the stress and hectic nature of a touring schedule, must have loved the beach
77. Nothing can be put past Florida man

and seed grows into a tree, as is the case with Fred, the famous tree of the Keys. Fred grows off the Old Seven Mile Bridge and welcomes locals on their return home. He reminds Floridians that nature will always persevere, despite governmental decisions. After they passed Fred, the girls kept the music going and Charlie double checked that Tabby had actually put in the correct destination.

CHAPTER SIX

Love Street[78]

The girls weren't sure what to expect when they arrived in the dark at the Key West home Alec described to them as "the compound", but they certainly weren't expecting the cute little group of welcoming homes at the end of a quiet lane surrounded by an actual white picket fence. The compound was hidden inside a neighborhood, or rather it seemed Key West had grown around this historic neighborhood and somewhat cut it off from the neighboring lanes. GPS couldn't find the houses which Apple seemed to think didn't exist. The girls used Alec's instructions via text which told them to punch in the Monroe County library as their destination and then to round the corner behind the library to tiny Love Lane, which was barely wide enough for Baby to drive down.[79] On the right side of the road, the bamboo and tropical flowering plants formed a natural barrier between Love Lane and the library. On the left side were Victorian Era houses of the variety only seen on Florida's coastal islands.[80] The houses hung in varying stages of

---

78. Morrison, Jim. "Love Street." Strange Days. Elektra Records, 1967.
79. Tabby nearly cried from the stress of easing Baby down the little shell-lined lane. Her stress was only navigable because she knew Alec also respected Baby.
80. Compared to lake islands

decay, held together by hope, heart of palm, and paint, and they brought a sense of stepping through a portal into another time—and it was this timelessness that drew millions of tourists to Key West annually. At the end of the lane was the promised spot of refuge for Baby—a parking spot that was tucked away from drunken tourists driving golf carts and carefully shaded from the angry sun by palm fronds.[81]

Upon entering the gate, the girls found an adorable little cottage with a bike chained to the front porch. The white shell path led beyond the house, which was in need of a paint job, and to the right, it led to a second house of identical size and color. An envelope on the screen door of the main home was addressed "To Professors Tabby and Charlie." Tabby stepped forward and opened the envelope:

> Dear Professors Tabby and Charlie,
>
> Alec asked me to prepare the main home for you. His brother is staying in the home to the right, but you are not likely to see him. The front door is unlocked. We only lock the doors when the house is empty or we are sleeping. Downstairs you will find a one-bedroom apartment with a stocked kitchen and clean sheets, towels, etc. You can get to the nearly identical upstairs apartment by the path to the left of the home. Climb the stairs and you will find the second apartment to be just as clean and comfortably

---

81. For a Florida girl, Baby enjoys the shade

stocked. Alec has instructed me to help you with anything you may need. Feel free to text me.

Regards,
Constance

P.S—I left the family pass to the library and Fort Zachary Taylor on the downstairs kitchen table. Feel free to use them both.

The girls agreed to tour the apartments together before settling in and foraging for food for the night. The front porch of the downstairs apartment had spindled porch rails and softened floorboards that had clearly been welcoming visitors and island dwellers for decades. The screen door opened easily and led to a small sitting area with a white leather couch and Italian marble top everything. This was clearly the apartment Alec's parents lived in. Every wall was covered with art that had Google worthy names and price tags in the five- and six-digit range. The efficiency-style kitchen was stocked with essentials, but its smallness made the kitchen seem out of place next to the adjoining living area. However, after a drive that took up the entire day and part of the night, Tabby and Charlie were more excited to see the coffee, tea, bacon, eggs, bagels, fresh fruit, chips, salsa, Champaign, and fresh seafood than they were to see the imported Italian artwork.

In the back bedroom, the bed used much of the space created by fourteen-foot ceilings on the first floor by filling it with a four post bed and a beige canopy, which easily connected them while also providing a sense of shade from a perceived sun for those on the bed, but the thick down comforter on the bed called to Tabby alone. Charlie's feather allergy led her out of the room and towards the upstairs apartment in hopes of a synthetic comforter. The upstairs apartment, accessible only by the outside stairs the girls had noted on entering the compound, didn't have a porch to sit on, but the wide French doors opened into wood floors and a space designed for writing and reading. Alec's mom had furnished the space with her author sister in mind, since she often wintered in Key West to attempt to get some writing done. There was a comfortable brown couch, of the kind that allows all sorts of dirt sins to be hidden in its midsts, and a wall of books for the girls to explore. Given Charlie's love of books, and the threat of the feather comforter on the first floor, the rooming situation was confirmed. Tabby and Charlie were glad for the gifts of Constance. Neither realized how tired they were until the choice was in front of them to walk to a restaurant for food or to eat the food left in the kitchen. Clearly it was a "staying in" sort of night. For the first time in years, the girls said goodnight and went their separate ways, eager to begin their time in Key West in the morning.

CHAPTER SEVEN

People Down There Really Like to Get it On[82]

The evening passed in sleep uneventful, but the morning began with a start. Charlie, a light sleeper by nature, had chosen to close her bedroom door to help block out lights and sounds, both real and imaginary. The house, like most homes in historic Key West, was built on stilts made of bricks a century ago.[83] As the years passed, just as is often the case with aging women, things began to settle and sag. The floors were no longer level, but she had served her purpose and was still standing strong.

The downside to settled floors is that the pocket door to Charlie's bedroom, which was added before Tabby and Charlie were born but after the house was built, was a bit deceptive in nature. One assumes that once closed, contrary to popular philosophy, a door can be opened again. However, the floors and walls had conspired while Charlie slept and alas, the door was jammed in the "closed" position. Charlie couldn't get out of her bedroom. Fortunately, after years of working together, Tabby was rather adept at getting Charlie

---

82. Morrison, Jim. "Maggie M'Gill." Morrison Hotel/Hard Rock Cafe. Elektra Records, 1970.
83. Like most things Hemingway, Hemingway's house is an exception to this expectation

out of jams,[84] and came when Charlie texted, laughed, and grabbed a pair of scissors for leverage.[85] The door was opened in a jiffy, and the girls swore off closed doors for the rest of the trip.

That done, the girls had two activities planned for the day: breakfast and Jim's jacket. The internet informed them that the Key West Hard Rock Cafe had Jim's actual jacket on a wall, and the girls had to go pay their respects. Even after Charlie's door escapade, it was only nine a.m., and the cafe didn't open until eleven, so factoring in time to get lost, the girls still had time to see some sights. Today was about Jim and not about jobs. After a light breakfast, the girls walked down Love Lane and headed right. They had no logical reason for going right, they just figured the ocean was to the right.[86] The girls walked for several blocks with no destination in mind. They knew they were going to find Jim's jacket, but they had no particular reason to hurry. The historic homes in the neighborhood lined both sides of the street with the occasional church or men's only/clothing optional spas breaking up the monotony of history on parade.

Eventually the homes gave way to the one constant in Florida cities—creepy, old, dingy cement store fronts—and the girls began to question if perhaps they'd wandered in a rightly direction for a bit too long. After walking a while more, they came to a large metal fence blocking off barracks, which in Florida could mean one of two things: a prison or a military base.[87] As Tabby and Charlie realized they were hitting the end of the road and must decide on a turn, they watched a shirtless man come out of the open gate leading into the barracks that was guarded by a shack and an angry looking,

---

84. Usually jams of the variety that comes from a boss named Mira, the perfect name for someone who wants to be stared at often
85. Math coming in handy
86. On an island, the ocean is in all directions, including to the right
87. Both are places one cannot escape from once sent there

armed, nineteen-year-old. Fortunately, the shirtless man did not look nineteen. His legs were like banyan trunks with muscles entwining around them that Charlie and Tabby had forgotten existed. While Charlie liked to joke that she had a six pack, but it was at the back of the fridge, this man had a twelve back right in the front for all to see in his shirtless wonder, with sweat dripping down all over his glorious body.

"Tabby. Tabby. He looks just like Christian Bale. Look at those eyes."

"You can't see his eyes from here. You left your prescription sunglasses at home."

"Oh no. This man begs to be seen. I can see him."

"Come on now. We won't ever get to the jacket if we stop to admire every shirtless man."

"Not every shirtless man is worth admiring."

"True, true."

"Maybe I could be like Jim on Venice beach and call out 'Hello, I love you, won't you tell me your name,'" Charlie said, half joking.

"I don't think either of us could pull that off, and I'm not sure he did, either," laughed Tabby.

And so, they turned to the left and walked until they hit government subsidized housing,[88] which led to the obvious choice to turn left again. After all, the last random directional choices led to the Christian Bale look-a-like, and as the decrepit cement buildings began to turn into historic homes again, the girls felt pretty secure in their left turning choice. As they passed a house marked as a national historic home, a man who looked like Johnny Cash, dressed in all black, approached them to ask directions.[89] While this is at

---

88. Having lived in trailers, both girls understood them to be a sign of being on the wrong side of the tracks
89. Surveys show 99.9% of all people who find men attractive would rather see Christian Bale at any age than Johnny Cash (shirtless or shirted).

times a pick up line, the man, halfway through a beer[90] and quite confused, really did seem to be hoping for help. Once they dashed his hopes, he walked on as they did, not yet realizing that confused middle-aged men would be a steady sample of the demographic of tourists in Key West.

Their confidence shaken, but not shattered, they continued on in no direction in particular except for straight ahead when another middle-aged man caught their eyes. This man didn't appear to be lost and instead seemed to be leading a parade of children and a wife who was likely questioning her life choices. Every time this leader of the pack approached a crosswalk, he held his right hand up high for all to see and crossed. This level of confidence suggested to the girls that he had read a map, or better yet, he *was* a map to the tourist area. While they didn't wish to join his little hand-holding-high-road-crossing parade, they decided to discreetly follow from the opposite side of the road. Confidence in this stranger's abilities was not misplaced as he inadvertently led them to the Studios of Key West Books and Books, a Mecca for readers and Judy Blume fans[91] alike. The three-story building had metal signage designed with a 1960s feel, like Cosmic Rays at Disney, and the inside didn't disappoint. Not only did the store's AC offer a moment of respite from the hell hot sun of Key West, once cooled off inside, the girls found themselves surrounded by books begging to be read. Charlie grabbed an autographed Tananarive Due graphic novel and a novel by a Yugoslavian author she hadn't heard of before, and Tabby picked up a Judy Blume, which the cashier said she could leave and it would be autographed for free by the author in two weeks when Judy came back to the island. She could pick up her autographed copy then. On their way out, they found a small advertisement for

---

90. Key West police are too busy with the craziness that tourists daily bring to have open container laws
91. Judy Blume in fact owns this not-for-profit store

an author event by the obscure Yugoslavian[92] author whose book Charlie had just bought.

"Want to go?" Charlie asked.

"Why not? Let's take it as it comes. We literally have nothing else to do."

And so, the girls moved on, not making it far before they came to the Key West Theater and saw a concert for the same night as the book signing but about an hour earlier.

"Take it as it comes?"

"Got that right. And, she's Irish," answered Tabby.

"But it's not St. Paddy's Day," questioned Charlie as they approached the box office window in the same way a millennial might approach a phone booth. They had no idea an actual person really was stationed inside. The box office person[93] was a little man with a tiny brown mustache and wire rim glasses sitting behind an IBM desktop.[94]

"Welcome, yes, the Irish do sing outside of the month of March. In fact, they're rather well known for both the singing and the dancing," said the box office person with twinges of sarcasm pulling at his voice. "We have two seats left in the first level of tables, but those seats aren't together. For that you would need to go to row twenty-five."

"What's the price difference?" asked Tabby.

"They're all the same price until you move up to the balcony level," said the man with a sigh, clearly repeating lines he said all day every day.

---

92. It's often a mistake to label someone from one of the many countries that were forced to form Yugoslavia, Yugoslavian, after the death of Tito and the violent war that brought freedom and separation. For more information, see House of Cards

93. The Society of Box Office Employees (SBOE) voted unanimously to change nomenclature from box office man to box office person ahead of the game in 1974

94. Always a mistake

"But we sit at a table of strangers?"

"Yes, if you want the single seats in the front row."

"There are tables, does that mean there's food?" asked Charlie.

"No, well, you can order snacks and wine."

"We'll take the front row seats," declared Tabby.

"Wait, how will we afford this?" asked Charlie, who was starting to think she should focus a bit more on the numbers.

"You're right," said Tabby, and then she did a very unexpected thing—she pulled out the FSU P card they'd been given for their Irish professional development trip. Truth be told, Charlie had forgotten the cards existed. They'd both been given one and had put their cards away safely in May so as not to lose them before their fall trip for professional development at the Irish Four Seas Conference.[95]

"We will bill it as networking and prepping for both study abroad and professional development," said Tabby, justifying the expense.

"I like the way you're thinking," said Charlie as Tabby handed the card through the window. The girls both held their breath as he ran the card through and sighed when their tickets were in hand. While they knew the wheels of college bureaucracy moved slowly, as this was their first time using the card without prior permission, there was fear.

Tickets in hand, the girls moved forward, this time in the general direction of the noise that was now emanating from Duval Street.[96] Unfortunately, the girls' instinctual sense of direction didn't hold out, and they walked right past Hard Rock Cafe and turned left once again, bringing them eventually past Truman's very own "Little Whitehouse."

---

95. They were not sure what the four seas were, but the conference was held along the coast in Ireland
96. Duval Street in Key West looks like someone put all of the French Quarter in NOLA onto one street in Key West

"There is nothing little about that house," said Charlie.

"Go ahead."

"What?"

"Say it."

"What?"

"Oh, you always need to comment on historical presidents, so, let it out."

"Well, since you asked, I actually don't have a strong opinion on him. He wasn't contradictory like Teddy, he didn't refuse to sign a federal anti-lynching bill at a time when lynching was at an all-time national high like Wilson, and he didn't leave the vets stranded in Key West without evacuation or shelter in the face of a Cat Five like FDR. So given those examples, I am neutral for Truman. Probably would change if I researched him."

"Is there a president you do like?" asked Tabby as they navigated the crowded streets that neighbor Duval, which was full of historic homes and tourists ready to spend money and get drunk.

"Lincoln."

"Lincoln?"

"Ya, Lincoln. I hear he was funny and not racist."

"High bar you're setting there."

"And yet, it is a bar so many presidents didn't rise to meet—hey, look, isn't that Hemingway's house?"

"Well, we can't come all the way to Key West and not see that," said Tabby.

"College card?"[97]

"College card . . . might have to work on justifying this one."

"We will find a way," answered Charlie as the girls made their way around the brick-lined wall that Hemingway allegedly had

---

97. In actuality, the home, which is for profit, is cash only

built to keep tourists out and was now used to keep the supposed descendants of his cats in and to give the tourists a feeling of being inside Hemingway's private world. Not surprisingly, given the free-flowing cat food, there were many cats inside the walls, following tour guides around the grounds.

A little guard shack sat inside the front gate to purchase tickets and to lead tourists to the front porch for admittance. The house was a wide, two-story structure painted cream with yellow shutters and green double porches wrapped all the way around on both levels. The fourteen-foot ceilings gave every room a lofty feeling, which seemed fitting for the giant of a man who'd lived there almost a century before. Charlie and Tabby successfully avoided the tour guides[98] and self-guided their way through the sparsely decorated home to the overly manicured lawns wondering, aside from the infamous penny[99] he'd left in the wet cement around the pool, if there was anything that actually still resonated Hemingway on the property aside from the cats, certainly not the hundreds of daily tourists. While neither girl was a literary buff, they were pretty sure from what little they knew of him that he'd want to be left alone,[100] much like they did, but in death we frequently don't get what we want.[101]

As they ended their self-guided tour looking at the penny Hemingway had thrown in his anger when he saw his second wife had spent over $20,000 putting in the island's first private swimming pool, Tabby interrupted their thoughts to say, "That would have been $355,681.40 in today's money."

---

98. Hemingway tour guides are notoriously based in fiction
99. Thus offering his wife his last penny
100. Thus the brick wall around his property
101. Which explains the naked pictures of Hemingway in his archives

"It wouldn't have just been about the money," countered Charlie. "That was the year he was a foreign correspondent in Spain covering a bloody civil war. He was shot at. People died. Probably brought back memories of WWI.[102] Then he came home to a wife who'd built a pool to achieve a higher social status than others on the island."

"To be fair," said Tabby in the silence that followed, "the pool is a bit of an over kill."

The girls stood in silence for a while as Charlie contemplated life on return from a war zone before Tabby broke the revelry with "well, should we go find Jim's jacket?" And with that they were off, but this time, they used the GPS in their phones so as not to walk by Hard Rock Cafe.[103]

When they made their way through the maddening crowd of people in their fifties looking to get drunk on Duval with their young children in tow, the girls were glad they'd used the GPS. One has an expectation of Hard Rock Cafe to look a specific way, like the Walmart of restaurants but cooler, and this cafe did not follow expectations but met them in typical Key West style. The Cafe had taken one of the historic homes in Old Town, Key West, and added gables and shutters that harkened more to a Bavarian style and added a large second story balcony to give the idea that one could NOLA-style get drunk on the balcony.[104] The front lower level porch[105] was also full of seating that somehow spilled over into and all over the lawn until reaching the mini bar set up in what must have been a driveway at one time, giving the masses many choices for where they would like to sit and drink. Drinking heavily was not Tabby and Charlie's mission, and they would not be distracted. They

---

102. Tabby knew not to enter discussions of WWI or Charlie would never stop talking
103. Something they did not realize they had already done
104. There is no bead throwing in Key West
105. In typical Southern style

approached the hostess whose umbrella stand stood in the midst of the lawn and asked for a table for two.

"Is it true you have Jim Morrison's jacket?" Charlie asked in nervous anticipation.

"Oh, is that a drink?" asked the hostess.

"No, Jim Morrison's actual jacket framed and hanging on the wall."

"But also, yes, please, that should be a drink," said Tabby with a laugh.

The hostess was clearly flustered as she tried to recover from a lack of amazing rock and roll knowledge of Jim Morrison while working in the restaurant home for rock and roll; she asked if they would like to sit inside or out.

"In," said both girls in unison, wiping sweat from their brows.

The girls made their way up the porch steps and past the tables of people who come to Key West to drink on vacation with their kids of all ages. The inside was like a cave of classic rock. The coolness of shade was much welcomed by the girls. The expected wave of AC didn't hit as all doors and windows were open, but the home did what it was designed to do a century ago—provide cool respite to all who enter. The girls were seated near the empty bar in a room where they could see guitars that at one point belonged to various artists and some Van Halen's drumsticks and TVs everywhere blessedly playing Springsteen concerts and not a single one playing sports. The girls were home.

But where was Jim's jacket? A fear of false hope spread as they sat and looked through the drink menu. The waiter approached, bringing hope in his wake. He was a slight man, but not slightly manly. He exuded testosterone in the way of Eddie Veder. His long brown hair was swept up into a bun, but it fought the system and was heading out in any way it chose. His eyes seemed to be pleading for escape, but his voice kindly asked the girls if they would like a drink. While they agreed this wasn't a skinny trip, they both hated sweet drinks. Since they'd just left Hemingway's house, Papa's Pilar[106] seemed like a good choice.

"Are these two Papa drinks sweet?" asked Tabby.

The waiter raised his eyebrows slightly, a motion barely detectable but suggesting a positive impression.

"Well, this one, yes," the waiter said pointing at the menu, "this one a bit less so. If you're looking for a less sweet drink, I could bring you mojitos and ask them to use less sweetener?"[107] he offered.

"Yes, please."

"Make it two," said Charlie in the way of women who go to bars and stress as they have absolutely no idea what they want to drink.

"Excuse me," Tabby said, interrupting the waiter's escape, "is it true you have Jim Morrison's jacket?"

"Yes, we do. It's on the wall right over there," he said pointing to an adjoining room.

"Can we go see it?" asked Charlie in anticipation.

"Sure. You can walk all around in here if you want to," he said with a friendly nod as he walked off presumably in search of their island mojitos.[108]

With that encouragement, the girls went to seek the holy grail of their trip and weaved their way through the maze of tables seated with patrons who were ignorant of the fact they were eating in the nearness of greatness: THE Jim Morrison's jacket. And there it was,

---

106. Papa was a nickname for Ernest Hemingway, which started back in the day when he was way too sexy for a name like Papa. Pilar was his boat, and Papa's Pilar is the name of a tasty rum company that has capitalized on both names and their associations

107. Bar tenders assume middle-aged women don't actually enjoy the taste of alcohol and so they hide the alcohol behind massive amounts of sugar

108. Island mojitos are better than those made and enjoyed off island. This saying is true for all islands and their mojitos

in all its glory, bigger than life, and framed in museum quality glass with appropriate lights shining on it, giving it the glorious appearance of an angelic halo.[109] Thankfully, there were no people eating at the table in front of the jacket's hallowed space on the wall because the girls were going to be hanging all over the table either way.

The jacket was snakeskin, and the sign explained it was a custom jacket bought and worn by Jim in 1966 before he gave it to his girlfriend/common wife (as Tabby and Charlie referred to her), Pamela.[110] The jacket was at the Rock and Roll Hall of Fame from 2004-2012 when it was freed and moved to the Cafe to sit before the masses who have no interest in ever going to Cleveland. They stood in awe and resisted the urge to pet the display. To the left was a staged photo of the band with Jim doing his best to look down and appear angry.

"He was already gaining a bit of weight in that one," said Charlie, who considered herself an expert on Jim's waist.

"Probably why he gave the jacket to the common wife. That thing is tiny."

"OMG—look at this one," Charlie said drooling over a picture of Jim leaning against a bar, his left leg provocatively resting on a bar stool to his left, his jacket[111] slipping off his shoulder, and his eyes boring into the camera, a beer in his hand and a come and get me look on his face.

"OMG, it is—"

---

109. Jim Morrison was many things, but he was not an angel
110. They also did not acknowledge the woman he had married in a Pagan ceremony
111. Not this jacket

"Autographed. It. Is. Autographed," yelled Charlie. At this point, other patrons were staring but my goodness, what are they even doing at the Cafe if not to fan girl over the memorabilia.[112]

To the right of the jacket was a picture of Jimi Hendrix above one more picture of the Doors with the famous Doors font on it.[113] The girls felt comfort in knowing the jacket was so rightly placed between Jimi Hendrix and Bruce Springsteen. A beautiful Bruce—Jim—Jimi layout.[114] They sighed a collective sigh and made their way back through the uneducated patrons who were unaware they were basking in the shadow of Jim's jacket and sat at their table just as the waiter came with their mojitos.

"Here you are ladies. Did you find the jacket?" he asked in a conspiratorial voice.

"It's so small!" said Charlie

"Did he have it tailored for Pamela?" asked Tabby, not thinking of the unlikeliness of a snakeskin jacket being tailorable.

"No, I don't think so. People ask about that a lot, but I think I could wear it," he said with a shrug of his shoulders as he returned to the other tables.

"Wow, the internet says he was 145 pounds and 5'11'," said Tabby.

"Looks like during what he called his fat days he was only 185."

"Wow," said the girls, in a real Owen Wilson moment, enjoying their own natural high and trying not to think of their own weight. They relished the moment of Jim's jacket and sat in wonder at the music videos ranging from live Mumford and Sons to younger bands they'd never heard of.

---

112. Surveys done by the Association of Bar Food show that no one who has eaten at Hard Rock Cafe comes back for the food
113. Despite numerous petitions asking them to do so, Apple has refused to make a Doors font
114. No other Doors band members matter

"Do you know this guy singing?" Tabby asked Charlie.

"No, and my god does he look young. He's dancing around and eyeing the camera like he is some sort of sex symbol, but I swear we have students who are older than him."

"Right? Go home. It's past your curfew," laughed Tabby.[115]

When the waiter returned, they both ordered a salmon noodle bowl, because who doesn't like salmon and uncooked ramen on top of a salad? While they waited for their meal, they sat in silence listening to the father at the table next to them explain the alcoholic drinks on the menu to his boys who were clearly not old enough to drink legally. He seemed to be bragging about his ability to drink, something that they didn't have, some sort of compensation for all the things they could likely do better than their father at this point in life.[116]

"Tabby, what do we do from here on? I mean I had kinda assumed eventually we would both go full-time at FSU, meet some guys, get married, settle down, maybe have a kid or two."

"Speak for yourself. No kids for me. I have 150 of them every semester and that is all I need."

"Ok, but where do we go from here?"

"Well, I think dropping off some CVs would be a good start. Want to try tomorrow?"

"Yes, let's. I haven't gone this long without a plan since elementary school. I saw a printer in the little office off the kitchen in my apartment."

"Great. Let's print some CVs up tonight and tomorrow we could hit the library and the college. Surely one of them is hiring."

"Sounds like a plan, and I like the sound of having a plan."

---

115. Likely Jim himself was younger than the band on tv at the time when they found his pictures to be so appealing

116. Like grow hair

"I know you do. Ready to get out of here?" said Tabby, forgetting about food.

"Yep. Veni Vidi Vici." And with the Latin words spoken, the waiter appeared with just one salad.

"I apologize, ladies. There was a mix-up in the kitchen, and, for some reason, they only made one salad."

"This is what we get for ordering the same thing," moaned Tabby.

"The second one will be out shortly, and, as an apology, the drinks are on the house."

Thus began the long wait for Charlie's meal, which seemed to have no end. Tabby felt guilty as she munched on her salad. She was stuck in that moment of "If I wait, my food will get soggy, but if I eat in front of my friend, I'll feel bad," but as often happens, the stomach won over the bad feeling.[117] Charlie sat in silence and focused on the jacket on the wall, which she could just barely make out from her seat. If she had to wait, at least she could wait in the shadow of Jim; she often considered herself to be in his shadow, but the lights on the ceiling actually were casting a shadow on the table where her food was supposed to be.

We can't be sure what Tabby and Charlie expected to happen next,[118] but what happened next was certainly not what they expected. An older man wobbled up with his cane, clearly reaching the stage of needing a walker and not a cane, and he stopped in front of their table with a nod, "You have to watch out for this place. I sat down and ordered lunch and look at me now. It's been fifty years," and then he walked off. The girls couldn't restrain their laughter, glad for the break in tension as they continued to wait for

---

117. Which is closely connected to guilt
118. Except for Charlie's food to show up

Charlie's meal, which took nearly another thirty minutes to come.[119] When the food was eaten, they asked for the check, only to find out the older gentleman had paid for their lunches on his way out. Feeling thankful, they headed out of the restaurant ready to take the afternoon on and grateful for Old Town hospitality. Having spent the day in Key West without seeing the water, the girls decided it was best to head towards where they thought the water would be, heading left but this time on a new street. After all, their sense of direction had led them to the shirtless Christian Bale[120] look alike, so they might as well stick with their instincts now that they had a broad destination in mind. After wandering the streets and stopping to talk to several roosters, the girls realized they were no closer to finding the beach than they'd been at any point in the day.

"Hey, I've got an idea. Let's stop at a place that has rooftop seating and see if we can find the ocean. We can get a drink and see if we can find a clear path to the beach."

"Ya, but let's pick carefully. I don't want to end up at one of those $50 a drink rooftop bars."

"Is that a thing you find often?" questioned Tabby.

"Well, no, but I was willing to pay about that for a salad and a drink at the Cafe."

"Still worth it. I would have paid that just to see the jacket."

"Me, too, but I'm worried about what we have left, and we can't keep using the college card," sighed Charlie.

"Too true, too true. Hey, this place looks good. Bit of a dive bar, but we're just getting a drink."

"Whistle Bar. Let's go."

The girls entered the bar on the first floor which was labeled "The Bull" and asked where the stairs were. The bar tender smiled

---

119. They were actually out fishing for the salmon
120. No look alike can actually compare to Christian Bale

and said "Alright, alright" in a very Mathew McConaughey sort of way before pointing them in the right direction.

"Remember, drinking is mandatory," he said and laughed as they went towards the stairs, missing the rest of what he said.

"People here are weird."

"That they are," Tabby said as they made their way up the stairs.

The doorway to the rooftop bar had a huge sign that said cellphones weren't allowed, which struck the girls as unusual, but they figured with all their degrees, they could remember the path they would see from the roof. Opening the door to the roof let in a wave of humidity similar to the wind from hell that hits as soon as one walks out of Orlando International Airport, but it wasn't the heat wave that shocked Tabby and Charlie. No. It was the people.

"Tabby, everyone is naked."

"I see that," Tabby said as they froze and let the door slam behind them.

"Tabby, the sign says 'Drinking is Mandatory, Clothing is Optional.'"

"Geez. And no. I am not getting naked in a rooftop bar."

"What do we do?"

"Take it as it comes. That's our theme for this trip," Tabby declared as she went and sat next to an older gentleman at the bar whose rear end enveloped the bar stool he was sitting on. As the girls looked around, they found what teenage boys find when they go to the French Rivera looking for naked French girls—a lot of overweight old men looking for naked women and not caring what anyone thinks of them.

"You know, I kind of envy their confidence."

"Me, too, but I'm not joining them."

"Nor are we taking any of that as it comes."

"Got that right," said Tabby as she looked around and realized they may be the only women in the bar.

"What can I get for you ladies?" asked the bar tender who was thankfully wearing clothes, along with a glorious mustache that was long enough to form some sort of a much-needed covering for the man sitting to Tabby's left.

"Mojito," said Charlie.

"Frozen or on ice?"

"Frozen is an option? I'll take frozen."

"Sounds good, me, too," said Tabby and the girls sat back looking straight ahead at the bar in front of them, enjoying the view of the fully clothed bar tender working on their frozen drinks.

"New to the naked bar scene?" asked the bar tender as he worked.

"How could you tell?" asked Tabby sarcastically. The bar tender laughed. "We get that a lot. No worries, there is no pressure to do anything you don't want to do here, and also, there is no sex allowed on the premises."

"I saw the sign," said Tabby pointing to the "No sex on premise" sign. "I bet that had to be custom made."

"You know, it actually didn't. There's a bigger need for those signs than you might think," he laughed as he brought the girls their drinks. "Here you go. Enjoy," he said as he placed the alcoholic slushies in front of them.

"Can you tell us how to get to the beach from here?" Charlie asked, not wanting to approach the side seats for a view due to the long line of older buns sitting and enjoying the sun along the edges of the roof.

"Well, you have hit on a well-guarded secret of Key West: there are no real beaches. Now, we do have a few small man-made beaches, but that is it. Your best option is to go to Fort Zachary Taylor. They have probably the best beach on the island and plenty of parking."

"Now you're speaking my language," said Tabby who'd been afraid to take Baby out anywhere for fear of the combination of drunk tourists and street parking.

"Is there anywhere we can watch the sunset?" queried Charlie, who was definitely not wanting to stay at Whistle Bar to watch the sunset. There were already enough moons out.

"Now that you want to do at Mallory Square, but you've got a few hours' wait for that. Best spot to watch the sunset anywhere in the world, and you can quote me on that," said the waiter as he twirled his mustache.

"Can we carry this out with us?" asked Tabby.

"Well, there is no open carry rule around here, but y'all don't look like the open carry sort," he said with a wink and went off to help another patron.

"Ok, let's finish these, eyes down, and then let's get out of here."

"Agreed," said Tabby. That was easier said than done. While the alcohol can at times cover the brain freeze effect of drinking a slushy too fast, this one had more sugar than alcohol and the girls found themselves needing to drink slower than they'd hoped.

When they were done, the trip down the stairs had more laughing than the patrons in the bar downstairs were expecting, but Tabby and Charlie really didn't care what others thought of them, as long as they all had their clothes on.

"Let's go back the way we came and head to that Mallory Square he mentioned."

"But this time let's use the GPS. Want to get another drink to wash out the memory of that place? We need to waste a few hours anyway."

"I think I've had enough alcohol for the time being; let's get some dessert and coffee."

"This place looks good," said Charlie, pointing to First Flight, which boasted of being the Southernmost Brewery in the United States.

"Can we ask the hostess if clothing is required," laughed Tabby.

"Looks like everyone has clothes on," Charlie said, leaning over the brick wall that surrounded the bar, much like the wall surrounding Hemingway's estate, "but look, let's ask for one of those tables in the garden that's far away from everyone. I'm done with people for a while."

"Agreed," said Tabby as the girls walked in and asked to be seated by the far wall in the garden. Unlike the rooftop bar, this one was pretty empty, but it was only mid-afternoon and with clothing required, they were not seeing the kind of action the Whistle Bar was getting.

The girls sat in the shade of the neighboring trees that leaned over the wall. The large garden area was really a giant brick patio, but the frequent placement of potted plants of various heights gave the patio the feel of a garden. Much like many bars in Key West, Hard Rock Cafe included, the backside of the brewery was an old historic home converted for the brewery's purposes. The brick wall to their right was taller than they were, so from their seated position they had privacy from the two houses on the other side, the smaller of which was very close to the wall.[121] The girls sat in the shade and rested, enjoying the time to kick off their shoes and relax. Tabby played solitaire on her phone, and Charlie pulled out a book from her purse.

---

121. The smaller of the two houses was the cottage Robert Frost had stayed in and written in, but Tabby and Charlie were unaware

"That looks new; is that the one you got from the Judy Blume bookstore?" asked Tabby.

"Yep. It's the one by the Yugoslavian author."

"Oh, right. What's it called again?"

"*I'm Not Going Anywhere.*"

"Oh, I'm sorry, no worries. I wouldn't ask you to go anywhere," said the waitress who'd just approached at the wrong time.

"Oh no!" said Tabby laughing, "It's the title of her book."

"Oh good. I was wondering. It's my first day, and it's not been going well. I keep going to the back and crying, and my boss keeps telling me to pull up my big girl panties."

"Oh," said Tabby, in that awkward moment of not knowing how to respond to an oversharing stranger.

"I'm sorry," said Charlie, falling back on the old stand-bye line of comfort.

"Can I get you a drink?"

"Sure, can I get a black tea with a little bit of milk, and do you have any scones by any chance?"

"No, but we do have pie. The best kind sold in Key West—Key Lime."

"Ok. I'll have one of those."

"I'll have the same."

"Ok, I'll be right back," said the waitress.

"Do you think she's ok?"

"Doesn't appear to be."

"Do you think she'll get our order right."

"Unlikely."

Both girls sighed and went back to their own thoughts. After spending so many years offering comfort to students who needed counseling and not just the listening ear of a professor in her office hours, they didn't have anything for the waitress but decided to tip nicely and be patient, and they remained so even when the green tea with sugar arrived without pie, and even when the pie never came.

The pie may not have come, but the waitress did. Just like their students, she seemed to sense some sort of motherly affection or tendencies in Tabby and Charlie, which was something neither understood as they'd never been mothers and hadn't even ever owned a cat.[122] The closest either ever came to mothering was their plants, and those only survived due to the kindness of Mrs. Bunderoff. Regardless, she sensed something and sat down at their table, causing a raising of eyebrows from each of the girls who were too polite to question.

"I just can't take it. I'm no good at this job. This is my second waiting job in as many days. There's no work here, and I can't survive on just one waiting job. I'll need two or three to make ends meet." With that said, she laid her head on the table and began crying.

"Have you thought of switching careers or maybe going back to school?" asked Tabby.

"I tried school and failed out of every class. Three semesters in a row. I have so much debt." The crying got louder, and the girls realized once again that their doctorates were not very useful—they were doctors of the sort that could correct commas, history, and math problems, not real-life problems.

"Well, have you tried across the street at the Whistle Bar?" asked Charlie, a plan forming in her head for this young girl, who was a bit of a mess, but very well-endowed.

---

122. Tabby in fact hates cats

"No, I just got here last week. I'm staying in my friend's houseboat and can only try places I can walk to. I haven't walked over there yet."

"Well, it's not very far. Are you on break? You could go over and see if they're hiring."

"Dressed like this?" the girl asked, looking down at her formfitting button-down uniform shirt and black pants.

"Just like that, but maybe put your hair down and unbutton a few of those buttons," and with that, Tabby realized what Charlie was doing but refused to join in.

"Ok, thanks. I'll go give it a try," she said, walking away from their table and out the gate to head to the Whistle Bar.

"Did you just send that girl to go prostitute herself?"

"No, I just thought all those old naked guys would surely rather see a topless or scantily clad female bar tender than they would our bar tender with his mustache. Maybe so much so they will train her to bartend. She can take that skill and go make some money with a shirt on elsewhere."

"I see your logic. I do not approve, but I see it."

"I'm not her mother."

"That you are not."

With the sending off of the waitress, the girls realized they could no longer pay the bill for their tea. They asked at the bar and were met with shrugs, so they headed in the general direction of Mallory Square, passing by the famous Captain Tony's just as a middle schooler was entertaining his drunk parents by repeatedly throwing a coin at the mouth of a fish statue on the roof. Charlie and Tabby felt validated in the life advice they just gave their waitress. After all, clearly parents weren't doing that much better.

Mallory Square is a courtyard right on the water not far from where cruise ships dock, which means it is surrounded by touristy shops and restaurants that cater to people who hope to spend money quickly and with little to no thought. The girls easily passed the trinket stores but were drawn into Kermit's with a promise of key lime pie on the door.

"Hey, I think this is the place I read about on TripAdvisor. Let's get some pie and sit in Mallory Square and wait for the sun to dip down." Tabby agreed, and they grabbed a piece of pie each; the pie was packaged in cheap plastic and paired with a plastic fork, so the expectations were low. However, no matter the pie quality, they were sitting on a concrete block wall looking at million-dollar yachts and staring out at the ocean. Life was good in the here and now, and nothing else mattered. They sat watching the street performers and listening to the live musicians around the corner, and watched as eventually the sun set in a glorious display of color, with a brief flash of green as it hit the water, and decided that life was what they made of it. They might not have jobs right now, but they would find jobs, and they would do what they could to stay here and make a life for themselves.

The morning came in the most uneventful way possible, which was what the girls needed. They packed a small breakfast of bagels and headed to Charlie's idea of the perfect picnic ground—the local cemetery, which really wasn't far from the compound they were staying in.[123] The cemetery was gated, although the front gate seemed permanently propped open. Since there wasn't a clear and present danger to those within the cemetery, they assumed the gate

---

123. Nothing in Old Town is really that far from any other point

was to keep others out, but that wasn't all that necessary as the girls were the only ones entering. They went through the gates as they entered most things—with no plan.[124] They wandered the pathways, which were blessedly crooked, and stopped to admire a gated section with a monument inside for the USS Maine. "Ah, the Maine," said Charlie as she went off on a mini lecture of the sad fortune of the USS Maine. Tabby did her best to nod accordingly as she read the numbers on each grave. She loved the opportunity to read the birth and death dates and quickly do the math to figure how much time the person underground had had above ground. What kind of life did they have? Was it enough? Did they see death coming? Most don't. It reminded Tabby of how short life is and the need to do what she could with the time that she had, and maybe that was why she hadn't argued when Charlie wanted to hit the cemetery.

As Charlie's lecture wound down, they made their way to a miniature brick house and sat on a bench to eat their breakfast and enjoy the view as the sunrise hit, lighting up the sky with beautiful hues of orange and red. They couldn't see the exact moment of sunrise, but its effects spread across the sky and made entering the cemetery in the dark just before dawn very worth it.[125] With breakfast done, they rose and started to make their way down towards Fort Zachary Taylor. The way was long but beautiful as they avoided drunken Duval Street as much as possible. The beauty of Key West made them glad they'd decided to walk and not to drag Baby through traffic.

Fort Zachary Taylor boasts of being the best beach in Key West and there in lies the problem—the boast. Tabby and Charlie arrived

---

124. In fact, like most professors, they often walked into the classroom with no idea what they would lecture on that day
125. Like all those who love old graveyards, Charlie understood and explained to Tabby that ghosts, if they should exist, do not come out at dawn. She used Hamlet's ghost as evidence to support her argument

after breakfast, with Tabby again asking why the cemetery came before the beach ("because you said you wouldn't go afterwards since it would be too close to sunset").[126] Knowing that Charlie wouldn't get her off the beach to tour the historical parts of the park, Charlie insisted on hitting the tour first before walking to the beach part of the state park. The fort is a pentagonal-like structure built to defend the southernmost point of the U.S. Charlie explained the history of the park and how it came to be preserved. Tabby dutifully nodded her head while inwardly questioning why she hadn't chosen a friend who was a captain of a cruise ship or something that was truly helpful rather than a best friend who was full of useless knowledge. Tabby sighed as she watched a Carnival cruise ship pull out of the harbor and head out to sea.

Finally, Charlie finished her historical discussion with mostly herself, and the girls set off on the trail they could see from the vantage point of the roof of Fort Zach (as Charlie liked to call it) and headed out to the water. They needed the view from the roof[127] because, as was typical of their wandering ways, they hadn't asked for a map at the front gate. They rounded the mangroves to the left of the trail, sand sticking between their toes in their open-toed shoes, and followed the long and winding trail of rock-lined ocean where man kept nature inaccessible for the sake of the shoreline. The path went on for so long that the girls doubted openly whether they would ever be able to access the turquoise water that called to them from beyond the rocks, but soon they found the crowd. Yes, Fort Zach had indeed advertised their beaches well; they'd been discovered by everyone. Tabby and Charlie made their way along the pebbly beach, dodging small children as they went, searching

---

126. "Historians love visiting cemeteries more than beaches", as was explained in Historians of America Magazine
127. Which was blessedly free of old naked people

for a place to sit. The only space they could find open was behind a small child who was digging a hole to China as if he was a dog, throwing all the sand and pebbles onto the empty space.[128]

"Charlie, let's rent chairs. I think the area down there is for people who pay for chairs. See—there's the host to pay."

"Twenty-seven dollars for two chairs and an umbrella? Deal," said Charlie, reaching for her wallet as Tabby pulled out the college card and reached beyond her.

"Again?"

"Again."

Tabby paid for their chairs, listening to nothing the man said about where they should and should not bring their chairs, which, although they paid for them, they still had to drag to the set location themselves. Given their academic and not physical nature, they stopped as soon as they could, not realizing they'd be next to the path everyone else would soon be dragging their chairs on. Nor did they realize they'd be sitting next to a group of college students who'd decided to skip the first week of classes and have their own spring break in the fall. Tabby and Charlie loved their students but only in certain contexts, and the beach wasn't one of those contexts.

The girls quickly tossed off their shoes and with the feigned confidence they appear to have in the classroom, they stripped off their shorts and shirts and walked calmly down to the water.[129] They soaked and floated, forgetting everything but the sun and the feel of the water supporting them back and forth towards the shoreline. Jet skis and boats passed by, reminding them that while the water appeared clear enough to swim for miles, they should stay near the shore. Charlie took the passing jet skis as her signal to go sun for a bit. Her beach pattern was dip, sun and get hot, dip again. Tabby was

---

128. No one wants to sit behind small sand throwing children at the beach
129. Like all mature women do at the beach

more of a dip, dip, dip, sun sort of girl.[130] Charlie lay on her chest on the chair that elevated her above all the beach goers who didn't pay for a chair and commenced to relax and read her Yugoslavian book she had picked up at Books and Books.

"Uhhmm, did you see my sign," interrupted a demanding voice.

Charlie, aware she may have placed her chair in the wrong spot, replied "I'm sorry," questioningly.

"My sign—you have to pay to rent the chairs. You can't just unfold one and sit where you like without paying," said the man standing over her. His white shirt clung to his chest, and his loose brown hair suggested a calmer nature than his words betrayed.

"Oh, I did rent a chair. Both of them, and the umbrella," Charlie said standing up and looking at the man, who wasn't much younger than them. At those words, he started to stammer a bit, stumbling over himself with apologies.

"I'm sorry, people just take chairs all the time. You wouldn't believe it. And those unpaid for chairs come out of my paycheck, as small as it is," and his words kept coming, words that Charlie recognized, after years and years of listening to students, to mean he just needed to vent, so Charlie listened and nodded until he moved on.

And so, the beach day passed in peace from there on out. The girls alternated between water and sun in their own set ways, and eventually they packed up and began the walk home, which seemed so much longer than the walk there had been. They slowly wound their way back towards Love Lane wondering if they should've driven, stopping at Kermit's for more slices of Key Lime Pie to go, and when they reached their cottage, they went their separate ways for some peace and quiet, and their own pieces of pie.

---

130. Florida girls all have their own beach patterns

CHAPTER EIGHT

Cancel my Subscription . . . Send my Credentials to the House of Detention[131]

The third morning in Key West began sunny and bright. The island breeze kept the morning weather at a cool 72 degrees, and the girls were ready to explore. Charlie had overheard at Hemingway's house that in his era, the restaurant Blue Heaven was a brothel/bar whose patio held a boxing ring; in typical Key West fashion, Hemingway boxed there regularly during his time in Key West. While the girls were never really interested in boxing as a sport, following on the heels of the literary giant seemed a good idea, and it was only a fifteen-minute walk with two left turns[132] and then one right turn. The girls headed out excitedly because apparently Blue Heaven served good pancakes.[133] At eight a.m. the city was still quiet, leaving the streets easier to navigate as the girls passed construction workers and locals on bikes headed about their daily routines, with the beauty of the city surrounding them for the backdrop. The sight

---

131. Morrison, Jim. "When the Music's Over." Strange Days. Elektra Records, 1967.
132. Their favorite way to go
133. Tabby's sole motivation for going

of others heading to work brought the girls' lack of employment to mind and reminded them of how unpleasant returning to work sounded. If only they could find a way to survive without work.[134]

"Charlie, we're going right by the library," Tabby said at the end of Love Lane. "Let's drop in and see if there's any work."

"Good idea. And after breakfast we can drive over to the college and look for work."

With that decided, they went back to the cottage, grabbed their CVs, and headed to the library, turning at the end of Love Lane towards the Monroe County Library, which, unbeknownst to the girls, was another Hemingway stop.[135] The pink stucco one-story building had architectural details that harkened back a few decades, cementing its place in the historic district. Next to the library there was a gated garden known as the Palm Garden, which was walled-in similar to Hemingway's house and many other gardens in Key West. The brick-lined walkways and benches were surrounded by plants Charlie and Tabby could only describe as being palm like, and thus assuredly came the name of the garden. The girls passed the garden by, eager to knock on the door of opportunity in the hopes of securing a place in Key West.

They ascended the steps into the front door of the library, finding the interior to be disappointingly modern, and walked up to the same front desk that is seen in every library across America.[136]

"Hello, how can I help you," asked the friendly looking older woman working behind the desk. Her hair was cropped short in typical librarian fashion and behind her glasses, her eyes seemed to anticipate being asked truly great questions from those

---

134. The true American Dream
135. The first girl to break Hemingway's heart and end up in a novel for it later worked as a librarian in this very building
136. Librarians adore sameness and familiarity

seeking answers only she could help navigate. However, to her disappointment, the girls asked if the library might be hiring. She sighed both inwardly and externally.

"No, we have a small staff and no budget to expand. We are, however, always looking for volunteers and Friends of the Library."

"Do you know of any open positions in the area? We're both professors looking to relocate," asked Tabby.

"Unfortunately, the island is full of retired professors, doctors, lawyers, and what have you. It's a tough job market. And rent here is 3-4 thousand a month for a one bedroom," she remarked, assuming the girls would want a one bedroom.

"How do normal people survive?" Charlie asked.

"They don't. They work 3-4 jobs at a time bussing tables, cleaning houses, what have you, and they leave as soon as they realize it isn't going to happen for them. My advice is this: Leave," she stated bluntly, "I'm sorry to be so upfront, but I've seen too many ruin their finances trying to stay."

Tabby and Charlie thought of the waitress at First Flight. "No, I appreciate the bluntness," said Tabby as they made their way back outside, leaving under a cloud of disappointment. The girls decided to call HR at the college rather than force Baby out of her shaded spot for a fruitless journey. They sat on the cement wall that both supported the very ground the library was built on and provided seats for the homeless population who gathered in small groups of one[137] or two to use the free Wi-Fi and sit in the coolness of the shade surrounding the library, enjoying the closeness of an aspect of a normal life they'd had at one point. The girls sat and searched online for the local college's HR department, realizing that they really were only a few degrees separated from homelessness themselves.

---

137. In true Kurt Cobain style, authors and the homeless population realize that their friends are in their head.

"Here it is," said Charlie.

"Good, are you going to call?"

"Well, looks like their hiring system is fully online," said Charlie, who hadn't applied for a job in over ten years and was surprised to learn how quickly life had evolved.

"Do you see anything?" Tabby asked, trying to read the screen over Charlie's shoulder.

"Well, I filtered the search to show just faculty, both full and part time, and I only see they're hiring for some vocational faculty."[138]

"Not even adjunct positions?"

"Not one."

"Let's call and confirm," said Tabby, getting her phone out to call the number on Charlie's screen.

"Hello, yes, my name is Dr. Tabitha Divine. I'm a math professor at FSU, and I'm looking to relocate to Key West, as is my partner in the History Department.[139] I'm wondering, I don't see any openings in any department on your website. Is that accurate? . . . umhm . . . I see . . . Thank you for your time," she said shutting the phone off.

"Anything?"

"Nothing. Apparently so many retired professors are in the area that they basically only use adjuncts, with no more than one or two full-time faculty positions in any department and those hardly ever open up."

"Well shit," said Charlie, whose dying dream of staying in Key West brought on the rarely used swear word from the professor influenced by a conservative grandmother who never swore. "Let's get some food and figure it out." With that, the girls continued on

---

138. Colleges are almost always hiring adjuncts to teach air conditioning and heating, the service most revered in the state of Florida

139. The girls often refer to themselves as partners as an inside joke and an easier way of explaining themselves. This might also contribute to their perpetual singleness

their second left hand turn of the day, wondering what their next move should be. Alec's invitation was for the entire semester, but they didn't want to overstay their welcome.

The girls wandered over to Blue Heaven and found a short waitlist, which was no issue as the girls had nothing but time. Once seated, they quickly ordered pancakes and mimosas, hoping a drink would ease their thoughts. The courtyard was comfortable, but it seemed to be full of ghosts of days past, as if one might expect Hemingway to wander back anytime. Chickens moved swiftly from table to table in search of generous gifts from tourists[140] and roosters rudely crowed, interrupting table conversations. Umbrellas were connected by black canvas tarps which worked together to provide shade for all patrons.

"Screw it, Tabby. What have we been saying this whole trip?" Charlie asked, expecting no reply. "Take it as it comes. Listen. All the good things in our lives are connected to Jim. Our friendship. This trip. Our jobs—ok, well maybe that one hasn't ended well, but you know what I mean."

"I know. He is the center."

"Yes, and what have we always said about his death?"

Tabby floundered at the mention of the death neither woman accepted.[141] "Charlie, he's not dead."[142]

"Exactly. Let's prove it. We're researchers. It's what we do. Let's go find him."

Tabby let that thought sink in. Really, in their shared office over the last several years she'd seen Charlie track down historical facts about presidents that she herself marveled at, and when Charlie did

---

140. In Key West it is legal to carry open containers, but it is illegal to feed chickens

141. Rock and Roll Magazine has published an article annually since 1974 that focuses on the faked death of Jim Morrison

142. As Jim had told the band he'd fake his own death one day, even they wondered if he truly died

hit a metaphorical brick wall while researching, it was Tabby who found a way to help her over that wall. Maybe they could. Really, if anyone could do it, it was them, and it needed to be done. Even if they didn't share their discovery with the world, they would know, and maybe they would even meet Jim. And that was the thought that really sealed the deal for Tabby.

"But how will we pay for it? He supposedly died in Paris. A trip like that will cost money."

"The same way we have paid for every fun thing here—the college card. Do you remember the limit?" asked Charlie, knowing that Tabby was incapable of forgetting any fact related to numbers.

"Just under ten thousand each."

"We could get pretty far on that combined amount."

"If we do it right, we'll arrive with money down for an apartment and start up money left over, when we get wherever we decide to settle, after finding Jim, of course. The wheels of the college move so slowly, we'd have months before they'd even notice and start looking for us."

"I think you might be right, and I also think that amount would be too low for another country to extradite us. In true Hemingway fashion, we could become ex-pats," said Charlie, a tone of awe in her voice.

"Alright, where do we start?" asked Tabby.

"Well, to save some funds, let's go with what we have. We start in Dublin."

"Charlie, it's more likely he went to Dublin, Virginia than to Dublin, Ireland."[143]

"True, but we have tickets to London and then to Dublin for the professional development trip, and we have hotel rooms in Dublin.

---

143. Due to his father's career in the Navy, Jim spent much of his childhood in Virginia and even went to high school in Alexandria

Getting over there is the biggest expense, and if we go to Dublin, from there we can fly or drive back to London, London to Paris and then figure out from Paris where he went after faking his death, and at a pretty low cost for us. Or we could cut Dublin out altogether."[144]

"OMG. This could work. We could do this. We will do this." And thus, a beautiful plan was born to throw caution to the wind and go find Jim.

---

144. Charlie's Irish heritage dictated that she could not in fact cut out Dublin, but the statement was made to appease the numbers member of the trip

CHAPTER NINE

Illegitimate Son of a Rock and Roll Star[145]

Despite the sweltering heat and humidity, the girls couldn't stay inside for long. They spent each day of their time in Key West out exploring the island. The sounds of the city called to them from outside of the compound walls.[146] After their trip to Fort Zachary, where they got to soak in the perfection of clear water, they decided they had to get in the water again before heading out for Ireland where they knew the water had to be too cold for these Florida girls. Charlie slipped into her bikini and headed down to persuade Tabby to go to the beach, only to find Tabby sitting on her front porch, soothed by the sounds of cooing doves and the neighbor's pool filter constantly humming behind the fence.

"Tabby, we are almost out of time in Key West. Let's get in the water one more time."

"I'm way ahead of you. Already have my suit on," Tabby said, rising from her chair and picking up the beach bag she'd already packed with towels and waters.

---

145. Morrison, Jim. "Maggie M'Gill." Morrison Hotel/Hard Rock Cafe. Elektra Records, 1970.
146. The sounds of the city being the dogs, ever present roosters, and noisy airplanes passing over head.

Charlie followed Tabby off the porch and down Love Lane onto Fleming Street and slowly through the humidity down Elizabeth Street and eventually Simonton Street to hit the local beach they'd heard would be worth the short walk. The streets were crowded, and as they got closer to the beach, they soon realized the reason for the crowds—another cruise ship was parked in port. The postage stamp sized beach was, despite the large parking lot, about the size of land that five or six people would spread out on at a beach in Clearwater or St. Augustine, but here in Key West the space had somehow filled with easily five or six times that amount like a Harry Potter bus folding in on itself to make the space work for something it was not designed for.[147] The people filled the white sand to the left of the pier and spilled out into the water and onto the pier. To the right of the pier, a boat was parked, and dogs were playing fetch in the water.

"Well."

"Yep."

"I want to get in, but do I want to get in with fifty of my closest strangers or with the dogs and the boat?"

"And which side do you think is least likely to mean swimming in pee?"

"Dog side for sure."

"Are we getting in?"

"Nope."

And so, the girls defeatedly made their way back through the parking lot, passing more families heading to the beach with children and wagons in tow. They headed right since the road was one they hadn't walked yet, and they saw the sun like a beacon of light streaming down on a brick Haagan Dazs store.

---

147. And indeed, it was designed as it is a man-made beach

"It's a sign."

"I don't know about you, but I'll feel a lot better about missing out on the beach if I can eat an ice cream cone while walking along the water."

"Agreed. I mean, we could also go for another frozen Margarita," Tabby said, pointing at a drink stand across the street.[148]

"Why get that when I can have ice cream?"

So the decision was made, and they waited their turn to get glorious waffle cones dipped in chocolate and filled with creamy goodness before walking back along the sidewalk to the water, where they stood gazing out at the barrier islands, stripped of their mangroves decades ago and filled with mansions and pumped in white sands, and they listened to a local sing her heart out for tourists over the loud speaker of a nearby bar. Thus ended their last attempt to swim at a beach of Key West. With their time in Key West coming to an end, they were glad to have one more fun evening event planned.

When Tabby and Charlie bought tickets to the random concert in Key West on their first day in town, they gave little to no attention to what or who was performing, aside from the Irish theme. In fact, as they walked to the concert, they actually didn't know what they were going to see or what to expect inside the revived theater. The Key West Theater was originally built over 150 years earlier as a Baptist church, but as with most buildings on the island, it'd had a variety of uses since its inception. It'd been a brothel, a dance club, a bar, and now a community theatre/recording studio. Key West was full of talented musicians, artists, writers, and more. Tourists

---

148. Fun fact, there are more places to buy frozen alcohol in Key West than there are bathrooms, according to the Restroom Association of America.

can't walk down the street without passing someone with immense talents, probably dressed like a bum. Along with this conglomeration of talent comes the opportunity for that talent to explore and grow and perform things that maybe shouldn't be performed, and that is what the girls were happening upon.

As they approached the theater, and they realized they didn't even know what they were going to see, Tabby pulled out the actual tickets[149] to see what the show was, and discovered it was a cover of Jon Bon Jovi with Irish dancing. While he was no Jim Morrison, the girls love a good eighties hair band cover, and in Key West, nonetheless! They entered the building and were stopped by a kind, young college student checking bags at the front door. Fortunately, no one appeared to have anything illegal-ish in their bags because the young girl was clearly not equipped to stop someone from entering and would likely move out of the way if someone said something even remotely mean to her.

"Thank you for coming tonight, I just need to look in your bags," she said as Tabby and Charlie held their purses open for her. "I hope you enjoy the show; it's for cancer."

"Oh, it's FOR cancer," Charlie said with a giggle. The young girl, not catching on to the giggle repeated herself, "Ya, it's for cancer."

Inside the doorway, the girls were stopped by a middle-aged woman who directed them to the left where items were being auctioned off in a silent auction "for cancer."[150] Charlie walked to the left laughing and got a sharp elbow in the ribs from Tabby.

"Shush, you should've been an English professor. No one cares. Everyone knows the money is being raised to fight cancer, not to give to cancer." But that just made Charlie giggle more.

---

149. No digital tickets were issued
150. At her age, the woman really didn't have an excuse for not knowing her prepositions

"Are you sure? I mean two grown people just told me the money is for cancer. Maybe if we come back next week, they'll be raising money for Stalin,"[151] she said with another laugh. The girls glanced over the silent auction table, but as the first item had an initial bid of $1,000, they figured they best get on their way to their seats.

The old-style theater had been renovated well, and instead of adding seating back in, as it likely had seating at some point, the theater had set up tables and chairs, like a dine-in-theater, but disappointingly without food—not even the snacks mentioned as a possibility. As the box office man had told them, their seats weren't together, but they were both in the front row. The volunteer ushers walked Tabby to the left of the stage and Charlie to the right where she was seated with a group of three very retired people from the Midwest. No one in this new group of four was very happy about sitting together, so they did their best not to make eye contact at the small table, but instead of remaining silent, they sat and discussed politics and the Republican/Democrat stance on inheritance laws.[152] Charlie's back was to the stage, so as the concert started, she had to crane her neck to the left to see the performers come out, and Tabby had to do the same to the right. Fortunately for Charlie, despite the neck craning, things got better as the lights dimmed for the performers because the talk of politics ceased.

Despite the darkened lights, or maybe because of them, the anticipation was high in the crowd. Who doesn't like some Bon Jovi? The crowd cheered in anticipation as a woman in her mid-sixties made her way out on stage in faux leather pants, very high heels, bright green polish on toes and fingers, hair done in the style of Olivia in *Grease*, and a fitted sleeveless green leather crop top. Her toes were tapping in Irish style as "Livin' on a Prayer" started, and

---

151. Who Charlie was aware reviled cancer for more people killed during his reign of terror
152. Something that matters a lot to many islanders

despite the look of the performers, who were all over sixty, the girls held out hope the concert would meet and surpass all expectations, but alas, sometimes things are just what they appear they'll be—not good.

The music started from a sound system in the back,[153] and the lead singer and her back up girls, whom Charlie couldn't see behind the piano as she was looking up at the stage, all sang Bon Jovi in impossibly operatic voices. The crowd went wild and didn't stop cheering and singing along to every song that was performed. Charlie knew she had to get out of there, but judging by how much the others at her table were enjoying themselves, they had friends up on stage. The singer had the energy of a forty-year-old, and she showed no signs of slowing down. Her tennis bracelet reflected the stage lighting, and Charlie thought again of the vast divide on the island between the have and have nots.[154] As the promise of intermission was mentioned on stage after a couple more songs,[155] Charlie texted Tabby "Headache?" just as Tabby sent the same text. Relieved they were on the same wavelength, both girls left as quickly as possible, apologizing to the others at their tables as they left, and not minding the doorman's warning that they would not be allowed back in. They laughed all the way to the compound and from their separate apartments, they both cleansed their mental pallets by listening to the Doors.[156]

Despite the odd ending to the night before, they knew Key West was full of nothing but promise and began the next day with

---

153. The band appeared to be there just for show
154. Something Hemingway was painfully aware of
155. A couple in this case being rightly interpreted to mean a few more songs, not two more songs
156. The decision was made not to go hear the Yugoslavian author speak as they had lost trust in what constituted as worthy of an audience in Key West

anticipation. They sat on the welcoming Southern porch of Tabby's downstairs apartment, looking out at the pebble-lined front yard and the white picket fence that kept their compound separate from the rest of the small homes on Love Lane, and they looked at Apple Maps to decide what they might want to go see.

"Oh, there's an Audubon house. That sounds good," said Tabby.

"Well, the Audubon house, yes, but he didn't actually live here like Hemingway did."

"And how, pray tell, did you know that?" asked Tabby, who was enjoying her morning caffeine enough to ask history questions.

"I am looking him up right now. Looks like he was a Napoleonic draft dodger."

"I like him already."

"Well, don't like him too much. I think his family had the money to help him dodge the draft because of enslaving others. And then he spent his time and the family money in the States going all over drawing birds."

"Living the life at the expense of others. Seems a common theme for that era."

"The life of the wealthy," laughed Charlie sarcastically. "Listen to how he describes the Keys: ' . . . seldom have I experienced greater pleasures than when on the Florida Keys, under a burning sun, after pushing my bark[157] for miles over a soapy flat, I have striven all day long, tormented by myriads of insects, to procure a heron new to me, and have at length succeeded in my efforts.'"[158] Charlie read with a laugh at another tourist from long ago who found the Florida heat and bugs a bit unbearable.

"Ok, that's funny, and he deserved it, but probably his house, which isn't his house, is less funny. And that area is right on the

---

157. Or small boat
158. https://fcit.usf.edu/florida/lessons/audubon/audubon.htm

water in a section we haven't walked yet," said Charlie, knowing Tabby was up for an adventure.

"Great, let's go, but for the water, not the enslaver."

"Breakfast first." So, the girls enjoyed a breakfast of cereal and fruit and headed out.

The streets in Old Town had begun to ring familiar to both girls at this point. They wound their way through the streets with ease, taking the literary route they had seen on a sign in the library and passing the house of Shel Silverstein[159] and the Windsor Lane compound where Ralph Ellison worked on *The Invisible Man*.[160] They followed their slow route through the neighborhoods of Old Town towards the Port of Key West and finally found the impossibly turquoise water separating Key West from barrier islands that served as bastions for the uber wealthy. As the Conchs like to say, the millionaires are being chased out of Key West by the billionaires. The girls, ever practiced at looking at the beauty in front of them, the shiny thing if you will, but not acknowledging the elephant in the room,[161] finally noticed the arrival of the newest cruise ship that was basically the length of a city block and easily twelve to thirteen stories in height above the water. The monstrosity blocked off a long stretch of the view, which was judged less valuable by the State of Florida than the tourist dollars the ship brings to shore, with little to no consideration of the ecological effect of city-sized ships dumping waste off the coasts of Key West.[162] The city had recently voted to

---

159. THE Shel Silverstein

160. Tabby read this once and was disappointed to find it was not, in fact, a sci fi novel about an invisible man

161. Such as ignoring the elephant in the room of their life as adjuncts that suggested they could easily and quickly be without work

162. Perhaps the federal government assumed the current would wash the waste down towards PR, DR and Cuba, places the feds cared little for

limit the port to only one cruise ship at a time, but the State, in all of its infinite wisdom, claimed eminent domain (ED)[163] over the coast and demanded two to three ships in port at a time, filling the pockets of lawyers across the state as the scramble began to stop the ED and causing doubt to spread across the island whether one man's vote truly did count.

Tabby and Charlie knew none of this as they stood on the water line, leaning over the railing and basking in the glory of the view to the right of the cruise ship. The moment was too much to let pass by, so they sat at a bistro along the water appropriately furnished with lime green tables and turquoise chairs. The girls sat in silence sipping their unsweet teas[164]and watching the jet skis and parasails, which provided depth to the view off in the distance. They were content in their people watching situation, watching as students, who clearly had more money than their professors, walked by on their false spring break, which seemed to be a trend among the COVID high school grads.[165] After eating the best grouper sandwich they'd ever experienced, which is saying a lot for Florida girls, Charlie and Tabby headed out to explore this new-to-them section of Key West. Charlie feigned surprise when they turned the corner to find the Key West Art and Historical Society. After all, no self-respecting historian could possibly go to a new city without seeing the history museum.

The museum is housed in a brick building that dominates the landscape with its archways and picturesque details. The building was constructed centuries ago entirely of brick that the federal government had shipped in complete with fireplaces on all floors,

---

163. ED, something the state was familiar with
164. Once again revealing some history of northern-ness and a bit of a desire for a skinny trip
165. Those outside of the field of education seriously underestimate the effect of the COVID years on kids in school at the time, who now enter college unprepared for life in general

since the feds liked the familiarity of building the same thing in all states. This created a sense of congruity despite the lack of need for fireplaces in the sub-tropics,[166] revealing the strong tradition of governmental stupidity and waste. The girls knew Jim wasn't featured in the museum,[167] so they went past the traveling exhibits on the first floor straight to the second floor to view the Hemingway exhibit. The girls felt they knew the man since they toured his bathroom, but this exhibit brought them a new depth of proximity. Incased in glass was Hemingway's WWI uniform, complete with blood and holes[168] in the pants from the mortar that blew up near him just before his 19th birthday. The hat with the uniform clearly didn't match; Charlie explained that it must've been Italian and thus a souvenir of sorts that Hemingway brought home from his time serving along the Italian Front.

The museum passed much in the same way as all museums do, and the girls made their way through the exhibits as Charlie narrated for Tabby, and Tabby dutifully nodded her head, aware she'd been tricked into more historical talks and wondering if they could get another alcoholic slushy afterwards. When the tour ended, they went for more ice cream and headed back to the compound, exhausted, as they always were after a day of walking and sun.

The days blended from one to another as their time in Key West wound down. They knew from the start that they'd only have a few weeks if they wanted to make it to Ireland, and with the Jim plan in place, they knew they'd be making it to Ireland.

---

166. If you ever feel useless in your job, remember the brick mason who had to create brick fireplaces in Key West

167. Although he does deserve a place in ALL museums

168. Which led to the blood

One thing they hadn't tried in Key West was actually getting out on the water. Charlie had insisted on no boats due to her extreme motion sickness, and Tabby acquiesced due to her extreme need to live on a budget, but they did want to get on the water. Key West is a spring break and vacation destination and the tourists pour in with a deep desire to get into the ocean, only to find the beaches are lined with rock and lead to the deep waters that are playgrounds for boats and jet skis, so no jumping over the sea wall for a swim anymore.[169] Fortunately, the internet held the answer—they could go kayaking with a guide. While cost was a factor, even with the college fraudulently covering costs, they did want to be sure money was left to chase Jim once they got to London and Paris. Airbnb experiences held the key—buy one, get one kayaking experiences through a maze of mangroves.

The girls made their reservations and looked forward to the experience. Both had kayaked extensively in their lives, although never alone and not for several months. A guide seemed like a good idea. The experience was nearly twenty minutes by car, so they had to let go of their vow to walk everywhere and ease Baby out of her shaded glory on Love Lane. The trip was stressful as they fought the hordes of tourists making their way on and off the island, which is both entered and exited by a two-lane road. They arrived on time and found themselves at the end of a shell-lined dead end with kayaking companies surrounding the end of the road. They walked to the nearest kayak hut and found a man with a mini bun, shaved sides of his head, and his arms, hands, and fingers covered in tattoos. While a fairly good-looking man, his eyes had that look that many women take as a warning to stay away—something Tabby and Charlie felt from his toe to head glances, but not from his tattoos.

---

169. Although while there the girls learned that Tennessee Williams used to do just that daily and in the nude

"What can I do for you ladies today?"

"We're looking for Blue Moon kayaking."

"Oh, they're over there, but I've canceled all my tours today because of the weather; I think we all have."

"We didn't get a cancelation notice," said Tabby, checking her phone.

"Well, I imagine they've cancelled. When you see that he has, come on back over. I can help you reschedule for another day," he said in a plea for more business.

"Thanks," said Tabby as they made their way in the direction the man had told them was where they'd find Blue Moon.

"They better not have cancelled," said Charlie. "The weather is fine. Just a bit windy."

"I agree. If they cancelled, let's just get a refund and leave."

The girls arrived at what was basically a plastic shed from Home Depot made into an office, and found a man in his mid-fifties[170] sitting in a chair, his scraggly, greying beard down to his chest, which was a feat, since his chest and stomach stood out far from his face.

"Charlie and Tabby?" the man asked as they approached.

"Yes sir, we're here for our tour. Have you cancelled for the day?" asked Tabby hesitatingly.

"Well, that'll be up to you. The family of four scheduled to kayak with you has cancelled due to weather concerns. If you want to go, we go, if not, we can reschedule or cancel."

The girls both looked up at the sky and the clear blue above them held no sign of rain, and there was barely a breeze on their cheeks.

"Does the water look bad?" asked Tabby.

---

170. Age is hard to distinguish on those who have spent excessive amounts of time in the sun

"Let's walk on out and see what you think," said the man.

The girls followed him behind a building and out on a little wooden dock covered in kayaks and lined with jet skis behind a mass of mangroves. The water around the dock was clear and still, without even a ripple, and looking out over the docks, they could see the channel of open water they'd have to cross to get to the mangroves, which had a few small waves but no white caps.

"This doesn't look bad at all," said Charlie as Tabby nodded in agreement.

"If you're comfortable, we can go out and turn around anytime you feel you're done," said the man, and Tabby and Charlie thought of their theme for this trip—take it as it comes—and got ready to go kayaking with the guide whose name they heard but didn't listen to. While they didn't listen to his name, the more he spoke, the more they realized they needed to listen.

Often academics get the idea in their heads that intelligent people look, speak, and smell a certain way.[171] However, this man broke their assumed mold. As he led them deftly towards the mangrove forest, he regaled them with stories of Florida biology that would put a biology professor to shame. He was a naturalist and had spent a lot of his free time studying and learning to appreciate the ecology of Florida. As they made their way past the houses on the sea wall overlooking the mangroves, he went from explaining why iguanas are bad for the delicate coastal ecosystem to showing them which house used to be Jimmy Buffet's and which local would sometimes come out to give him a free frozen margarita. As they approached the mangrove forest, he explained how to separate the paddles and told them they could also just spider monkey their way through the forest. The girls took this last bit to be a joke, but as they made

---

171. A very ill placed assumption considering the appearance of many professors, who cannot be fired for appearances

their way through the small tunnel into the midst of the mangroves, they could see him in front of them choosing to reach out and grab the mangrove branches and pull or push himself through the water. Soon they followed suit, gliding over the brackish water as they reached out and grabbed onto the branches, some of which were sturdy and others were broken off or their growth was stunted into the shape of something humorous.[172]

At first the girls struggled to stop and take pictures. They knew that Jim had wanted to be a film maker, so part of them always felt they should be documenting their trip in photos, but as they had no real talent in that area,[173] they weren't planning on actually making any documentaries. In this instance, in order to take pictures, they had to get their phones out of their dry bags, turn them on, open the camera and take a picture before their kayaks either floated away, crashed into a tree, or crashed into the tour guide. After stressing about pictures for a while, they decided to tour like it was 1999.[174] After all, once they were fraudulent felons out on the run, they would have to get off of social media and rely on their memory alone to document their experiences, or maybe a really well-made scrapbook.[175]

With the decision made to let the cameras stay in the bag, the girls laughed their way through the mangroves, spider monkeying every chance they could get. They stopped at two separate swimming holes, getting out to swim in the first one that was shallow and had visible white sand. They sat in the cool shade soaking in the water while watching the mangrove crabs scatter around the branches and listening to the guide explain the importance of the crabs for the

---

172. "So, these are male trees" Tabby said jokingly as they moved through the tunnel
173. Jim, whose IQ was 149, was always able to sort how to do the things he wanted to do
174. Without pictures
175. Tabby's mom, while she did not like to talk about her, had managed to raise her with the ability to make a really impressive scrapbook

environment and all that the mangroves offered the shoreline of Florida. He warned them that some people wanted to remove the mangroves for the sake of the view and the tourists.

Climbing back in from the shallow swimming hole was challenging for the girls, so when they got to the second one, which the guide warned was over their heads, they skipped the opportunity feeling sure that they couldn't pull themselves up and out of the water and back onto their kayaks.[176] When they came to the circular opening between much of the mangrove maze, the guide stopped to show them the upside-down Medusa jellyfish that were dotted all over the sea floor and told them about the shorebirds flying overhead.

"See that tower over there?" he asked. The girls nodded as they watched the beauty of the jellyfish which seemed harmless when they were out of reach. "Well, that is Hawk Missile Station, which was the anti-missile station that would've been used to send a counter strike to Cuba. Thankfully, it was never used, but it has stood as a reminder of the danger in which we once lived in the state of Florida. But not for long. The government has decided to expand the airport. Now it is one of those small airports that you have to walk from the tarmac to the terminal, but they want to have full terminals and more planes to enable more tourists to come down here, so they are taking out the missile station and building over that piece of land to connect with the main runway."

The man stopped and stared at the skyline, shaking his head as yet another airplane flew overhead. Between the commercial flights and the military flyovers, there seemed to be a plane flying overhead every few minutes. The girls couldn't imagine what it would be like once the airport was expanded or the impact this increase in tourism

---

176. "I'd like to see you try" laughed Tabby when the guide mentioned the possibility, knowing full well Charlie could not pull herself up out of a pool let alone on to a floating kayak

would have on the environment. The guide explained he was living in a bedroom he rented for over a thousand dollars a month, just for access to the bedroom. He didn't have a car, so he biked everywhere, and he regretted the loss of the one room boathouse he rented for a thousand a month before a hurricane took it out. His dream was to own one of his own one day.

As they made their way back out of the mangrove forest and into the Florida sunshine, the girls faced the open channel and the opposing current with vim and vigor, refusing to stop and rest when the guide offered and not stopping until he found some nurse sharks napping on the ocean floor close to the Blue Moon docks.

"You see, these sharks sleep. They are actually sleeping on the floor of the ocean now," he said with child like glee as he looked down into the water. Tabby and Charlie were pretty sure this was a great way to close out their time in Florida, possibly forever.[177]

---

177. They realized that if they used up the college credit card fraudulently, coming back would mean a free place to live and free meals every day for at least several years in one of the many prisons that decorate the swampy regions of Florida

CHAPTER TEN

Waiting for the Sun[178]

All good things must come to an end, this the girls knew, so they planned on making the most of their last day in Key West before boarding the plane headed for London, Dublin, professional development, and fraud. Well, Charlie did. The night before, Charlie laid out the plan to see the sunrise and the sunset on the same day on opposite sides of the island—all on foot. Tabby responded with something along the lines of "you do you" and slept in. Waking up to an alarm before 6:30 a.m. on a day when she could've been sleeping in felt like a mistake when the alarm broke Charlie from her slumber, but she persevered, had some water and threw on her bikini, sweatpants, and an adventure shirt[179] before heading down Love Lane to find Higgs Beach, a beach the girls had yet to explore. The internet informed Charlie this was one of the top places on the island to view the sunrise. Tabby countered with the reminder that rooftop bars are likely better to view from, but they'd sworn off rooftop bars for fear of naked old men, so Charlie made her way through the dark and winding streets of Old Town, Key West,

---

178. Morrison, Jim. "Waiting for the Sun." Morrison Hotel/Hard Rock Cafe. Elektra Records, 1970.
179. Doesn't everyone have an adventure shirt?

walking under the cacophony of roosters greeting the morning from the treetops lining the sidewalks, and sometimes descending on their kingdoms to howl at Charlie from the streets as she walked by.

Walking through the dark streets had Charlie rethinking life. Why was she up so early? Aside from roosters, the streets were near apocalyptic in their silence, and she was convinced for sometime that she was alone as she weaved her way down the sidewalks, avoiding the tropic bushes that reached out into the sidewalks at the passersby, of which Charlie was the only one. The silence was deafening, and when she came upon two college students out in the morning, she was surprisingly glad for the company. They were also wearing sweatshirts, which is Florida for "I knew I was going to be out in under 80 degree weather," suggesting they weren't still out from the party the night before.[180] She found comfort in their chatter as she made her way to Windsor Lane and turned right near the cemetery. The street was dark and here and there a man would come out walking his dog or heading to work and Charlie was reminded of the words of John Muir in his essay about Bonaventure graveyard outside of Savannah.[181] Muir realized the danger in life lay with the living, not with the dead, and so she crossed the street to avoid a lone man on the street and to take comfort from the nearness of the empty graveyard in the dark, knowing it offered more safety than a dark street with a stranger passing by.

Eventually, as she got closer to the beach, the sky started to lighten up a bit. The walk was a solid thirty minutes, and Charlie didn't feel like running in flip flops. Every now and then, she turned the GPS on so the sound of Siri's voice could bring comfort, as if Siri could

---

180. Fun fact, some of the bars Charlie passed were not empty but still had patrons from the night before
181. Muir, John. "Camping Among the Tombs." A Thousand-Mile Walk to the Gulf. Houghton Mifflin Company, 1916.

offer help if she wandered into the wrong neighborhood.[182] The sky was fairly light by the time she could see the man-made white sand beaches of Higgs,[183] and there were women out running and men working on park maintenance before the crowds descended. Charlie took off her flip flops and took the slow walk through the sand towards the pier to watch the sun put on its show. Man-made or not, there was much comfort found in running her feet through the sand and watching the darkened brownish color of the waves as the sun wasn't yet over the horizon. She thought of the words "waiting, waiting, waiting for the sun,"[184] as if Jim was becoming a theme and a sound track for life and not just for the trip.

Charlie made her way past a young couple posing for pictures along the water and went out onto the pier which led into a California-style brick paved walkway, complete with benches and lamp posts that looked like they were fresh out of Narnia. She chose a spot along the vacant portion of railing and left the benches to the crowd, preferring the silence at the front end of the pier, and watched as the sun slowly began its daily ascent above the horizon, first lighting the underside of the clouds, and then beginning to change the color of the water as the light lit up the waters that began to be turquoise once again as the sun made its way to its spot up in the sky, something it does daily, and yet the process is worth watching as often as possible.

The sun once again where it belonged, Charlie turned to walk back to the apartment and find some breakfast and hopefully Tabby awake and ready to take on their last day. The couple on the beach was still posing for pictures, only in her youthful stupidity, the woman had gone pants-less and was only wearing a brightly

---

182. She wasn't positive Key West had a truly bad neighborhood, but now was not the time to find out
183. A hidden beach that tourists and locals often forget exists
184. Morrison, Jim. "Waiting for the Sun." *Morrison Hotel/Hard Rock Cafe.* Elektra Records, 1970.

colored T-shirt that the wind kept blowing up, revealing the rear end all people have, but that young people feel pretty spectacular about. Charlie was surprised to see what she'd assumed to be an engagement shoot becoming an acted out sexual assault on the beach, being repeated for the camera often with screams from the girl as the boy tossed her onto the beach and the wind showed her rear over and over as she was pushed onto the sand and then helped back up by her cohort. The ignorance of protected youth made the scene a game to the young girl who didn't seem to know the dangers of the world, nor did she seem to be aware of the old man standing several feet behind her discreetly taking pictures of her ass before walking off to whatever cave he crawled out of. All this played out in front of a monument for enslaved people who were rescued from ships taking them to market in 1860. Unfortunately, of the 1,400 and some rescued, nearly 300 succumbed to death after their brutal treatment on the passage over. Their remains were buried below in unmarked graves. Charlie imagined the souls of those below wouldn't have understood the young couple pretending to be caught in an act of sexual aggression.

However, remembering that Key West is a city where anything goes, Charlie made her way back towards Love Lane, enjoying the walk much more in the morning light. The light showed the neighborhoods to be safe and inviting with their old-world charm and their young soldiers running bare-chested through the streets before the heat of the day began baring down. A man with dreads biked past her pulling a cart with mysteriously tarp-covered items and nodded with a "Morning love," as she passed, smiling at the friendliness of the city. While the tourists, such as the couple on the beach, brought a certain distraction and disruption to the city, Charlie had learned to see and love the locals who managed to find a way to move here or a way to let their roots grow deep into the bedrock of the city like the banyan trees did and cement the ability of their children to stay. The city was waking up, and it was time to find some food and adventure before they left one island paradise for another.

She made her way down Love Lane and pet the neighborhood cat who'd learned when Charlie was passing by so he could come out for some pets and comments of adoration, which all cats love to hear. Tabby was sitting on the porch waiting with a pot of tea.

"Oh, thank God. I need some caffeine," said Charlie.

"I figured you would."

"How was it?"

"So beautiful. That moment when the sea turns turquoise as the sun hits it is even better than the red glow of the sky at sunset."

"You know what's also great?"

"What?"

"The inside of my eyelids as I get an extra hour of sleep."

"Whatever. You know what's also cool, there's an unmarked African cemetery along the beach."

"Of course you found history on your walk," laughed Tabby, who at this point was very aware of the depth of history woven into the very streets of Key West.

"So, what do we do on our last day?"

"Well, all the boring stuff. We need to do laundry, pack, clean up after ourselves . . ."

"And then go see the sunset in Mallory Square," interrupted Charlie. And with the plan set, the girls got ready to head to Miami the next morning.

Packing was faster than they'd thought it would be. Tabby had kept up on laundry, Charlie didn't care if she packed clean or dirty clothes, and Constance had made it clear the cleaning expectations were minimal for the two-house guests who didn't really make a mess anywhere they went. With everything packed in Baby's trunk, except for what was needed in the morning, they made their way towards town, deciding to hit the Southernmost Point, a necessary Key West tourist destination they'd somehow missed, and then to head over to Mallory Square, which was amazingly enough on the same street, just at the other end of the tip of the island. The girls were realizing the main streets of Whitehead, Truman, Elizabeth, and Fleming could get them to many of the places they wanted to go, and this time Whitehead was for them. They turned left from Eaton onto Whitehead and started their long walk towards the Southernmost Point. The heat and the sun were blinding by the time they could see the end of the street, and what they saw first wasn't the famous Southernmost Point marker, but instead was a man standing in the sun, tilting his head back and pretending to blow on a conch shell. Charlie watched in awe at his ability to hold the position for so long.

"Dang. That's some balance, but why not just take the picture already?" asked Charlie.

"Right? Talk about vanity. Take the pic and move on," said Tabby in full judgement.

As they made their way closer to the water, and the sun shifted, or rather the one cloud in the sky shifted to provide some clarity, the girls realized they'd been casting judgement on a statue,[185] which brought on a cascade of laughter and prepared them for the

---

185. The statue was built to honor Albert Kee who was Key West's unofficial goodwill ambassador https://www.roadsideamerica.com/story/46913

quarter of a mile line that waited to pose for a picture in front of the Southernmost Point.

"Do we—"

"No," said Tabby and the girls quickly took a picture of other people posing in front of the Point from across the street and made their way instead to the mobile stand selling frozen alcoholic slushies to get some for their walk up Whitehead towards Mallory Square and the sunset of a lifetime.[186]

As they walked on, Charlie started to notice the hearts carved into the sidewalk. Many towns have hearts or names carved into the sidewalk, but she was seeing a pattern.

"Tabby."

"Yes," said Tabby as they approached the adult slushie sales cart.

"Have you noticed how many hearts are carved 'Lisa and Nancy' here?"

"No, can't say I have," Tabby said as she approached the cart and ordered a strawberry daiquiri.

"Ah, so you girls have noted the Lisa and Nancy hearts now have you," said the man with an accent the girls couldn't place and a trim Hitler-like mustache that was somehow making a comeback.

"I swear, I've been seeing these all over town," said Charlie as she ordered her strawberry daiquiri.

"That you have, love. Lisa and Nancy retired here a few years back from somewhere up north and didn't know how the town felt about, you know, things like that."

"Like women living together," said Tabby between sips.

"Exactly, love. So, they didn't know Key West well, yet."

"Clearly."

---

186. Or so they thought

"And they didn't understand wet cement either. They carved their heart and names and when it would settle into the drying cement, they thought someone had removed their names in an act of homophobia, so they carved more and more. As it turns out, the cement held their love and now their names are all over town."

"That is hilarious," said Tabby, enjoying the man's accent and story.

"This town is full of funny people," he said, leaning his thin forearms on his cart and adjusting the visor he was wearing. It was bright green and didn't go with the 'Hitler-stache.'

"We've noticed," said Charlie.

"Take this guy here," the man said, pointing at a guy going by on a skateboard. He was thin—very thin. Meth addict thin. His hair was dirty brown, a color he seemed to take seriously by not washing it. His skin and clothes all seemed to be in need of a bath, but his arms and legs were clearly defined in muscles and not only dirt. His right arm held a speaker that was blaring gospel music.

"Does he always play gospel music?" asked Tabby.

"No, I swear I saw him go by playing rap earlier this morning."

"Oh, he plays all sorts of music, he does. What do you take him for?"

"Most entertaining place to pick up some meth in town," said Tabby as she took another sip of her daiquiri.

"That's the look he gives off, I'll give you that," said the man with a deep laugh that seemed to emanate from a body larger than his. "No. That is Dr. Phelps."

"Dr., as in that tv show where the teacher made meth and sold it in town?"

"No, as in award-winning financial advisor. He made his fortune before he hit thirty-five. He was some kind of groundbreaking analyst who made so many people gads of money, he was able to retire early and decided to fix his own life by leaving whatever city he was in and moving to the Keys."

"And giving up bathing?"

"Apparently."

"He is a bit gruff looking, that one, but the locals all know him. Walk alongside him and he will hear you out. Give you financial advice. Free of charge. Of course, that only matters if you have money to invest."

"Which we don't."

"Me either," said the man with a sigh, "but if I ever do, I know where to go. You ladies have a nice day," he said with a nod as he turned his back to the girls and began organizing his supplies.

As the girls left the cart and walked along the water, sipping their drinks, they weren't sure what they would do for the next few hours, but if they could see the water and walk the streets of Key West, the afternoon would be well spent. Of course, they'd be walking the streets and not shopping, given their financial status as unemployed middle-aged women, but it would be fun, nonetheless. Without discussion, they headed towards Kermit's for another piece of Key Lime pie, which they gladly ate at a fountain near the water while looking toward Mallory Square. When the pie was done, Charlie led Tabby through a garden of statue heads[187] and told her stories about the statues she knew, speaking quietly when they got to the section with a homeless man sleeping on the ground between heads. The statue towards the front of the garden was Charlie's favorite. It was a nearly life-sized boat and showed people caught in distress in an apparent storm, muscles ripping and life looking grim. The plaque spoke of Key West wreckers who went out and valiantly saved those

---

187. Which was not creepy at all

left clinging to ship remains or rocks after harsh storms left them to the elements. In return, of course, they were able to help themselves to any goods on the ships.

"My favorite bit of this piece of history—" said Charlie.

"Of course you have a favorite bit," said Tabby, wishing she still had more to drink.

"Turns out, sometimes the wreckers let the light go out in the light house so that ships would wreck, and they would have someone to save."

"How heroic."

"I'm sure they appeared that way to the people clinging to the rocks."

"Indeed."

The girls made their way to Mallory Square, arriving early enough to get seats on the sea wall and let their legs dangle over the ocean as they sat and waited for their final show of nature's beauty in Key West. Eventually, the sun set in all of its glory, lighting up the sky in shades of orange, yellow, and red that can't be seen in northern parts of the country. In the morning, Constance would get up early with them and drive them out of the Keys and to Miami airport for their flight to London. The hardest part wouldn't be leaving the country, perhaps forever, but leaving Baby. The only comfort they had was in Alec's offer to store her in the compound under a cover, which was a truly generous offer in a town with such small amounts of real estate available.

The morning drive out was before the sunrise, so they missed a lot of the views. As they made it to Islamorada, Tabby and Constance agreed to stop so Charlie could see one more monument, this one for the Labor Day Hurricane of 1935. Charlie walked up to the monument explaining that the storm was likely one of the biggest

Cat 5 storms to ever hit the nation, but, of course, the instruments to measure the storm's intensity didn't exist then. The storm was known to have killed a few hundred veterans in a government camp.

"However," said Charlie, "the Floridians among the veterans knew the storm was coming. Many did. In fact, the National Weather Bureau had given enough of a warning that residents in Key West knew to get ready, and even Ernest Hemingway, who was living in the Keys at the time, was able to prepare for the storm. The veterans were part of one of FDR's WPA camps—"

"Ah, a reason to hate another president," said Tabby with a sigh.

"Yes, actually, the reason I don't like FDR. He vacationed enough in Florida to know the danger, yet when the vets who were stationed here requested a hurricane shelter because their camp was so low the tide put out their camp fires—and yes, I know what you're thinking, the request did make it all the way to FDR—the request was denied over expense and then when the storm was coming those in charge didn't know what they were doing—"

"They often don't."

"And they wouldn't let the vets leave until it was too late. The escape train came so late it was washed off the tracks. Hundreds of vets were killed due to government neglect."

"And with that uplifting story, we head off on our adventure?"

"Exactly," said Charlie, ignoring the sarcasm. The girls got back into Baby, along with Constance, and drove off to Miami airport.

CHAPTER ELEVEN

Elementary Talk[188]

Miami airport is surrounded by the kind of frequent and incessant traffic that has always kept the girls away from Miami at all costs, that and the semi-rational fear of floods and buildings collapsing. Surprisingly, there were no crowds, and the airport was easy to navigate, which made the girls thankful that at least one thing in Miami was easy. The girls pulled their not-so-sexy luggage behind them as they made their way towards the check-in counter. They'd given up on the idea of wild travel years ago. The closest they came to planning sex into their trip was a Sixt rental, which at least had two of the letters right. Nothing else would be hit today.

They walked past miles and miles of customers and ticket counters and many slow-moving lines, and eventually found their very own long, slow-moving line. After what felt like ages creeping along between red roped lines, they made their way around the rope and right up to the counter where three agents stood waiting to serve the masses. Airlines have a reputation for being understaffed, and today was no exception. The girls weren't surprised since the tickets were the cheapest, and the college, who is all about degrees,

---

188. Krieger, Robby and Jim Morrison. "Twentieth Century Fox." The Doors. Elektra Records, 1967

always went for the cheapest airline, which is also how the girls were about to find themselves with the worst seats on the plane.

"Checking in together?"

"Yes," said Tabby.

"Ah, a couple's trip. How nice."

Tabby and Charlie looked at each other briefly and shrugged. While they've only been heterosexual friends, they've learned to keep quiet and take the congratulations, which at times come with free upgrades. Alas, not this time, but who can blame a girl for trying?

"I've got you seated together, last two seats in the same row on the flight," she said with a wink.

"Told you we should have stayed in and checked in by phone last night," moaned Tabby as they walked away.

"Well, I looked, and it was expensive to pick seats."

The girls headed off around the line of people still waiting their turns. Charlie has a "no bathrooms on a plane" policy, but that won't matter. Unbeknownst to them, their flight from Miami to London will be next to the plane's bathroom, with all its crowds, scents, and noises in the way back of the plane.

Charlie and Tabby, aside from finding room for their Morrison bobblehead and a few other memorabilia (as one does), had packed light and avoided the punishments and humiliations that come with the sin of packing a 50.2-pound bag instead of 50-pound bag. Curses avoided, they slowly made their way through the remaining tantrums in the other check-in lines and went straight to TSA. As they made their way, their plans motivated them through the stressful line like a carrot in front of a donkey. Orlando TSA always seem like they're directly willing to kill you or themselves.[189] Their

---

189. So much so that one of them did kill themselves in the airport by leaping off a hotel balcony inside of the terminal

job is stress inducing for all. For years now, passengers had made their way through TSA shoeless, leaving a highly questionable amount of filth in the carpets, all while being yelled at for leaving their laptop in a bag and alternately being yelled at for taking the laptop out of their bag. The girls hoped the Miami TSA would be easier.

Unfortunately, Tabby had worn her favorite sequined shirt as a reminder that even if they were currently homeless and jobless, she was a bright light. That this was a mistake became apparent when Tabby made her way through the naked body scanner and was pulled aside by a very big lady who wanted to pat her down in all the awkward places, before whispering to her the sweet nothings of knowledge: the naked body scanner can't scan through sequins, "so you will always get a pat down when you wear that shirt through TSA." Charlie didn't get the pat down, but she did have to let them have her full tube of toothpaste.[190] She offered to squeeze out some toothpaste in order to get the tube down to three ounces.[191] However, she was firmly told, "it doesn't work that way." And they took her toothpaste. Tabby watched it all go down in silence, pulling at her sequined shirt and doubting her own fashion choices. Eventually, they made it to their assigned gate and just in time to get in line to board.

Upon boarding they realized how full their flight was going to be. Alas, they weren't meant to be in the luxury of two friends sitting next to each other in a tiny three-person row. As they filed into their seats by the bathroom, a tall and thin European man took the seat between the girls. Length doesn't matter in most parts of life, or at least it doesn't for two short women, but as the man folded himself into his seat, and his knees into the seat in front of

---

190. Key and Poole have a very informative video to explain the logic of the TSA
191. Three is the magic number

him, it was clear that height made things a bit more difficult on a plane. Charlie looked at Tabby. Tabby rolled her eyes and sighed. Apparently, two seats together hadn't mean directly next to each other, and the girls had hoped to keep the empty seat between them, but alas. Compassion won over.

"Fine. Excuse me, did you maybe want the aisle seat?" asked Tabby who always took the aisle seat, but the combination of the man trying to fit into what was a child sized seat for him and the weirdness of having a stranger between them for so many hours pushed her.

"Really? Yes," he said with an accent. "Hvala, thank you," he continued as the two of them did an awkward dance of trying to switch seats now that their bags were comfortably stowed, or at least Tabby's were. The man hadn't even tried to get a bag under the seat in front of him. He needed every bit of square inch he was given in that seat.

"Are you Americans?" asked the man as Tabby looked at Charlie and shot a "now I'm stuck talking to this guy" look.

"Yes, we are."

"I'm Croatian. You've been to Croatia?"

"No."

"Oh, you must come," he said as he paused and waited for a response from Tabby that was sure not to come. "You know, Croatia is the best country. We have the best beaches in Europe, and we have the best singers, and you know, we invented the pencil and the tie," he said with a nod and an ear-to-ear smile.

The girls were wondering where the world would be without the tie as the man went on about the wonders of Croatia. Charlie, thankful for her window seat, put on her headphones and opened her book, ignoring Tabby's pleading glances as she dove into an

Agatha Christie book she had managed to buy from an airport gift shop as they quickly passed by. It was the only book that didn't scream conspiracy or cheap beach read. She had taken the "don't throw up" medicine she always traveled with, thanks to Tabby's packing abilities, so reading would be no issue.[192]

Time passed as it always does on an international flight: slowly, but more pleasantly for those on the plane who, like Charlie, were drugged. Charlie read, Tabby nodded her head, amazed this man could talk about his country for as long as he could. The girls were very international and not overly focused on nationalism, despite loving their country, so he was a new level of exposure.

The regret for the seat purchase, or rather the college's lack of specific seat purchase, came not over the man who joined them, but over the row. They hadn't realized how difficult sitting in the row directly in front of the bathroom would be.[193] There was a constant line of men, women, and children coming to wait for the bathroom.

"Geez," said Tabby "What have they all been eating?"

"This line is out of control," said the man who was not enjoying the ability to stretch his legs into the aisle the way he'd thought he would. As he spoke, a large man stood in the aisle right next to their row, and apparently struggling to hold in whatever he was holding in, felt the need to sit to contain everything, so he sat his rather large rear on the arm rest of the Croatian at the end of the girl's row, his back to them.

"Ok. Glad I changed seats," said Tabby.

"Excuse me, you can't do that," said the Croatian to giggles from the row across the aisle as the large man ignored him. The Croatian looked to Tabby for help, but Tabby just turned away, glad the stars

---

192. Tabby always carried a medicine bag inside her carry on. Math people like to be prepared

193. While statistically the row in the back is the row one is most likely to survive a plane crash in, it is also the smelliest of rows.

had aligned, and she wasn't in her usual aisle seat. The seated man ignored them until blissfully the bathroom opened and his turn was up. In that second, the Croatian made every effort to claim his arm rest with blankets and appendages.

The flight passed with awkward stories between strangers, long bathroom lines, unfortunate smells, and even more unfortunate food. Most importantly, thanks to modern medicine, Charlie didn't throw up, but also thanks to modern medicine, she said exactly what she was thinking at all times. When the Croatian asked if he was boring them with his stories, she said "a little." When the stewardess was foolish enough to ask if they were enjoying their dinner, she responded with "not at all" and kept eating as Tabby and the Croatian, finding common ground, raised their eyebrows in judgement of Charlie's open response, and finally, when the plane landed, and everyone applauded, Charlie said, a bit too loudly, "that landing was a 2 out of 10 at best." In the end, they landed in London and waited until most of the plane de-boarded before their row was finally able to escape the plane and head into England. Tabby was glad for space and for Charlie's medicine to begin wearing off, which she realized would take another 6-12 hours to be fully out of Charlie's system, leaving Tabby to be the only adult in the pair navigating their way to a hotel in a foreign city.

CHAPTER TWELVE

Break on Through to the Other Side[194]

Landing at Heathrow was like landing in any other airport,[195] but where it differed was the British TSA. While the name might not be TSA, much like Sherlock, the girls throw out all information that isn't helpful to their actual daily lives, like the names of airport security or the word "customs." They were all TSA, and their common bond over the size of toothpaste one can and cannot travel with made them equal in all countries. This time, however, the girls were thinking of Bill Murray and his extensive experience in this same TSA line when he was the man who knew too little.[196] They waited in the very long line that wound around and around, much like a labyrinth a laboratory would put mice in for experimentation. The tired masses from the recently landed planes wound slowly through the roped barricades, screaming babies providing background noise. When the girls found they were finally at the front, standing at the invisible line on the old linoleum that one mustn't step over for pain

---

194. Morrison, Jim. "Break on Through." The Doors. Elektra Records, 1967.
195. Aside from all of the tea and British accents
196. Amiel, Jon. The Man Who Knew Too Little. Warner Bros., 1997.

of possibly being denied entrance into the country, they saw a little old man in a box, glasses sliding down his nose, waving them up annoyedly.

"Passports," he said with his hand reaching out towards the little gap in the plastic wall that caged him in from all the rabble that passed by him on a daily basis. "Where are you going?" he asked, assuming they would know the exact address of their hotel and everywhere they would be heading. Fortunately, because Tabby was insanely good at Excel,[197] they did have a spreadsheet of their hotel's address and a list of places they intended on seeing. As the man read the address of the hotel his eyebrows raised but he only said, "I hope you like rice," laughed, and asked them why they were coming to London.

"Well," Charlie started, "we are headed for professional development here and in Dublin officially, but unofficially, we are thinking of tracking down Jim Morrison's last known steps in an attempt to prove he is alive." Tabby looked at Charlie with judgement over her still lingering openness, but Tabby had already had eight hours of honesty on the plane, so this was no surprise.

"That sounds like a much better plan than trusting the Irish with any kind of professional development," he said as he stamped their passports and waved them through into the British side of the invisible line where they made their way past the shops selling little tin buses full of dry cookies and stale teas and found the doors that opened onto England.

Fortunately, unlike other cities they'd visited, the taxis were easy to distinguish as distinctly British. London taxis, like Cuban taxis, have an extra cool factor to them. Instead of following the American rule of painting all cabs yellow, or yellow and black checkered,[198]

---

197. A talent few humans and mostly AI have
198. Yellow taxis are consistently voted the ugliest and least desirable

London uses specially made vehicles that harken back to days of old that are now instantly recognizable as London cabs. Unlike Cuba, where the vintage cars are actually vintage and are persistently maintained by individuals and serve as a sign of the determination of the Cuban people, London's vintage cabs are made in China.

Knowing none of this, the girls filed into the back of their cab and gave the address of their hotel. What the girls also didn't know is the notoriously infamous nature of London cabbies who can sense a tourist arrival at any hour of the night and then charge the tourist exorbitant rates for a short ride. The girls watched in the peaceful bliss that comes from ignorance as they rode through trash lined neighborhoods full of signs written in a foreign language. As they pulled up to their destination, a sense of unease settled over the girls. Contrary to the online pictures, the hotel was anything but welcoming for anyone except working girls and their clients. The small front door was painted in Tardis blue with clearly too much paint in an attempt to hide signs of the decay the building was experiencing.

As the cabbie came to a stop, he turned around and in a fatherly tone said, "Ladies, I don't feel comfortable leaving you here."

"I don't feel comfortable being left here."

"Are there other hotels nearby?"

The cabbie shrugged his shoulders as Charlie remembered that this hotel was already paid for. The girls sat and discussed their options as the cabbie continued to express concern with no better hotel options offered in his best dad-with-a-London-accent voice.

"Fine. I'll go in and see how bad it is," announced Tabby, always first to brave new situations. Charlie waited in the cab with the bags and Tabby opened the door with the solid pull a door coated in thick paint requires. The narrow doorway opened to a steep and apparently winding staircase covered in thick red carpet that harkened back to the hotel's harem days that Tabby hoped were in the past as she ascended the stairs, and even though she was the lesser germ-a-phobe of the two, she chose not to use the handrail.

The man at the top of the stairs rested behind a wall of thick glass of the kind that stopped bullets and germs long before COVID arrived. He greeted Tabby and handed her an actual key and explained in a dull voice only slightly lightened by an exotic Indian accent that breakfast was included and held daily on the ground floor between six and ten in the morning. Not feeling confident, but knowing that the hotel was already paid for, and knowing that they needed a place to lay their heads for the night, Tabby descended the red stairs to convince Charlie to come, which was easier than she thought as Charlie's motion sickness meds made her a bit more pliable. As they got their bags from the cab, the cabbie notified them their fare was 100 pounds.

"Pounds?"

"Isn't the pound 2-1 over the dollar?"

The cabbie remained silent as the girls handed him the college card, knowing this was at least a justifiable expense and swearing not to take another London cab.

The harlot red path led quietly to their shared room, which was tightly bound with two beds and a small bathroom that inexplicably contained a dingy looking bucket in the shower. The girls stood in silence as they looked around the dark grey room.

"I'm not showering in there," declared Charlie as she sat on a bed. "I'm not sure I even want to sleep here, but what are our options?"

"I suppose it's not that bad. I've stayed in Bosnia," said Tabby as she started unfolding her pajamas from her suitcase.

With that said, Charlie and Tabby picked their respective beds and started to settle in.

Unfortunately, as is the case with much of Europe, there was no AC, and the girls were forced to open the rusty metal window. A further unfortunate occurrence came when they opened the window and realized there were no screens so bugs could get in, but, as they were tired, they decided that just as Ireland is an island with no snakes, England is an island with no bugs. They didn't think about bedbugs.[199] The trip had been long, so they decided to head straight to sleep. They'd brought their own towels in the hopes of getting into foreign waters, but for now they decided to spread their towels on top of the beds so they could curl up and not have their skin touch the blankets, which, like the room, were a nondescript grey.

They slept fairly well, as Americans do after a sugar-infused, restless night on a plane. In the morning, they woke to find the sunlight did nothing to improve the room, and they both had suspicious rashes from their knees down where their legs had stretched off the towels and onto the grey blankets. Alas, the bedbugs they'd forgotten, had not forgotten them, but the sight of the moldy shower strengthened their resolve not to shower. Despite their itchy legs, they headed out on the town.

After they paid the steep cost of a cab from the airport, they knew they needed to find their way to public transportation and breakfast. While they'd been excited about their hotel because of the free breakfast, the unforgettable level of mold and the mysterious bucket in the shower made them choose to walk for food. They stopped at the first grocery store they found and after perusing the vast selection of British crips,[200] they settled on crisps and bananas. They stood on the street corner eating and making a bit of a mess,

---

199. A common mistake
200. The British think themselves superior for calling chips crisps

which the pigeons appreciated. They had planned for two full days in London before heading to Dublin. The plan was to go to the Isle of Wight as the Doors performed there twice,[201] but first they had to go to London and see where the Doors had performed in 1968 and explore a bit before heading to a ferry and the Isle of Wight.[202]

First things first—navigation of the Metro so they could see more of London than they could by foot. The Metro in London is often below ground and is fairly well marked for tourists to be able to find their way.[203] Finding the Metro wasn't the problem. As girls living much of their lives in Florida, which has a high water table, they'd never had the chance to regularly take a Metro or subway.[204] They stood in awe of those who came in and seemed to know exactly what to do. When a small child came in unattended and easily got her ticket, they knew that they had to sort themselves.

"Ok, so I think we need to go to that machine marked oyster cards."

"Why an oyster? Didn't they know that word is taken?"

"They do what they want," said Tabby as they approached the machine and, thanks to the kind man behind them, sorted out how to get a card that would allow them to use the Metro as much as they wanted over the next few days.

The Metro did not disappoint. The stations they stopped at were something out of Harry Potter. While they struggled to follow the map, Tabby's math skills got them to their first stop—Big Ben. They came out at Westminster Station and couldn't believe the change in scenery. The tall, formal buildings spoke of success and comfort.

---

201. One of those times Jim required special permission due to the charges he was facing in the States for indecent exposure
202. As true professionals, none of their plans included actually going to the professional development the college had sent them on
203. Truth is the Brits got tired of helping Americans find their way, so they made their signage clearer and less British-y
204. And they had no idea what the difference was between the two

The girls walked straight to Westminster Abby, and Charlie began her long speech about who was buried there. They approached the tall, stone building, built in an era when churches weren't metal buildings or barns, but were representations of God's glory, and hoped to go in and see the tombs Charlie had been speaking of. Unfortunately, what they didn't expect was the price to get in.

"Dang."

"That is a lot more than we paid to go in Hemingway's house."

"Well. This is God's house."

"Still. What happened to let the people come, or something like that."

"I imagine too many came."

And so the girls decided to settle on a view of the inside of the gift shop, which had free entrance, and then walked over towards Parliament, the backside of which was fairly visible, and then headed towards the bridge that spanned the river in front of Big Ben and Parliament. The view was stunning, and they could think of no better way to spend their time in London than seeing the sights.[205]

---

205. Certainly not attending a conference for professional development

CHAPTER THIRTEEN

Take Me, Spanish Caravan[206]

The day was long, and as two broke ex-professors, they didn't have the funds to tour all the sights.[207] They walked along the River Thames, passing by St. Paul's, where Charlie made incomprehensible comments about robot aliens invading,[208] and they continued across the bridge to see Shakespeare's Globe, where Tabby put her foot down, insisting that she wouldn't be seeing a play on this trip. They walked by Jim locations, including Roundhouse, but as with Westminster Abbey, the girls didn't have the funds to get in, and they were sure Jim wasn't inside anymore. As with many other Jim locations, just as in Clearwater, the need to keep making money had caused businesses to shift and grow, and little to nothing of Jim remained. Disappointment, little food, and lots of exercise led the girls down a path of tiredness and hunger that even a Snickers bar couldn't solve and that didn't set the girls up for the best of nights.

Walking through the streets of London alone at night wasn't how Charlie saw her night going, but alas, here she was. The girls rarely

---

206. Krieger, Robby. "Spanish Caravan." Waiting for the Sun. Elektra Records, 1968.
207. Or use the bathrooms, as public restrooms cost money in London
208. Davies, Russell T. "Aliens of London." Dr. Who. BBC, 2005.

argued, but like an old married couple, occasionally[209] the conversation turned into an argument. This day was the day for their argument. They had travelled long, and now as they sorted their path to Jim, decisions had to be made, and these were decisions they'd put off until they got to London in order to live in the moment in Key West and to deal with their talkative neighbor on the flight over, as well as Charlie's buzz from her motion sickness meds. Sitting in their room in London, everything came to a head. What had started as an argument over whether or not they could afford a trip to the Isle of Wight grew out of control.[210] For privacy sake, and because other people's arguments are only marginally interesting if they are not juicy and instead are academic, we will move past the argument only to say that one of the professors felt that the history of Ireland meant that going to the professional development would be worth the trip to the west coast of Ireland, and the other one, who shall remain nameless, felt that math wouldn't actually be that prevalent in the professional development, despite what she'd said to the college. Thus, that one had pushed for a move straight to Paris to look for Jim's resting place and to set off in pursuit of Jim, for money's sake. In the end, they compromised on a few days in Dublin and then taking the ferry back to England without seeing the west coast of Ireland, which the college had already paid for. The choice led to a heated discussion and a decision to spend their evening headed in different directions.[211]

Charlie walked in one direction for quite some time. The neighborhoods she initially walked through looked like cute townhouses from *Notting Hill*,[212] although she was fairly certain she

---

209. This word can be interpreted as daily or weekly, depending on the couple, according to surveys done of people who live with or near old couples

210. The conclusion was that as they had no income, they could not

211. Which could be interpreted as Charlie walking out to cool off and Tabby saying "fine"

212. Mitchel, Roger. Notting Hill. Universal Pictures, 1999.

wasn't in the area the movie had been filmed in. The neighborhoods surrounded little hidden parks, like the one in the movie, and she began romanticizing her walk. As the sun set, the parks were beginning to look like safe havens, and Charlie felt the peace and security one often feels in new cities where one has no idea what the crime rate is and one doesn't watch the local news.

She wandered wondering what her life would become, angry at Tabby, but mainly wanting to sort things with her oldest friend.[213] They could lose their jobs and their home, but they needed each other. The homes faded away as Charlie kept moving in a straight direction knowing she would only have to turn around and walk back in the same direction in order to find their hotel. As she thought out her reasons for feeling anger and the path to making amends, she felt eyes on her and finally glanced around only to find she had somehow reached what must be the beginning of a shipping district along the Thames. She became aware of a group of men who were eyeing her, wondering what she was doing there about the same time that she wondered what she was doing there. Her anger was real, but the sense of security wasn't, and so our girl turned around and headed back the way she came, working with the theory that similar to bears, if she acted confident, she wouldn't be attacked.[214]

While safety and darkness dictated the need to head home, she didn't feel her anger agreed with their decision, so Charlie made a left when she approached a recognizable area. She remembered there was a McDonald's to the left, and familiarity seemed to call her towards a safe port where she could have some cheap food and Wi-Fi. The walk only took five minutes, but when she got there,

---

213. Both her oldest friend in time and her oldest friend. Charlie tended to make friends with younger people
214. This may not be a great practical theory for avoiding bear attacks, but as Charlie only approached bears safely at the zoo, it had worked well thus far

she realized she didn't bring any money. She sat outside and sighed, knowing it was time to go back to the hotel and hoping Tabby felt like apologizing so she wouldn't have to. The London street glistened from a recent cleaning, and couples walked to and fro laughing, but Charlie thought back to the shipping port, wondering how quickly the streets might feel unsafe for a woman walking alone should she stay out longer. She sighed and rose to head back, wishing she'd at least brought her Beats so she could have Jim with her, even if that meant she would be less aware of her surroundings.[215]

As she passed a train station,[216] a crowd released in front of her, bringing the warmth and comfort one feels being ignored in a crowd of people. However, the crowd thinned quickly, and before Charlie knew it, she was alone with just one tall man[217] who was walking beside her in the dark, confidently heading in the same direction as Charlie. Glancing to her right she saw he was wearing a turban and an older coat that had some wear. His beard was thinner than he probably wanted it to be, but long enough to reach his jacket collar. She thought she'd looked stealthily, but as with most things the girls thought they were sneaky about, she, in fact, had been seen.

"How are you?" he asked in a kind, musical voice.

"Good," Charlie answered, wondering why this man was speaking to her, but sticking with her bear theory.

"You've been in this area long?" he asked. Charlie felt glad in that moment that their hotel was oddly placed in a very residential area, even if it was a questionable hotel at best.

"Just a little bit. We live around the corner," she said, pointing randomly to the rightish and aiming for confidence and plurality.

---

215. Generally that is the purpose of wearing Beats
216. As she actually had no idea what street she was on, Charlie did not know the name of the station and she didn't care to know
217. A woman alone in the dark always feels the height of the male stranger next to her

"It's not been long for me either," he said as he started humming. "Great weather," he added with a sigh. "You know what?" he said in a way that invited Charlie to listen and match the halt in his stride.

"What?" Charlie answered, wondering if she'd be murdered on this dark and suddenly vacant London street.

"Tonight is too beautiful to waste," the Indian man said as he turned and faced Charlie who kept with her feigned confidence and gave a cautious smile.

"Hold up your hands," he said, and for some reason, Charlie did. The man took her hands in his, repositioning her fingers so they weaved into his in a way that felt both awkward and at home, and suddenly, they were dancing. Charlie wasn't one for dancing, but here, in the dark with this strange but musical and friendly man, she felt compelled to dance. With no witnesses around to see, she danced on the sidewalk, weaving in and out and under his tall arms until, just as suddenly as he'd started, he stopped, gave Charlie a smile, wished her a good night, and headed off in his direction with a wave. As the sound of his humming continued down the street, Charlie knew life was too good to continue being mad at her best friend, and she headed back to the hotel, aware that she could never tell anyone about that encounter as no one would believe her.

CHAPTER FOURTEEN

Petition the Lord with Prayer[218]

Charlie guessed that on her return there would be no need for apologies or a rehashing of their discussion. Charlie and Tabby always came back to the starting ground of friendship. They remembered who they were to each other despite any disagreements. What she didn't expect when she returned was to find Tabby cowering on the edge of her bed staring at a mouse running around on top of Charlie's bed. We all have weaknesses, and this was Tabby's. While she would rarely discuss her personal life, she'd been raised in poverty surrounded by filth and mice and insisted that as an adult she would never be around either.

"So, we need a new room," said Tabby as Charlie walked in the door.

"I see that. Have you been down to ask?"

"This sort of just unfolded."

"I see."

Tabby got up from the bed, and both girls left the room to walk down to the front counter and ask for a new room. The front desk clerk showed no concern for their situation, and also no surprise,

---

218. Morrison, Jim. "The Soft Parade." The Soft Parade. Elektra Records, 1969.

which suggested the mouse was a regular visitor and confirmed their need for a new room. The man explained that there were no more rooms available with multiple beds, but there was one empty room with a twin bed.

"We'll take it," said Tabby with no room for a disagreement from Charlie. Her fear of mice overwhelmed any concern for personal space. The girls got their bags, which Tabby had managed to pack up while watching the mouse, and went towards the two flights of stairs as the elevator wasn't working. When they got to the top of the narrow stairs, they found only the door to their room, which opened to a long, grey hall and ended at one small twin bed. The door didn't seem to want to lock, so the girls used their bags to hold the door shut and walked in to see the bathroom, which was even smaller than the bed and even dirtier than the last bathroom.[219]

"Well."

"Yep."

And with that they were reminded that they only had one night left in London, and they would survive. They spent the night in relative discomfort trying to sleep in the twin bed without accidentally touching each other. They didn't often discuss what their close friendship looked like to others, nor did they care, but they did care for clear physical boundaries, and this was crossing the line. The stupidity of their situation eventually led to reliving childhood sleepovers and a late night of laughing over memories, as the very best awkward nights often do. In the morning, they briefly discussed whether they would take the free breakfast in the mice and bed bug invested hotel and then walked across the street to the closest store. The street to the store was lined with trash, as many side streets in London are, as if trash day is perpetual in London.

---

219. But was blessedly bucketless

When they made their way in, they realized they didn't know what most things were and there were slim pickings.

"Do we want chips?"

"Crisps."

"Whatever. Or ice cream, or cereal—oh look, they have some form of Rice Krispies."

"Well, we had ice cream for dinner last night, so let's branch out and have cereal." Tabby grabbed the box and then, realizing once again there wouldn't be bowls or spoons, decided against buying milk.

Once she'd paid, the girls stood to the left of the trash pile heaped in front of the store and along the street and opened their box of cereal. After the night in the twin bed, sharing breakfast seemed minimally invasive. They stood there taking turns grabbing handfuls of cereal and eating out of their own hands while discussing what would come next. They had left their luggage with the front desk of their hotel,[220] and they had a few hours to explore London before they would need to head to Heathrow. Late the night before, as a peace offering, Tabby had offered to go to see Shakespeare's Globe Theatre. Charlie had always struggled between history and English, and she couldn't pass up the chance to see both in action in the modern version of the Globe.

"Shakespeare's theatre was originally built on the opposite side of the Thames River. However, when their lease was cancelled, the men in Shakespeare's acting guild had gotten drunk, stayed up all night, and taken the theatre apart to rebuild on new land across the river. The current Globe Theatre is a recreation of what would be built on the new land," explained Charlie between fists full of cereal.

---

220. Where it would be extra safe behind the bullet proof glass wall

"I didn't need all that history," said Tabby. "I would've gone with you to see it anyways."

The girls began their trip by heading down to the closest train station. Every train station in western nations is relatively the same—confusing for people from other countries that don't rely on public transportation. Tabby, being the more responsible of the two, studied the train maps and sorted the route they would need to take. In other words, she found the way to get there without having to change trains. Charlie did her part by standing and listening to the frequent reminders to "Mind the Gap," sure that she wouldn't have fallen onto the tracks without the reminder. With Tabby's navigational skills, the girls boarded what they hoped was the right train and made their way towards the Globe.

"Are there any more Jim locations we want to hit?" asked Tabby, looking at her phone and trying to hold on to the bar to steady herself as the train made its way through the darkness.

"The last few we walked by were pretty disappointing," said Charlie with a sigh as she strained to reach the bar between the British citizens who'd crowded into the train on the recent stop. Tabby, standing behind her, let go of the bar in the crowd and strained to see her phone screen with the motion of the train.

"Well, there are more to try."

"Ya, but we know he isn't here. If he faked his death—"

"Which we know he did."[221]

"Correct. Then we can also deduce he wouldn't have come back to London."

"For sure he would've been recognized in London at that point."

"And he'd been advised to go to France to avoid extradition for the charges out of Miami."

---

221. Among other reasons, Jim's use of "Mr. Mojo Risin" as an acronym for Jim Morrison was a sign to them that he had planned to "rise" from the dead

"That's right—avoid arrest in France, like The Rolling Stones."

"Exactly."

As the girls made their way through the logic that would inevitably lead them to decide to stick with just seeing the sights and trying to pick up the Jim trail in Paris, unbeknownst to them, the train eased into a station. What they'd not expected was that while they'd entered the train on one side, it would be the door on the opposite side that would open when the train stopped. Tabby, focused on their conversation and the list of Jim locations in her phone, failed to notice that, and despite the signs warning her not to, she'd leaned against the train door behind her—a fact she would come to know as the door opened, and she fell towards the platform outside of the door.

"Watch out, love," said a tall, thin man with a close haircut and bright blue eyes who winked at Tabby as he grabbed her hand and pulled her back into the train before heading out onto the platform.

"Oh my gosh," said Charlie as she fell onto a now empty seat and laughed at her friend. The girls laughed through the rest of their trip to the Globe and right out into the sunny walk outside of the station.

The Globe was exactly as pictured online, supporting Tabby's thought that there was no need to go inside. However, they also arrived just in time for a tour[222] and an early matinee, and they were given an educators' discount, so Charlie's wisdom prevailed, and the girls entered. The Globe felt like stepping back in time. The girls followed the tour guide around as he regaled the group with explanations of Shakespeare's life and the history of the theatre, making sure to warn them not to say the name of the Scottish Play. As they made their way into the balconies, he explained the

---

222. Tabby was suspicious that this was no accident

importance of the stage names, the heavens, hell, and earth where Shakespeare's plays were still being performed hundreds of years later.

"Unfortunately, as there is a rehearsal scheduled, followed by our next performance, we will not be able to tour backstage, but we can sit down and watch the rehearsal," he said with a nod as the group took seats.

"So, since we're getting to see a free rehearsal, can we skip the play?" asked Tabby.

"Uhm no," said Charlie with an eye roll. "They're not the same show."

With those words the stage came to life in the city of Verona as actors made their way around, reciting Elizabethan English as if it was today's vernacular.

"Wait, isn't that the guy from NCIS?" asked Tabby, trying to hush her voice as she excitedly pointed at a rather good-looking actor on stage.

"Yes," said the tour guide, "big name actors from both sides of the pond frequently perform here." Charlie smiled, glad she had pushed her friend to see a show that was clearly already working out better than their last show.[223] After a few minutes of rehearsal observation, the tour ended, and they made their way to the gift shop where they walked around looking at all the overpriced Shakespeare-themed souvenirs and wasted some time before their matinee began.

When the start of the show was announced, they made their way back into the center of the Globe. Just as in Shakespeare's day, the standing room in front of the stage was left at an affordable price for all, and it was made even more affordable for educators and students. As they were there waiting when doors opened, they

---

223. Which wasn't hard to do

were able to stand close to the stage. When the show began, the minimalist setting let them know they were in Rome.[224] Charlie was entranced as the actors made their way from scene to scene.

"Charlie," whispered Tabby.

"Yes."

"I keep getting spit on every time that guy comes over here."

"The NCIS guy?"

"No, he's not in this one. Every time they walk over here, really any of them," Tabby silenced herself after a glance from a rather intimidating looking security guard.

Thus, the girls experienced true Shakespearean theatre and the sad, quiet fact of all live theatre: While the front row offers the best seats, it is also often the "spray row" as actors work to be in character and to project their voices, particularly in a theatre without a sound system. Fortunately, part of their agreement was to stay only until halftime, as Tabby called it, and so it wasn't long before they made their way back out onto the London streets to sort an early afternoon picnic and the Tower of London, which they had somehow missed yesterday, and before picking up their luggage and making their way back to the airport.

---

224. The togas were their biggest clues and the sign that said "Rome"

CHAPTER FIFTEEN

Streets are Uneven When You're Down[225]

The girls had gained confidence in their train riding skills over their short time in London.[226] They managed their oyster cards and were able to make their way to the correct train, minding the gap every time. After their pre-performance metro ride, they were more careful not to lean on doors.[227] They flowed into the train with the Londoners, silently laughing at "Mind the Gap" and even managed to find seats near each other while still holding on to their suitcases. They would make it to Heathrow with time to spare. The train filled and the doors shut.

The girls had chosen Paddington Station not because of the bear, they told themselves, but because they wanted to picnic in Hyde Park before heading to the station. And indeed, Hyde Park had been worth a picnic and a stroll for our heroines, and they did in fact enjoy being in Paddington Station more than they'd enjoyed trying to see the Harry Potter location at King's Crossing where they found

---

225. Morrison, Jim. "People are Strange." Strange Days. Elektra Records, 1967.
226. Navigation confidence as a tourist in London is often misplaced
227. Jim was the only door they should lean on

the line was long enough to lead the best of friends to argue and the food was truly limited. In Paddington, just being in the station brought them joy. Like many professors, they grew up reading[228] or being read to,[229] and they had an innate love of Paddington. As the train pulled out of the station and into the bright sunlight, they readied themselves for the stress of plane travel, even if it was for a short flight. The trip from Paddington to Heathrow wouldn't require them to change trains, something they still didn't feel confident in, so they sat back and relaxed in the comfort of their good choices and Paddington Bear memories.

Walls are built in life to keep things out or to keep things in. Some promise walls will keep everyone and everything on the other side, but human determination, for all its faults, can overcome walls. The Great Wall of China, for example, was built to keep people out and now it brings tourists from all over the world. No wall works every time. Long discussions could be had on where walls fail, but in this instance, all that mattered to the girls was that walls can and do fail to keep everyone out. The how can be left for designers to discuss. And thus, just as soon as their train began to move, it came to a stop. Tabby and Charlie looked at each other, but at the moment all the Londoners appeared calm,[230] so they figured it was a slight hiccup in their travel and went back to their own thoughts.

The train sat for a while, and the girls realized it was getting a bit warm. A group of college students at the back of the train had come forward to see why the train had stopped. As they passed the girls, their Scottish accents rang out above the quiet discussions

---

228. For Tabby, who grew up poor, the library was a bastion of comfort and cleanliness, and Saturday scrapbook building classes with her mom
229. Because as Barbara Bush said, reading to kids is good for them
230. British people always appear calm and thus their ability to conquer much of the world

in British accents. The words "casualty on the tracks" caught their attention.

"Casualty on the tracks? What does that mean?"

"There must've been a death," answered Charlie, thinking only of their flight and a lifelong ambition instilled in her by her father to see Ireland.

"Yes, dear," answered a British man sitting to their left. "There appears to have been a death on the tracks. Poor bugger must've jumped over the wall," he said, shaking his head and going back to his papers.

At these words, the Scottish students[231] nodded to each other and moved towards the front of the train, pulling their cameras out of their pockets as they went. The doors of their train car weren't open, but the cars connected, and apparently the doors further up had been opened to let air in. The girls watched with interest as the boys made their way towards the front of the train and then appeared outside of the train. From their vantage point, they could see the boys from the shoulders up, but without a serious attempt, they couldn't see the tracks under the train. They watched as the boys moved forward and posed with their cameras, only to see their faces change quickly and the boys move separately to nearby tracks to sit down, heads between their knees, looking a bit green as more officers and officials moved towards the tracks under their train with tarps and official cameras.

"Serves them right," said Tabby, completely uninterested in seeing what lay beneath the train.

"Why would they want to see that?" Charlie asked.

Collectively, without discussing it, the individuals in the girls' car decided not to follow suit and attempted to see nothing at all

---

231. College students are always listening except for during lectures

from the windows. The time passed slowly as the train warmed up from human occupants and no air running. No one discussed how the man had managed to get past the walls protecting this portion of the tracks, as they knew that he had. Officials came on with water bottles but only confirmed what the girls feared: they were stuck and wouldn't be able to leave their train until the police were done and the tracks had been cleared. Once that was accomplished, they would be brought to the next station. The train would need repair. They were reassured the train was safe to drive them to the next station, but at that point, they would be on their own.

Once the train official moved on to bring water and news to the next car, the occupants began discussing their situation together. One of the locals had been texting with a family member who worked at the station and was happy to share the news.[232] The man, as it was a man who'd jumped, spoke at large with someone before doing the deed. The man, named Justin something or other, was upset upon returning from some sort of family court. After twenty years of not paying child support for any of his children, and not wanting to be a part of their lives,[233] he'd been ordered to pay back-pay to all the mothers of his children, and there were many. He decided they could fight over what he had after he was gone. Probably wasn't much anyways.

"And now we all get to sit in the heat and wait? Great," moaned Tabby.

"I mean, he could've just paid his child support."

"That would've been great. Do you think we'll make our flight?"

"We've already been here for an hour at least. How long do you think this will take?"

---

232. The individual was not in fact British but had immigrated from another country where open discussion was acceptable
233. He felt this justified not paying for the children

"Last month it took two hours," said the man to their left with a sigh.

"Two hours?"

"Apparently there's a lot to clean and document," said the man with a grimace.

The girls decided to ask no more questions and to spend the time listening to Jim on their headphones. The time passed as fast as one might expect time to pass as one sits and waits for a body to be recovered and processed. The girls were careful not to make the mistake of the Scottish students and even look out the window the entire time. They had no interest in finding out what was going on. Compassion for and curiosity over the dead are two vastly different feelings. When the train finally switched back on, the air was a welcome relief, as was the forward surge. The girls began discussing what they'd do when they got to the next station. Neither one knew the route, and they quickly agreed their time on trains was over. As Floridians, the promise of a train[234] had been proving false for decades.[235] They saw no reason to continue seeking out trains. They would find a taxi to Heathrow.

---

234. Outside of the monorail in Disney, which was always on time and delivered only joy
235. The state of Florida had no interest in building public transportation to lessen the traffic on highways or the impact on the environment that traffic was causing

CHAPTER SIXTEEN

Driver, Where Are You Taking Us?[236]

Arriving at the train station after a "casualty on the tracks," made the doors of the train opening feel like the doors to heaven opening to let the girls and their luggage out of the heat and anxiety of death into the possibilities of life. Glancing at their watches, they realized the chances of arriving in time for their flight to Dublin were slim. They headed out to find a taxi but given their current financial status of unemployment and the cost of the only cab they'd taken thus far, they were hesitant. They headed to the edge of the group of taxis lined up outside the train station[237] and discussed options. They had to get to Heathrow, even if they missed the flight. Maybe the airline would understand and help them out. As they discussed their dilemma, a man quietly approached. His wire rim glasses hid his understanding dark eyes, and his accent kept his speech low and buried in insecurity.

"Ladies, are you looking for a taxi?"

"We need to get to Heathrow, but our last taxi was so expensive," said Tabby.

---

236. Morrison, Jim. "The End." The Doors. Elektra Music, 1967.
237. Likely word had spread of the casualty on the tracks and taxis rightly guessed many passengers would not be eager to get back on another train

"I am the cheapest here. I can get you to Heathrow for half price. Come," he said as he picked up Charlie's bag and headed towards his minivan.

"Well, can't be much worse than how the rest of our day has gone," said Tabby.

The girls watched the nameless man load their bags into the "boot" of his van, as the British say, and took their seats in the middle of the van. In no time at all, the man was behind the wheel and navigating out of the city. They watched from their windows as the van wove its way through the crowded traffic of London and out on to open highway. Getting space from the direct hustle and bustle of the city felt relieving.

"Tabby?"

"Yep."

"Do you see one of those counter things? You know, those things on the dash that count the distance travelled by cabs?"

"Uhhmm no," whispered Tabby.

"Do you see signs that this is in fact a cab?"

"Well, we're in now, and he has our bags, so we're not getting out anytime soon," said Tabby as the van took an exit into a neighborhood that had no signs of nearing the airport.

The girls sat in silence wondering if this was how their trip would end. Thoughts of movies such as *Taken* and *Ransom* went through their heads while they contemplated their next move as the driver pulled into an empty gas station and up to a pump on the backside of the station.

"Only a moment," he said as he got out of the van.

"What do we do?" asked Charlie.

"We don't have a good phone signal. We don't know where we are. Let's see where this goes. After what happened earlier, we deserve some good energy. We said we'd take it as it comes. Let's keep going."

The girls sat quietly ignoring their fear as the man climbed back into the van and rejoined the other cars on the highway. Being on the highway brought the comfort of witnesses and the hope that they were heading towards the airport, and as they made progress, the girls started to see signs for the airport. Their anxiety and fear stayed high until they pulled up alongside the curb at Heathrow, jumping out as the man got their bags. Tabby handed him some pounds as the girls both ran for the door.

"Did you pay him? Was it half?"

"It was, but I gave him a nice big 'thank you for not killing us' tip."

"Seems appropriate."

"Let's not take an illegal taxi again."

"Agreed." And so, the girls made their way into Heathrow, following the signs and weaving their luggage amongst the crowds to head towards the Aer Lingus counter.

Heathrow, like many airports, was a crowded mess crammed into a modern building built to distract from the immense crowds shifting through long lines[238] wondering whether their luggage would make it to their destination. Because British food isn't very good, there was only tea and chips designated as crisps and hidden under questionable flavors. No worries, the girls had no time for food. They made their way to the Aer Lingus counter to attempt to check-in. As their flight was now less than two hours away, they stopped and asked the requisite airline employee stationed at the end of the long check-in line if it was possible to still check-in. The woman was about twice Tabby and Charlie's age, and she compensated by

---

238. Much like Walmart

wearing twice as much make-up. However, her blue eye shadow was not enough to hide the "please fuck off" look on her face. Charlie saw the look but dared to interrupt the woman's clear intentions of doing as little work at work as possible.

"Excuse me," said Charlie carefully, with Tabby standing behind Charlie's suitcase pretending to casually look at her phone.

"Yes, dearie," said the woman with a British accent, who, as she turned, appeared to see the girls for the first time. Her face lit into a smile revealing teeth that suggested an even older age or a complete lack of dental care.

"Yes, we are trying to catch our flight to Dublin, but there was a casualty on our train, and I am worried we've missed our flight."

"Come now, dearie. Is it a honeymoon we're on? That sort of thing wasn't allowed in my day, but I'm glad times have changed," she said with a wink, clearly missing the bit about the suicide. Charlie gave her a quiet smile and let her interpret what she wanted.

"Now, I'm supposed to send you to the help desk since you are clearly not going to make that flight. But I'll tell you what. Us girls need to stick together. Let's get you two on your travels the best way possible," she whispered in a conspiratorial voice as she led the girls around the line to the very front and right to the first open desk.

"Good luck, girls, and have a great time," she said with a wave.

"You're horrible," said Tabby.

"Hey, we've got a flight to catch, and I didn't even have to hold your hand this time," Charlie said with a laugh.

"Passports," said the man behind the desk in a bored tone with an outstretched hand that had clearly never done manual labor. The girls handed over their passports and quickly went into their story of how they'd left with enough time to make it to the airport, but there'd been a casualty on their train. The man, despite having heard the news of the casualty on his way into work by car, thought only of the stereotype of Americans oversharing and nodded his head without listening.

"Unfortunately, this flight has closed for check-ins. I can offer you seats on a future flight; however, I can tell you our Dublin flights are fairly booked for the next few days. You may have to fly standby."

"Standby?" questioned Tabby, who did know the meaning of the word but was shocked at the possibility they were facing—more time in London and limited funding.

"Do we have other options?"

"Of course. You could always hire a car and head over to Dublin. It's a lovely drive."

"Can we get a refund?"

"You can call our customer service and petition for a refund."

"Does anyone answer those numbers?" asked Tabby.

"As I said, you can call."

"Ok, could you point us in the direction of the car rentals?" asked Tabby.

"Sure, you're going to follow the signs for the Metro," he said as he pointed in a vague direction, "and board the Piccadilly Line. Be sure to head towards Terminal 5, not back in towards London. Next," said the man with his hand in the air, clearly moving on to the next customer.

"Well, I guess that's decided," said Tabby as Charlie lamented boarding yet another train and hoping that the people of London would have the decency not to kill themselves on this train.

Miraculously, the girls were able to follow the signs to the Metro, which they located after asking a lovely, elderly, Irish woman on her way back from a London holiday. They boarded the train headed, they believed, in the right direction, but there were no more seats as they apparently boarded at a time when many others were also headed to "hire" a car. There was a veritable run on cars. However, they didn't worry. They stood by the far door and waited for the train to take off. Tabby, having travelled enough for the day, sat down on her luggage and leaned against the wall of the train, waiting for it to take off and very careful to be away from any doors. The door behind Charlie was still open, allowing others to come on until the girls were pressed on all sides by apparent Londoners and fall vacationers. Charlie found herself surrounded by people who needed a shower, and she focused on her phone for distraction from the smell of bodies surrounding her as the train started to go. Fortunately, the train worked as trains are supposed to work, and no one jumped on the tracks. They reached their destination and exited, making their way towards the Sixt sign. They approached the counter, which had a surprisingly long line compared to the long line coming into the hall from the Hertz line.

"Don't worry," said a plump middle-aged man as he passed the girls with his keys. "That line is long because they try to get every penny out of you. This mate is honest. He'll get you right to your car," he said nodding in the direction of the counter. "Bye, Travis. See you next week."

"See you!" said Travis with a wave. The girls waited their turn and slowly made their way through the red velvet ropes towards the front counter.[239]

"How can I help you ladies?"

"We've missed our flight and need to rent a car to Dublin."

"So, you'll be needing to hire the car here and then leave it in Dublin?"

---

239. Much of travelling is just moving slowly in roped in lines

Charlie looked at Tabby to make the decision as both girls were too exhausted to think of the next step.

"Right. We have a flight out of Dublin."

"Well now, if your flight to Dublin didn't board you, they will cancel your return flight."

"Fuck me," said Charlie.

"Thank you for the offer," said the man in an accent that brought forgiveness for anything he said, "but I can help you with a car for just monetary exchange," he said with a wink. At which point Tabby took over. "So, we should rent a car but still leave it in Dublin. We have a conference there for a few days and won't need the car. We can sort ourselves from there and call the airline."

"Ok. Just the two of you? Two bags? Right. I can get you in a two-door car and on your way. Will you take the ferry over?"

"Right, because this is an island, and Ireland is a different island."

"And a different country."

"Right, yes. I'll work on the ferry, and you get the car?" Charlie asked.

And so, the girls found their way forward as they always did—together. Having rented the car, they headed out into the parking lot. Their car was easily found by numbered spot. They started to load their bags into the car and looked to find a way to Dublin, even though their hearts were in Paris with Jim.

"Tabby, my stomach has about had it from all this motion. Can you drive?" asked Charlie, knowing Tabby would always be the driver in a foreign country.

"Sure. Want to grab some Pepto-Bismol from my medicine bag? It's in the small bag I already put in the front of the car."

Charlie headed to the front passenger seat, reminding herself it was on the wrong side of the car, opened Tabby's medicine bag and took two pink bills, deciding on a third for good measure as her stomach continued to lurch forward with the motion of a train she was no longer on. With the hope of some relief, she sat in the passenger seat and waited for Tabby.

"It's four hours, closer to five, to the port. Tickets on the ferry are one hundred pounds each, so I didn't want to purchase until I was sure we could make a ferry tonight. The last one is at ten pm."

"We haven't had the best luck today. The college paid for our hotel in Dublin tonight. Let's call them and reschedule a night so they don't cancel us for not showing, and then let's just find a hotel on the way to the port, or close to it, and stay the night. That way we can sleep in and head to the port when we're ready."

Charlie began looking for a hotel that was affordable, payable online, and close to the Holyhead port. Unfortunately, what Charlie had thought was Pepto-Bismol was actually Benadryl. Before she could find a hotel, she was out cold and snoring for effect.

"Charlie," called Tabby, having made her way out of the abysmal London traffic and finally finding some smaller roads on the way out towards the port.

"Charlie—"

"Hmm," said Charlie, wiping drool from her chin.

"Good god, what did you take?" asked Tabby, trying hard not to look at Charlie as she navigated driving on the wrong side of the road using the wrong hand.

"I don't know. I thought stomach meds, but I'm really tired. I don't think I took the right pill."

"Apparently not. How many did you take?" Tabby asked with a laugh.

"Three. I think."

"Ok, so you're probably not going to die, but you're also no help. Did you get a hotel?"

"I don't think so," said Charlie as she opened her phone and checked her last open screens. "No, looks like I didn't make it very far," she said, looking at a kayak.com screen with no search bars filled in.

"Great."

"Sorry, I don't think I can stay awake long."

"No, I mean great. We are probably never going to be in England again, we need a new hotel room, and I want to explore Wales."

"Wales?"

"Wales."

"Why Wales?"

"Ok. So, you probably won't remember this anyways, but there's this one poem—"

"You have a poem you like?" interrupted Charlie with what any drunk person would feel was a laugh but what actually came out as more of a chortle.

"Yes, now, don't laugh, but there was this one poem about an Abbey. My grandma loved it. She had a picture of the place on her wall, between those giant wooden forks and spoons all grandparents had."

"That checks. Mine had some too. Not the pic, but the fork and spoon. I always wanted to use them," said Charlie, leaning her head against the window and yawning.

"Grandma had always wanted to go but never did, and I always wanted to go for her. It's not that far out of the way, and it's rural, so I bet the hotel and food are way cheaper."

With Charlie passed out once again, the decision was made. Of course, with no voice command in the car, and a complete inability to tap the screen on the dashboard with her left hand, Tabby had to pull over into a parking lot to adjust the address. Fortunately, she'd made the decision by the time they were passing Oxford, so they only had to shift their path to the left a bit. There would be an hour and a half until they could get out and rest, and then four and a half hours the following day.

Tabby was pleased to see they'd make sunset at the Abbey and could then hopefully find a hotel in nearby Chepstow. What she was surprised by was the narrowness of the roads. As they neared the Abbey, every road seemed to be a one lane road that somehow was supposed to house two cars speeding in different directions. While the speed limit was pretty high, she found herself going uncharacteristically slow as a line of cars formed behind her.[240] Signs popped up occasionally reminding drivers to "Mind the Verge," and Tabby persisted through the path, occasionally swearing under her breath as she flinched when Brits sped past her in the opposite direction. As the roads got narrower and the speed limit lowered, she began seeing the words SLOW and ARAF painted on the roads.

"I don't know who ARAF is, but he and I are both slowing down," said Tabby with a nervous laugh as she followed the GPS into a small parking lot. When she parked, Charlie awoke from her drug-induced coma.

"Are we in Dublin?"

"No, that would require a ferry."

"What in the world," said Charlie, stepping out and seeing the bones of what must have been a giant wonder-of-the-world cathedral at some point. The structural remains rose to the sky surrounded by green grass and pastures. A surprising amount of the walls remained

---

240. Unable to pass due to the narrowness of the road.

as if God himself was holding them together against the oppression that led to the destruction of so many cathedrals.[241]

There was a cute little café near the parking lot, so the girls popped in for the bathroom and a scone with tea to go. They quietly walked over to the Abbey and went inside with their picnic dinners.[242] Entering the ruins felt somehow holier and more solemn than entering a church. The floors were grass interrupted by the remains of the stone floor. They slowly walked the inside of all the walls, looking out the empty holes where windows once were and soaking up the silence and peace of having what must be a national treasure all to themselves. The archways spoke of perfect craftsmanship and furthered the feeling of solemnity brought by only the holiest of churches. The missing roof seemed to bring in the feeling of nothing separating guests from heaven itself. Even Charlie had nothing to say or nothing that she felt worthy of breaking the heavy sense of peace and solitude that exuded from the stone walls as if the centuries of monks who had prayed, chanted, and sang into these walls had left something behind, or like God himself was watching closer at this location where his friends once lived.

As the girls settled on some large rocks left in the middle of what must've been the sanctuary to eat their food in peace, a bus of middle school boys parked and sent the boys spilling through the doorway, interrupting the silence with a noise level only middle schoolers are capable of. The girls weren't sure if anything could be worse than more students finding them, but middle schoolers finding them was certainly a start at being worse.[243] The goal of middle school boys[244] is to disrupt life all around them and to never

---

241. As a wise man once said, the British oppressed everybody
242. Because scones are good for any meal of the day, even second dinners
243. Unlike their hero, Jim, they didn't ever choose to sit at the kids' table
244. Regretfully, this was an entire small bus of boys and chaperones who were hating life

shower. As the girls began packing up their food and rolling their eyes, the boys assembled on what was left of stairs to one side of the cathedral while their chaperones circled around them. Without warning, the boys broke out into perfect pitch a-cappella singing in Latin. The girls were entranced. Music transformed the little monsters into angels, and the girls could do nothing but sit back and enjoy the show.

The chaperones divided their roles into filming and conducting seamlessly; clearly, these were roles they were very much accustomed to. As the group began their third song, Tabby suggested they leave while life inside the cathedral was still peaceful and before the little monsters no doubt returned to explore the ruins. Tabby led Charlie out to the surrounding maze of what remained of the cathedral and took her turn in telling long-winded stories of what the buildings must've been before leading her to a centuries old tree with one gravestone at its roots. As they made their way around the slumbering tree to see the gravestone up close, they found it wasn't actually a gravestone but a commemorative plaque letting visitors know that the tree had been planted to commemorate the coronation of George V in 1911.

"So, not centuries old," said Charlie, always eager to correct her friend.

"That felt good, didn't it?"

"Actually, yes," said Charlie.

The girls sat at the base of the tree, more relaxed now that they knew it wasn't a gravestone indicating a sleeping neighbor under the tree, and they finished their tea and scones.

"Want to see the river before we go?"

"There's a river?" asked Charlie, who hadn't read the poem and whose drugs weren't worn off completely. Tabby stood up and led the way down closer to the River Wye where they breathed in the solitude that can only be found in nature, before heading back to their rental car to find a place to stay the night.

Driving into Chepstow didn't take as long as Charlie had worried it would. They drove into town and found The Coach and Horses Inn. The building looked older than America, so they figured it was worth a shot. As they dragged their bags up the front steps, they found themselves in a perfect pub rounded with mahogany wood that spoke of decades of polishing and spilled beer.

"Can I help you ladies?" said a kind voice that sensed the need for English.[245]

"Do you have a room for tonight?"

"We certainly do. Our last room is on the third floor. Is that okay with you?"

Tabby turned and saw the elevator before agreeing as Charlie managed to break out the college card for what might truly be their last justifiable charge on the card, and the man behind the bar explained that the doors locked at midnight, at which time they could access the third floor by the fire escape in the back.

"As much fun as that sounds like, we will be asleep before then," said Tabby with a laugh.

The girls brought their luggage into the tiny elevator and up to the third floor. Once again, the room opened with an actual key, and inside they found two twin beds in a room that was clean, comfortable, and that had clearly housed guests for hundreds of years, despite the level of polish and the added modern comfort of a private bathroom. They lay on their twin beds and stared at the ceiling in silence for a while, thinking of how the afternoon could begin with death and end with reverence. Before long,[246] they

---

245. Americans can be spotted yards and yards away
246. About five minutes

realized scones don't hold one over for dinner, and they wandered back to the pub.

Like any good pub in Wales or Ireland, the pub was full of locals laughing, drinking, eating, and watching sports. The girls found a seat and were glad to see the same man was working. Charlie had noticed how good-looking he was. His brown eyes looked tired, and he seemed to hide a laugh that was likely at the expense of his patrons. His shoulders were strong, and his trim build kept her eyes coming back.

"What can I get for you girls?"

"Do you have any hot cocoa?" asked Charlie.

"We do, the very best in town. Shall I get you some?"

"Yes, please," said Charlie, captivated by his eyes and his accent.

"Two then?"

"Unless you want to make it three and join us?" Charlie said with uncharacteristic boldness. He smiled and said he'd be right back with their drinks.

"What was that?"

"Well, we're only in Wales once, right? Might as well try."

"Not sure that was trying."

"Whatever. Don't they say Americans are more interesting when they travel? Maybe he'll take me up on it."

"On what? Cocoa?" said Tabby with a laugh as the man came back with two mugs of steaming cocoa and menus in case they wanted dinner and quickly left.

A woman came to take their order afterwards, cementing their rejection, but the girls did as any sane and yet rejected person would do and ordered pizza.[247] The late hours of the evening passed calmly as they ate their pizza. One of the good things about most countries

---

247. Carbs erase all pain

in Europe is that since waiters are not paid by tip, they don't care how long one person stays at a table or if they are ordering more food. In fact, if they don't order more food and continue to take up a table, the waiter benefits from less work with the same pay, so the girls felt no pressure to leave until they noticed that the rest of the crowd was leaving and floors were being swept.

"Want to go up to the room?"

"Or we could go out and explore town?"

"It is our only night in Wales."

The girls made their way out of the pub and into the narrow brick roads of the town that had seen kings and monks come and go. The shops were all closed for the night, but they spoke of a quiet town: book shops, bridal shops, secondhand stores, and antiques. They regretted their need to get to Dublin tomorrow as they explored the narrow pathways and quiet roads.

"What in the world does that sign say?" asked Charlie, pointing at a small sign on the opposite side of the road.

"Oh my gosh, it's an old people crossing sign." The girls laughed and explored the town that cared enough to warn that old people might be slowing traffic by crossing the road willy-nilly, and eventually they found themselves at a crossroads, well, a bridge. The stone bridge passed over what they assumed was the River Wye and the sign explained this was the border of England.

"Wait—this is the border of England—want to walk to England?" Charlie asked and like giddy school girls, they walked across the bridge to England, and then walked back to Wales a few times, each time laughing about how many times they'd had to walk to England that day.[248] Eventually, their adultness took over, and they decided they should get some sleep if they were ever going to get to Dublin

---

248. Things that entertain Americans to no end

tomorrow. When they walked back to the front of the pub, they remembered what their good-looking friend had said: The doors were locked and there were few lights on.

"So, outback?"

"Outback it is."

Having never climbed a fire escape before, the girls didn't mind the climb as much as maybe they should have, and eventually they arrived at the third floor and were surprised to find the door was propped open.

"So, we are definitely using the extra locks on our bedroom door tonight."

"And stacking the luggage in front of the door." And with that, they headed off to sleep, ready to take on a new country in the morning.

CHAPTER SEVENTEEN

Keep You Eyes on the Road, Your Hands upon the Wheel[249]

In the morning, they packed up and headed downstairs for breakfast before hitting the road. They were both glad to see that the man who rejected Charlie's cocoa offer wasn't working, and they sat down to have some croissants.[250] The tea was markedly better in Wales than anything they'd found in England, and for that, they were grateful.[251] They sat and sipped their tea as Tabby explained how the ferry to Ireland worked and that they had until that evening at nine to make their ferry to Dublin, which should give them some time to slowly drive through the winding roads of Wales and England to the port in Holyhead, allowing for time to return the car and head over to the ferry by taxi. Charlie nodded, more than willing to let Tabby lead the way as she took her don't-throw-up-in-the-car meds and helped Tabby get the luggage out of the pub/hotel and into the "boot" of the rental car.

---

249. Morrison, Jim. "Roadhouse Blues." Morrison Hotel/Hard Rock. Elektra, 1970.
250. Which are somehow available in every European country, even those practicing Brexit
251. Likely this was because prices in England kept them from accessing any good tea

Tabby made her way out of Chepstow and back onto the small winding roads of the countryside. The roadside blurred together for Charlie, whose medicine helped her sleep as Tabby nervously gripped the wheel and fought the urge to drive off the road and into the verge. The cars coming at her on the wrong side of the road weren't any more comfortable today than they'd been the day before, and she questioned her life choices that brought her to this moment of driving while her friend slept. The four-hour drive stretched into five hours and beyond as Tabby's fear of crashing on the wrong side of the road kept her far below the speed limit. Eventually, they arrived at a Sixt rental on the north-western coast of England.

"Charlie."

"Hmm."

"We're here," said Tabby with a sigh, finally letting go of her grip of the wheel after parking in front of the rental store.

"Oh, that was an easy drive."

"Sure," said Tabby with a laugh as they took their bags from the boot and headed into the "car for hire" building.

"How can I help you?" asked a short, fat woman behind the counter without looking up from her phone.

"Hello, we're just here to return our car," said Tabby handing the keys over.

"Oh, well, these are Sixt keys," said the woman in disgust.

"Yes."

"This is Hertz. We don't handle Sixt," she said trying to hand the keys back.

"The GPS said this was Sixt," said Tabby, "really" she said in defense, looking at Charlie.

"This used to be Sixt. They moved up the street on the other side of the highway a few months back. GPS still lists their address as here. The boss has told Apple and Google maps. No one listens. Have a good day," she said, placing the keys on the counter and heading back to the refuge behind a "Do Not Enter" sign and away from the customer counter.

"Well, now what?" asked Tabby as they headed back out into the parking lot.

"Well, now we find out where Sixt is," said Charlie, still feeling the effects of her motion meds.

"No shit, Sherlock."

"Nice British reference."

"Well, I had to get it in once while we're here."

"Wouldn't be a trip to England without it. Hey, let's ask those cops over there," said Charlie pointing to a few police cars pulled over alongside the ramp leading from the parking lot onto the highway.

"They seem like they're setting up for some detail or whatever."

"You have any better ideas?"

"Nope, go ahead," said Tabby waving Charlie on as she sat in the car to see if Google could sort the way to the right Sixt. Her wait wasn't long as Charlie quickly returned.

"No help, huh," asked Tabby without looking up.

"Actually, they're giving us an escort to Sixt. They said it happens a lot, and one guy said he wouldn't want his wife driving on the wrong side of the road alone in America or something like that."

"Perfect," said Tabby as she started the car and took off following the small police car as it broke from the pack and headed off to Sixt. The drive took all of two minutes, but it was two minutes they couldn't have handled on their own. Plus, the drive was accomplished quicker because when you are following a cop, you get to take the access roads that are closed to traffic. Unfortunately, this secret back path meant that the girls actually didn't know where they were or how they got there. This was something they thought of after returning their car to Sixt and discovering they had no signal on their phones.

"Great," said Tabby with a sigh, ready to give up.

"Wait, I think you were right."

"About what?"

"Those cops were setting up for some kind of detail. Look, there's more of them over in that parking lot," said Charlie pointing to the parking lot of the business next to Sixt.

"Are you sure those aren't the same guys? They all look alike."

"They do, but look, that one looks just like Gerard Butler.[252] I would remember someone looking like that in the last group," said Charlie as the girls walked towards the group of officers, naturally drawn to the tall, broad shouldered, muscular officer with brown hair flowing over his ears[253] and greenish-blue eyes piercing them as they got closer. Charlie explained their situation—no signal, lost, on the way to the port, as Tabby chimed in with the difficulties of driving in England, and likely the charm of accents did its work as the man smiled.

"No worries, love. We'll get you sorted," he said as he told them to follow him to his car. He drove them over to the port, which was only a few streets away, and he regaled them with stories of the time he took his family to Disney and struggled to drive in America. Before they knew it, they were at the port and on their way to Ireland.

The ferry didn't look like much from the outside, but once they were inside, they saw it was like a moving casino with a movie theater and more places to eat than they wanted to consider. There

---

252. Who is in fact not British or Irish
253. Which would suggest an undercover officer in the States

were rooms to sleep and shower, but they wanted to live as they always did—on a budget—so they found their way to some free seats and sat down to wait out the time until they made it to Ireland.

"Take more meds," said Tabby as the ferry left port.

"Already done," said Charlie as she leaned back in her seat to attempt some sleep. Given the stress of driving, even Tabby was able to sleep, and the ride over churning dark waves passed quickly for our sleeping beauties.

The girls arrived in Dublin confused and exhausted in the dark. They were glad they'd left the car in England so they didn't have to navigate the Dublin streets by car. The streets in old European cities were built for pedestrians and horses, not for cars, and many of the streets through old cities haven't been remodeled in a way that Americans can safely navigate, especially on the wrong side of the road. As the girls exited the port, they were thankful for Tabby's research about taxis and used the FREENOW app she'd found to quickly get a taxi to Temple Bar. The college had gotten them reservations at the conference hotel, Camden Hotel, for the first night, but then they were supposed to go with the conference to the Wild Atlantic Way, or the west coast of Ireland. They'd missed the bus, even if they'd wanted to make the conference, and despite their attempts to move their reservation a night, they'd had to make their own reservations elsewhere. According to Tabby's research, Temple Bar was the main tourist attraction in Dublin. She'd found a hotel with solid reviews, large en-suite bathrooms,[254] and rooms named after literary heroes. They'd gotten the James Joyce room and couldn't wait to check in.

---

254. Always double check for ensuite bathrooms when travelling to Europe as Europeans are way too comfortable using non gendered shared hall bathrooms

With the taxi located, the girls headed to Temple Bar, entranced by the River Liffey and the old buildings of Dublin. The taxi stopped at the end of a narrow brick street and eased them into an alley that was clearly only one way, which was possibly not the way they were going.

"Here yous are," he said coming to a stop and getting the girls' bags for them. The hotel door was behind a chain gate with a sign informing them they would need to ring for service. To the left was a similar door, but with no glass to see inside, and to the right was an adult shop.[255]

"Well, this looks great," said Tabby.

"Feeling at home already. Didn't you say there were no kids allowed in this hotel?"

"Ya, I figured that would be great. No screaming babies."

"I'm thinking there was another reason and there still might be screaming."

"The shop to the left is a massage parlor, isn't it?" asked Tabby, head down.

"Not thinking it's a normal massage parlor based on the need for a code to enter."

"What now?'

"Well, we did say we'd take it as it comes."

"We did."

"And it's late."

The girls decided one night between the adult store and the shady massage parlor on a small back street of Temple Bar would be passable and then they could find options for the next day. They rang the bell and eventually a man came down who was thin and in his fifties. He was stylishly dressed and had a few piercings. He

---

255. The kind only certain adults shop in.

seemed annoyed to see them and perhaps aware the feeling was mutual.

"Welcome to the Merchant House," he said as he opened the gate and helped them bring their bags inside. "Your room is on the third floor. Check out is at eleven. Breakfast is around the corner; here are your breakfast tickets. These will get you free breakfast. Do not lose them. If you lose them, they will not be replaced," he said as he made his way up the winding staircase to the third floor with their luggage, continuing with what felt like a lecture. "When you head out tonight—"

"We're not heading out," said Tabby.

"When you head out, and you get lost, which you will, here is the map marked with where we are. I say when because you will get lost. Americans always get lost. Here is the map. Do not call for help if you get lost. Here is your room. Quiet hours have already started, so do be considerate of other guests in the hallways. Goodnight," he said and left the room.

"Well."

"At least the room is nice."

Tabby and Charlie walked into the entranceway that was tiled and ended in a beautiful, old brick fireplace surrounded by candles that couldn't be lit and deep plush chairs to sit in. To the right was a comfortable bed surrounded by more chairs and tall windows closed off by dark, thick blinds. To the left was a large bathroom shut off by a glass door.

"Great door."

"Lots of privacy."

"At least the bedroom is nice."

"I do prefer my own bed, though."

"Well, given the neighborhood, we only have to make it one night, and at least it's a double bed."

"How long do you want to stay in Dublin?"

"I've always wanted to go to Dublin. It's something my dad passed on to me, and his dad passed to him, and so on, all the way to my great, great, great grandparents who came over in the Potato Famine."[256]

"So, let's give it a few days, assuming we can get a better place to stay."

"Agreed. Sounds great."

"Why don't we see if we can get rooms at that Camden Hotel the conference was using, at least then we have the people running the conference saying it's an ok place to stay."

"Ok as in no whore house next door?"

"Hey, no whore shaming."

"Ok, but I prefer to keep my whores at a distance."

The girls laughed, as they always did, found their way to bed, and made plans to move to the Camden Hotel after free breakfast the next morning and then to explore Dublin for a few days.

---

256. The famine involved more than potatoes, and the starving masses would have been glad to eat anything—not just potatoes. Thus, the Irish call it the National Famine, not the potato famine

CHAPTER EIGHTEEN

I'll Say it Again, I Need a Brand New Friend[257]

The morning came and the girls were excited to explore Dublin, as Americans always are when in Dublin. They had slept in and woke up to the sound of the city moving around them.[258] Since their time was short, they had to get right out and explore. However, they were sure they were done sleeping next to the questionable massage parlor, so they packed their suitcases, put them in a closet marked "luggage storage" behind the vacant front desk, and went out into the city. The cobblestone streets wound around Temple Bar inviting the girls to keep walking as they headed in the general direction of what they felt would lead to the River Liffey.[259] More important than food was checking off one of their goals, but since food was needed, and they had slept past the time of free breakfast, they decided to get the best ice cream[260] on God's green earth.[261] The goal for the day

---

257. Morrison, Jim. "Hyacinth House." L.A. Woman. Elektra Records, 1971.
258. A common occurrence as there isn't a lot of AC in Dublin
259. In fact, they were not headed towards the river at all, but their stomachs were honing in on ice cream like pigeons narrowing in on their destination
260. The day starts best when it starts with dairy products, according to a survey down by The Midwestern Cattle Society of Canada.
261. The greenest of which is in Ireland

was a new tattoo for each of them. Getting a tattoo was something Tabby and Charlie had talked about for years, but never actually planned on doing. After all, there would be pain of the sort one brought on oneself and the risk of infection.[262] Only the love of Jim could cause them to pull their shirts up and get a tattoo. But first, ice cream, and this ice cream shop had really great reviews online.

"Tabby."

"Yes," answered Tabby as they joined a line that came out of the shop and wound around like a queue at Disney.

"Are we seriously going to wait in a line this long?" asked Charlie. Generally, their rule was if there is a line to wait and eat, and that line might require twenty minutes or more of patience,[263] they don't wait in it.

"For ice cream?" answered Tabby rhetorically.

The idea of a tattoo seemed a bit odd as they stood in the extensive line at Murphy's Ice Cream, but they chatted about it nonetheless. Should they get one? Should it be matching? This was all discussed as the line slowly progressed, winding into the small but beautifully decorated ice cream store. Unlike many lines, which lead to grumpiness and anger as one questions one's life choices and why in the world one would wait in a life-ending-line for five dollar ice cream, this line was frequently interrupted by teenage employees offering unending samples of any flavor ice cream patrons could possibly want, indicating a business owner that finally knows how to work a line. If only doctors worked in free ice cream samples, patients wouldn't mind waiting for hours beyond their scheduled appointment. Anyways, the girls continued making their way through the line, discussing their tattoo options when the lone Irishman in line spoke up:

---

262. As a researcher of historic events, Charlie took into consideration all sorts of horrible possibilities
263. Which, as the person used to being in charge at the front of the class, they were not used to having

"If you ladies would really like a tattoo, the perfect place is around the corner," which was met with silence as the girls were reminded they were actually not alone in this line of patrons enjoying the bliss of unending free ice cream samples leading to the promised land of the ice cream dishing counter. "Sorry to interrupt, but the line is long, and I couldn't help but overhear. What flavor are yous gettin'."

"Well, I really liked that raisin one."

"Raisins are dead flies," said Tabby with an eye roll.

"But I usually go with cookies and cream," said Charlie, ignoring Tabby's comment.

"Ah, the gold standard. Good choice," he said with a wink in the flirtatious way of all Irish men as Charlie took a longer look at him. His thick brown hair curled into little half waves that seemed to be praising God for making the Irish, and he had just a hint of grey filtered into his beard that welcomed a closer look at his full and beckoning lips as he took another bite of his sample ice cream.

"What are you getting?" Charlie asked the stranger, in an effort to regain her composure.

"Well, it's not for me, ya see."

"No, shopping for neighborhood children?" asked Tabby with her usual level of sarcasm.

"My sister is pregnant and on bed rest. Today is my day to visit, and I find it's best to open with ice cream, plus I get free samples while waitin'."

"That you do."

"So, you mentioned a tattoo place?" asked Charlie, thinking this gift from God to the eyes of all may be a sign that they should get a tattoo.

"Yep. It's right around the corner next to an Italian place and a hidden downstairs barbershop, which is a secret sort of place, but I suppose you're not in the market for a barber now, are ya?"

"Not really," said Charlie, hoping to get the name of the tattoo parlor out of him before reaching the counter, which, after so many ice cream filled winding minutes, was finally approaching the girls.

"Can't remember as there's actually a name on the front. Put Faction Barbershop in your GPS. If you get there, you won't see the barber, he's downstairs so as only locals can find him, but you'll see the sign for the tattoo place. Guy is known by locals as the Godfather of Irish tattoos. Don't rightly know where he got himself a name like that, but he's the guy I'd go to. He's the guy I do go to when I want another tattoo."

"Thanks," said Charlie as the blessed ice cream girl asked for her order. The girls both ordered cookies and cream in cups, having sampled every other flavor in the shop on their descent to the counter. They happily paid and made their way out, waving to their new Irish friend on their way.

"Dude. Where can I get one of those?"

"Seriously," said Tabby, knowing Jim was the only man in their lives.

"I think it's a sign. We need tattoos."

"I'm game."

"You are?"

"Ya, I mean, we've talked about it long enough; it's been a goal. Let's just do it, but nothing matching, and definitely something for Jim."

"Of course. A tribute and a way to lead ourselves into the search in Paris."

And so a plan was hatched and the girls walked, following their GPS and making their way towards Faction Barbershop, hoping to find the Godfather and hoping he had time for walk-ins, preferably after they finished their ice cream.[264]

The walk from Murphy's to Faction Barbershop took the girls over the cobblestone streets that make their way through buildings that have been inviting visitors for centuries.[265] They made their way quickly, looking intently at all the windows and doors, wondering what life was like for the average Dubliner, and like most Americans who visit Ireland, wishing to join them. But alas, their's was to find Jim. Their's was not to stay and become a Dubliner.[266] The phone alerted the girls that they'd arrived at Faction before they saw it. Remembering the advice they were given, they realized the secret shop, known only to locals on the inside track, was likely in the basement of the music store in front of them, so they stood in the street looking for the tattoo parlor. Lucky for them, as they may have been standing in the middle of the road either way, this was one of the many cobblestone streets in Temple Bar that are pedestrian only. Across from the phone's decided spot for Faction stood a copper door about two stories high with a glorious tree embossed in it. Charlie stood transfixed by the door and the idea of what stood behind it, but Tabby, ever the focused one, kept her wits about her and saw that a few doors[267] down on the right was a vertical sign that simply said "Tattoos" in front of a green door.

"There it is," said Tabby pointing.

"So, we're doing this."

---

264. Tattoo artists do not respect patrons who come in eating ice cream, unless they bring some to share
265. The British were in fact not invited
266. 78.6% of American visitors wish to move to Ireland, according to Travel International's 2020 survey.
267. Normal sized doors down

"Yes, we are," said Tabby as she finished her ice cream and found a nearby trash can.

The door to the tattoo parlor led to a small, dark sitting room furnished with one padded bench. The walls were lined floor to ceiling with pictures of tattoos inviting tourists to select them and take them home. The light in the waiting area came from the room where the magic happened, but the girls found themselves separated from the magic-maker by one of those half doors that preschools use to keep the toddlers in one room while still being able to keep an eye on them.[268] Inside the room sat a thin, grey-haired Irish man wearing a black leather jacket and smoking a cigarette in a way that invoked all the James Dean vibes. He didn't acknowledge the tourists gazing at him over the door.

"Excuse me," said Tabby. The man slowly turned his head and raised an eyebrow.

"Are you taking walk-ins today?" Charlie asked. He sighed deeply and nodded his head.

"Great," said Charlie, "we're hoping to get tattoos while we're in Dublin."

"Of course you are. Wanting Celtic crosses are yous?"

"No, sir," said Tabby, unsure of how to respectfully address the man known as a godfather of anything. "We want this," Tabby said, holding up her phone. He rose and took the phone from her in one stride, moving smoothly as if worldly concerns didn't weigh him down.

"So, it's a lizard king you'll be wantin' then?"

"Yes, sir," the girls said sheepishly in response.

"Well, then. I can do that for ya. Have a seat," he said pointing to the bench.

---

268. Tourists in fact do behave like toddlers who need supervision

The girls sat in silence, unaware of the pain[269] that awaited them but smiling inwardly at the devotion they were about to write on their bodies for all to see.[270]

"Where will you be getting these?" called the Godfather from over the half door.

"I'm going for as big as will fit on my ribs."

"Well, at your height that won't be too big," Tabby said quietly.

"The rib is very painful," said the tattoo artist, rising to look questioningly at Charlie over the door.

"How much?"

"Like no pain you've ever experienced." Wondering how this stranger felt sure of the level of pain she'd experienced, she knew she must rise to the challenge.

"I can take it," she responded.

"Right. That'll be 200 cash."

"Is there an ATM nearby?"

"Yes, on the other side of this building on the next street over. Now where'll you be gettin' yours?" he asked, turning his steady gaze to Tabby. His eyes reminded Tabby of the calm before a hurricane hits.

"Where would it be least painful?"

"Back of the calf," he answered without breathing, giving an answer he had definitely given before.

"Can I add some books under the lizard king?"

"Books?"

"Yes, so he's sitting on copies of Blake's *Marriage of Heaven and Hell*, Morrison's *American Prayer* and Huxley's *The Doors of Perception*?"

---

269. People without tattoos know it will hurt, but underestimate the pain
270. Only, very few people would see their bodies

"Doors Tattoos?" asked a voice from around the corner. The girls hadn't realized there was another person in the room.

"Don't mind him. He takes up space here, but he never pays rent," said the Godfather.

"I've paid my share in tattoos," said the voice, walking around the corner and into view.

"That you have," said the Godfather to the short, thin Irish man.[271] His hair was blonde and closely cut; his eyes were brown and searching. The tattoos which covered both arms were slowly creeping up his neck attempting to cover the kind spirit behind his eyes.

"Are yous Doors fans?"

"Who isn't."

"That's what I say," said the man with an approving grin.

"Do you have any Doors tattoos?" asked Tabby, assuming he had space for all kinds of tattoos in the midst of his arms.

"I prefer art that reflects my music, my life," said the man, "but as a musician and a songwriter, I have a lot of respect for Morrison."

"You're a musician?"

"I am. Name's Rob," he said with a nod.

"That'll be 200 Euros each. Who's going first?" interrupted the Godfather, unconcerned with the conversations of others. Tabby looked at Charlie.

"I'll go."

"Right. I'll set you up."

"Since Tabby is adding books, could I add some words—veritas vos-"

"Let's see how you feel when the lizard is done," interrupted the Godfather as he turned and began setting up his workstation.

---

271. Irish men are 85% more likely to be thin than American men, according to studies done by Trinity University sororities in the spring of 2015.

The girls took that as a sign and made their way back outside to the cobblestone street, turning right at the dead end, as instructed, and heading around the back side of the building. They made their way towards where they assumed the backend of the store was and found the ATM machine the Godfather had mentioned.

"Look! It's a thrift store," said Charlie, pointing at a store just past the ATM. The store spilled vintage clothing out into the street, beckoning in fans of classic rock era clothing and music, and the girls felt the call.

"Tattoos first?"

"Tattoos first."

So, they headed back to the store, ready to lay under the needle as a sign to the world of their devotion to Jim.

"Step right up," said the Godfather, pointing to a black-covered bed that looked like one that might be in a massage parlor.[272]

"Alright," said Charlie, untucking her shirt.

"Which side?"

"Left," she answered. He nodded in response, and Charlie hiked up her shirt, tucking it into her bra as she'd read online was the best way to get a rib tattoo.

The Godfather sat next to her, arms wrapped over her left hip and poised to begin.

"Sure, love, could we be off with some of this?" he said, motioning towards her shirt.

"Oh, sorry," said Charlie, standing and removing her bra without removing her shirt.[273] Charlie eased back down and knew immediately when the needle hit her skin. Her entire world became focused on a sign on the wall: "Good Tattoos Aren't Cheap & Cheap

---

272. As a massage was the only thing Charlie and Tabby had to prepare them for this experience, they were in for a ride

273. Middle school gym class paying off

Tattoos Aren't Good." She hoped 200 Euros was enough to lead to a good tattoo, but breathing was her only focus when the needle hit her. Speaking was no longer in her realm. The Godfather gripped her hip with the crook of his arm, holding her back against him, which was oddly comforting for a woman who hadn't been held in years.

Tabby and Rob's voices droned on, discussing the trip the girls were on, why the tattoos, Rob's travels, and the fact that he once had a nephew but now had a niece;[274] it was all the sort of white noise that helped Charlie move through the pain she was experiencing. Once the outline was done, Charlie was granted a break. The Godfather sat and smoked in the shop while Charlie stood and carefully lifted her shirt to see the outline in the mirror.

"Looks good," said Tabby with a nod. The sight of the tattoo made Tabby eager to get hers, but as she knew Charlie well enough to know the pain she was masking, Tabby felt her hesitation building.

"Looks great," said Rob, before starting a football conversation with the Godfather. The girls zoned out, as they often do during sports conversations.

"Right, ready?" asked the Godfather after a sufficient amount of smoking and football conversation had been had. Charlie nodded and laid back down on her right side, bracing for the pain she knew to expect, only to find it had eased a bit and the strokes had changed, as any artist might change his brush strokes for a different effect.

"Not as bad, eh?" asked the Godfather.

"No, it's not," said Charlie, meaning the words but still wincing.

"The shading is the easy part," he said as he went back to his conversation with Rob.

---

274. The shrug of acceptance was somehow audible

The football conversation went on longer than Charlie and Tabby would have wanted,[275] and even included discussion about how they knew life was no longer worth living when they couldn't enjoy a live game anymore, when the girls were saved by a new voice entering the room. Charlie was still on her right side, not facing the door, so she didn't see the voice, but it was long, deep, and strong, bringing very specific images to Charlie's mind as she lay looking at her designated sign on the wall.

"Hello! Oh, hello, Rob," said the voice, "Howerya?"

"Good. What brings you by?"

"Wanted to show you I finished my sleeve," he said, holding out his tattooed arm. "Remember, you did this part."

"Yes, and you went somewheres else to get it finished," mumbled the Godfather unforgivingly.

"Just finished it," said the voice, not hearing what others were saying. Charlie wasn't fully listening to the man either. While she'd read the bit on her ribs would hurt worse, she found the work closer to her hip to be causing a mix of pain and upset stomach so that she couldn't listen to what others were saying. As the new voice left, the Godfather paused[276] and told Charlie the man who just left was the "biggest drug dealer in town, which is funny because his brother is a police detective," he said with a laugh. "There now. Finished," he said, putting down his tool. Charlie rose, nearly fell, then rose again, making her way to the mirror to admire her new look, swearing she would never do that again and knowing that she was lying to herself.

"I'll just need a few minutes to clean up," said the Godfather while working on disinfecting the space.

---

275. Any football conversation was too long for the girls
276. A much-welcomed pause

"I'm not sure I want to do this still," whispered Tabby to Charlie. In truth, Tabby had never been able to intentionally seek out pain, and as someone who was good at remembering numbers, she was aware of the exact likelihood of an infection or disease from a tattoo.[277] Even though it was a small number, it was a number, and that divided by the pain was intimidating.

"Nope. You're doing this. We're only in Ireland once."

"Well, you say that, but you don't know that. And besides, do I really need it?"

"Yes."

At that moment, Tabby reached into her brown bag of medicine and pulled out a small jar[278] of lotion; she'd come prepared.

"What's that?" asked Rob, who now seemed to be an old friend who'd seen one of the girls through battle.

"It's numbing cream."

"You had numbing cream, and you didn't offer me any?" asked Charlie.

"Well, I told you about it on the plane, and you said you didn't want it if we got tattoos."

"I did?"

"You did."

"I can't be held accountable for the things I say while flying."

"Now that's the truth," said Tabby, as one who was never able to take the unmedicated route when pain was involved. She covered every inch of her calve in numbing cream. By the time the Godfather cleaned up, set up and had another smoke, Tabby's leg and hands felt numb.

As Tabby lay on her stomach, the jet lag, travel, and dehydration, combined with her numb hands and leg, lulled her to sleep. She

---

277. 5% according to Brock Webster with Tattoos Daily Online.
278. Under three ounces so as not to appear to be a bomb

drifted off to the sound of the Irish accents and the knowledge that Charlie was awake and aware. Feeling no pain and only a gentle massage on her leg, she drifted off to sleep. Unfortunately, she wasn't listening to what the voices were saying.

"Did she have the cream on for long?" asked Rob. The Godfather shrugged.

"No time to wait," he mumbled as he began cleaning Tabby's calve in preparation for the tattoo. "The outline is always the worst part, and it should hold for that part. She could always finish it somewheres else."

"We all know how you feel about those who finish it somewheres else," said Rob with a snicker as a new man approached. The new man's milk chocolate brown eyes seemed to be laughing, and his long wavy brown hair had a life of its own, falling in a perfectly uncontrolled way around his shoulders. His jaw was firmly set, and his body was lean and long and invited Charlie's eyes towards him, drawing her and every woman around him in.

"Cathal Barnes, you made it," said Rob, rising to greet his friend.

"Well, you told me to come. You said it was important," he said in a deep, drawing Irish accent.

"It is. I've found your people," he said with a wave of his hands.

"Ladies," said Cathal, waving quizzically.

"Doors fans. More specifically, Jim Morrison fans. It's not just you," said Rob just as Cathal stepped into the room to get a closer look at the work in progress on Tabby's leg. He leaned over her leg, intent on the Doors image and nodding in approval. "The books are a nice addition," said the newcomer.

When Tabby awoke at the sound of his voice leaning over her legs, she turned and looked towards the deep, strong Irish accent entering through the half door, and her eyes were met with a man who exuded sexuality without trying. His brown hair had just the right amount of wave to give it body and invite attention. It wasn't short, but it was well cared for hair of the length that Tabby saw as perfection. He was the Irish Christian Bale she'd been waiting for.[279] His broad shoulders spoke of confidence and strength, but his stance didn't speak of arrogance. He smiled when he saw Tabby was looking at him. He seemed happy, as if his impression of his first view of Tabby had been met and exceeded. Charlie knew immediately that she would play the role of wingman.

"You're a Doors fan?" asked Tabby, laying still as the Godfather went back to work. The pain was starting to hit, which was honestly the reason she was waking up before she heard the voice of the Irish angel.

"I'm a fan of good music," he answered and was met with a laugh from Rob.

"Come on, man. You're the biggest Jim Morrison fan I know, and I know a lot of musicians."

"It's getting to the point where I'm no fun anymore. I am sorry,"[280] Cathal said with what sounded like a laugh and not any apology.[281]

"A non-Doors quote? I'm surprised," laughed Rob good-naturedly.

"Ok, we're not making fun of people who quote the Doors are we?" asked Tabby with a bit of a grunt as the Godfather dug into her leg with a needle.

"Are you feeling that?" Charlie asked.

"Of course she is. Only Americans would try for a tattoo with no pain," grumbled the tattoo artist without looking up from his work. He was grumpy, but he was focused on perfection in his art.

---

279. The girls do not look for a Jim Morrison because there is only one Jim
280. Stills, Stephen. "Suite: Judy Blue Eyes." Crosby, Stills and Nash. Atlantic, 1969.
281. Indeed, he was not sorry, but he was lonely

Every tattoo that left through that half door was an example of who he was, an extension of himself, and he insisted on perfection every time.

"I don't think the cream was on for long enough," said Rob as he explained that he'd gotten a few tattoos while he was in Florida and someone near him had used the cream. "It was great until it wore off, and once it wore off, the pain was worse for the guy who'd put it on than it'd been for anyone else getting one that day," he explained.

"But you didn't warn me not to use it," grunted Tabby between moans.

"I thought maybe he just hadn't used it right," said Rob with a shrug.

"Wait, you've been to Florida?" asked Charlie over Tabby's complaints.

"My band played at a punk rock festival in Gainesville a few years ago."

"In Gainesville?"

"It's a pretty big festival," said Rob, "bands come from all over."

"How have we never heard of this?"

"We don't like punk rock," groaned Tabby.

"Hey now," said Rob.

"Present company excluded," Tabby managed to say jokingly.

Cathal sat down next to Rob and asked Charlie about what started her interest in the Doors. She explained that her father, Tom, had raised her with a love for all things rock and roll. He was the definition of cool. In his youth, he was a hippy climbing telephone poles in Boston to see Jethro Tull in concert for free. Charlie's mom had left when she was young, and Tom felt he had to be twice the father to compensate. He taught her to read using Doors' lyrics. He gave her both her love of music and her love of fast cars. As it was always just the two of them, they never needed a four-door car or a minivan—

"Americans love those," interrupted Rob.

—so, he always had a Dodge Challenger. He gave Charlie both her love of music and the strength to become a professor, granted an unemployed professor. But he approves of her hunting down Jim. After all, she got her love of conspiracy theories from him, as well.

"When did you tell your dad about what we're doing?" interrupted Tabby.

"During *Breakfast with the Beatles,*" said Charlie nonchalantly. She and Tom listened to the podcast weekly and talked in chat about their thoughts on that week's podcast.

"Well, then," said Tabby, focusing again on the pain and the spot on the floor that was getting her through the searing of her leg.

"And you?" asked Cathal, turning his attention to Tabby. "What brought you to the Doors?"

"There's no excuse for me," said Tabby grunting and struggling to speak.

"We should probably give her a few minutes," said Charlie. "What started your interest in the Doors?"

"I got hit by a car," he said as Rob rolled his eyes.

"What?"

"Well, the good news is, I was in a car when it happened," he said, laughing at his own joke.[282] "This woman, American, was drivin'. Guess she couldn't get how to turn and follow signals on the right side of the road—"

"Wrong side," moaned Tabby. Cathal grinned, enjoying her perseverance.

---

282. Sometimes we have to laugh at our own jokes or no one will be laughing

"Well, anyways, I don't remember the accident, but the cameras showed it was her fault. She hit my car, spun it around and drove it into a pole. Turns out it wasn't my first head injury," he said with a laugh, "that's the thing about head injuries. You don't remember them," he continued with his deep laugh that sounded like the laugh one would expect from a large, overweight man. It barreled up from the depths of his belly and filled the room.

"Too much Gallic football, this one," said Rob with a nod towards Cathal. The Godfather nodded in understanding.[283]

"Well, at first there was the pain and the feeling of being massively drunk."

"That's a feeling I understand," said the Godfather, who seemed to speak more when Cathal was in the room.

"And as the world came back together in my head, I had to rest. I was Wilson Fisk staring at the wall all day.[284] The doc didn't want me watching tv or reading. Couldn't read anyhow. The words moved on the page—"

"Like, they actually moved?" asked Charlie.

"Yes, and once that passed, my head would read things the wrong way. Almost like mild dyslexia, if there's such a thing. My head was spinning, my ears were ringing, but I had this record player my dad left me with all his vinyls."

"Quite the collection," said Rob with a nod that hinted of jealousy. "The store is still willing to buy 'em," he said pointing towards his music store a few doors down that hid Faction.

"I sat and listened to records. My head remembered all the lyrics. I couldn't read, my voice didn't sound like me, my walk wasn't mine, but I knew all the lyrics. That gave me hope that my head would be

---

283. Gallic football uses all volunteer players who are not paid for the athleticism
284. Goddard, Drew. Daredevil. Marvel Television, 2017.

all me again at some point, that the spinning would stop, and that I could get back to life."

"Wow," said both of the girls, not sure what to say.

"It's ok. I work at the music shop with Rob now."

"When you work," said Rob with a laugh. "Great employee; he knows all the music."

"Not the rap. The beat gets to my head."

"It gets to all our heads," Tabby said to the floor.

"The Doors were the most healing. Jim was right. The music—"

"Is your special friend," laughed Charlie.

"Exactly."

"Show them your Doors tattoo," said Rob.

Cathal pulled up his long sleeve to show the sleeve beneath, and right in the center of his left forearm was a bird sitting in a window that hovered over a piano.

"'Piano Bird,'"[285] said Charlie, describing the masterpiece to Tabby who wasn't allowed to turn around and look anymore, even if the pain wasn't stopping her from doing so. "Why 'Piano Bird'?" asked Charlie. "I mean, I love the song; it's one of the only ones I like from that album, but . . ."

"Well, the mosquito one, too," laughed Tabby mumbling about a burrito and going back to her moaning.

"That's it," said Cathal, excited to be with anyone who understood his tattoo's reference. "See, the record wasn't the same as the past Doors records, but it was a start at getting back to life without Jim. The guys had to move forward. Sometimes we have to move forward, and it isn't the same, but we can have life after disaster. It's a reminder to me."

"Now that's cool," said Tabby.

---

285. The Doors. "Piano Bird." *Full Circle*. Electra Records, 1972.

"But do you think Jim is actually dead?" asked Charlie.

As the three of them dove into a discussion of Jim's apparent death, the Godfather interrupted. "There you go, ladies, you're all set." Tabby rose to admire her new tattoo dedicated to the Lizard King, happy to be in a room of three such tattoo references.

"Ladies, I hate to be forward, but do you want to get a beer and talk about Jim? You can drink until I'm funny," he said with an awkward laugh, the Irish lilt making the uncomfortable joke roll off their shoulders. And so, a plan was made to walk down the street to a pub he recommended.

CHAPTER NINETEEN

Easy Ride [286]

The girls weren't sure where this gorgeous stranger was leading them, but they didn't care. Between the view of the cobblestone streets in Temple Bar, the old buildings, and his backside, they were willing to follow where he was leading. Plus, in Temple Bar there's always a pub nearby, so they knew they could dip into safety at any point. As he rounded the first corner, he surprised them when he stopped in front of a tea and scones shop.

"I told the guys I'm headed to the pub, but truth be told, my head can't stand the sound and lights in pubs," he said reluctantly.

"Geez. When was this accident?" asked Charlie.

"A year ago."

"Were you at least able to sue?"

"That's a very American response," he said with a laugh. "I mostly go to places I know," he continued explaining as he walked into the tea shop and was greeted by friendly smiles and waves from the girls behind the counter. Tabby felt certain that was the response he received everywhere he went.

---

286. Morrison, Jim. "Easy Ride." The Soft Parade. Elektra Records, 1969.

"And the guys think you're going to a pub?" asked Tabby as they approached the counter and looked at the plates piled high with cranberry scones, blueberry scones, plain scones—if there was a flavor possibility for scones, the Irish had tried and perfected it and placed it in this shop.

"I'm fairly certain they know what I'm up to," Cathal said with his deep, rumbling laugh that took any nervousness away from the girls.

"What do you recommend?" asked Tabby.

"Well, I always order a black tea with a little bit of milk and a blueberry scone."

"Always?"

"Always."

The girls didn't question what Cathal needed to do to ease his head, but they did question his name, which they still had no idea how to pronounce.

"Well, black tea with milk and scones it is," said Charlie without telling him that they always ordered the same thing whenever possible. "I'm sorry. Can you tell me how to pronounce your name again?"

"Cathal—try to say alcohol, but without the al."

"Ya, that doesn't help," said Tabby.

"Americans usually call me Carl."

"Well, you do deserve to be called by your name, Cathal," said Charlie with a bit too much emphasis on the H.

"I once worked for a year in Germany, and everyone called me Carl."

"No one got it right for a year?"

"Right."

"That's terrible."

"Not really. Every time Carl fucked up, I just said, 'I'm Cathal, not Carl,'" he said, laughing at his joke again. "Why don't you ladies take a seat and let me get the food, show you some Irish hospitality," he said with a wink.

The girls wandered over to a window booth that had padded, curved benches, a chair at the end, and a view of the streets, although it seemed unlikely that they would be enjoying any view other than the one in front of them. Cathal returned in short order, balancing a tray of tea pots, cups, and scones like a pro. He set table in front of them and returned the tray as if it was something he did daily, and as the girls observed him, they suspected it was something he did daily.

"So, tell me, what brings you to Ireland?"

"We lost our jobs," started Charlie.

"And we already had tickets to come to London and Dublin for some professional development," finished Tabby.

"How's that been going?" he asked with an easy laugh and a glimpse in the direction of Tabby's tattoo.

"Well, we haven't been going," said Tabby between bites of her scone.

"No, we decided to prove Jim Morrison is alive instead," interrupted Charlie.

"Have you now," said Cathal.

"Well, we haven't really started, it's just something we've been thinking about."

"You plan on gettin' yourselves to Paris?"

"That's what we've been discussing," said Charlie, sipping her tea, wondering if their plan sounded as silly to Cathal as it did to her in that moment.

"Well, we're still undecided."

"What's the decision between?" asked Cathal as he held his teacup in both hands, soaking in the warmth and fully absorbed in the conversation in front of him.

"To fund this, we need to use the college credit card. We lost our jobs and have no savings," said Tabby, feeling so at ease around this Irish man that she said more than was characteristic for her.

"And you have the card now, do you?"

"We do."

"Well, I should've had you pay," he said with another laugh. "What's holding you back from going?"

"Knowing that we'll likely charge up the card and not be able to go back home."

"Do you have much to go home to?" he asked, looking only at Tabby.

"No," said Charlie as Tabby sat blushing and drinking her tea.

"Are ya waitin' on a sign?" he asked with a grin.

"That would be nice," said Tabby.

"Ya, a sign from Jim would definitely steel my resolve," said Charlie with a laugh.

Cathal got up with a nod and not a word, leaving the girls to wonder what they'd said and if they'd made the wrong choice in oversharing details about their unemployment and fraud. As they sat, the sound of a soulful blues guitar eased its way into the room. The girls were tapping their feet and nodding their heads when a voice they knew so well came over the guitar with words they didn't know:

"Well I wish I was, girl of sixteen . . . be the queen of a magazine . . ."[287]

"What—"

"What . . . how? What?" asked Charlie.

---

287. The Doors. "Paris Blues." Paris Blues. Rhino Entertainment Company, 2022.

"So you haven't heard it?" asked Cathal returning.

"What is this? Sit down, you have explaining to do," said Tabby. Cathal took that as an invitation, moving from his seat at the end of the table to the bench next to Tabby.

"It's 'Paris Blues', a brand new Jim Morrison song that just came out last week."

"How's that possible?" asked the ever-practical Tabby, not willing to take a miracle as it came.

"From what I read, the song was recorded and there was only one copy. Originally, one of the band member's kids recorded over part of it, and it was set aside. Recently, it was decided that the technology exists to bring the song back, and here it is."

"It's a miracle," said Tabby.

"It is," said Cathal, looking into Tabby's eyes. "And it's a sign," he said, looking over at Charlie.

"It is," and there and then the girls' resolve was sealed as Jim's voice belted smoothly across the speaker system of the tea shop *"going to the city of love, gonna start my life over again."*

"You can really hear Sinatra's influence in this one," Charlie said as she hummed along.

"He *was* Jim's favorite," said Cathal, nodding his head. "I think you can hear Sinatra in a few of their songs," he said as they discussed Jim's style and voice.

The discussion of whether they would go find Jim was over, and the three sat for hours discussing Jim, the music, and the band. As time passed, Cathal brought out three bowls of Irish seafood chowder with brown bread and butter on the side. He reminded them that it was important to eat well before and after a tattoo, and they gladly ate the warm, creamy soup with dill, peas, carrots, and every kind of seafood one could possibly want in a bowl of warmth.

They discussed their love for the Doors and even the band name. Not every fan was aware the name itself came from a William Blake poem, but Cathal, a true fan, did know.

"Do you think Jim read that Agatha Christie book?"[288] asked Charlie.

"Which one?" asked Cathal, enjoying his soup to the last drop as he used his brown bread to sop up any leftovers clinging to his bowl.

"*Endless Night*, and no, Charlie, no one has read that one," said Tabby in judgement. "Boy, you eat that soup like your mom made it," she said with an uncharacteristically teasing laugh. Cathal grinned and went back to his soup, responding to Charlie with a nod.

"I read that one and wondered myself. The timing isn't right. The book was published in 1967, and the Doors started in 1965," he said, not looking up, "but I'd wondered."

The conversation moved from Charlie's lone idea, that she hadn't taken the time to Google having only read the book on the plane ride over, to all things Doors. When Cathal started talking about the healing power of music, Tabby, feeling open after the hours of conversation, the searing leg pain, the soup, and the dimming lights, decided to talk about what really brought her to the Doors:

"Music *is* healing. That's why I listen to the Doors. When I was in elementary school my brother Jeremy killed himself."

"Oh, I'm sorry."

"Ya, so am I. We'll never know why, but then again, why does a fifteen-year-old do anything that they do? The day he did it, I'd argued with him. I knew he was upset, but he'd said some mean things, so I didn't care. I went to a friend's house, and he shot himself."

---

288. Christie, Agatha. Endless Night. Collin's Crime Club, 1967.

"That's horrible, love," said Cathal. Charlie sat quietly, having heard the story before, but only one time.

"It is. My parents couldn't handle the loss. Dad turned to drinking. Mom turned to other men for comfort. I was alone a lot, and a friend made me a tape with this song 'Center Aisle' on it.[289] It's by a random band, but it had the words I felt. He described that kind of loss so well. He said what I thought and had no one to say it to, so I would lay in bed and sing the words to the ceiling. By the time my dad died in a drunk driving accident, and mom was fully checked out, I'd moved on to better music. The lyrics helped me heal."

"That they do," said Cathal. The three sat in silence sipping the cups of tea as Cathal refilled them. With a full cup, Cathal sighed, "Well, music has been in my family for decades, you see, so I was raised to love music."

"A family of musicians?" questioned Charlie as she sipped her fresh cup.

"Well, no," said Cathal with a laugh. "A family obsessed with music would be a better way to describe them," he laughed again. "Have you heard the Beatles' song 'She Came in Through the Bathroom Window?'"

"Who hasn't?"

"Right," said Cathal with another easy laugh. "Well, the song was inspired by a group of fans who would hang around outside of McCartney's house, and one day, one of the women broke in," he said, pausing to let the information settle.

"Wait, are you saying—"

"Was this your mom?"

"No, she was home sick that day. It was my aunt."

---

289. Webb, Derek. "Center Aisle." Nickel and Dime Studios, 1997.

"Wait, really? Is this a joke?"

"No, she stole some pictures from the house. McCartney asked for them back and most were given back. I inherited what I think is the last one, and at this point I don't know how to give it back. I mean, do I walk up and knock on his door? Seems a bit intrusive."

"Says the guy whose aunt went in through the bathroom window," said Charlie laughing.

"So, you could say I was raised to be obsessed with music. Teenagers rebel with music sometimes, but I rebelled by not listening to music, and then with my head injury, I needed music."

"And now you're obsessed."

"Well, not like my aunt," he said with a laugh.

The girls were very curious about what picture Cathal had that belonged to *the* Sir Paul McCartney, but asking seemed likely to bring out an invitation to his place, and while they liked him, they weren't willing to go home with him. So, they sat and sipped, listening to music playing over the sound system. Cathal charmed them with stories of how he liked to put on "The End" when he left so the patrons in the tea shop would have to listen to the entirety of the nearly twelve minute song[290] as he announced that he was leaving through the gift of music. The girls seemed unwilling to come to the end of their time with Cathal as they'd finally found another person who felt like they did. But eventually, they had to call it a night. When they realized they were the only ones left in the place, and the cleaning had been done around them, they decided they had to go.

"Where are you staying?" asked Cathal.

"We're moving from Merchant House to Camden Hotel today," said Tabby, remembering that they still had suitcases to move.

---

290. Morrison, Jim and Ray Manzarek, et al. "The End." The Doors. Elektra, 1967.

"That's not far, but let me make sure you get home ok," he said with a concerned look.

"I'm pretty sure the two without head injuries are the ones most likely to navigate."

"Alright then, but text me tomorrow. I want you to meet my girl," he said on the front stoop of the shop with a wink and then disappeared around the corner.

"What do you think he meant by my girl?" asked Tabby with concern.

"What did he mean by anything? His conversation isn't the easiest to follow."

"True."

"Only one way to find out."

"Right. Text him tomorrow," said Tabby as the girls wandered in the dark towards their hotel.

"Maybe kids?"

"I mean, most men our age have them."

"Deal breaker?"

"Did you see his eyes? And just like Jim, he had a car accident that changed how he saw life."

"Well, Jim *saw* an accident, he wasn't *part* of the accident,"[291] corrected Charlie.

"Stop splitting hairs," said Tabby, who (against her math-logical brain ways) was seeing this connection to Jim as a sign. So it was decided, they'd be seeing Cathal again.

---

291. Jim claimed to see Native Americans in a car accident that had a great effect on him, and he wrote of it in several songs.

CHAPTER TWENTY

Lazy Diamond Studded Flunkies[292]

Now that their minds were made up about their purpose in life,[293] they had time to enjoy Ireland. They had their tattoos, no intention on going to the professional development sessions on the West Coast of Ireland, and they'd visited pubs with live music.[294] Now they were down to see a museum and have some lunch. Because days start off better if one starts with bog bodies, they set off to the National Museum of Ireland. The building itself was miraculous. The stately columns curved around with each of the three porches. The section of the building in the middle holds Parliament whose head is a Chieftain. As session is held there, tourists can't gain entrance to the middle section, which didn't bother our girls because they like to ignore politics at all times. On either side of the building is the National Library and the National Museum. So, they set off to find the 5,000-year-old bodies that'd been pulled out of the bogs and placed in the National Museum.

The girls wandered all three levels of the museum. They saw Celtic gold and Viking exhibits, but they didn't see the bog bodies.

---

292. Morrison, Jim. "Love Street." Strange Days. Elektra Records, 1967.
293. The purpose is to find Jim, which they feel is the highest greater good possible
294. Or walked by them, which was enough for them

Not being the sort to be easily brought down, they found a man in uniform to ask. After all, Mr. Rogers had taught them to "find the helpers," and so they did. Unlike Mr. Roger's helpers who save lives, this helper informed them of the proper floor and room to find the bodies. The reason they'd missed the bodies is that the museum placed the bodies in circular cubicles[295] to show some decency and respect.

"The circular walls are there to show respect to those who died. All were murdered and all were men. Men who had families most likely.[296] Show respect, but yes, you can take pictures without flash," the man told them as he pointed them in the right direction.

With that encouragement, the girls headed down the grand marble staircase back towards the bog bodies with determination. Inside they entered cubicles and found leathery remains encased in glass. One man still had a clear man bun. While the girls usually find those attractive, there was nothing attractive about this Irish man. His leathery body was open where he'd been disemboweled, and his arms were locked in a grasp around his stomach, which suggested to our historian that he'd been alive and bleeding when tossed into the bog, yet here he lay—murdered in his life and now serving the purpose of educating the world about the life of those who'd lived thousands of years before. Of the bodies, one had distinct leathery hands, and another's toes were frozen in a clutch one might do after a violent and terminal attack. Having seen the bodies, they regrouped on the porch.

"What do we want to do next? Lunch?"

"Right after seeing the bodies? We're not here for long, so let's fit in one more fun activity."

"I heard the Literary Museum is nice."

---

295. Everything in Ireland is circular
296. This point was lost on two single, childless women

"From who?" asked Charlie, who usually liked literary events but was surprised at Tabby's interest.

"I don't remember. I already got tickets at the hotel and printed them. Thought you'd want to go?"

"Why not? Let's maybe have a picnic and then head to the museum?" said Charlie, surprised at her friend's thoughtfulness and wondering where it was leading.

"You know, I think the museum is fairly close to St. Stephen's Green, which we haven't hit yet."

"Perfect—Picnic in the park and then one more museum."[297]

"I saw a Spar[298] near here. Let's pick up sandwiches." And so, a plan was devised.

Shopping in a foreign country is always a cultural experience. The nuances of grocery stores are somehow the same and yet different. Cocoa Pebbles exist, but not how one might expect them to exist. Fruit is the one constant next to chicken sandwiches with bits of stuffing or cheese sandwiches with pickles. However, being fairly open-minded women, they were able to find ham and cheese sandwiches and fruit, narrowly escaping the European way of drinking sparkling water by finding the water bottles labeled "still" water, and they headed to the register.

"College card?" asked Charlie.

"No," said Tabby, "after all, we were given per diem in advance."

"True, let's use that to eat today, if you still have some left after Key West dining. I used all the rest of mine to pay the light bill before we left."

---

297. As professors they are actually bound to visit museums when travelling, even if their travel serves a higher purpose.
298. The only way to pronounce this name is to follow the Germans, "Shpar"

"Why pay the light bill? Do you plan on going back?"

"I like to keep my options open."

"Fine, I still have enough left of my per diem. I'll pay."

Fortunately, the Irish are very patient, so while there was a line forming behind the girls as they sorted themselves, no one got openly angry.[299] With lunch purchased, they headed out into the Dublin sunshine,[300] and used their map app to find their way back to St. Stephen's Green. They'd walked by the park earlier when they were headed to their room at Camden Hotel, and the walk to the museum had taken them by the park, as well, and now was finally their chance to sit and spend time in that space.

They walked the smooth asphalt paths of St. Stephen's looking for the perfect spot as Charlie regaled Tabby[301] with stories of the Easter Uprising of 1916 that had held control of the park. She told Tabby about how they'd allowed for a daily ceasefire so the park supervisor could come and feed the ducks. When Charlie got to the part about the ducks,[302] Tabby thought it was a good time to speak up and suggest a picnic spot, but the rolling green hill to their left had a man sleeping on the ground. He wasn't your average sleeping-on-the-ground sort of man. He was wearing a business suit of the variety that the men Tabby and Charlie had dated surely couldn't have afforded. He was younger than the sort of guys Tabby and Charlie dated, fit and trim with black hair cut closely to his face—the kind of hair cut that said he spent a lot of money on fancy weekly haircuts, and yet he didn't seem to care about his suit. With no blanket spread under him, in the middle of a workday, he was curled up on his stomach, arm around his lunch container,[303] with

---

299. While the anger was not apparent, once they left, some were heard to mumble "stupid fecking tourists"
300. Which is to say it was not very sunny
301. Who wasn't listening
302. She wasn't hearing anything until the word "ducks" was spoken
303. Priorities

his right leg up so his knee was closer to his stomach. He was the kind of passed out and completely relaxed that made passersby also want to take a nap.

"How do you think he sleeps like that on the ground?"

"I mean, I'd be afraid someone would rob me."

"Well, he does have a grip on that lunch."

"But no other fear. Must be military."

"Must be. Military guys can sleep anywhere," murmured Tabby as they rounded a curve in the cement path and found an open space to their left and a large, ominous statue to their right.

"How about right here?"

"This is so perfect," said Charlie. "I love willow trees. They're my favorite."

"How did I not know that about you? You have a favorite tree? Are there any other favorites I should be aware of?"

"Don't you have a favorite tree?"

"The question is why would anyone have a favorite tree?"

"I think most non-math people do."

"Well, let's just sit down and eat," said Tabby.

The Florida girls settled directly on the grass, reveling in the space where one could sit on the grass without being stabbed by sand spurs, bit by red ants, poisonous snakes and spiders, or attacked by ticks. Their sandwiches were eaten in no time, and as they sat on the grass relaxing, Charlie noticed the statue of three people and a dog on the other side of the path from them.

"What do you think that statue means?"

"It's a statue, does it have to have a meaning?"

"All art is political, Tabby," responded Charlie with a sigh.

"Well, it doesn't look political. It looks like starving people."

"Ah, but it is political, loves," said a tall, thin Irishman with closely cropped brown hair, laughing eyes, and muscles filling in the space in his upper sleeves, but what really caught their attention was his dog.

"Oh my gosh. He is so cute."

"Yes, she is, would you like to pet her?" he said in the way of dog owners who like to be sure strangers know the gender of their pet.

"Yes, yes, we would," said Tabby as the man came closer and kneeled on the grass a bit behind and beside them, allowing the dog to sit between the girls.

"What breed is she?"

"She's a springer spaniel. She's a bit hyper, and she needs lots of walks, she does."

"She deserves all the walks," said Tabby as she pet the dog who politely rolled over for belly rubs.

"Yes, she does. Now, yous was asking about the statues?"

"Do you know what they're for?

"Yes, they're for the National Famine when about 1.5 million Irish moved to America to escape starvation and another million or so died of starvation while the British insisted on all Irish crops being sent to England, and they took all the cattle back to England, too."

"So, mass genocide?"

"Technically, no, as the Brits claim it wasn't their fault, but yes, mass genocide," he said with a sigh. "Our population still isn't back to where it was before the famine, but we can't only talk about death and mass starvation on this lovely day. You two are too beautiful for that."

Charlie and Tabby weren't used to being flattered by strangers, and they found that in the moment, they didn't mind it one bit.

"Are yous Americans?"

"Yes. We are," Tabby managed to say.

"What parts are you from?"

"Florida."

"Florida! And what brings ya to Dublin?"

"We lost our jobs so we're travelling around trying to prove Jim Morrison is alive."

"Jim, did ya say? Now, who's that?"

The girls were stunned and unsure of how to respond but also confident this man was too young to be knowledgeable in the ways of Jim or to be interesting to them.

"Well, never mind. Looks like she's ready to go," he said as his dog led him on after some birds. "Enjoy your time in Dublin, and good luck finding Joe."

"It's Jim," they said in unison.

As they shrugged off the stranger's ignorance, they sat relaxing in the green grass, reflecting on the beauty of Ireland, the lilt of the Irish accent, and the sun shinning perfectly through the willow branches.

"If Jim was alive today—"

"Tabby," said Charlie.

"I mean, we know he is, but my question is, do you think he kicked the drug habit?"

"Of course. He's too smart. He was reading Nietzsch in high school—by choice. He did drugs as an experiment. When he went to Paris, he stopped drinking and went for the clean shaven and sober look. I think he left all that behind when he faked his own death."

To cover for the ignorance of their young friend, they discussed Jim in-depth, debating topics they'd long over-debated, enjoying the sun and the promise of the possibility of proving the love of their lives, Jim, was hiding somewhere. Both agreed that should they find him, there was no need to blow his cover. They could live on forever knowing they were right, he lived, and they could keep his secret for the rest of his life.[304]

"So, what's next?" asked Tabby, ready to take on the day. "Did we want to go to that Oscar Wilde Museum?"

"I think we planned on the literary museum. Aren't the tickets time stamped?" Charlie asked, "do you have the tickets?"

"Yes. I printed them at the hotel this morning, and I put them in my purse," Tabby said as she reached around behind her to get her purse. "Crap, I didn't leave my purse open."

"Is it open now? Anything missing?"

"My wallet."

"Shit," Charlie said under her breath to no one in particular. "Were all your cards in there?"

"Not the P card. I didn't want to use it—doesn't feel right."

"So, now you have nothing?"

"Except the P card."

"Well, there wasn't much money in your wallet, right?"

"Or in my bank account."

"This is another sign we move forward. We have nothing to lose. Let's get that P card and go find Jim."

"I didn't know we had any other options."

"When did you see your wallet last? We haven't used it since the grocery store, right? Did you leave it there?"

"I put it back in my purse."

"Are you sure?"

"Yes, of course."

---

304. Which, given his age, couldn't be that long

"OMG. It was that guy!"

"What do you mean? He was right next to us; we would've seen him."

"Yep, he was right there, and we were listening to his great accent and petting the dog, not looking at him."

"So, if we were both distracted by him, even if for different reasons,"[305] Tabby nodded in agreement, "someone could've easily come up behind us and grabbed your wallet."

"Why not take the whole purse?"

"By just taking the wallet maybe you won't notice for at least a few minutes."

"But he was so polite. Did he really do this?"

"Yes, but in the end, at least it was polite thievery?"[306]

"It was, and you know, I think our literary museum tickets were in there."

"Shoot."

"Ya, I don't want to buy more tickets."[307]

"Should we call the police?"

"And say what? Some really good-looking Irish guy politely stole my wallet, but also, I'm currently committing fraud with my college's money."

"You have a point. Was there anything valuable in your wallet?"

"My drivers license, but that's it."

"And we have our passports, so that's fine."

"No literary museum."

"That's a disappointment, but we can find free things to do, and we'll head to Paris soon."

---

305. Tabby knew it was the new historical knowledge that distracted Charlie
306. "Polite Thievery" a term coined by Dr Naimh Hammell on 24 September 2022
307. 87% of tourists agree the literary museum is not worth the visit

And so, the girls decided to let the polite thief go, but for good measure, they agreed it would be in their best interest to call their favorite Irish man and ask for his advice.

CHAPTER TWENTY-ONE

Everybody Loves My Baby[308]

The girls had agreed that calling Cathal from their hotel might be the best thing to do. Slightly influenced by the need to find a bathroom and brush up her appearance, Tabby explained that the lobby was a great place to sit and talk. The lobby of Camden Hotel was a large room that had been broken up into multiple sections of cozy home spaces with careful placing of comfortable living room furniture that matched the other furniture only in its own area. To the far right, by the restaurant, and to the far left by the bar, hostesses stood able to take orders and bring food out into the living spaces so guests could relax and eat while feeling at home.[309] And as the largest bonus for hotels on the trip thus far, it was clean, didn't have mice, and wasn't next door to a brothel or an adult shop. When they reached the Camden, they sat in the lobby, and Tabby texted Cathal to see if he might want to join them for dinner.

"Is that a bit forward?"

"Well, we did sit and talk with him for hours yesterday, he's seen our tattoos, and we already had dinner together."

---

308. Morrison, Jim. "Break on Through." The Doors. Elektra Records, 1967.
309. Without in fact being at home or having access to Netflix with dinner, guests were forced to watch the news or sports

"Did we pay for that dinner?" asked Tabby who hadn't been paying attention to much.

"No, we did not."

"How long do we wait for his reply? If it's a long time, does that say something about his interest level?"

Charlie laughed, "No, it might say he's in the bathroom or at work. The man must work. Didn't one of the guys at the shop mention he works with them?"

"Does he? I didn't think to ask. I mean, his head is a bit loopy."

"That much was clear," said Charlie with a laugh. She was so happy to see her friend interested in a guy, and a good-looking one at that, that she didn't care much about his head. Besides, the accent covered a multitude of sins.

"Oh—he texted back and asked if we could meet in St. Stephen's Green. Something about having his girl with him."

"There again?"

"I mean, we can't get robbed every time we go to St. Stephen's, right? Surely there's a rob-one-tourist-one-time sort of rule?"

"When does it get dark?"

"I don't know. Let's ask the front desk."

Tabby walked to the front desk and asked the young girl whose dirty blonde hair was swept into a bun at the nape of her neck about the sunset and whether or not St. Stephen's would be safe in the dark. The front desk lady explained in the Ukrainian accent many of the employees sported that the park would be locked and cleared before there could be a concern.[310] The Ukrainian accent had become quite secondary for the girls on this part of the trip. The Irish, more than some countries, understood what it was like to have your country overrun by a stronger foreign power, and when

---

310. It's always important to clear the park before locking it

Russia invaded, they opened their doors to Ukrainians, housing them in hotels and apartments and helping them find jobs in the hospitality industry until they could return home. While the girls hadn't had the chance to interact with many Ukrainians at their smaller FSU campus, they found the people to be inspiring as they found them in Ireland—overcoming and persevering.

Despite the words of the Ukrainian woman, they sat and decided to try once more for dinner in the hotel, and when Cathal pushed for the park because, as he said, "his girl can't be counted on in public spaces," they decided to meet him at the park.

"So, kid then."

"I mean, if that's his girlfriend, I have multiple levels of concern."

"Agreed."

After freshening up a bit, they walked back to the park, reminding themselves at every stop light to wait for the green light to walk across the street. The cars all drove on the wrong side of the road, and the girls hadn't managed to grasp traffic patterns as of yet, so they stood with the tourists waiting and watching the Irish jaywalk. As they stood, an elderly lady stepped out right in front of a car, but with the confidence of a mom who knew the kids in the car would indeed stop for her, as they did.

"Let's not do that," said Tabby.

"Arrive alive is what I always say," said Charlie.

"You do not."

"I do now."

"Well, it's a valid concern here. They drive on the right side of the road in Paris, right?"

"Yes, but I still don't want to drive there."

"Got that right," said Tabby as they made their way across the convergence of roads down the street from Camden and heading to St. Stephen's.

The paths through St. Stephen's Green were becoming familiar, but no less desirable. The paths wove through welcoming green areas that were sprinkled with Irish men and women relaxing and dogs walking; people running on the paths balanced the relaxed atmosphere but didn't challenge the girls to exercise as they made their way past the little brick cottage at the entrance of the park. They paused to wonder what it was like to live in a little brick cottage backed up against one of the world's best parks.

"Invasive, I'd say," said a welcome voice behind them. The girls turned and grinned, agreeing, there would be little privacy in a house that backed into a city park.

"I like my back bits to be private," Cathal said with a laugh.

"So, where's your girl?" asked Tabby

"Ah, she's off terrorizing some ducks I imagine," he said with a laugh. "I need to get her back on the lead before she scares someone."

"The lead?"

"Ah, so. We're supposed to keep them on the lead at all times, but she hates it," he said as he led them around the corner behind a headless statue to find the largest dog they'd ever seen. The dog was standing in front of a bench, eye to eye with an elderly woman who was sitting and talking to the dog like a small child while patting it on the head.

"Now, there's your daddy," said the woman, giving the dog a treat from her purse.

"Mary and Joseph. She found you again now, did she," said Cathal with a laugh, "she can find you no matter where you sit in the park, Mrs. Hamill."

"Now, don't you go telling her what she can and can't do, Cathal. She is a free girl, and she can do what she wants," said the woman, more to the dog than to Cathal.

The dog stood at least four feet high while on all fours. Her hair was long and shaggy, and while her size said she could eat everyone in sight, her demeanor was gentle and kind. She clearly loved the old woman in front of her, and judging by Cathal's interactions, so did he.

"Are ya goin' ta introduce me to your friends?" asked the woman, her eyes still locked with the dog's eyes.

"Sorry, ma'am. These are my American friends, Tabby and Charlie, over here for some professional development, coming all the way from Florida."

"Coming from Florida I imagine they need all the professional development they can get," she said with a laugh. "Well, you kids enjoy yourselves. The sun is out, and the rain is not," she said with a nod. "Baby, I will see you tomorrow," she said, holding out her arm, which Cathal took, helping her rise from her seat, before putting baby back on her lead as the woman went on her way.

"So, this is your girl."

"That she is. This is my baby," he said, looking up from the dog, "everyone loves my baby,"[311] he said with a grin, knowing the girls would get his reference.

"Of course they do," said Tabby, reaching out to pet the dog on the head. "What breed is she?"

"Irish wolfhound, well, not pure bred. Her name is Maeve. Queen Maeve. My parents used to breed Irish wolfhounds, years back, when they lived outside the city. Sort of a hobby for my dad. They stopped several years before my accident[312] and by the time

---

311. Morrison, Jim. "Break on Through." The Doors. Elektra Records, 1967.
312. Cathal tracks all things as before or after his accident

they'd passed, all their dogs were gone, too. I spent months tracking a descendant down. She's not pure, but she's a link to my parents, and a reminder that the future is still out there, undecided."

"I'm sorry," said Charlie, "I didn't know both your parents had passed," she said awkwardly, not knowing what to say to an oversharing European.[313]

"I'm an orphan," he said with a laugh, "but I'm old enough to take care of myself," he said with the wink that he gave the girls so often that Charlie wondered if it was a twitch. Tabby didn't seem to mind.

"Let me show you my favorite bench," he said, leading them down the path a bit further, Maeve at his side.

"You have a favorite bench?"

"Indeed," he said, "that's why all the ladies here know me," he said as he passed another bench with an elderly woman waving at him and Maeve.

"I see that."

"Like I said, everyone loves my baby," he said as Maeve paused to take a treat from another woman's purse.

"Speaking of taking treats from a purse," said Charlie as Cathal led them to a bench and sat down, leaving just enough room for the girls to fit in with no space between any of them.

"Yes, my purse," said Tabby as she sat down next to Cathal. "My purse was robbed."

"What was taken?" asked Cathal.

"My wallet."

"But not her passport or the college card."

"Did ya get a look at the guy?"

"Funny that you assumed the gender of the thief."

---

313. It requires a head injury for a European to become an oversharer

"Well, we do have our share of lady robbers," said Cathal, "but sitting on this bench here, I mostly see polite thievery."

"And you watch it happen?" asked Charlie.

"I've managed to stop a few. Well, Maeve has," he said with another laugh. "It's usually young guys using their charm on unassuming Americans. Can't get enough of the accent ya see."

"So, you're aware of the power that you hold," said Tabby.

"That I am," he said jokingly. "Does this thievery hurt your plans any?"

"Not really. My bank account was empty, the college card is in the hotel room, and I have my passport. If we go home, I'll have a lot to sort, what with my driving license and all," said Tabby.

"But you can still go after Jim?"

"As planned," said Charlie.

"Well, that's good. Nothing lost then?"

"They left my purse, so no," said Tabby. And while the violation of a missing and worthless wallet still existed, the girls were distracted by Maeve and her daddy.

"What kind of name is Maeve?" asked Charlie.

"I'm glad you asked. Queen Maeve was a Celtic Queen."

"So, she married a King?"

"No, she was the queen, and someone married her. She was strong, powerful, and beautiful, and you best believe she was in control. She is the focus of much of *The Táin*, which is kind of like an Irish *Beowulf*." Charlie's ears perked up at the mention of *Beowulf*, but both girls listened on to the Irish accent, sure that anything he said would be interesting, even if it wasn't, in fact, interesting.

"She defended her people, and they say she is buried in her cairn standing up, holding her sword, and facing her enemies."

"Oh, I think that was on our itinerary for the Irish portion of professional development."

"Was it now," said Cathal, turning to Tabby sitting next to him on the bench, his voice and eyes a magnet that continually drew her in. "Where all are ya goin' on that itinerary?"

"Well, Bundoran mostly, with day trips to Derry and all over county Donegal."

"Ah. County Donegal. Are ya goin' on this trip?" The girls sighed and their eyes met, determined to stick with what they agreed on and not to argue anymore.

"No, we decided we should move forward with finding Jim. We made it to Dublin, and now we are going to go to Paris, and we are going to find Jim. We don't need professional development since we don't have jobs to develop."

"And unlike London, this portion of the professional development is run by a small group operating out of the hotel we would be staying in."

"So, they would notice if ya didn't actually go to the professional development."

"Exactly," said Tabby, who liked to think her mind had been made up from the beginning.

"How are ya gettin' to Paris?"

'Well, driving didn't work out so well for us coming over, so we wondered if maybe we should fly."

"Don't like driving on the right side of the road?" asked Cathal with a laugh.

"Wrong side of the road."

"No, we don't," said Charlie, feeling like a third wheel.

"Well, you can fly non-stop to Paris from Dublin for less than 200 Euros. Cheaper if you're willing to fly Brian Air, which I imagine you're not." Cathal explained that it was one of those cheap airlines that charges for everything once you have a ticket.[314] They imagined domestic airlines they'd had bad experiences with and agreed it was sometimes worth paying more for a flight.

Cathal got out his phone and showed the girls Aer Lingus,[315] which could get them to Paris in less than two hours, and they agreed it would be a lot better than trying to drive on the wrong side of the road down country lanes again all the way from Dublin to Paris.

"Plus the tunnel and the ferry," added Tabby.

"Ya, that ferry was expensive," said Charlie.

"That it is. Flying is the best way," said Cathal. So, the girls bought tickets using Charlie's college card, one way from Dublin to Paris, with a departure the day after tomorrow.

"Are ya sure now that you don't want to stay for a bit longer?" asked Cathal.

"We have to do this."

"Our path is set in front of us. We've got no job and might as well sort this," said Charlie, who was not willing to let a man derail their carefully made plans, no matter how good-looking he was.

"Well, how about dinner?" asked Cathal.

"What about Maeve," said Charlie, watching Maeve sit next to them and guard Cathal from unseen dangers.

"Well, for tonight, I can offer you the best boxty you can get from a cart, but for tomorrow, if you're willing, I have reservations at my favorite place to eat in Dublin."

"You already have reservations? That's rather forward of you," said Tabby.

---

314. Want a seatbelt, there's a charge for that
315. Ireland's favorite airline

"I liked my chances," he said, turning to Charlie, "reservations for three; Maeve will be home. Does four work for you?"

"Sounds good to me," said Tabby.

"I'd love to try a local place before heading out to Paris."

"Great," said Cathal rising.

"What's a boxty?" asked Charlie.

"It's an Irish potato pancake, basically. Now, I wouldn't normally get one from a cart, but we can't take Maeve to eat anywhere inside, and this cart is especially good," said Cathal, leading the girls towards a park exit and around a side street where a cart stood waiting to serve patrons. There was no queue, and the street was quiet, which seemed to fit in with Cathal's expectations for a good place to eat.

"Dia Duit, Cathal, Maeve," said the woman behind the cart with a smile.

"Dia duit. Tri boxty agus tri tae le bainne le do thoil," said Cathal. Tabby shot Charlie a look that clearly said this man was even sexier in Irish than he was in English. The girls sat at the nearby metal table and chairs as Cathal sorted dinner. The boxty, as he called them, were warm and comforting. The girls had been discovering throughout their visit that the Irish food they'd grown up eating on St. Patrick's Day alongside their green beer was not, in fact, Irish food. Cathal explained that the boxty is Irish food, but that when Irishmen and women left Ireland for America in the nineteenth century, they brought versions of what was being eaten at the time. Once in America, they had to adjust recipes based on what ingredients were available to them in the States. From there those recipes continued to evolve through generations of Irish Americans, while back home in Ireland, the same recipes took different paths of evolution. So, Irish American food is a version of Irish food, but not truly up to date with what the Irish are actually eating. And in that moment of a long, not necessarily needed, historical explanation, Charlie knew that she and Cathal could be friends. The girls parted from Cathal as the sun began to set, time once again getting away from them, and headed back towards the Camden, ready to sleep and have one more good day in Ireland, hopefully one that included lots of Cathal and no polite thievery.

CHAPTER TWENTY-TWO

We Want the World and We Want it Now[316]

Breakfast in the morning was in the Camden. The girls had just remembered that breakfast was included. While the front desk likely told them it was included at check in, they most certainly were not listening. They went down to the plush lobby on the first floor and headed to breakfast off to the right. A young man with an accent and styled blonde hair checked for their name on a list of those staying at the hotel and then helped them find their seats at a small table off to the left.

"Help yourself to breakfast when you're ready," he said, pointing them towards a large breakfast buffet. As he left, a woman came and offered them a pot of tea, which Charlie gladly accepted, happy to be in a country that realized tea was a superior breakfast drink.

"Tabby."

"Yes."

"Have you noticed that the British brand Irish breakfast tea is better than actual Irish tea."

---

316. Morrison, Jim. "When the Music's Over." Strange Days. Elektra Records, 1967.

"Maybe it's not breakfast tea?"

"But it is breakfast, and we are in Ireland."

"I've got nothing, but I'm pretty sure we shouldn't tell them the British make better Irish tea."

"Probably not," said Charlie as they headed up to the buffet. The left side of the buffet was a meat eater's paradise of sausages, eggs, and the weird, disappointing sort of European bacon that has been letting Americans down since its invention, but the girls headed to the right to gather plates of parfaits, fruit, lunch meat, cheese, and pastries.

While the tea wasn't as good, the hotels in Dublin were certainly more accommodating with 100% less mice and bugs. The girls sat in silence sipping the disheartening tea and eating pastries[317] and cheese when the table behind them started to get very loud.

"Listen, I don't care who you are, American television is better than anything these Brit wannabes can put together," came a loud voice from over the glass partition.

"Got that right."

"And if I have to get another one of these tiny drinks with no ice . . . ," a large man said, his belly hanging over his knees, his face permanently red, and his hand wrapped around a small glass filled with soda.

"Oh my god, I know," said the woman next to him. "When we land, I'm gonna get a big ol' cup of ice."

"Get in line," said the woman across from her. "I'm gonna kiss the ground in New York and run for some ice."

"And free ketchup."

"Seriously. What is wrong with these people and their stupid fucking ketchup charges? Land of the free for me."

---

317. Which come first amongst the breakfast foods

"Got that right. Free refills and free ketchup."

Tabby rolled her eyes at Charlie. One thing they'd noticed in travelling is that Americans really could be spotted from afar due to their loud speech and arrogant comparisons. While everyone loves free ketchup refills, what the girls enjoyed even more was breakfast in peace away from loud, demanding patrons. When the table got up in their MAGA shirts and left, the girls sighed a not-so-silent sigh of relief and went back to sipping their Barry's tea.

"What time did Ca-H-al say?" asked Charlie, with emphasis on the H.

"He texted to change to a park by the literature museum at one."

"We're not going in the museum, right?"

"Don't think so."

The girls sat in silence, enjoying their breakfast, and second breakfast, before heading out to find the park by the literature museum. They had plenty of time to wander on their short walk from Camden to the museum. Charlie led them on to Cuffee Street, making jokes about coffee all the way. They detoured a bit into St. Stephen's Green and sat beside the water on a bench to watch the ducks swimming and the children playing. Charlie got out her book and read, soaking up every minute of peace.

"What are you doing?" asked Tabby.

"Reading."

"I know that; what are you doing with the pages?"

"Oh, I like to see how long I have to the end of the chapter," she said as she flipped a few pages ahead in her paperback.

"If it's that bad, why are you reading it?"

"No, I just like to check the progress."

"Repeatedly?"

"Ya."

"So, you flip back and forth to see with one hand while reading?"

"Yep."

"Ok. I don't know how we've managed to live together all these years," said Tabby with a judgmental laugh.

"Said the girl who's not reading."

"Fair."

"We should probably go anyways. It's getting closer to one, and we don't want to be late for your date."

"It's not a date."

"Sure."

"He probably wants to see both of us."

"Tabby, that man can't keep his eyes off of you."

"Well, he does have a head injury."

"True, but give him a chance."

"Whatever. Let's head out," she said, changing the subject and walking back towards Cuffee Street.

As they crossed the street to the median, they saw Cathal and Maeve waiting for them.

"Is it a dog friendly museum?"

"Can't imagine it is, especially not for a horse-sized dog."

"So, maybe we're not going in."

"Thank god," said Tabby as they crossed the second street over to Cathal who stood tall with his back to them. He was wearing Beats headphones and talking to Maeve, who seemed to be listening. His curly brown hair was swept up on the top of his head and his shoulders were stooped as he pet Maeve, telling her what a pretty girl she is.

"Hi," said Tabby.

"Oh, hello," said Cathal with a start, "Sorry, we just passed a small little dog that was a bit rude," he said, taking his headphones off.

"Poor Maeve," said Charlie, who found Maeve was a lot easier to say than Cathal.

"Do you always wear headphones when you walk?" asked Tabby, who'd noticed he was wearing them around his neck every time they saw him.

"Ever since my head injury. Background noise can set off symptoms."

"What kind of symptoms?" asked Charlie, curious.

"Well, mostly lack of focus, confusion, kind of a bit of a tipsy feeling, but if I let it go, I become dyslexic and start to see things that aren't really there."

"So, you're a lot of fun at parties," said Tabby.

"No, I don't go to parties." Charlie giggled a little at Cathal for not getting Tabby's sarcasm.

"Dublin is so loud. How do you live here and stand all the noise?" asked Tabby, fishing for information.

"I wear headphones in my apartment when it gets bad, otherwise I play music a lot."

"That's right. You said music helps."

"Music is my special friend,"[318] he said with a wink, "especially living in Temple Bar where it's rarely quiet."

"So, are we going in?" asked Tabby, with a nod to the museum.

"I know I said everyone loves my baby, but, in fact, not everyone does," he said with a laugh as he led the girls on a sidewalk around the museum that opened on to a garden hidden from tourists. To the left, a young couple was posing for wedding pictures in a small

---

318. Morrison, Jim. "When the Music's Over." Strange Days. Electra, 1967.

garden area behind the museum and in front of them there was a large open garden with statues and benches to sit on.

"There are so many gardens in Dublin."

"We like a bit of green," said Cathal with another wink. "This is the Lveagh Gardens. We like to come here when St. Stephen's has been our usual for too long. Maeve likes to have herself some new smells."

"I bet she does," said Tabby who was absentmindedly patting Maeve on the head, which was an easy accomplishment with a dog as tall as Maeve.

The girls followed Cathal as he led them along the crunchy pathways that were lined with small stones and weaved their way around the green spaces back towards a rose garden before sitting down to rest on the grass. The three sat down as Cathal threw a ball for Maeve that he'd pulled out of his pocket.

"Ah, the ever-ready dog dad," said Charlie.

"I've got to take care of my baby," he said as he took the ball from Maeve's mouth and threw it again. When Maeve was worn out, the four lay in peace on the grass, looking at the clouds.

"Girls, I don't want to sound too crazy, you know, head injury and all, but doesn't that cloud there look a bit like a cat."

"You know, I see it," said Tabby.

"Could it be running for that cloud over there? It looks a bit like a glass."

"Probably, what cat doesn't want to knock a glass over," said Cathal with a laugh.

The hours passed as the four lay on the grass and talked about nothing but the clouds, laughing, and playing the Doors on Cathal's phone. The girls had never felt so relaxed around a man, particularly one as good-looking as Cathal. He exuded manliness and strength, but he didn't seem to know what he had.[319] As he lay on the grass next to them, he started singing along to the music and before they knew it, they'd joined in. While they never would've sang aloud at home, here in Ireland, they felt relaxed and just went with the moment, singing and not caring what anyone else thought. In that way, Cathal was a good influence on them.[320]

"Girls, have you heard the live recording from Isle of Wight, 1970?"

"Of course," answered Tabby.

"So, you know they watched *Sound of Music*?"

"I mean who hasn't, but no."

"Ok, let me play it for you. Here, it's the 'Light My Fire' performance, about minute eight—"

"And of course we can't fast forward."

"Of course," he said. They lay on the grass, listening to Jim's soulful voice as clear as if he had been recorded that day. Lost in the moment of cloud watching and Jim, they almost missed it, but as Cathal said, around minute eight there were chords played from "Favorite Things."[321]

"How have we never noticed that?"

"You weren't looking," Cathal said with a laugh.

"And you were."

"Cathal, you are a wealth of Jim knowledge, and that says a lot coming from us," said Charlie. Cathal blushed and pet Maeve. "Hmmm," said Charlie, who felt her Jim knowledge level was challenged, and that she must now give a bit of Jim trivia. The girls weren't used to being around someone else who held such

---

319. Due to his head injury, there were a lot of things he didn't know
320. Irish Psychology Today stated in 1974 that the portion of society who did not care about what others thought was 75% happier.
321. Hammerstein II, Oscar and Richard Rodgers. "Favorite Things." Sound of Music, Concord Music Publishing, 1965.

vast amounts of knowledge. What they'd gained from Cathal, the knowledge of the Easter egg in the song and "Paris Blues," was priceless, but they had to share that pricelessness.

"Have you heard where Matthew McConaughey got his famous 'Alright, alright, alright' line?" questioned Charlie.

"Can't say as I have."

Charlie grinned. "Well, he was getting ready to film a scene from *Dazed and Confused* and was listening to a recorded interview of Jim in his car while prepping. He was thinking that his character was all about girls, drugs, cars, and something else—four things. I forgot the fourth, but it's not important. Anyways, as he thought about that, in the recording, Jim said, 'Alright, alright, alright, alright'—four times. Matthew thought, well his character has three of his four things he's about so 'alright, alright, alright'—three out of four," Charlie said with a laugh.

"And an iconic line was born."

"From Jim," Cathal said with a smile as one who enjoys getting new knowledge, but more as a man who knew he'd found his people.

"Ladies, let's head over to St. Stephen's. We've got dinner reservations, and I want to show you some things before dinner," he said. As he rose, Maeve instantly followed suit.

"Hey, on the way, could we maybe stop and get one of those Irish rings, you know the ones with the hands holding a heart?"

"A Claddagh ring?"

"Is that too touristy?" asked Charlie.

"Well, you're only in Dublin once, so you should get one, and there's a mall on the way. We can stop by. Maeve and I will wait out front," he said as he led the girls back out to the street and across to St. Stephen's Green, one park leading so closely to another, as seemed to be the way of Dublin to the girls who'd been fortunate enough to stay in the right part of Dublin. Cathal led them across St. Stephen's to another street to cross, this time with a maze of train tracks.

"Wait," said Tabby, "let's look both ways. Twice."

"And check for anyone trying to throw themselves in front of the train?" said Charlie with a laugh and a question.

"The light says we can go," said Cathal. And so, the girls told him about their adventures in London which ended with "Ach, so. Well, if I lived in London, I might throw myself in front of a train, too."

The girls made their way across the train tracks, and they found a brick road bordered by old buildings filled with modern shops and in the center a woman singing "Zombie."

"Is this song popular here?" asked Tabby.

"Of course it is," said Cathal, surprised, and he led into a lesson in history about the Irish Troubles, British violence, and IRA response that led to children dying, something that shouldn't ever happen. The song, he explained, was the band's response to the cruelty of man that could lead to the violent death of children with no mourning response from society. Society had grown cold to death in Ireland at that point.[322] When his story was done, he walked the girls over to the left where a three-story building full of windows stood.

"St. Stephen's Shopping Centre," he said by way of introduction. "Maeve and I will wait here. She likes the music," he said as he walked up to the shopping center to hold the door open for the girls.

---

322. Cathal's history lesson was in fact longer than many Charlie had given to Tabby, who didn't seem to mind Cathal's stories.

"Hold on. No dogs allowed. Can't you read the sign? Ya feckin' idiot," yelled a voice to their right. The girls turned to see what must've been shopping center security.

"Excuse me," said Tabby, ready to face the glorified mall cop. As they turned to the voice, they found a man of average height who'd managed to stay thin into his sixties. His face was both arrogant and angry. This was his mall, and they were not going to question him.

"Listen, ladies. There are no dogs allowed in this mall. You need to step back outside."

"But we're not inside yet," said Charlie.

"Step back," repeated the man.

"Hello," called out a voice from inside. The girls turned away from the angry, arrogant, small mall cop to find a short, round, Black man with a strong Irish accent walking out towards them wearing a uniform similar to the one the man at the door was wearing, but with more brass. "Now, Ed, it looks to me like this man is just holding the door open for the ladies, like any fine Irish man should do," he said with a nod towards Cathal and a pet on Maeve's head. "Let's let the ladies get on with their shopping and this gentleman get on his way. There's been an incident in the refreshment area, and they're needing assistance with cleaning. Why don't you head that way?" he said, as he held the other door open and nodded for Ed to head over to the food court.

"You ladies enjoy your day," said the second officer with a smile from ear to ear.

"Maeve and I will wait out with the music," said Cathal as he turned to step back to the singer who'd moved on to an Ed Sheeran song. The girls smiled as they passed the second security officer, who smiled back and wished them well.

"Can you tell us where we can get Claddagh rings?" asked Tabby.

"For those you'll want to head to the back. My daughter sells them. Tell her Captain Woods sent you," he said with a smile and a "good day."

"Amazing how one person in the same job can be so kind and useful and the other—"

"Should rethink their life."

"Exactly," said Charlie as they walked into the building.

Inside they found a large atrium with glass ceilings like a large greenhouse. The natural light was relaxing. The girls wandered around the kiosks and shops selling home goods and touristy shirts. The mall was long and thin, like a train station, so they made their way to the back without issue and found a kiosk with a smiling young woman selling rings. Her red hair was tied back, and she quickly asked if she could help.

"Hello, Captain Woods told us to head this way for Claddagh rings."

"Ah, so you've met my father-in-law now, have you?" she said with a laugh.

"Father-in-law. This makes sense," said Tabby.

"He does love confusing the tourists. Did ya get into some trouble with Ed?"

"Who is that guy?"

"He was yelling at our friend with the dog outside."

"Ed hates dogs," she said.

"Who hates dogs?"

"Horrible people."

"I can't argue with you there," said the young woman, "can I help you find a ring?" she asked, waving towards a display of rings in front of her. The girls leaned over the display and decided on matching rings, something they'd been doing on their travels for years. Once the purchase was made, they thanked the young woman and headed out to Cathal, looking carefully for Ed who was apparently still handling whatever situation had happened in refreshments.

"Did ya find what you was looking for?" asked Cathal with a grin.

"We did," said Tabby, pulling the rings out of the bag.

"Oh, they're matching, are they?" he said, his smile shrinking just noticeably.

"We always get matching jewelry when we travel."

"Well, these are special," said Cathal, looking at Tabby. "These let the fellas know if your heart is taken. You see, if the heart is down, your heart is taken, if it is wrong side up, your heart is available," he said, watching Tabby, who pulled the ring out of the box so quickly she nearly dropped it and placed it upside down on her finger. Charlie laughed and followed suit.

"Ah, so you're not," he said, pointing back and forth. Charlie laughed more than she should have.

"Sorry. No," she said to Cathal's grin as they walked forward.

"Where to?"

"Well, this street is a bit crowded, but if we head about two blocks to the right, there's a little shop I want you two to see. I think you'll like it," he said, looking at Charlie, but then slowing down to walk with Tabby as the girls headed past the Coach and Pandora shops to the right and then past the LGBTQ center and to the right again until they were at a small bookstore that the girls would've walked right past.

"Go on in. Me and baby will wait here," he said.

"That's ok, let me know how it is. I'm shopped out," said Tabby as Charlie headed into the most perfect antique bookstore she'd ever seen.

Charlie wasn't sure which part of her conversation with Cathal had let on that she loved the smell and feel of old books, but she was thankful he'd listened and led her here. She found a first edition signed A. A. Milne, a first edition signed Oscar Wilde, and early editions of Tolkien, Lewis, and Stoker. Milne and Wilde were behind glass, but the others she could pick up and feel. She made her way through the shelves in awe of the books that existed and could, for the right price, be owned. The store was a time machine into a different world and a different time, and the storekeeper seemed to know this as he let the few patrons that came in wander in silence and reverence.

Charlie wasn't sure how long she stayed inside; she had known when she entered that she would have to leave empty-handed, but with a goal of one day having the funding to buy books like these for herself—to hold a book in her hand that Oscar Wilde had held in his. When she came out, a bit dazed and confused by the wonder of the bookstore, she found time had also passed unnoticed for Tabby and Cathal, who seemed to come to when she exited and asked her if she liked it.

"Loved it. One day I'll need to come back and buy a book."

"One day when you have a job?" asked Tabby.

"Exactly."

"Ok, we're getting close to dinner time. I've got to bring baby over to her sitter."

"She has a sitter?"

"That she does. Rob watches her for me."

"Tattoo Parlor Rob?"

"The very same."

The girls followed Cathal and baby through the streets of Dublin back into Temple Bar and to the little tattoo parlor with the green door, just past Faction and the music shop.

"Rob, you in?" asked Cathal, leaning over the half door into the parlor, ignoring the Godfather who was working on a client that seemed to be getting some sort of Celtic symbol on his chest

"Always," said Rob standing from around the corner. "Ah, I see. You ladies heading out on the town with our Cathal now, are you?" he asked with a grin. The girls smiled in response.

"Don't sound so surprised, like anyone heading out with me is strange."

"Anyone but baby, yes," said Rob with a laugh as he took the lead and pat baby on the head.

"Come on now."

"Well, you do have that head injury. No idea how anyone puts up with you, right Maeve, how do you survive?" he asked, looking into the dog's eyes and rubbing her chest. Maeve seemed to smile as she wagged her tail and placed her head on Rob's chest for a head hug.

"Even you now, Maeve? Everyone is against me."

"Have fun now, you kids," said Rob. "Me and Maeve will behave ourselves and maybe chase some pigeons."

"Don't take her off the lead, Rob."

"Never."

Cathal led Tabby and Charlie down the street back towards the River Liffey and the Ha'Penny Bridge. On the way, they passed Temple Bar where U2 used to perform, but Cathal explained that he never ate there; it's too noisy and full of tourists. They arrived at the Ha'Penny Bridge, which was lit up in the dark and Cathal explained that the bridge used to cost a ha'penny to cross as he led them over to another street of old Dublin buildings with their brightly painted doors and half moon windows above the doors. The Winding Stair was to the left, and they wouldn't have noticed it if Cathal hadn't taken them there.

"Now Cathal," said Charlie, "you said the other day you only go to the same places, for your head, right?"

"Right."

"So, you've been here before?"

"My mom used to love the place. It was where we went for special occasions before she passed."

"So, you bring girls here often then?" asked Tabby.

"Mostly I come by myself. It's quiet and the food is good, and wait until you see the view," said Cathal, holding the door and leading them up a winding staircase to the second floor.

"So there really is a winding staircase?"

"That there is," said Cathal as they reached the top and he held the door open for them.

They entered a dimly lit room that wasn't bigger than a large bedroom with a bar to the right. The large windows on the opposing wall looked right over the river, and the dim light gave a quiet and serene feeling to the room. Similar to the bookstore, Charlie felt that time would pass unnoticed here. As with the tea shop, Cathal had led them to a quiet oasis in the middle of a bustling city. The waiter came and checked their names on the reservation list and then led them to a table for four right next to the windows. Cathal held out his hand gesturing for the girls to take the seats with a view and then sat down next to Tabby.

The menu was short, but the dishes were all gourmet, and they were fancier than what the girls would normally go looking for. The meals were all several courses, and as the waiter brought them appetizers, salads, main courses, and desserts, all with paired wines, the girls weren't sure they'd be able to get up after the meal. They talked quietly about Dublin and whether the band should've ever tried to get back together after Jim's disappearance. They'd agreed to call it his disappearance and not his death for the sake of the adventure the girls were leaving on the next day. Cathal sipped his water glass throughout, sticking with his "I don't drink" announcement from the first day they met. While they couldn't believe not all Irishmen drank,[323] they found his company to be relaxing, and every place he took them felt like home.

When dinner ended, they headed down to the river. They didn't feel ready to part, and yet they knew they needed to leave in the morning. Standing on the Ha'Penny Bridge, with a FREENOW taxi waiting on the other side, the time had come. Cathal leaned in to give each girl a quick hug and made them promise to let him know when they found Jim. While the temptation was strong to invite him along, they were not ones for inviting men they just met to travel with them, and so, as he nodded and said, "May the road rise," they let him walk away, slightly dejected.

"Charlie."

"Yes."

"That man."

"I know."

And so, they got into the taxi and went back for their last night at the Camden. The following morning, they would endure one more breakfast with tourists and one more cab to Dublin Airport before their flight into Charles de Gaulle Airport in Paris.

---

323. A stereotype pushed by British colonizers for centuries

CHAPTER TWENTY-THREE

Changed One Degree[324]

Breakfast was thankfully quiet and full of Germans who were efficiently eating and preparing for a conference in the hotel. The girls sat and ate in silence with their suitcases next to them, ready for their midday flight. When they were done, they called a FREENOW taxi and headed out to meet the cab, ready to take on the next portion of their trip. Leaving Dublin is never easy, especially when leaving a good-looking man and his dog behind,[325] but the girls got into the taxi as the driver loaded their bags, and they sat in silence as the Dublin views passed by their windows.

They hadn't walked out along the canals in Dublin, but Cathal had mentioned them and the poets who would sit and write along their banks. As the cab drove by the canal, Charlie could imagine sitting and reading on a bench by the canal all day. Life in Dublin was tempting, but Jim was beckoning, and they must answer. So, the cab made its way to Dublin airport, which isn't really any different than any other airport that the girls had been to, except this time they arrived without a casualty in the road or the tracks.

---

324. Morrison, Jim. "My Wild Love." Waiting for the Sun. Elektra Records, 1968.
325. Leaving a dog is always hard

They got their bags, thanked the driver, and went inside.[326] The line for Aer Lingus was long, but with forward moving progress. Tabby always felt they were being herded like cattle in those lines, but she remained silent this time. When they came to the desk and handed over their passports, the woman at the counter greeted them kindly and asked if they enjoyed their time in Dublin.

"Indeed, we did," said Tabby with a sigh.

"Well, we hope you'll come back soon. Enjoy your time in Paris," said the woman, handing the girls their passports and plane tickets before pointing them in the direction of their gate.

The girls made their way through the crowds. Taking Cathal's example, they wore their noise canceling headphones, which are essential on any trip,[327] and wound their way through the crowds and security lines. They passed the maddeningly crowded shops full of tourists trying to get one last Irish gift or duty-free alcohol before boarding the plane[328] and made their way to their gate to sit and rest before what should be a blissfully short flight.

"Did you take your motion sickness meds?"

"Of course."

"You sure you took the right ones?"

"I'm never going to outlive that, am I?"

"Nope. Movie, books, or music for the flight?" asked Tabby.

"Movie. Something dark."

"Because we need more darkness in our lives? I'm going to grab us some tea and snacks from the cart by the gate."

"The flight isn't very long."

---

326. This is the way all taxi and train rides are intended to be
327. The Academy of Pakistani Psychiatrists discovered in a 2019 survey that the screaming of babies in public raises heart rates to an alarming degree and recommended combating this danger with Beats headphones
328. Fun fact. Cuban cigars can be bought in these shops

"Ya, so there won't be food, and when we land, we'll have to go through customs, get our bags, find a cab—all before we find food."

"Good point. Did you get us reservations in Paris?" asked Charlie, who'd been too distracted by Dublin to think of the next step.

"Of course. I got an Airbnb this time. I found one with good reviews, and since it's last minute, I got a price break."

"Sounds perfect."

"Ya and apparently it has a view of the Eiffel Tower."[329]

"Even better," said Charlie as Tabby went to get them snacks and drinks.

When Tabby returned, the girls sipped their tea, not wanting to bring drinks on the plane, and put their scones into their bags for later. When the call came, they made their way on to the plane and took their seats, immediately looking for movies.

"Same movie?"

"Probably not. What are you watching?"

"*Insidious.*"

"Definitely not," said Tabby with a laugh as Charlie started her horror film, not caring if the small children behind her could see through the seats.[330] Tabby picked a comedy, and they sat watching their movies, taking the bottles of water when they were passed out by the stewards. They ate their scones and drank their water, letting the time pass until they landed in Paris.

Since the flight was only two hours, the flight and movies ended about the same time and the plane landed to a resounding cheer

---

329. What the girls didn't realize is that since the Eiffel Tower is so massive and central, most apartments have a view of the tower, as do many, many hotel rooms

330. Viewing horror films between the seats of the preceding row is a risk all parents take when bringing small children on flights.

from the other passengers.[331] The girls waited their turn to deboard, which was always long for them as they often took seats in the back of the plane. The walk from the plane to customs took them on a tour of an airport that seemed to always be under construction or protest or both. Eventually, after walking for what felt like two or three miles,[332] they found the customs line, apparently faster than the other passengers who'd stopped to use the bathroom. They approached the line and were called forward by an intimidating Frenchman who stared them down while waving them forward.

"What brings you to Paris?" he asked in a thick accent while looking down his nose at their passports.

"We're coming to find Jim Morrison." His eye roll was visible.

"And you will find him in Cimetière du Père-Lachaise," he said with a sigh. "Enjoy Paris," he said with a stamp in the second passport and a wave to the tourists behind them.

The airport felt much like the one they'd just left—full of gift and duty-free shops—but this time there were male and female officers with mohawks, muscles, and large automatic weapons patrolling every corner. The girls had no idea the Parisians took security so seriously, but in retrospect, they did remember a few very unfortunate attacks in Paris. Apparently, that wouldn't be happening again. Perhaps distracted by the large weapons, the girls missed the exit for taxis and ended up in some sort of a pickup area they couldn't sort. Their phones were having trouble finding service, and they were stuck.

They stood for a while, realizing their options were to walk along the road and see if there were paths that connected to highways or to head back inside. Deciding inside was the safer option, they went

---

331. The girls did not clap as they felt landing the plane was inherent to the pilot's job and did not deserve applause.
332. More for Charlie who was on meds

back in. Unfortunately, they still couldn't sort the correct exit for taxis and ended up outside where people who actually had friends in Paris were being picked up. They sighed as they realized their error, but as they headed back in, a balding man with dark skin and an African accent called out to them, offering a ride. He waved towards his minivan and encouraged them that he would be faster and cheaper than any of the other rides to Paris. The girls looked at each other.

"Another illegal taxi?"

"Well, legal modes of transport haven't always worked out for us," said Tabby, thinking of the suicide on the train.

"And illegal cabs have."

So, the girls followed the man who politely put their bags in the back of his van and shut the door behind them. As he pulled out on to the highway, he told the girls about Paris, highlighting areas he thought they might be interested in.

"What brings you to the city? Maybe I can recommend something specific to your trip," he asked with a smile.

"We came to find Jim Morrison."

"Morrison. I know this name. Is he a politician?"

"No," said Charlie with a laugh.

"He's the singer for the band The Doors."

"Can you name one of their songs? Maybe I know them. What genre?" he asked, his brown eyes attempting to connect with the girls in the rear-view mirror.

"The Doors are classic rock. American Classic rock."

"Is there any other classic rock?" he said with a knowing laugh. "Ok, I do like classic rock. What is their best song."

"Now that is hard to pin down," Tabby laughed.

"'People are Strange', 'Roadhouse Blues', 'Love Me Two Times.'"

"Oh, I know this one," he said with a laugh as he started to sing. "Isn't he dead? I think tourists have asked me how to get to his grave."

"We think he isn't," said Tabby, a bit too tired to explain their thought process and years of research to another stranger.

"Like Tupac?"

"Who's Tupac?" asked Charlie. And so the girls descended into conspiracy theories and discussions, which inevitably led to a discussion of Princess Diana as they neared the scene of her death and the cabbie recounted his knowledge of the accident as someone who lived and worked as a cabbie in Paris at the time. The girls, while not predisposed to conspiracy theories, did enjoy a good one, so they followed the cabbie down the rabbit hole until he pulled up in front of an apartment door on a side street and thanked them for the opportunity as he got their bags out of the back of the van. They exchanged virtual money, and the girls waved him on his way.

They didn't see the Eiffel Tower, but the side street looked like every picture of Paris streets and cafés that they'd ever seen. They used the key code to enter the door and went up the stairs with their bags to the door numbered for their Airbnb. The door opened into a small entrance way and then an open dining/living room with floor to ceiling narrow windows that were shuttered off. To the right they found a small but functional kitchen with another floor to ceiling window. When they opened the shutters, they saw a view of the street they'd just come from. Disappointed at the lack of tower, they put down their bags, got glasses of water, and headed back into the living room to sort the rest of the apartment. Past the dining area was a narrow hallway. On the left was a room with a small toilet and sink and a shower room, separate from each other so one could shower while the other uses the facilities.[333] Across from the toilet room, or WC in European, there was a large bedroom with two twin beds, extra long, and two floor to ceiling windows, shuttered. At the end of the short hallway, and just past the shower, was a bedroom of similar size with a double bed and two large windows. Tabby asked for the larger bed as she preferred to stretch out, and Charlie was tired enough not to care.

As they came back into the living room and sat down, Tabby questioned where they could see the tower from and opened the shuttered window on the front facing side of the living room. As she did, the room filled with light and fresh air, and just above the Persian buildings across the street they could see the Eiffel Tower. And so, having done enough for the day,[334] the girls made tea using the supplies in the kitchen and sat on the couch to sip tea and look at the tower. Later that night they would walk to a café and get sandwiches to bring home, but for now, their day was done.

---

333. A great example of European innovation
334. Having taken a two-hour flight and found a window facing the Eiffel Tower, they had no more goals for the day

CHAPTER TWENTY-FOUR

The Future's Uncertain and the End is Always Near[335]

The best part of waking up in Paris, is waking up in Paris. The city lies waiting just outside the door, and in this case, just outside the window. The girls dressed quickly and headed down to a café they'd seen when they got sandwiches the night before. They walked the quiet streets, which had been cleaned that morning by a Zamboni-looking street cleaner,[336] and headed straight into the café. Tabby used her DuoLingo knowledge to point at the pastries they wanted and said the number in French she'd learned. The man behind the counter smiled and spoke to the girls in English, wishing them a pleasant morning.

They took their food and walked over to the shadow of the Eiffel Tower. What they hadn't realized until they got there was the length and width of the lawn in front of the Eiffel Tower. The lawn stretched out in front of the girls like the Mall in Washington D.C., and tourists were dotted throughout the green space on blankets,

---

335. Morrison, Jim. "Roadhouse Blues." Morrison Hotel/Hard Rock. Elektra, 1970.
336. Zamboni Street Cleaner is an illusive career many Parisians strive for in order to perfect their Zamboni street racing skills, a sport not yet traveled to the US, which is less concerned with street cleanliness.

relaxing, so the girls joined them and stretched out on the lawn in the shadow of the tower and sat eating their pastries, which, while amazing, they found lacked the something the Irish scones had given them.

"So, should we start where it ended—the grave?"

"Yes. I've brought the words Pamela spoke over his grave."

"Because we want to repeat anything the common wife said?"

"Well, seemed like a good idea."

"No, it's fine."

The girls sat and contemplated life and death and flipped through a book of Jim's poetry[337] while they finished their tea and pastries. When they were done, they waved goodbye to the Eiffel Tower and headed over towards the Louvre, which was on the way to the cemetery.[338] This time the girls decided they could indeed try another form of public transportation. Surely not every European[339] train would lead to a suicide? They managed to load the path they wanted into Tabby's phone and went to a bus stop, only to learn from a friendly Parisian that the bus stop was closed for construction, so they followed his directions to the nearest train station. The station was underground, but as they were becoming world travelers, they were able to navigate the ticketing machines, turnstiles, and escalators to find the right train. As they arrived at the train, Tabby motioned to Charlie's purse, recommending she move it to the front of her body.

"Why?"

"Well, I read robberies are common on Paris trains."

"Could we possibly be robbed twice on one trip?"

"Do we want to find out?"

---

337. Charlie brought the poetry; Tabby did not approve as it contained little math
338. In the sense that it was in the general direction and they had little to no navigational skills
339. They did not stop to ponder if London was in fact European post Brexit

Charlie moved her purse to the front of her body, both girls holding on to their purses, and they got on the train as it came to a stop and the doors opened. The train wasn't full, but the only seats open were next to strangers, except for one that someone had left an open and mostly brown-looking banana on. The girls chose to stand and hold on to the poles in the aisle. Tabby, as the more responsible of the two, kept an eye on the map as they counted down stops to the one by the Louvre. They'd decided to get out and walk to the cemetery from there. As the train came to a halt, the doors opened, a small, hunched-over, elderly Parisian woman entered and made a move to sit in the banana seat near Charlie. Charlie quickly grabbed the woman's shoulders as she lowered herself on to the seat and, when she turned with an angry glance at Charlie, who was keeping her from the seat, Charlie shook her head and pointed at the banana. On seeing the offending fruit, the woman's face softened, and she nodded and gave Charlie's arm an appreciative squeeze before moving to sit near a stranger.

"Good deed done for the day?"

"We need all the good karma we can get."

"True, true," said Tabby as the train took off just after letting in an American couple who stood near the girls.

Their plan when traveling overseas had silently been to never admit to being American when they ran into Americans. They hoped, by not speaking to or acknowledging the other Americans, that they could go on in their private trip without long discussions with home sick strangers. As they did their best to avoid eye contact, they noticed a group of young men join the Americans on the handrails by the door. The train had enough space to avoid this kind of close quarters, but well, the door was near, so the girls went on ignoring all. As the train came to a brief stop, one of the boys quickly grabbed something from the backpack of the American man, who was too busy watching over the small woman with him to really see what the stranger behind him was doing. As soon as the item was grabbed, the doors opened, and all the strangers went out; the door closed just as the Americans realized what had happened.

"He just robbed me," said the man. The woman responded in shock, but the Parisians, used to train side robberies, ignored the event, and Charlie and Tabby were off at the next stop, so they followed the Parisian example and left the Americans to sort out life without whatever item was stolen from the backpack.

"Not even polite thievery," said Tabby as the girls got off the train and headed in the direction the GPS told them would walk them by the Louvre.

"Not polite at all," said Charlie with a laugh, silently glad Tabby had warned her to move her purse to safety.

As they neared the Louvre, the girls were taken in by the calm serenity of Paris. They walked through a garden that had small bodies of water and a simple amusement park for children. Parisians and tourists sat on benches watching the water or the children playing. While the sight didn't draw the girls in as Dublin did, they could understand why generations of Americans had chosen to be ex pats in this city. As they followed the wide path, they soon found the monstrous building the overly rich French kings had built. As a good friend had once explained of the beautiful buildings French aristocrats had left behind, it's amazing what a group of people who steal all the money from society can build. The Louvre was bigger than anything they'd expected. The small, in comparison, glass pyramid in front of the museum buildings was a sight in and of itself. They contemplated going in, but as they were fully on the college card at this point, they decided they needed to conserve funds and time, and they walked on to the graveyard. The walk was about an hour long, but as they were entranced by the city, they spent a couple[340] of hours strolling their way to Jim's highly debatable last known whereabouts.

They walked along the Seine River. As the sun was out, there were artisans sitting and painting the city and selling their wares all along the river. Notre Dame stood on an island in the river, something the girls hadn't known before they came.

"Tabby."

"Yes?"

"Uhm, what are those cops in scuba gear doing under that bridge?" she asked as a police boat was sending divers into the river.

"Let's think that's a training exercise and not a body recovery," said Tabby as they hurried on to the cemetery.

They weren't sure what to expect, but there is something finalizing about seeing a grave. Once they made their way through the graveyard to the correct lot, they felt a sort of sadness and peace settle on them. They sat around the foot of the grave, and Charlie read soberly:

> "Now Night arrives with her purple legion
> Retire now to your tents and to your dreams
> Tomorrow we enter the town of my birth
> I want to be ready."

"Ah, Pamela's eulogy, yes," said an older voice behind the girls. They turned to find a little, old woman, hunched over, wearing black, and walking up the aisle between the graves.[341]

---

340. While the debate is still raging, as a math professor, Tabby knew the word "couple" could mean 2 or 3 hours
341. Scholars are unclear if the pathway between gravestones is indeed an aisle, or if it is a pathway. The argument has continued for the betterment of none.

"Yes, are you familiar with it?"

"Yes, dear. I've been coming here for decades. My mother was here that day."

"That day?" asked Tabby, her ears perking up.

"Yes, dear, the day Jim was buried. You see, my mother was French and my father was British, and we've always split our time between Paris and London, but now that it is just me, and I am old, I prefer to stay in Paris," she said sitting on a nearby bench.

"And your mother was here the day Jim was buried?"

"Yes, dear. That's what I said. She always told me it was a very small funeral that seemed to be in a hurry, as if they were getting him in the ground before they got caught. Didn't even leave flowers. My mother moved a flower from another grave and placed it on the fresh dirt no one had stayed to see placed over the poor boy. Or that's what she told me."

"I've heard it was rushed," said Tabby, moving closer.

"Yes, quite. But my dears, don't get any ideas. He *is* in there."

"Did your mother see inside the coffin?"

"No, of course not."

"Well, only a handful of people did see him, and none of them had seen his ID."

"Well, surely there was an autopsy," said the woman, a bit disgusted with their level of silliness.

"No, no autopsy, and the authorities were given the wrong name. No one who knew Jim, aside from his girlfriend, his drug dealer, and a friend saw the body. Jim was supposedly nailed into a coffin before anyone else made it to Paris."

"That's right, and when they were asked to surrender his passport to get the death certificate, they said they didn't have it with them."

"So, the authorities said to turn it in at the embassy after the Fourth of July holiday."

"So, no official word got out for days."

"So, there was time for a conspiracy?" questioned the woman.

"There was."

"And members of the band said for years they thought he could've faked his own death."

"Even some of his family questioned if he was really gone."

"And the common wife—"

"Pamela."

"Always referred to him in the present tense."

"Maybe that's why it took the estate so many years to add this," said the woman pointing at the gray slab above the supposed burial site.

The older woman took a seat closer to the girls, leaning forward in a conspiratorial manner and whispered, "so if he's not in there," she said pointing at the grave, "who is?"

"No idea."

"I mean, there had to be a body. A few firemen and emergency doctors or personnel did see a body," said Tabby.

"Just not Jim's."

"They certainly didn't do their due diligence to identify the body. This explains why my mother thought the ceremony felt strange. She was right," the woman said with a nod of her head. She paused and then asked, "So, would he still be in Paris then? Seems like someone would've found him by now."

"Agreed," said Tabby. "He was strongly influenced by a French poet, Arthur Rimbaud—"

"Who also was known for disappearing to go have adventures after he gave up writing at a young age."

"So, we think Jim faked his death and ran off to focus on being a poet."

"He did have a warrant out for his arrest in the States, no?" asked the woman.

"Exactly," said the girls in unison, feeling conspiratorial with this woman they just met, but who made them feel comfortable the way many elderly grandmothers did.

"Where did he go?"

"We think Africa. Europe could only hide him for so long. The States and Canada would've been hard, if not impossible, to hide in."

"Canada would have kept him," interrupted Tabby, who loved all things Canada, "after all, they were hiding a lot of draft dodgers at the time."

"But people would've figured out he was there, which he didn't want."

"Correct," responded Tabby, glad to have vindicated Canada in the eyes of this stranger.

"South Africa wouldn't have extradited him. There was space for a wealthy foreigner to come in with faked papers and disappear. Eventually, if he was found out, there may've even been pride in having hidden this odd American."[342]

The elderly woman nodded, and started to slowly rise up, holding her back as she did so. "Ladies, I think you might be right. I believe my mother, God rest her soul, would've agreed with you," she said as she signed a cross over her chest. "I need to get back to my apartment for dinner. Julianne does not like his dinner to be late," she said with a nod as she clasped their hands in hers and wished them well.

---

342. Said Charlie, in the tone of someone who is so convinced of a conspiracy theory that no matter of logic can convince them otherwise

The girls weren't sure what else to do. They'd made it to the grave. They felt validated by the Parisian woman, but they weren't sure where else to go. They punched a couple of cafés that Jim had frequented into their GPS, but found what all Americans find when they seek out the remnants of their American heroes/expats from the previous century—the café is either gone or has learned how to both blend into Paris and capitalize on their famous historical patrons. They decided to walk past the cafés, and they made their way to the place Jim died, 17 rue Beautreillis, which looked like any other apartment building. While they enjoyed being in the city he'd faked his death in, and it in a sense made them feel closer to Jim, they didn't feel like they were actually closer to finding him. So, the girls made their way to a café in the basic direction[343] of their apartment, after stopping at Notre Dame to light a candle, as they read Jim had done on several occasions.

The café they chose, or the one they felt chose them, was across the street from a macaroon place they could go to for some ice cream decorated with macaroons after a light dinner, and it was around the corner from Shakespeare and Company, which they'd hoped to check out. They sat at a table outdoors[344] and ordered salads which eventually came and looked nothing like what they expected a salad to look like. Charlie had varied by ordering some tartare salmon, which she'd mistakenly taken for salmon with tartar sauce. Needless to say, they planned on filling up with ice cream and macaroons on their way to the bookstore. As they picked at their food, they sorted their plans: they would enjoy another few days in Paris, since the apartment was booked, and they would work their way to South Africa. Life would be cheaper there. They may be able

---

343. Basic in the sense that any American who has only a few days in Paris is willing to walk extreme distances in order to fit in as much as possible
344. One should always sit out of doors whenever possible when dining in Europe

to sort finding any trail Jim left in Africa in an era before digital records. South Africa still had lax extradition laws that they felt might shelter them, as well. So, they rested in the knowledge that they had a plan.

As they sat, a man walked from across the street, stumbled a bit on the curb, and then headed towards their table. He appeared to be in his mid-forties, disheveled, bearded, and dirty, and he was carrying what looked like a wine bottle in a brown paper bag. He approached their table and spoke to them in a slurred version of French.

"We don't speak French," said Tabby in a condescending voice for someone who always tried to speak the local language.

"Americans!" he said with a cheer as he came around the small bar that protected those eating from those walking by on the street. He sat down at one of the two empty seats at the table. "Do you watch TV?" he said good-heartedly.

"Sometimes," said Charlie cautiously, glad they were out in the daylight.

"Good, me too, but not those shows with commercials. I like to stream American shows," he said as he listed off several American TV shows that were obscured by the combination of his drunken voice and his French accent. The only show the girls understood was *Pysch*, which seemed an odd option.

"I watched that," said Charlie, finding herself more willing to speak to strangers in Europe. The waiter walked by and seemed to be keeping an eye on the situation.

"Ah, Shawn and Gus. Love them," said the man as he dove into a long (and one sided) discussion of the show, episodes, and guest stars. He seemed most interested in Cary Elwes, who he claimed to have met once. The girls imagined Cary Elwes also cornered by a drunk Parisian and unsure of what to do. The man sat and laughed with them for several minutes about the show before telling them he must go and saying goodbye.

"Well," said Tabby

"Yep."

And with that the girls paid their bill and headed over for some ice cream, which they ate while overlooking the Seine before heading into the bookstore. The bookstore was full of rooms of books that famous visitors had poured over in decades past. Charlie felt at home and welcomed by the love of old books, but she knew they didn't have the money nor the space in their luggage, so the girls took the long walk back to their apartment empty-handed and headed to sleep for the night. While they had not found Jim, they had a plan and a few days to play in Paris.

CHAPTER TWENTY-FIVE

Follow Me Down[345]

A few days is never enough in Paris. It would take years there to really feel everything had been seen, felt, and understood. The girls were only one day in, and they were in love.[346] They woke in the morning to their tea and the fresh bread they'd brought home from a local bakery the night before. While they did enjoy the pastries of their first full day, Parisian fresh bread was more their speed. So, they sat in the living room on the couch facing the windows and ate while looking at the Eiffel Tower peering over the rooftops at them.

"Where to today?"

"Did we consider Versailles?"

"We did. Well, I did, but I read it can take literal hours just to get through the entrance line, and it's not a real Jim site."

"Ya, let's skip that."

"I was thinking, it's not every day we're here. The Jim spots are cool, but he's not in the cafés. There's no Jim archive—"

"Should be."

---

345. Krieger, Robby. "Tell All the People." The Soft Parade. Elektra Records, 1969.
346. With Paris, not each other or anyone else

"Ya, but there isn't. Let's just keep enjoying Paris, and that way we can absorb the vibe, like Jim did."

"Take it as it comes. I like it. In that case, let's go back to the Eiffel Tower."

"I could do that." So, it was decided—they would hit the Eiffel Tower again and go from there. The girls got dressed, grabbed bread for their bags along with some bottled waters[347] and headed out the door. While they were never really sure of the way, since they could see the Eiffel Tower over building tops, it was easy to make their way in the right direction, if not the fastest direction. When they got there, they decided to get a bit closer, and then they settled down on the lawn to relax and bask in the shadow of the tower.

"Ladies," called a voice behind them in a heavy accent. As they turned, they found a freshly shaved man with clean, styled, dark hair approaching them wearing a suit that came from the sort of place they'd never shopped at. Dollar signs rang in their ears as he approached, and while they recognized the value of the suit, they had no idea who he was.

"It's me; we had drinks together the other day," he said with a laugh as he approached.

"Oh—you brought the wine?" said Tabby, trying to grasp if this could actually be the drunk who invaded their space the day before.

"Did I?" he laughed. "I must have had more to drink than I realized. Come," he waved them up for a Parisian greeting.[348] "Forgive me. When I start writing, I lose all sense of myself," he laughed again.

"Are you a writer?" asked Tabby.

"Yes, from Switzerland. I come here to write, for the inspiration," he said waving his arms around. The girls were starting to realize

---

347. Like all good Americans, they liked to travel with bottles of water
348. Strangers kissing their cheeks would never be welcome outside of Paris

that what had sounded like a drunken French accent was masking a wealthy Swiss man and a soft German accent.

"I can see how this place would inspire some writing," said Charlie, wondering what in the world this man wrote that bought him the clothes he was wearing.[349]

"Yes, yes. Have you been up?" he asked, pointing at the tower.

"No, not yet," said Tabby.

"Oh, you must. You must come. I have reservations today. Join me. Be my guests."

"You can eat up there?"

"Oh, yes. I prefer Jules Verne. It's a Michelin." Tabby and Charlie had no idea what that meant, but they were a bit hungry, and the bread inside their purses, which was not wrapped at all, was surely stale by now.

"Is that something we should have had reservations for?"

"I have a table for one. They will extend it. Come," he said waving them on and heading towards the tower.

As they got closer, questioning their pattern of eating with strangers, they found that like all attractions, there was a queue to go up the Eiffel Tower. However, their new friend was waved around, and they followed him to the elevators where he seemed to know exactly what he was doing. They rode in the elevator, which was very much like all elevators, but felt special because of the location, and when they exited, they found themselves in the belly of the beast, so to speak. The inside of the tower was metallic with giant bolts, and didn't feel romantic at all, despite all the engagements there, celebrity and otherwise. But as they turned, the aerial view of Paris struck them, and the romance was clearly understood. There is no view like the view of Paris that stretches out in front of the

---

349. Tabby, always more sensible about numbers, assumed a trust fund bought the clothes and funded the writing

tower on all sides. The girls headed to the rail and stood looking as strangers took selfies beside them. They didn't feel the need for pictures. The view itself was enough to live in the moment,[350] but soon they noticed their strange friend observing them with a smile.

"Come, ladies, we must go in," he laughed as he led them inside an unassuming door that opened into a blissfully air-conditioned room.[351] The walls were entirely made of glass, and the ambiance screamed opulence. The waiter took their friend's name, which they really should've been listening for as they had no idea who he was, and he explained there would be two more joining him.

"Of course, this way," said the waiter who nodded at another employee who scrambled to bring more place settings to their table, which was a prime spot right next to one of the windows. As they sat, he ordered wine.

"You didn't bring your own," laughed Tabby.

"No, forgive me. I have my days," he laughed. "Please, order what you like. I want to hear more about your trip. I know we talked, but I have no memory. You're Americans, yes?"

"Yes, from Florida," said Charlie.

"Ah, Florida. That is the Wild West," said their friend, and so the discussion began that often hits Floridians who travel and speak to locals. Between the politics and the long list of animals that can kill you, there's always something to talk about. While he'd told them to order what they wanted, as they sat discussing Florida, he motioned to the waiter speaking in French and food appeared. The girls ate and regaled their friend with stories of giant dinosaur fish that leap out of the water in certain seasons and kill boaters.

---

350. Their nineties upbringing keeps them from joining true desires for selfies or constant pictures to share
351. Europe should come with a warning label for Americans: "Low Air Conditioned Area Ahead"

"You're kidding. No, this I cannot believe. I will believe snakes, alligators, and spiders, but not killer fish," he said with a laugh.[352]

The girls ate and laughed, and having no desire to prove the existence of killer fish, they moved the conversation to life in Switzerland. Their friend laughed and explained his village was rural—rural and beautiful—and on a lake near the Italian border. He spent most of his days writing at cafés or staying in his mountain house.

"You don't get out much?"

"No, I get out when I come to Paris."

"Which clearly you do often," said Tabby as she motioned towards the waiters who all appeared to know their friend.

"Yes, quite often."

"And do you work?"

"My writing is my work," he said and laughed again. The girls were starting to think the Swiss laughed a lot, but maybe it was the wine.[353] "Have you tried this yet?" he said as he grabbed a bottle from the ice bucket next to the table. "It's champagne," he said as he began to explain to them that true champagne is only produced in Champagne, France, and all other champagne is false and just bubbly white wine. The girls, whose salaries were quite restricted, nodded and laughed but had no plans to pay more for "true" champagne moving forward.

The girls ate and laughed, enjoying their nameless friend, the food, and the view of Paris that surrounded them. The tables were lit with candles, which provided softness, even though the natural light came in from all sides. Before long, the food was gone, and the girls had no idea how much time had passed.

---

352. In fact, according to Florida Fish and Wildlife, sturgeon cause boating accidents, often fatal, annually
353. The Swiss do laugh a lot when at home, but due to the strict nature of borders that take no stand on international politics, they keep the laughter at home, unless a lot of Parisian wine is applied

"So, what is on your agenda today?"

"No idea."

"Have you been to the catacombs?" he asked.

"No, should we?" asked Tabby who was always skeptical of vacations that included any kind of graves.

"My American friends usually do," he said as he explained where they would need to go. "Ladies, I am sorry, but I must return to my writing. I've had an idea," he said suddenly rising.

"Oh, well, thank you for lunch. Will we see you again?" asked Charlie.

"If the fates have it," he said as he kissed each of their cheeks, said "Ciao," and headed out the door after asking if they could find their own way down.

"Do you have any idea who he was?" asked Charlie.

"No, but you know what, I don't think he knew our names either."

"Really?"

"Ya, that's why he kept calling us ladies." The girls laughed and headed back out, in no hurry to take the elevator back down.

Even as they relaxed, in awe of Paris, they knew they needed to move on. The beauty of Paris could entrance them indefinitely, but they wouldn't find Jim here. The graveyard discussion had convinced them. He must've gone to South Africa. Whatever evidence was here of where Jim went was swept up by his few friends or, in later years, was buried by officials who signed a death certificate without seeing ID or drug dealers who didn't want to be pinned with another celebrity death.[354] Once in South Africa, they

---

354. Fun fact, Count Jean de Breteuil is said to have dealt the fatal doses of heroin to both Jim and Janis Joplin (who is most certainly dead), and Jim referenced him in "Love Street."

were convinced they could do what they do best—hit an archive and figure out if he came through the border using an assumed name, and if not, research what other African[355] nation might've been open to a not-so-closet bisexual, sexually active man in the early 1970s. So, from their vantage point on the Eiffel Tower, they shopped for tickets to South Africa.

"Tabby."

"Yes?"

"Ok, we can get a reasonable ticket to South Africa from Paris without too long of a delay, or we could take this deal from Turkish Airlines that involves a long layover in Istanbul."[356]

"How long?"

"Overnight."

"Ok."

"We could go see Istanbul."

"Pretty sure we won't find Jim there."

"No, but we've never been to Istanbul."

"Is it a really good deal?"

"Really good," Charlie said, showing Tabby her screen. "The government must be running some kind of deal to bring in tourists."

"Well, they did blow up their own airport a year or so ago, right?"

"Only part of it."

"Well, if it was only part, I say we go for it. Are the hours right to get a tour or something?"

And so, a plan was born. They would buy tickets that gave them a bit more time to explore Paris, eat Parisian food, and relax before heading down to Africa. They made plans for twenty-four hours in

---

355. Currently, South Africa is the only African nation that is openly welcoming to LGBTQ individuals
356. Countries with random incidents of bombs at airports set off by locals often offer tourism deals to entice visitors

Istanbul. A tour guide with strong reviews was easy to find online. Since the airport was fairly far from the city, and they didn't feel comfortable driving in Istanbul, the tour guide seemed a reasonable expense.[357]

---

357. For the college

CHAPTER TWENTY-SIX

Death Makes Angels of Us All[358]

The days passed in Paris as the girls rotated between museums, historical stops, cafés, and places they knew Jim had been. They spent an entire afternoon in Musée Rodin[359] and were in awe of the Van Gogh exhibit in Musée d'Orsay. They could see why Jim found Paris so inspirational for his poetry, but, as their last day came around, they realized there was one place they hadn't gone. Well, Charlie realized.

"We've hit enough graveyards," moaned Tabby as the girls lay around on the couch looking out the window at the Eiffel Tower.

"It's not a graveyard."

"No, because apparently in the catacombs, they don't actually bury people."

"That guy told us we should."

"You mean that guy whose name we don't know? Ya, he said his American friends went there, not that he would."

"Which means Jim most certainly went there."

---

358. Morrison, Jim. "A Feast of Friends." An American Prayer. Elektra Records, 1978.
359. Mostly because they got massively lost on the way there

"Ok, you're probably right on that," said Tabby, agreeing that they would spend their last day at the catacombs of Paris.

Getting to the catacombs wasn't difficult as they were able to take the subway and then follow GPS to the entrance. However, there was a long line to get in as tourists are required to go with a guide.[360] They stood and waited in the line of tourists as it made its way to a gate that led into a tunnel. At the head of the tunnel, they purchased tickets and were shuttled into a waiting area, much like the ones found at the start of Disney's Haunted Mansion.[361] The room had already cooled off several degrees, so the girls got their sweaters out of Tabby's grab bag and waited until the tour guide led them through the open stone door with the French words "C'est ici l'empire de la mort!" The tour guide explained these words meant "Stop! This is the empire of the dead!"

"We should probably take that warning," said Tabby, pointing back towards the way they came in.

"We're already here; let's just see what's in there," said Charlie, pulling Tabby through the door below the warning.

As they made their way through the winding stone pathways, the girls found literal walls of bones. The bones had been stacked and organized by some poor soul, so the bones could rest not with their original bone-mates, but with other femurs, skulls, etc. The first few rooms were fairly interesting, but as they made their way further and further through the bowels of the city, the girls found themselves wondering how long this tour of death would last.

"Ma'am, how much longer is this tour?" Tabby asked the young tour guide during a pause for tourists to take selfies with the bone walls. The young girl swung her long, black hair off her shoulder

---

360. Even in the catacombs, tourists will steal items, according to Paris Weekly.
361. Only this line would lead to actual dead people.

to turn and look, her brown eyes clearly pleading to be free of this place.[362]

"Madam, this is an hour-long tour, and we have completed the first," she paused as she checked her watch "ten minutes," she said as she turned to wave the tourists on to the next section. They were on a tourist track, and unlike many other tours, one cannot turn around and leave when one realizes the enormity of one's mistake.

"Fifty minutes. We've got fifty minutes left," said Tabby with a sigh.

"Glad you could do the math. Well, at least there's some Latin," said Charlie, aware they both had a secret love for trying to unpuzzle Latin phrases, the only words Tabby enjoyed unpuzzling.

"Memento irae in die consummationis"[363] read Charlie in her best *Supernatural* voice, attempting to distract her friend.

"Tempting with Latin will not get you anywhere," said Tabby as they made their way around a skull so many tourists had touched it shinned like the bronze boobs on the Molly Malone statue in Dublin.[364]

"Well, we've got to distract ourselves somehow," said Charlie as the tour guide explained the bones in front of them were from the June Uprising,[365] which inspired the book *Les Mis*.

"Ok," said Tabby as they worked together to translate the Latin.

The long hour passed as the girls made their way from one Latin sign to the other, turning the macabre tour into a dark passage in Latin studies.[366] "Melius est mihi mori quam vivere," read Charlie. "Oh, I know this one—it's better for me to die than to live."

---

362. It's amazing what college students will do for money
363. Remember the wrath of the end of days
364. Statue boobs and skulls—two things only tourists would touch
365. Charlie was beginning to wonder if the tour guide knew what she was talking about
366. As horror films have confirmed, Latin is a dark art

"Just had that one down, did you? Well, I guess the words aren't too complicated on that one," said Tabby, checking her watch for the time.

"That one is a bible verse. I remember that one from Sunday school."

"You learned that in Sunday school? No wonder why you grew up wanting to tour graveyards."

"Dude. My second-grade class took a field trip to a graveyard."

"What? To visit someone?"

"No, to do crayon rubbings."

"Of course you did," said Tabby as they finally made their way out of the tunnel of death and into the light and fresh air of Paris.[367]

"Let's not tell anyone we did this."

"Seriously. This was a low light for sure."

"Let's get something to eat."

"Because nothing inspires hunger like an hour with bones?" asked Tabby.

Not wanting to speak with anyone else on the tour, they wandered away from the crowd leaving the catacomb and decided to walk until the smell and sights of a café called them in. When they found a place a few blocks over, the waiter seated them and asked if they came from the catacombs.

"Ya, how could you tell," asked Charlie.

"You have the look," said the waiter whose name was unfortunately Agatha.[368] "I've been here my whole life, and I've never understood why people want to go there," she said with a shudder. "That is a place of the dead."

"I can tell you, I'm not going there again," said Tabby as she looked over the menu. Experience had taught them at that point

---

367. They would have welcomed the fresh air of any place at that point
368. Studies show women in any country that are stuck with the name Agatha are not happy

that beyond bread and pastries, they weren't fans of French food. They both picked a pizza and ordered. They were in no hurry. Leaving the catacombs left them feeling alive, happy to be above ground, and ready to explore a new city.

When their pizza came, they relaxed and ate slowly. They had no desire to take food home and every goal of enjoying their last meal in Paris.[369] When they were done, they made their way back to their Airbnb, but as it was their last night, they decided not to stay in their apartment. While they'd made a habit of spending the nights in the Airbnb while in Paris, since they didn't know anyone and would honestly rather be in every night anyways,[370] tonight was their last night, so they packed up the last of their cheese and the wine they'd barely touched and made their way to the Eiffel Tower. Tabby had read online that the tower was amazing at night, but as they made their way onto the lawn, the sight was more than they could've expected.

Against the backdrop of a dark Paris night, the tower seemed to be lit on every square inch.[371] They sat on the lawn and stared at the lights, sipping their wine and munching on cheese, aware that life likely couldn't get better than this. Around them were scores of tourists from around the world. The lawn was crowded, but peaceful, as everyone stayed in their groups and basked in the beauty in front of them. They were alone in a crowd of people who were all enjoying being alone.

"Excuse me, ladies, something to remember your trip by?" said a man's voice with a deep African accent. Charlie turned to see a thin Black man with big muscles and an even bigger smile.

"Hello," said Tabby. "How much?"

---

369. While large, most European pizzas are designed for one—a true inspiration
370. Unless they were in Dublin
371. Or centimeter

"For you, ten euros," he said with a wink. "Look, it lights up," he said as he lit up the miniature Eiffel Tower Tabby had asked about.

"Now how can we say no to that?" asked Tabby. The girls bought the Eiffel Tower, and the man made his way on carefully so as not to disturb the peaceful crowd. The girls watched as on the hour the tower shifted from steady lights to a twinkling light show. They were in awe and decided to stay for another hour to watch it again.

Their evening passed as evenings in Paris do—in beauty and in rest. In the morning, they would get up early, throw what they had into their bags,[372] and head to the airport. Tabby had thought to get the phone number of their illegal Parisian taxi, and they decided that since he'd gotten them safely to their destination the first time, they would take him again, thus ending their European tour with one last illegal cabbie.

---

372. Including their miniature Eiffel Tower

CHAPTER TWENTY-SEVEN

Away, Away, Away, A—way in India[373]

When they boarded the plane to South Africa, they weren't sure what to expect. Like many Americans, despite their education, they had the idea that anything from the Middle East[374] would be shabby and uneducated.[375] When they boarded the plane, they found it cleaner than expected. Basically, Turkish Airlines is a typical airline with A-typical service. All the flight attendants seemed actually happy they had arrived and sat them down with a genuine welcome and a promise of food.[376]

They sat in their window and aisle seats; this time they'd picked seats on the side of the plane with only two seats in the row so they wouldn't be stuck with a stranger again. They each went through their preflight rituals of motion sickness meds, downloading movies, and getting out noise canceling headphones.[377] As the plane started

---

373. Morrison, Jim, Ray Manzarek, et. al. "The End." The Doors: Live at the Isle of Wight Festival 1970, Eagle Rock Entertainment, LTD. 2018.

374. Even an airline from a country that balances itself between Europe, Asia, and the Middle East

375. When in fact there is so much wealth in the Middle East, quite likely God has his bank there.

376. French airlines also promise food, but sometimes that food is raw fish. Raw fish should never be on a plane.

377. Bring it, screaming babies, they will not be hearing you.

to take off, they were buried in technology and drugs and didn't even notice. The time passed quickly, as it does when you have technology, and before they knew it, they were being served food and ice cream.[378] They ate in silence and chatted briefly about their plans. They had chosen the flight with a 24-hour layover in Istanbul. They knew there wouldn't be Jim history or Jim there,[379] but they were up for adventure. They couldn't pass up the opportunity to explore Turkey.

When the flight landed, they followed the signs leading to customs that are navigable in all countries, and once again, they wound their way through the cattle-like corral that leads to the country of destination. Tabby had arranged for a tour guide. They typically preferred to explore new cities on their own, but this one was very foreign to them, and it was also about an hour from the airport, so they decided to go with local knowledge through My Local Guide. When they left the airport with only their carry on bags, which were really just big purses, they felt a bit odd, but that oddity was comforted by exiting the airport to find a man holding a sign with their names on it.[380] He smiled as they walked up and waved them over to a van that was waiting on the street behind him. It was not lost on the girls that once again they were boarding a random van with no labels in a foreign country and hoping that this man, who didn't speak English, wasn't kidnapping them.[381] They sat in the back of the van and listened to the man speak to the driver in what they assumed was Turkish as they both buckled up and the van headed off towards what they hoped was Istanbul.

---

378. Airlines that give dessert are truly an inspiration
379. Jim's ability to behave was not high enough to move to a Muslim country, and they doubted that changed after his fake death.
380. Life goal accomplished
381. In truth, they had seen too many Liam Neeson movies

The streets were full of traffic of the sort they hadn't even seen in Miami. There were so many lanes of traffic weaving in and out and following rules they couldn't understand, they were glad these strangers were driving and not them. Eventually, they parked in front of a sidewalk and were encouraged to get out.[382] As they stepped out of the van a tall, thin muscular man with thick, wavy brown hair and large chocolate eyes smiled and greeted them both.

"Welcome to Istanbul, ladies. Is this your first time here?"

"Yes," they both replied.

"Wonderful. Welcome. My name is Salih, and I will be your guide. Come, we have much to see, and since it is just the two of you, we can alter plans as you wish," he said as he walked up the cobblestone street between buildings that looked older than anything they'd seen in Paris or London.

"We're not really sure what to expect, but we heard the Hagia Sophia is good to see, and is it true we can go to Asia?"

"Yes, Istanbul is a city that spans two continents. We can take a ferry to Asia, if you wish, and grab some lunch and come back?"

"That would be amazing," said Tabby.

"But first, maybe you are hungry after your long trip?"

"Not really, we came from Paris and had food on the flight."

"Coffee, maybe, or tea?"

"Tea always," laughed Charlie.

Salih led them between buildings to a beautiful tea shop in a stone building that seemed older than their home state. The decorations were minimalist but welcoming. The girls sat and Salih ordered them tea and Turkish Delight, which they were surprised was not something C.S. Lewis had made up for the benefit of Narnia. They had no expectations for what Turkish Delight would

---

382. It never ceases to amaze how much can be communicated without language

be like, but had they imagined, this was not what they would have imagined. They worked to mask their disappointment that what Lewis had promised would be worth selling out siblings for was actually a gelatinous mess hiding under some nuts.[383]

As they sat and sipped tea, Salih regaled them with stories of Istanbul—the glorious history and culture. He explained that as the westernmost Muslim country, women from more strict countries like Saudi Arabia came to Turkey to let their hair down.[384] He smiled as he explained this, and waved to some Middle Eastern women who weren't wearing a Hajib. He explained the women were there for a holiday. As the conversation and tea died down, Salih led them out to walk toward the Hagia Sophia. On the way over, they walked between buildings that had seen Roman emperors come and go. There were cats roaming the streets who were all well cared for. The girls were entranced.

Similar to Disney, they walked for what felt like hours but was actually a very long, hot walk accomplished in minutes. As they entered the Hagia Sophia, Salih explained that they were okay to enter as they were dressed, but they would need to use a scarf to cover their heads. Fortunately, the mosque had scarfs available for that purpose.[385] They entered and Salih pointed out where women went for services, as services and prayer were segregated by gender. For tourism purposes, they were allowed to tour the mosque. They walked around, amazed at the artistry in what had originally been a church. The colors and heights of the building were more than can be explained, and they were in awe. They stood in wonder for a while before Salih encouraged them to head to the port if they were going to make the morning ferry to Asia. The girls exited the

---

383. Edmund was even worse than we realized
384. literally.
385. As they had planned on visiting a Muslim nation, they had picked their outfits carefully

mosque and returned the borrowed scarves.[386] They followed Salih through the city and out to a harbor. As Salih bought the tickets, the girls wandered and found a café named The Orient Express.

"There's your Agatha Christie for you," said Tabby with a nod.

"That looks amazing," said Charlie. The outdoor seating was organized alongside an old brick wall built around oak doorways with circular stained-glass windows above them, surrounded by beautiful off-white bricks with mauve trim. The place looked like something that had stepped out of a bygone era.

As they stood in wonder, Salih approached them with tickets in hand. "Ladies, I see you found The Orient Express. This is one of the many great places to eat in Istanbul. However, the ferry is departing soon, and we can eat in Asia, if you would like," he said with a smile and a wave towards the water where a ferry sat waiting.

"Eating in Asia sounds good."

"Can't say I've ever done that," said Charlie as the girls followed Salih towards the ferry. He handed the tickets to a man standing at a podium by the plank walkway to the boat. The men exchanged a few words in Turkish as the girls waited, and when they were waved towards the ferry, the man behind the podium handed them back the bottom half of their tickets with instructions that they would use the bottom half to reboard the ferry back to the European side of the city, should they wish to return.

"Should we wish to return," said Charlie with a giggle. "That's a rough thing to say as we walk the plank."

"It's hardly a plank. There are railings," said Tabby with an eye roll.

The girls followed Salih to seats he had gotten for the three of them. The seats gave a perfect view of the harbor as the boat started

---

386. Which would be washed and reused for sustainability purposes

to take off. The water was entrancing, as it is in all ports, but it was a different shade than the water in Key West.[387] The water leading into Asia was a darker blue, but it invited them in all the same. They sat back and enjoyed the rocking motion of the boat.[388] The ride was fairly short, and soon they were disembarking, a word they don't get to use very often. They weren't sure what they were expecting from their first view of Asia, but it was not this: the Asian side of Istanbul looked the same as the European side. Salih led them down a sidewalk along the water which opened into a beautiful park. They stopped at a small building on the water that had a roofed patio and seats.

"Maybe you would like to get a sandwich to eat while we sit by the water?" Salih asked, motioning towards the window for ordering.

"I could eat," said Tabby. The girls ordered hamburgers and Diet Cokes. The food was quickly sent down to the second window, and once the food was obtained, the girls followed Salih towards some benches that sat in front of a brightly colored playground overlooking the water. They sat in silence and ate their burgers to the sounds of children laughing and playing on the playground while they looked over at the water.

Time in Asia went quickly, as the ferry was scheduled to leave only thirty minutes after arriving. Salih explained that they could stay, but they could also go back and shop at the spice market. He also hoped to take them to the Galata Tower and Taksim Square. The girls were hoping to see as much of Istanbul as they could, and now that they had a sample of Asia, they followed Salih willingly back to Europe.

---

387. The Florida state government has copyrighted the exact shade of the water in Key West so that other ports cannot have the same shade.
388. Motion sickness meds make the rocking motion of boats 99.8% more enjoyable, according to a survey done by Pediatrists of America

The ferry ride back was beautiful and very much the same as the ride over.[389] They disembarked again and followed Salih back into the city. On arrival, Salih let them know that they would first walk to the Galata Tower and then would slowly walk towards the square, and along the way they could shop. After the square, they would dine once more and then be driven back to the airport.

"Do you have a hotel room at the airport?"

"No, is that an option?" asked Tabby.

"Yes, since you will have several hours, you could rent a room for those hours inside the hotel."

"Is that legitimate?" asked Charlie, who'd only heard of hourly rates applied in a different context.

"Yes, airports in major cities often have them, but they are very nice in Istanbul. The rooms are clean, and you can shower and rest in privacy and then head down to your flight when it is time. You can also eat there in the hotel, but you will probably not be hungry," he said with a laugh as they walked past more restaurants and cafes.

The girls followed Salih down more cobblestone streets. Along the way, they found a few more healthy-looking street cats that Charlie of course had to stop and pet. Salih explained that the cats, and all stray cats and dogs, were cared for by the city and the people. Stray animals were believed to have value and to offer protection to the city.

"Key West is similar. The city takes care of stray cats. They're all fixed and fed," said Charlie.

"And the chickens."

"And the chickens?" asked Salih. "Are the chickens wandering the streets? Or do you eat them?"

---

389. The same route was taken in both directions

275

"Oh no. The chickens in Key West are not for eating," explained Tabby as they walked towards the tower.

"No?"

"No," said Charlie. "They live in the streets and in the bushes; they are protected, and people are also not supposed to feed them."

"Someone must feed them."

"Or maybe they eat whatever chickens naturally eat."

"What do chickens naturally eat?"

"Bugs?"

As the three of them discussed what chickens in the wilds of Key West ate, they arrived at the Galata Tower, and Charlie listened to Salih explain the vast history of the tower in this ancient city. Unfortunately, due to her motion sickness medicine, she would remember none of what he said. All the same, the short trip up the tower gave the girls a fabulous view of the old city. They stood overlooking the cobblestone streets and narrow passageways that are common in European cities until Salih encouraged them to head back down so they could walk towards the Spice Market. The girls followed Salih and listened to more of his historical discussions. As they walked up to an old, white stone building, Salih paused.

"Would you like to try a Hookah Bar?"

"Is that a real thing? Not just something in *Alice in Wonderland*?"

"Well, you won't find any caterpillars smoking in here, but it's very real, and it is a part of Turkish culture."

"Well, if it's a part of the culture, I say we give it a shot," said Charlie, awakening to the adventure of the city. The girls followed Salih in, who spoke in Turkish to a waiter. The waiter led them in through the bar that looked like something out of an old cartoon and gave them seats that had plush cushions to sit on before bringing them a large contraption that they assumed was a hookah.

"So, what are we smoking here?" asked Tabby.

"This is a water pipe," said Salih, holding up the smoking end of the instrument. "You will breathe in the water, tobacco, and rose here," he said, handing the pipe end to Charlie. Charlie smiled, took a big drag, and handed it to Tabby who did the same. The three of them passed the pipe around and listened as Salih told them about the history of smoking in Istanbul. While Salih assured them there was only tobacco and rose in the smoke, the girls found the situation increasingly ridiculous as they smoked and thought of caterpillars and little lost Alice. Looking around, they realized they were the only women in the bar, which added to the ridiculousness of the situation, and the level of ridiculousness wasn't decreased as they giggled and men continued to stare at them from around the bar.

"Let me order you some coffee," Salih said, interrupting their fun as he rose and walked to the coffee bar, returning with a tray of coffee in ornate little glasses. "Turkish coffee is the best coffee in Europe," he explained, "but we should not drink the last few drops as that is where the coffee grounds settle."

The girls sipped their coffee, ate a few more regrettable and yet socially expected Turkish Delights, and smoked hookah through their giggles until Salih, who'd likely had enough of their shenanigans, led them out of the hookah bar to find the nearby and yet elusive Spice Market, which looked like something out of *Aladdin*. There were people with wooden tables with cloth awnings all lined up making cobblestone pathways for the girls to follow. The tables were covered in goods ranging from various tins of aromatic spices to perfumes, to clothing, to olives and the basic tourist goods. The girls weren't sure where to start, but at this point in the tour, they trusted Salih's wisdom and followed him. He led them to a vendor who greeted him in Turkish. "This is the best tea in the market," said Salih with a nod.

"You must try some," said the vendor with a smile. He quickly made the girls samples of his apple tea, which he informed them was the best in Istanbul. He also gave them samples of black tea and a tea that was good for sore throats. "Guaranteed to cure all throat illnesses, including COVID," he said with a smile and a story of how the tea had cured his great aunt of COVID. The girls happily sampled and decided to bring some different teas along for their journey. They also purchased some Turkish Delight, which the man explained was made by his family and would stay fresh for a very long time as all the ingredients were fresh, so the honey wouldn't ferment as other processed sugars would. The girls thanked him as he packaged up their purchases and sent them on their way.

"Salih."

"Yes," he answered as they made their way through the spice market, looking at all the interesting wares along the way.

"Is it true that it is illegal for Americans to buy saffron from Iran?"

"Well, I cannot say what is illegal in the United States, but I can say that we do sell saffron from Iran here, and it is quite wonderful. After we see the square, I will take you to a wonderful place to eat and you can try some saffron dishes."

"Oh, I just googled it," said Tabby, who was increasingly grateful for the international plan on her phone. "It *is* illegal for Americans to buy and bring home saffron from Iran."

"So, we have to buy some. It's an illegal spice."

"I think we may need some of this illegal spice."

Salih led the girls to what he said was the best saffron vendor in the market. The girls gladly made their purchases, grinning at their cunningness in buying a spice they weren't allowed to bring home to the country they could no longer go home to.[390] They took their packages in hand and followed Salih to the promised square, which opened up into a beautiful stone area centered around a gorgeous statue and fountain. While the statues were pretty much of the sort of historical statues found all over Europe, which often are much better to enjoy with fictional accounts of their history,[391] the girls were in awe. They wandered around the square with the other tourists and took photos of the statues.

"Excuse me," said a small voice in broken English. Tabby turned and found an adorable little boy with dark hair and large dark eyes that betrayed his fear.

"Madam, how are you?"

"I'm good. How are you?" asked Charlie.

"I am good," he said with a smile.

"He must practice," said the man standing behind the boy with his hands on the boy's shoulders, before turning to Salih and speaking in Turkish.

"Aha. This boy has been assigned by his teacher to find tourists who speak English and have a conversation. He must then turn in the assignment to his class. The father is asking if you are willing to speak with him in English," said Salih with a smile.

"Yes, of course, we are teachers," said Charlie with a smile. Salih relayed the response to the father who smiled and nodded.

"Do you like football?" asked the boy in a thick accent.

"Yes, I do," said Charlie, understanding he likely meant soccer. "I played football when I was a little girl. Do you play football?"

"Yes, I do. Who is your favorite football player?"

---

390. Unfortunately, like most Americans who buy this illegal spice while traveling abroad, they would have no idea how to use it.
391. American statues would also often be better with creative historical histories

"Messi," said Charlie with a smile. The boy smiled in return.

"Me, too. Why do you come to my country?"

Charlie thought for a moment. How to explain their obsession with Jim Morrison to a boy who is clearly at the very beginning of speaking English? "Hmmm . . . we are traveling to learn more about the Doors."

"You come here to see doors?" he asked, clearly confused. Charlie looked at Salih and explained the band the Doors. Salih smiled and nodded.

"Ah, Jim Morrison," he said and turned to the father to explain something in Turkish of which Charlie only understood "Jim Morrison." The father smiled and spoke back to Salih.

"Yes, he knows Jim Morrison. He is also a fan," Salih smiled. "He thanks you for helping his son." As Salih spoke the father nodded and bowed.

"Thank you for your help," said the boy and the two left. Salih explained as they headed out of the square that he'd had similar conversations with school children before, and he thanked the girls for their willingness to help the boy as he led them to a restaurant he promised was the best in the area.

They walked up a long cobblestone path that turned and curved as it headed up a hill. Eventually, they came to some outdoor seating on both sides of the path. The seating was attached to a small, quaint restaurant. Salih told them to have a seat, and he went to get them water. The girls sat and watched Salih move with ease behind the counters as he gathered them waiters and waters. Soon the girls were looking over menus. Salih told them the dishes with saffron in them that would be best to try, and as the girls were both game, they ordered a chicken dish with a creamy saffron sauce. They sat and sipped water as they waited for their dishes. Music came from the restaurant and the girls relaxed, realizing how much they'd walked over the last few hours while they explored so much of an entire city in a short span of time. Soon they were digging into a creamy chicken delight that they knew they would never be able to recreate on their own.

Their time in Turkey was short, but they'd enjoyed every second, and while they had no evidence of Jim to follow up on here, and they were pretty sure Jim wouldn't have gone to any kind of Muslim nation with his overly sexualized self in the seventies,[392] they were glad they'd taken the time to explore this city that felt both ancient and exotic. When dinner was done, Salih took them to a meeting point where their ride was waiting, and they said their goodbyes. The girls felt they were saying goodbye to a friend at this point, but when friendship is built on monetary exchange, it never really is friendship, so they said their goodbyes.

The girls struggled to stay awake on the drive back to the airport, but the fear that comes with long rides in foreign cities in unmarked taxis kept them awake. When they got to the airport, which was surrounded by large men with even bigger guns than the guns they'd seen at the Paris airport, they left the cab with a wave and followed the picture signs to the hotel inside the airport that Salih had connected them with. They were able to get a room and check in immediately. The room was a small, basic hotel room, which followed the modern European trend of full glass walls for the bathroom and a curtain for the bathroom door.

"Well, this is private," said Tabby with her usual sarcastic tone.

"I think I'm tired enough not to care."

"I'll sleep first, you shower first?"

---

392. They weren't sure of what to think of Marrakech

The girls went about their showers and naps. A few hours of sleep and a shower were completely restorative; when their alarms went off, they both felt ready to get on the next plane. Tabby had booked the room with access to the buffet downstairs before heading out, so they headed down to the buffet room with their carry-on bags. While they'd decided they were comfortable leaving the carry-on bags with the unmarked cab driver, they didn't feel comfortable leaving the bags in their seats at the buffet, so they took turns getting plates and babysitting[393] the bags. The food was familiar but strange and consisted of fruits, nuts, lunch meat, unrecognizable foods, and parfait. The girls marveled at the internationalization of the parfait, which they'd found in each country they'd stopped in thus far. When they were full, they headed back to airport security.

Istanbul Airport had an initial level of security, which everyone must pass through[394] to gain entrance to the building. They'd already passed through that to get to the airport hotel, but now they had to pass the next level of security. In Turkey, the airport security officers were of the sort that were very intimidating and carrying large weapons.[395] The girls kept their heads down and made their way through security as directed. They wanted nothing more than to board their next flight and head to South Africa. They felt hope that they would find what they wanted. They were researchers, and technically, they were both doctors. They were good at researching and felt that they had found Jim's trail, and they would track him down—if he was still alive. And so, they boarded their plane, went back through their flight habits, watched movies, ate, slept, and listened to music until they landed in Cape Town.

---

393. Always grateful they were babysitting bags and not actual babies
394. And have bags screened at
395. But without the mohawks of the Parisian security officers

CHAPTER TWENTY-EIGHT

You Remember When We Were in Africa[396]

South Africa isn't what people expect it to be, but fortunately, the girls had only the hope of finding Jim and no expectations of what South Africa would be like. They arrived at the airport and got a rental car, thankful that Sixt had followed them all the way to Cape Town, and headed out, with GPS guiding the way. While they were driving on the right side of the road, the roads were winding and dark and seemed endless.

"It's so dark," complained Charlie in her Dramamine enforced grumpiness.

"Well, it is nighttime, and it's still dark at night, even though we're in Africa," said Tabby with a laugh.

"We've been driving forever."

"*I've* been driving forty minutes."

"These roads are so curvy."

---

396. Morrison, Jim. "Wild Child." The Soft Parade. Elektra Records, 1969.

"Well, we like curves," Tabby said with a laugh. "Fifteen more minutes according to the GPS. You've still got your motion sickness meds, right?"

"Right. Where did you get reservations?"

"Some place called Misty Cliffs. It's right on the ocean, like the house backs up to the ocean. I figured if we're going to use the college card, we might as well enjoy it. Plus, it was surprisingly affordable."

"Is this the off season?"

"Maybe? I don't know the seasons in South Africa."

"Me either."

The girls drove on in silence, with only the GPS voice speaking, which they'd set to British for entertainment purposes. They watched the car drive past Table Top Mountain on the GPS screen and felt they'd now seen a landmark.

"Table Top—isn't that a cool hiking spot? I think I remember reading that."

"Yep, but of the sort where you could actually fall off the mountain and you will need mountain climbing skills of some sort."

"And we have none of those."

"Exactly. I was thinking we could hike the Cape of Good Hope instead."

"Isn't that the southernmost point? Like, where all those adventurers/colonizers used to try to make it around to get to Asia or somewhere?"

"I think so? Math, not geography."

"Does it look like good hiking?" asked Charlie who'd done the research for exploring Istanbul on layover, not Cape Town.

"It does. Plus, there are baboons."

"Like actual baboons or baboons in cages?"

"Baboons in cages are still baboons."

"Well, ya, but they're in cages."

"I don't think they're in cages."

"Ok, we're definitely doing that."

"I don't think we'll find Jim there hanging out with the baboons."

"But you never know where we might meet someone who knows something."

"Hanging out with baboons?"

"You know what, I don't need your negativity. We're going to see the baboons and that is that."

Indeed, that was that, as Tabby signaled her way off the main road to the right, following an awkward one lane driveway down the side of a small mountain.[397] They parked in the dark, unable to see the house, and found a small path down a hill to a door, which opened with the code they'd been sent by the Airbnb host. They entered into a large living room painted in white. There were white couches and a few light wood tables with minimalist decorations and light brown shelves that held board games and puzzles for visitors. Taken by the childish drive to explore, the girls locked the front door behind them and took the stairs up to a narrow hallway with four doors across from the stairs and an open door to the left that led to a large bathroom. Next to the bathroom was a door that led to a small laundry, and as they explored each door in turn, they found all the other doors led to enormous bedrooms, each of which had a balcony. The doors to each balcony were floor to ceiling and entirely glass aside from the metal framework and locking system, which still had the skeleton key in place to unlock the door. They opened the door of the middle bedroom and went out onto a balcony that stretched the length of the backside of the house. They

---

397. Normal sized hills are in fact mountainous for girls from Florida

were immediately struck by the sound of waves crashing loudly on the beach below them. While they couldn't see the ocean in the dark, the noise was loud enough that they knew it was close, and down below they could see a small patio area that led onto dark sand, not like the white sand beaches of home.

"Wow."

"Ya."

"We could afford this?"

"Dude. This was cheaper than that place in London with the mice."

"We're not going to London again."

"We are not."

"As Ca-h-al would say, London is no craic,"[398] said Charlie.

The girls laughed and headed downstairs to explore the rest of the first floor. On the first floor they found another bedroom, which was easily rejected since it had no view of any kind, another bathroom, and a large open-floor plan kitchen with an eat-in area that seemed to have been an enclosed porch at one time. The windows ran the length of the room and benches lined the windows behind a long wooden table. The girls stood in awe of what would certainly be a great view of the ocean when they woke up in the morning.

"Want to go out there?"

"Uhm, yes" said Tabby with a laugh.

They went out a sliding glass door to the small patio area they'd seen from the balcony on the second floor and immediately threw off their shoes and went for the sand, which was a welcome coldness to their feet. They ran to the water, letting themselves get wet up to the knees, and embracing the coolness only water brings. The

---

398. The Irish word for all things fun, which may or may not include crack

weather was getting to be what the girls would consider to be spring or early summer, but in the evening, for these Florida girls, there was still a coldness they found refreshing, especially after a long trip on a plane followed by a dark drive. Eventually, they went back into the house and started looking through the pantry.

"Well, there's some tea in here. Oh—and some biscuits."

"Like British biscuits or Southern biscuits?"[399]

"British."

"Oh, that sounds good. I'll make the tea, and you order some food delivery for tomorrow morning?"

"Sounds good," said Charlie as she made plans for a few days' worth of food.

When the tea was ready, they sat together looking out into the dark at where they knew the ocean was.

"There won't be any milk for the tea today."

"But there will be tomorrow."

"Good, so you sorted how to order food?"

"Yep, wasn't that hard. They've got all the traditional ways of ubering and ordering food."

"Great," said Tabby as they both started to sip the tea.

"Oh, man. What kind of tea is this?"

"The box said Roobios."

"Roo-boys?"

"Something like that."

"What kind is that?"

"No idea, but it's the kind that was in the cupboard."

"I see."

"Some kind of South African tea. It's caffeine free."

---

399. A very important distinction

"It's going to take some getting used to. Kind of in the Turkish Delight category."

"Good thing we loaded up with tea in Istanbul," offered Charlie.

"Ya, I think it will be British or Turkish tea from here on out. Not sure if we will be here long enough to get used to this tea."[400]

"Well, if we find Jim, we might be here a while."

"Can you imagine? The greatest research find for decades, and we can't tell anyone."

"Not can't, won't."

"Right. Won't."

The girls sat and dreamed together about finding Jim and exploring South Africa, a country very foreign to both of them, and eventually they went up to the bedrooms, each of them picking a large room for herself. They climbed into their beds and slept better than they had in days, letting the sound of the waves lull them to sleep and wake them up again in the morning when they were ready to face the day.

They started the day with a walk on the beach, which they cut short when Charlie's phone alerted them to the grocery delivery. When they went in for the food left on the front doorstep, they realized they were ready for food and questioned what they'd eaten in the last twelve hours aside from biscuits.[401] They unloaded the groceries, which were easily sorted in the biggest kitchen the girls had ever stayed in, and Charlie began making American pancakes and Turkish black tea with milk.

"Pancakes?"

---

400. She said knowing their options were limited and if possible, they might not ever leave

401. Long travel days lead to forgotten meals, according to We Travel magazine, which has been voted Azerbaijan's number one travel magazine three years in a row.

"Yes, I am so glad to have a kitchen again."

"We had one in Paris."

"Ya, but we didn't in London, Wales, Dublin, or Istanbul."

"True."

"I'm enjoying being able to have a bowl of fruit out and to make my own pancakes."

"It *is* nice to have fruit again."[402]

"It really is and look how great that fruit is," said Charlie as she whisked up the pancakes using her dad's from scratch recipe and poured a small cup of batter on the hot griddle she had waiting. She poured a perfect pancake circle and sat watching as the edges slowly started to firm up, waiting for the telltale bubbles that would let her know to flip the cakes. The secret, she knew, was to only flip them once.

"Pancakes, my dear," said Charlie as she set a plate in front of Tabby who was staring out at the ocean. The waves were hypnotic, and Charlie doubted how much work they would get done in the house. Only Jim could pull them from this view. Charlie returned to the griddle to make her cakes and explained to Tabby that there wasn't any maple syrup in the grocery store so they would have to make do with butter and jam, but at least the jam was fresh and tasted great, unlike the Rooibos.

They weren't really certain where to look for Jim. They were following a trail that was decades cold. They were confident he had come here,[403] and it seemed unlikely he went home afterwards as that would call for a lot of fake documentation, and it would go against the knowledge that if any country had fans who wouldn't let him rest, it was the States. Plus, there were the charges against him in Miami. They knew the charges had been dropped, but that was

---

402. Studies show that the Irish and British combined eat even less fruit than Americans
403. Through logic that possibly only made sense to them

only a handful of years ago. Did Jim know? Or had he let Florida go over the past few decades? Looking out over the ocean, the girls doubted he left a spot that offered such peace and obscurity.

"So, where do you want to start looking?" asked Charlie as she ate her pancakes.

"Well, we found great Jim contacts at the tattoo parlor in Dublin."

"That we did."

"So, why not start at another tattoo place?"

"Another tattoo?"

"Well, I wanted words added to mine, so I could get those added, or maybe do another one on my wrist or something."[404]

"I don't think it's been long enough to make progress on mine."

"I think I read you have to wait a few months to work on a fresh tattoo again."

"Well, I'm game for a new one. Did you have a place in mind?"

"I found this one called More Than Hype in Cape Town."

"Does it look good?"

"Ya, solid reviews, and it looks like he does really good line work, which apparently is pretty difficult."

"Maybe we should call and see if we can get in today?"

And so, a plan was made, a call was placed, and the girls started to get ready for their day.[405] They decided to take it easy by driving into Cape Town first and exploring a bit before getting the tattoos. No need to try to fit in the Cape of Good Hope, which is in the opposite direction, on the same day, since they had no tickets or plans to leave South Africa anytime soon.

---

404. Charlie was experiencing the tattoo curse, or blessing depending on viewpoints: once you have a tattoo, there will need to be more tattoos. According to a survey by Tattoos.are.us.com, 99.8% of people who get tattoos, get more soon after. .2% die not long after their first tattoos, due to unrelated risky behavior

405. As they were new to tattoos, they were unaware how unlikely it was that they got into both of their tattoo parlors of choice without placing an appointment weeks in advance. This phenomenon of availability was due to COVID restrictions both countries had placed in the not-so-distant past.

The drive out in the morning was remarkably better than the drive in the night before. In the daylight, they realized the curving roads were following the curve of the shoreline, and the views of Cape Town were astonishing. The girls continued to drive in silence, without music even, as they looked at views they never thought they would see. The drive through mountains was barren and beautiful at the same time. As they got closer to Cape Town, they noticed some shanties along the left side of the road where houses made of tin roof panels little bigger than an outhouse stood in clusters. The shanties were organized along dirt pathways in straight lines, connected by confusing networks of satellites and wires above the houses. There was an ominous Porta Potty at the end of each row.

"How do you think neighborhoods like that survived COVID?"

"Not very well. I imagine any sickness would plow through there."

"I didn't realize places like this were real."

"Me either," said Tabby as she drove into Cape Town in silence.

The streets were becoming more city-like, surrounded by businesses and people on bikes heading to work. As traffic slowed, they realized they must be getting closer to the city.

"What's that up there?" asked Charlie.

"I don't know, some kind of construction?"

"I guess you might need a flag for construction."

"Ya, to wave cars around, right?"

"Seems likely," said Tabby as she inched the car forward behind the car in front of them. When they got close enough for a glimpse of the young woman in a bright orange construction vest waving a large color guard style flag with less flair, they could see an entire family of baboons walking along the side of the street.

"OMG monkeys."

"Baboons."

"Whatever."

"Well, it's not the same thing," said Tabby.

"Whatever, there are actual baboons walking along the road," Charlie yelled out like a child. "This is the best," said Charlie with a sigh.

"Better than when we saw Jim's birth house?"

"There were no monkeys there. Only a lot of tourists and traffic."

"True. 100% less monkeys. Better than Key West?"

"Also, no monkeys."

"Is that the scale that we judge all places by now? 'Are there wild monkeys out where we can see them?'"

"Maybe it should be."

"A lot less places would be cool."

"There is that one place in Florida, where is it, near Ocala or something? In the middle of the state. Those monkeys escaped years ago and now they live in the wild? I hear you can kayak under them."

"I'm not sure kayaking *under* monkeys is a good idea, but probably you should've mentioned wild monkeys when we were driving across the entire state of Florida."

"Lost opportunity for sure," said Charlie with a laugh. "Did you want to grab some lunch before tattoos?"

"Yes, because eating before tattoos is important."

"Exactly, but did we find a place? I don't remember."

"Hout Bay."

"I thought we were going to Cape Town."

"Listen now, I'm the driver. Hout Bay has places to eat on the water, and we can maybe see sea lions in the wild."

"Ok, sea lions and baboons in one day. This is insanity."

With no idea where to start looking for Jim, they arrived at Hout Bay and parked the car, glad that even though the country was clearly different than their own, parking signs were mostly universal and fairly easy to navigate. They walked towards the water and found a few places to eat that were facing the bay, picked the one closest to them and headed inside to ask for a table. The restaurant was made of wooden beams connected with walls of windows that gave tourists a complete view of the ocean.[406] The decor was rustic and comfortable, like something they would expect to see on the water in a more rural Florida setting. They sat down where the hostess guided them and read over the menu.

"They call shrimps prawns?"

"Apparently so."

"Do we want prawns for lunch?"

"I think we do."

When the waitress came for their lunch orders, they asked for Diet Cokes and prawns, finding joy in asking for prawns.

"Is there anything else I can get for you ladies?" asked the waitress.

"Well, actually, odd question."

"Go for it," said the waitress who'd likely heard it all from tourists before.

"Do you know Jim Morrison?"

"As in the Doors?"

"Yes."

"Ya, great singer. There's never been his like again."

"That's for sure."

"So, we have this theory he faked his death and came to South Africa."

---

406. Because the desire to sit and stare at the water is also universal

"South Africa? Really? Why South Africa?" asked the waitress, now invested in the conversation.

"Well, Jim idolized this French philosopher, and when that guy had enough, he faked his death and moved to Africa."

"And you think Jim did the same? Why would he want to leave all that fame?" said the waitress, sitting down in the empty seat on the outside of their table.

"Well, he did have a warrant out for his arrest for that concert in Miami, and he'd tried to get out of the band a few times."

"Really? And he would've come to South Africa in the early seventies?"

"We think so. Of course, that's assuming we're right."

"Seems like if he came to hide in Africa, South Africa would be the place to come in the seventies."

"Or anytime, really," said Tabby as she looked out at the bay.

"Well, I'm studying genealogy for a history project in university, and the records for South African immigration have been translated and scanned."

"What?"

"Yes. They're actually pretty easy to sort through," said the waitress, who by now was fully sucked into their conspiracy theory.

"Are they posted on a government website?" asked Tabby

"Actually, I've been using the American site, well, I don't know if it's American or British, but it's ancestry.com. They have access to a lot of international government records for immigration. I bet you can sort through those," she said standing. "I'll put your food order in, and you let me know if you find anything," she said as Tabby and Charlie pulled out their phones.

The girls quickly found the site and added one of the P-cards so they could have full access. In a basic search of South African immigration papers, they found that no one had immigrated in 1971, the year of Jim's apparent death.

"Bad year to move to South Africa."

"Apparently."

"So, we try 1972? Do we hope no one moved in 1971 and not that all those records were lost?"

"I mean, we have to start somewhere."

The girls put Jim's birthdate in the search bar, assuming he would be ballsy enough to stick with his original birthdate and not to make one up. They found no white men who moved to South Africa in 1972 with his exact date, but 202 white men who moved to South Africa who were born in or around 1943, Jim's birth year.

"202."

"202. That's not bad. So now we individually seek out these men to see if we can find any information?"

"I think newspapers.com has international papers. Of course, they might not be in English, but it's probably worth trying."

"And if we find the name we're looking for in an article, we can always use Google translate to help."

"Look at you being all tech savvy," said Charlie with a laugh as the food arrived.[407]

As they sipped their Diet Cokes and ate prawns, they divided the list into 101 men each and started to dig for anyone who could possibly fit Jim's description. They assumed he must've taken being private seriously, or he would've been found in the last fifty years or so. By the end of lunch, they were happy to report to the waitress that they had the list down to a total of 150 men. It would be slow going, but they hoped to continue shortening the list.

---

407. Food arrives very quickly in South Africa

"Come back and let me know if you find him," asked the waitress as the girls got ready to leave. Never sure if they should or should not tip when traveling, they decided to air on the side of generosity and left a tip.

"Do you know where we can find sea lions?" Tabby asked the waitress as they got ready to leave.

"Well, it's always worth a walk along the water. You might see one, but usually from here you'd need to take a boat tour to find them."

"Oh."

"I could point you in the direction for a tour."

"No thanks, we've got tattoo appointments today."

"Really? Where are you going?"

"More Than Hype."

"Oh, that place is good. I've had friends recommend it. Well, you girls enjoy your day," she said with a smile as she walked away.

Ever the optimists, the girls headed down closer to the water where they found no sea lions but plenty of coast to admire.[408] With no sea lions to see, following so close after seeing actual baboons in the wild,[409] they decided to drive to the tattoo parlor. They'd need extra time to find parking in a new city, so it seemed wise.

---

408. Thus local knowledge prevailed, as it usually does
409. They weren't really in the wild, they were walking along a highway

CHAPTER TWENTY-NINE

Summer Sunday and a Year[410]

When the girls drove into what appeared to be the economic hub of Cape Town, the city took on the look of all cities—tall, beautiful buildings as far as the eye could see.[411] The girls were amazed that South Africa was so similar and yet so different. A cliché, yes, but one that was accurate in South Africa. They parked in an underground garage below one of the tall buildings and came up through a mall that reminded the girls of malls they had visited up north as kids.[412] The street level opened up onto the four-lane road they'd just left, and the GPS in their phones led them to walk across the street and around a few blocks into what seemed like a residential street in the Bronx. The brick buildings looked like brownstone homes that had been made into offices and businesses. They followed the GPS to the designated door and found a button to buzz into the building. Above the buzzer was a sign that read "Not a brothel."

"Are we sure this place is for us?"

"Well, yes, because it is NOT a brothel."

---

410. Morrison, Jim. "Love Street." Strange Days. Elektra Records, 1967.
411. Which wasn't far because the tall buildings block the view
412. Because there is no below ground parking in Florida

"Ok," said Charlie as she rang the buzzer and waited.

The door was opened by an average size man with an above average smile that seemed to stretch from ear to ear. His arms and neck were covered in tattoos.[413] His jeans, T-shirt, and Converse showed his easy-going mood, and he quickly welcomed the girls inside.

"How can I help you two today?" he asked with an eagerness to welcome them in.

"We have appointments for tattoos," said Tabby.

"Great, let's head upstairs and get you checked in," he said as he led them through a building that, had it been in the States, would have likely been a speakeasy in the 1920s. The pillars, décor, and floor to ceiling mirrors would have fit in a speakeasy or brothel.

"This *isn't* a brothel, right?" asked Charlie, which the man answered with a relaxed laugh.

"No, no," he said as he led them up a short flight of stairs to an open room set up for tattoos and staffed by two women who were also tattooed and smiling. "A lot of our clients are wealthy men from the Middle East. The bossman was tired of them assuming that after a tattoo they could buy one of the girls," he said with a shake of his head as the girls collectively made disgusted faces.

"Eww."

"Exactly," said one of the female tattoo artists.

"Does the sign help?"

"Some of the time. What kind of tattoo did you two want?" one of the artists asked. Charlie explained the two tattoos they'd gotten in Dublin and how they hoped to add to them.

"When were these tattoos done?"

"About three weeks ago," said Tabby embellishing.

---

413. A good sign for a tattoo artist

"Let me see the rib tattoo," asked one of the girls. As Charlie pulled up the edge of her shirt to show her, the girl nodded. "Ok, so lettering here, Louis can do that, since it's not going over any of the skin that's still healing, but," she said, leaning over to get a better look at Tabby's calf tattoo, "this is too fresh to go over. Maybe there's something else we can look at?"

As Tabby and the tattoo artist went into another room connected to the parlor to look over tattoo books, Louis led Charlie back down the stairs to a room on the right that she hadn't noticed on their way up. The walls were covered with hand-drawn art.

"Are these all yours?" she asked, looking around at drawings of mythical beings and a few movie characters she recognized.

"Ya, we were closed a long time for COVID. I had no work at all, so I focused on my art and building my portfolio. Sold some online. The rest serves as ideas for clients."

"They're beautifully done. Great detail," said Charlie as she walked around looking and Louis arranged tools.

"Thank you.[414] What color and font were you thinking?" he asked, sitting down at a computer in the back of the room.

"Hmm, well, I think something softer, and big enough to be read, but small enough to fit all the words."

"Ok, what do you think of this?" he asked. Charlie walked over to the computer screen and saw "The Doors of Perception" stretched across in a lacy font.

"Maybe something less girly?"

"Ok, that was Bradley Hand, how about Chalkduster?"

"Oh, I like that. Will it fit ok?"

"Yep, I'll print up the size I'm thinking and put a temporary printing on your ribs so you can see if you like how it fits."

---

414. Artists always like hearing their work is appreciated

"That sounds great," said Charlie, sitting on the black bed that seemed to be the international standard for tattoo parlors.[415]

As Louis printed the paper, she wondered if Tabby was ok, but since she'd abandoned Tabby in NOT a brothel, and there was no yelling, she assumed Tabby was fine.

"Ok, here it is," said Louis, bringing back the paper for her approval. Charlie loved the look of the tattoo from first sight and quickly settled on a shade of green for the print in order to better match the tones of her Lizard King tattoo.

"I'll add a few gold flecks as decoration to help pull in the color from the crown," he said with a nod, getting out bottles and tubes.

"You can do that?"

"I sure can," he said with a smile.

Charlie lay on her side again and tucked her shirt up, this time having known in advance to remove her bra all together. She braced herself for the pain and settled on a black and red drawing of a rabbit eating something that appeared to be part of a femur. She wasn't sure what had inspired the drawing, but it reminded her of one of her favorite childhood books—*Bunnicula*, where the bunny doesn't actually eat people but is still pretty exciting for an elementary age kid.[416] The book had made her want a bunny her whole life, but Tom had insisted a bunny was not for them. They were a bunny-free household. Charlie lay and breathed through the pain, thinking of her lost childhood bunny experiences and staring at the vampire bunny drawing.

Louis was done in what seemed like minutes, and Charlie was able to breathe freely again as she walked to the mirror to see his work. The lines were impressive—exactly as the drawing appeared.

---

415. It was in fact
416. Howe, James. Bunnicula. Atheneum Books, 1979.

Charlie was in awe, and Louis enjoyed hearing her gush about how perfectly he had matched the colors of her lizard king.

"Why a lizard king?" he asked as he began cleaning up his workstation.

"It's for Jim Morrison, the Lizard King."

"Wasn't that sort of a sexual title for him?"

"With Jim, it's safe to assume most things he said had some sort of sexual connotation," she said with a laugh. He laughed as well and asked if she was a big fan.

"That's actually what brought us to South Africa."

"Really, why's that?" he asked. Charlie told him their vast conspiracy theory while he finished cleaning and disinfecting.

"Huh. I don't really get into conspiracy theories, but you say he had warrants out for his arrest in the States?"

"Ya, and nothing that he would've been extradited over."

"And he had syphilis?"

"Yep, so the public love life wasn't looking like a good idea," she said with a laugh.

"I'd move out of the country and away from the spotlight, too. But how did no one find out? I mean, there was a body."

"Was it his, though?" asked Charlie as she explained that only the common wife and a drug dealer had seen the body and known who Jim was. There was no ID used to identify the body.

"His family didn't see the body?"

"No."

"That's strange," he said, sitting down with Charlie on the sofa by the window that looked out onto the street.

"Well, he and the common wife didn't get along with his parents, so it isn't as sketchy as it sounds. He told the band members that his parents were dead."

"All together there's a lot of suggestive details."

"There are."

"So, how do you go about looking for him in South Africa? Cape Town seems like a good place to start, but where to now?" Charlie explained the search they'd started at Haut Bay. Intrigued, he asked for the list and began looking it over.

"Since it sounds like your friend's tattoo is still going, let's see if we can shorten this list through Facebook."

"Facebook?"

"Sure, Cape Town is a massive city, but it's more likely I have mutual friends with one of these guys than you do."

"Maybe so," said Charlie, holding out the list on her phone as Louis opened his phone to a Facebook account that had 10,000 friends. "That is a lot of Facebook friends."

"I like to make connections with people I've done tattoos on or people who've reached out about tattoos."

"So more of a professional page."

"If you like, but it's also my page, and it's not set to business settings, so we'll have an easier time searching for people."

Louis and Charlie started searching and finding names on Facebook, and confirming birthdates with those who had public birthdates listed. Of course, in that age group, fewer men use Facebook, but many have a profile of some sort set up by themselves or a loved one who is hoping they'll connect with the world on social media.[417] They were able to cross several men off the list by finding condolences and soppy death messages on their Facebook page. While the girls realized Jim could be dead of natural causes at this point, they hoped that the universe would align with this time in their life when they had the means, albeit fraudulently, to find

---

417. In fact, according to research done by AOMU, or the Association of Old Men United, about half of all male seniors have a Facebook account, a statistic that would help Charlie today.

Jim. Several others were crossed off the list because their profile picture had the wrong facial features or skin tone[418] to possibly be Jim. In the end, by the time Tabby came down to check on her, they had the list down to 124 possible men.

"Wow, nice work," said Tabby looking at all the artwork lining the walls.

"You should take that list to the Cape Town Archives," said Louis, standing and heading towards the door to his room, leading the girls back up the stairs to the counter where the other tattoo artist was ringing up their costs.

"Where are those?" asked Tabby as she got out the college card.

"Let me pull it up on my phone, and I will airdrop the link to you," he said as he pulled up the page for the Western Cape Archives. "There," he said as he airdropped the link. "I don't know if you'll find what you need, but maybe you will. It's free, so it's worth a try," he said with an easy grin.

"And you're already here, so might as well give it your best go," said the other artist, who Tabby had apparently also brought into the fold.

"Agreed," said Tabby.

The girls sorted their bill, thanked the artists for their work, and promised to leave reviews before heading out.

"Oh, I didn't see yours," said Charlie. "I got distracted by all the talk of Jim."

"I was wondering if you were going to ask," said Tabby, as she got out her phone. At this point the tattoo was wrapped up and out of sight, but she had taken pictures, of course. The tattoo was a fish, metallic in nature, curving on her left shoulder.

"A fish?"

---

418. While they had limited their list to those who had checked white on their immigration documentation, since there were only two boxes, there were inconsistencies.

"The Salmon of Knowledge."

"The fish of knowledge."

"Salmon."

"Is that the story Cathal told us in the park?"

"Yes, the fish has all the knowledge in the universe, and whoever catches and eats him gets all the knowledge."

"So, in this situation, are you the fish to be eaten? What's going on, I'm confused."

"No, back then, when the story was created, only some people could fight for and achieve knowledge, but now I get to give that knowledge out. Anyone can gain knowledge if they want to. Last names and money don't matter anymore. If you're willing, you can learn."

"And that used to be your job."

"Exactly. This is my hope that I will get to teach again."

"I didn't think you'd miss it that much."

"Neither did I. This is my hope that I'll get back to it some day. How'd your lettering work out?"

Charlie showed Tabby her picture as they made their way back to the underground parking garage. They decided the day had been exciting enough, and they would take Cathal's advice to eat before and after a tattoo. They got in the car and headed back towards Misti Cliffs, finding a pizza place on the way to pick up some takeout. The great thing about travel in the Information Age is everything is available online. Reviews and details such as "can the pizza be ordered to go" are easy to find. The girls had no problem finding a pizza place on the way that had good reviews and to go orders. Charlie got on the phone as Tabby drove, and she ordered a large pizza with mushrooms. When they arrived at the plaza with the pizza place, they found it behind a McDonald's and parked the car.

Charlie went in for the pizza while Tabby walked next door to the grocery store for a few more necessities[419] they'd forgotten in their food delivery.

---

419. Necessities, at times, are things like ice cream

CHAPTER THIRTY

Poor Otis Dead and Gone[420]

The concept of driving is always challenging internationally. There are signs that look like pretzels and railroad signs to Americans, but they appear to have some other basic meaning in the country they're placed in.[421] The girls navigated towards what they were calling home, but through roads and signs that were very foreign to them. Tabby had gotten more lotion for their tattoos and a bit more fruit and tea from the store, so they were ready for a night spent in.

When they pulled into the driveway, the stress of driving went away, and they took their groceries and pizza into the house so they could eat looking out the large windows at the ocean behind them. Charlie grabbed some plates, and they sat to eat the pizza.

"Tabby."

"Yep."

"Thoughts?"

"On life in general?"

"No, on the pizza."

---

420. Krieger, Robby. "Runnin' Blues." The Soft Parade. Elektra Records, 1969.
421. In fact, they do have a meaning, a meaning Americans will never know

"This is the worst pizza I've ever had."

"I mean, I had pizza in Cuba, and it was a world ahead of this one."

"That tracks. Third world nation of oppressed people can still make better Italian food than this."

"Yep."

"Of course, that's setting the bar low."

"Indeed."

"We need to figure out what food South Africans are known for."

"Right?"

"It's definitely not pizza."

"For sure," said Charlie.

"I'll do some research online. That place we had lunch was good."

"It really was. Great shrimp. Great view."

"And a list of Jim possibilities."

"Let's get the list and see if we can make a bit more progress."

The girls spent the rest of the day looking over what was left of the list, researching names on newspapers.com, and planning a tomorrow that would involve a bit of archival research, all while listening to the sound of the waves crashing and enticing them off to bed with open balcony doors to keep listening to the ocean.

When the sun rose in the morning and lit up the ocean to the beautiful turquoise green the girls had loved in Key West, they were both asleep. South African peace and tranquility had lulled them into a rest that they both needed, but eventually they woke up and had breakfast on the patio before walking along the beach[422] and heading towards the archives. The drive out of Misti Cliffs was beginning to be familiar, but the beautiful and oddly shaped mountains around them continued to amaze as they headed back into the city for their archival research.[423] South Africa, after the green of Ireland and the thrills of Paris, was a completely different sort of adventure, like heading to the lion enclosure at the zoo after a day at the mall, only the lions were actually in the wild, and the people were in the enclosure.[424]

When they arrived in the parking lot, they were surprised at the beautiful, modern nature of the building they were approaching.[425] After passing wild baboons in the street, and seeing the villages of huts outside the city, they weren't sure how far the city landscape they'd found yesterday spread out, but Cape Town is indeed a large, beautiful, and successful city full of businesspeople working, as they were in every city the girls had adventured through thus far. They entered through the large glass door and approached the woman at the front desk.[426]

"How may I help you?" she asked.

"We were hoping to do some research in the archives," said Tabby.

"Do you have an appointment?"

"No, do we need one?"

"It's preferred, but the archives are slow today. Can I see your ID?"

---

422. Living along the coast is not very productive, according to the Center for Productivity in Bulgaria
423. Something that excites all academics
424. Actually, the lions were quite far away from Cape Town, unless they had in fact visited the zoo, which they did not
425. Like most Americans, they really had no idea what South Africa was like
426. In every country, there is a person at the front desk

"Yes," said the girls as they got out their passports and handed them over.

"Ok, I'll hold on to these. Leave your bags in the lockers to the right. You are allowed to have pen, paper, and a laptop with you. Documents may not be scanned without first signing forms located at the help desk inside the archives."

Tabby and Charlie nodded, feeling at home in an archive in any country. They thanked the woman and headed back to the lockers where they deposited their bags and went back into the archival rooms. The archive was well organized, so they were able to easily work their way into boxes of information about the men who had immigrated into South Africa from Europe in 1972. As they dug into the boxes, they discovered that what had been digitized and listed as 1972 was actually a combination of 1971 and 1972, and since they only needed dates from Jim's supposed death date in 71 through the end of 72, they felt pretty confident of their chance of success. The work was tedious, but so were their PhD's, so they fell into a rhythm quickly. Within a few hours, they had the list down to thirty men by locating death certificates and those who'd returned to Europe. While they did run the chance of Jim having returned to Europe, or anywhere but the States, they were in South Africa, so that's where they decided to focus their research. When they rose to go, they had a list of names and addresses for all thirty men, although they couldn't be confident the list was up to date.

As they made their way out of the archive and retrieved their belongings from the lockers, they thanked the front desk woman and headed out the glass doors towards their parked rental car.

"So, where do we start?" asked Tabby. The archive had been a no talking zone, so they'd only split the list and worked with no opportunity to discuss their plans.

"Well, this guy Otis on my list is out near the Cape of Good Hope."

"And we did want to go there anyways."

"We did."

"I say we go hike the Cape and then drive by this Otis guy on the way out."

"Sounds like a plan."

The girls put the Cape of Good Hope into their GPS and headed out. The drive was a bit long, but since their research had only taken a few hours, they felt good about fitting in a quick hike, especially after all the sitting they'd just done.

Charlie slept through the entire drive. The windy roads of South Africa had proven to be too much for her stomach, so unlike the rest of their travels, she was living on motion sickness medicine. For Charlie, they got in the car at the archives and then were immediately transported to the Cape of Good Hope. For Tabby, the drive was long and ridden with signs warning about baboons, signs that Charlie woke to see towards the end of the drive.

"Why do we need warnings about baboons?"

"So Americans don't try to hug them?"

"Are they violent?"

"Well, I imagine there are reasons for the signs."

"Maybe South Africans just want to be the only ones who get to hug baboons."

"Yes. That's right. They want to hug all the baboons, so they stop tourists through a long line of scary warning signs."

"Did that one have stick figures being dismembered by a baboon?" asked Charlie.

"I believe it did."

"So maybe we don't hug the baboons."

"Maybe not," said Tabby as she pulled into a parking spot.

They parked and walked out towards the water to see a new view of the ocean. The cliff was high, and the water looked like a deep blue, endless wonder. The girls sat on a bench and looked out over the water for a while. When they were ready, they went in the small building that exists at tourist locations the world round to sell junk to tourists.[427] The tickets were listed in South African money, so they had no idea how much they were paying, but they decided that no matter the cost, they were hiking this cape.[428] They headed back out into the parking lot to find some baboons sitting and looking at the cars right next to the bench where they'd just been.

"Tabby."

"Don't go hug them."

"I won't, but I've got to get a selfie with a baboon. This is a once in a lifetime opportunity."

"I mean, you could've gotten one from the car yesterday, so technically it's your second chance."

"Whatever," said Charlie, laughing as she snuck up as close as she felt comfortable to the baboon.[429] She quickly crouched down and snapped a selfie before running off to join Tabby, who'd had the sense to stay away from the selfie she'd wanted nothing to do with.

The trail was a basic black asphalt path leading up the Cape with a deep drop to the ocean below on their right. The girls were silent as they made their way up the path, smiling at the tourists who came and went as they slowly made their way, snapping pictures of the ocean—the water was the one constant in their trip that had met them as they left Panama City, and again in Clearwater, Key

---

427. Junk you can only get at that location
428. And besides, FSU was actually paying through the P card
429. Which was in fact too close for safety but also not as close as Charlie wanted due to the stick figure she'd seen dismembered on the entrance sign

West, Dublin, and Istanbul. Whether through a pond, a channel, or a bay, or directly the ocean, the water always brought them comfort. They felt at peace[430] as they made their way to the top. Once closer to the top, their breath began to be more labored as Florida girls aren't actually ready for climbing mountains or capes.[431] They stood on the top and looked out at the ocean below. Charlie started explaining the path the explorers took to find a path around Africa and pontificating on the importance of piracy in history, even talking about her own pirate relative, John Whiddon, who'd pirated his way out west to find eternal life.[432] Tabby nodded but ignored Charlie's babbling while she relaxed and looked out at the ocean.

"You know," interrupted Tabby. "I think there's another path over there, down the left side of the Cape," she said as they both looked down the other side of the Cape.

"We have to go."

"That goes without saying."

They made their way down the asphalt path to the point where the small winding dirt path led off down the other side of the cliff.

"Are we sure this is a path?"

"Probably," said Tabby as they started to make their way down the switchbacks and out closer to the tip of the Cape. Tabby looked back at Charlie, who was moving very slowly behind her. "Oh, are you still feeling the motion meds?"

"A bit. The ground is only moving a little," she said as she stopped. The narrow switchback had no guard rails which, as an American, was both freeing and terrifying. Tabby, who had no fear of heights, went back and linked arms with Charlie. Charlie gripped

---

430. But still jobless
431. In fact, one of the largest hills to practice climbing on in Florida, although it is discouraged, is the large garbage dump outside of Miami.
432. He didn't find it, but he did find Indigenous people willing to kill potential colonizers

tight as they made their way both with one foot on the path and one off.

"This is slow going."

"Yes."

"You know who wouldn't be afraid of this?"

"Who?"

"Jim."

"Jim isn't afraid of anything."

"Maybe of fame."

"True. He was willing to fake death to get away from that."

"And don't forget, he was so afraid of singing in front of crowds that in the beginning he'd have to perform with his back to the crowd."

"That's right. If he can overcome his fears, so can we."

"Let's sing 'Hyacinth House'"

"What about 'Tell all the People' starting at the chorus:'Follow me down'?"

"Ok, I'll admit, that's more appropriate."

The girls sang the Doors at the top of their lungs,[433] and eventually, they made their way to an old cement bunker built into the hillside. While the path continued straight on, there was a path of sorts likely made from all the tourists who'd left the actual path to go explore the bunker.

"Are we going?"

"Of course," said Charlie as they let go of each other and started climbing the somewhat grassy path towards the cement bunker.

When they got closer, they could see it was a one-story, small room that opened through window frames that had never been windowed, or the glass was long since gone, and then there was

---

433. Since neither of them is actually good at singing, it's good there was no one else taking the odd path off to the left that looked suspiciously like an animal footpath in a country of dangerous wild animals

a second story, not above, but behind the room and built into the hillside. Likely there used to be stairs, but they were long gone. Charlie charged ahead into the room through a window, ducking to avoid an odd long pipe that stuck out from the building.

"Oh, shit," said Tabby. Charlie turned to find her sitting on the ground holding her head.

"You ok?"

"Hit the pipe. Went all black for a second."

"Dang," said Charlie laughing. "I mean, it's sticking out from the building, how'd you miss it?"

"I know," said Tabby as she got up and made her way carefully through the window.

The two of them walked around the small cement room and looked out onto the water through each of the three windowless windows before climbing up through the hole that used to have stairs and hefting each other up into the second dirt floor story built into the cliff. The second level no longer had a roof, but enough of the walls remained to suggest what the building had been, or appeared to have been, which they decided must've been some sort of watching post during a world war.

"I suppose it would've been important to watch for enemy boats from this location."

"Back before satellites."

"Exactly, and now there's no use for the building," said Charlie as they gazed out to the other side of the Cape.

"Well, I've seen—"

"And felt—"

"Yes, and felt," said Tabby rubbing her head, "enough, so let's head back to the path. I think we can get a closer look if we finish the path, and then we should still have time to head out and find that Otis guy."

"Are we just going to knock on his door?"

"I mean, I think crazy and honest might be better than just crazy," said Tabby as they slid down the dirt wall and into the first room.

"True," said Charlie as she climbed back through the open window frame and headed back to the path.

"Shit," she cried out as she hit her head on the same pipe.

"Doesn't seem so dumb now, does it?" laughed Tabby.

"They really should do something about the pipe."

"I'm pretty sure we're not supposed to be here, so . . ."

"It's kinda our fault."

"At least there were no baboons."

"So, we get to keep our limbs."

"Exactly," said Tabby as they made their way down the final portion of the switchbacks and stood looking out at the lighthouse at the bottom of the path.

Their minds had reached a point where they'd absorbed more beauty in one day than they could contain, like the moment when they'd seen so much art at the Musée Rodin that they couldn't see anymore, so they turned and went back up the hillside. Heading up switchbacks is more work, and yet the fear of falling to death is less going up, so they passed the walk quickly in peace and quiet and headed back to their car, no longer excited to find baboons, but excited to find the drinks they'd left sealed up in their car.[434] They got in and put Otis's address in the GPS. The GPS said the address was only a few minutes away and in the same direction as Misti Cliffs, so from Otis's, unless he was actually Jim, they could head

---

434. For baboon safety

back towards home and rest. After their hike, they'd be ready to lay in bed and listen to the waves crash.

The drive from the Cape was quiet and brown. The hillside was beautifully barren in the way only South Africa can be. The low growing bushes and trees dotted the landscape as they took the short drive towards a cute cement house surrounded by beautiful vineyards and gardens. The front yard was full of cars parked around a large fountain, and people were walking slowly up towards the house.

"I think we got here just in time for a party," said Tabby as she parked the car and started getting out.

"I don't think this is a party," said Charlie pointing to a large banner on the outside of the fence with Otis's name, dates of birth and death, and a picture of a man with darker skin smiling into the camera with a come and get me sort of face.

"Now *that* is a Jim smile, but not a Jim face," said Tabby.

"I'm sorry, dears, are you looking for Jim?" asked a small, old woman bent over a cane behind them. She was wearing a beautiful but casual black dress and a smile, despite her clothes and her reason for going to Otis's house. "This is Otis's house. There's no Jim here."

"I'm sorry, ma'am," said Tabby. "We're looking for Jim Morrison. We think he came to South Africa in the 1970s about the same time as Otis, but under an assumed name."

"Ah, 'the future's uncertain and the end is always near,'" she said with a grin that matched Otis's. "My brother was a big fan of music. Not the Doors, mind you, but of music in general. He used to play in a band, but clearly, we're not Morrisons," she said with a laugh. "Come in, dears. Otis was never one to turn away a visitor, and I will not end his celebration of life by turning away two foreigners," she said, looping her arm in Charlie's and leading them towards the backyard where the girls found a large group of people wearing black, but smiling and laughing.

In the backyard, they found a fire going with a large, black pot positioned carefully above it. The girls weren't sure what was in the pot, but the smell drew them in, as did the music that was playing over a sound speaker. As the woman had said, the music wasn't the Doors, but it was good music. The woman brought them towards a group of younger mourners and introduced them as old friends of Otis's from overseas and left them to their own discussion. The girls sat and talked with the group who quickly welcomed them and gave them bowls of what looked like stew that had chunks of vegetables the girls didn't recognize and a circular bone with meat on the outside of it.

"Here, have some dinner. That's ox tail," said the man who handed them their dishes. "It's called Potjie. Have you had it before?"

"No," they both replied, questioning how brave they felt in that moment.

"Oh, you're going to love it," he said as he handed them each a spoon and an empty glass.

"Red or white? Now, you can't say no, we're all toasting Otis."

"White would be great."

"I'll try red."

Their glasses were filled by a young smiling girl who reminded them of many of their students. They cautiously tried the stew, only to find it to be a medley of all sorts of flavors that shouldn't work together, but somehow did. The stew was warm and comforting, and the oxtail melted off the bone. This was one of the best dishes they'd had since leaving Panama City, and they both helped themselves to more while the South Africans laughed and discussed Otis, and life, always smiling and including Tabby and Charlie where they could.

When the conversation seemed to be happily and deeply enmeshed in old times, the girls took the moment to escape, being sure to wave and thank their hosts for what was actually a great evening, despite the reason for the gathering.

"Well, that was amazing."

"It really was," responded Charlie while they climbed into the car and put Misti Cliffs into the GPS.

"If only all the doors we knock on could be that kind."

"Maybe South Africans are just kind."

"You know, so far that tracks," said Tabby as she drove off into the dark towards home. "Who next?"

"Well, you know that wine region they were talking about," said Charlie, reminding Tabby of the conversation they were listening in on around the fire. "I think there are a few guys off the list in that area."

"So, maybe some wine tasting and door knocking tomorrow?"

"Sounds like a plan to me."

They drove on as Charlie began sorting the digital list of who they would visit next. When they arrived at the Airbnb, they were exhausted and happy. They both went straight to bed, ready to rest and head out for more Jim hunting in the morning.

CHAPTER THIRTY-ONE

This is the End . . . of Our Elaborate Plans[435]

In the morning, they woke up and sat alone on their portions of the balcony, sipping tea and nibbling on toast for a long while, neither one eager to face the day. They'd made it to South Africa, but they were realizing how difficult it would be to find a man who'd disappeared decades ago. Men grow and change over forty-some years. How would they know it was Jim, even if they did find him? After forty years of lying about names and backgrounds, how would they get Jim to out himself, if he was even still alive? The ocean remained constant and comforting as they sat, eventually working their way inside towards showers and a plan. While neither of them was a big drinker, they were finding South Africa to be a place to drink wine. Tabby had read online that one of the wineries on their list was Napoleon's winery. The actual Napoleon.[436] He used to order monthly deliveries and would drink a bottle a day. While they were pretty sure they couldn't each drink a bottle of wine, they were ready to head out and try. When they met in the living room,

---

435. Morrison, Jim. "The End." The Doors. Elektra Records, 1967.
436. Not the dynamite one

they agreed that it would be their first winery. It came with a tour and an explanation of how the winery had been in existence for as long as it had.

As they got into the car, they realized that while they'd argued for years if Jim's eyes were blue, light blue, grey or blue-grey, the eyes were the key to finding Jim—his eye color would be the same. They guessed his ears would be large and in charge, like his dad's had been in old age, but the eye color would be the same.[437] They set out towards Napoleon's winery, as they liked to call it, with a few doors to knock on in that direction. Their list was now down to a third of its original size just by asking questions and searching through archives and the internet, and knocking on Otis's door. They were pretty happy with themselves, despite the slightly discouraging lack of success, and Tabby said so as she drove.[438]

The scenery away from the coast continued to be what they'd seen already—dry, brown, and barren, but in a beautiful way that invited the girls in, leaving them wanting to explore and maybe find more wildlife. The hills were barren more often than they'd imagined, but the wild beauty of the place fit what they knew about Jim. This was a place where one could disappear and have adventures. Real adventures. As they didn't have a lot of hope of heading home, or anywhere else, South Africa became more and more inviting.

"Looks like we're coming up on that town," said Charlie.

"Odd that two of them settled in the same town."

"Maybe they knew each other."

"Maybe," said Tabby as she followed the GPS to a small salon with parking on the street.

---

437. They knew about color contacts but assumed Jim wouldn't use them because, well, that would make finding him nearly impossible
438. The effect of breakfast, ocean views, and wine in their near future

When they got out of the car, they found themselves hoping the salon took walk-ins. They'd found the business registered to the man they were looking for, but hadn't thought, in all that researching, that maybe they might need an appointment. They approached the door, walked into the salon and were struck again by how something in a country as foreign to their own as South Africa could be so different, and yet have amenities that looked so similar to their own. The salon was laid out just like any salon would be at home. There were men and women working at stations and gossiping as hairdressers do apparently on any continent. They approached the black front counter as a smiling young woman with smooth dark skin and curly brown hair greeted them.

"How can I help you ladies? Do you have an appointment?" she asked, smiling and looking at the calendar in front of her.

"No, but we were hoping you might take walk-ins."

"Hmm, well, I can fit one of you in, possibly, depending on what you want done." Tabby stepped aside, indicating that if one of them was going to experiment with South African hairdressers, it wasn't going to be her.

"Well," said Charlie, "I was thinking of a wash and cutting a bunch of this off," she said, stroking her long, brown hair that had gotten pretty disheveled on their trip.

"Really?" said Tabby with her eyes raised.

"It's time for a change."

"I can help you out with that," said the hairdresser as she led Charlie behind the front desk and towards the only empty chair in the salon.

While Charlie made changes, Tabby went out to see if she could find the second man on their list for this town. His name was Edgar, and she felt there couldn't be too many Edgars in one town. In

Dublin, she would've popped in a pub and asked if anyone knew Edgar, but in South Africa she wasn't sure where to go, aside from just knocking on his front door or his place of business. Edgar didn't seem to own a business, so she started walking in the direction of his house. The walk along the sidewalk was quiet as traffic sped by. No baboons came out to greet her, and she was struck again by how similar things could be, like sidewalks, even on the other side of the world. We all need social order, and that order is achieved through traffic rules and sidewalks, apparently. The walk led Tabby into a neighborhood full of small, quaint homes surrounded by waist-high fences and dry little gardens.

She approached the house and found the gate unlocked. She took that as a sign that the owners were open to knocks on their door. The door itself was a strong, wooden door, but the paint around it was peeling and neglected. She knocked and waited as she heard steps and voices heading her way.

"You get the door, Ed. I'm watching my shows," yelled a female voice behind the door, which was answered by loud mumbling she couldn't make out.

"Can I help you?" the voice barked as the door opened. "Oh, hello, I thought you were one of those kids trying to sell me something again."

"Ed, no kids knock on our door," yelled the female voice from inside. "That was in your TV show," she said with an audible eye roll.

"Well, anyways, how can I help you?" he asked with a smile. When Tabby looked at the man, she knew. His eyes were a beautiful color that made her want to get to know him more, and his smile was welcoming, but his left arm that held the door open was his only arm.

"I'm sorry to have bothered you. I'm looking for someone, and I think I'm in the wrong place," said Tabby, trying to sort out how quickly she could back away.

"Now, deary," said the female voice heading her way, "come on in. We don't get many visitors here," said the woman as she came into Tabby's view. She was a short, plump woman with her grey hair in curlers. "Who are you looking for?"

"Jim Morrison," she said, realizing how she sounded but unable to come up with a lie she was willing to tell a cute old couple with a missing arm between them.[439]

"You mean from that band?" asked the woman.

"Yes."

"Well, that's a first," said the man with a laugh.

"We, well, I believe he faked his death and moved to South Africa, and I'm going through a list of men that could possibly be Jim."

"Really, so Jim could be one of our neighbors?"

"No, honey," said the man, "she means me. Don't ya dear?"

"Yes, you see, you moved to South Africa from Europe about the same time he would have."

"And I'm the same age."

"Yes."

"I see it," said the man with a nod. "But I have been missing this since birth," he said holding up what should have been a full arm. "There weren't too many of us that moved from Europe to this area. Things were closer back then. Why don't you come sit on the porch with us and let us see that list of yours."

"Oh, that's a good idea. Like one of our mystery shows. We can help you sort yours," said the woman rubbing her hands together

---

439. With all of their time for discussion, the girls really should have come up with a cover story

in excitement as the three of them sat on the little metal chairs that overlooked the dying garden from the front porch. Tabby pulled her list up on her iPad that she'd fortunately carried in her big leather bag.

"Ok, so we started with a bit over 200 men."

"Were there that many of us?" asked the man in surprise. "Felt like only a few of us foreigners back then. Don't consider myself a foreigner now, mind you, but we certainly stuck out then, didn't we dear?"

"That we did."

The three of them looked over names, and Tabby got to hear the background stories of several of the men on the list who were familiar to the elderly couple. In doing so, she was able to knock a few more off the list based on who didn't have the right back story or eye color. While she was disappointed by not finding Jim, she found it heartening that so many people she spoke with agreed that Jim was out there somewhere, and loved him enough, even decades later, to want to help her find him. When the list was done, she got up to leave and shook their hands in thanks.

"Sorry we couldn't help you more, dearie," said the woman as she toddled back inside towards her shows with a smile and a wave.

"Just keep at it; I'm sure you'll find him," said the man with a pat on Tabby's back as she headed off the porch and back towards Charlie, hoping she'd had better luck so they could be done knocking on doors.

As she approached the salon, Tabby found Charlie surrounded by hairdressers who were all smiling and laughing at something on Charlie's phone.

"Oh, hey, Tabby," said Charlie as she looked up. Her once disheveled mess was now styled better than Tabby would've imagined Charlie getting done in New York City. She was glad to see the laughing was over something on Charlie's phone and not about her hair.[440]

"She was just telling us about your Jim idea," said one of the girls with a laugh.

"They're not into conspiracy theories," said Charlie with a shrug that was met by a series of giggles from the crowd.

"Thanks for the laugh," said one of the girls as they went back to work and Charlie paid. The two of them walked outside, glad to be away from the laughter that continued, and possibly got louder, as they exited the salon.

"So, nothing?" asked Charlie.

"Well, really nice couple. Helped me sort a few names off the list."

"But for sure it wasn't Jim?"

"He was born missing a right arm."

"Oh."

"Any luck here? I'm guessing not," said Tabby as they got back into the rental car.

"Nope. They're all Greek. Came through France, but they've got a strong family history. They claimed they could trace themselves back to Alexander the Great. They're all cousins."

"Seems doubtful, but ok."

"Not Jim anyways."

"Not Jim." So, the girls put Napoleon's winery back in the GPS and headed out on to the highway, out of the city, and back into the wilderness of South Africa.

As they were led by the GPS on the short drive towards the winery, they found themselves entering an open gate to what

---

440. According to hairdressersrus.com, hairdressers often realize the hair style they have created does not in fact look good, but they will not admit or laugh until the client is well out of hearing range, as a matter of policy

appeared to be a several million-dollar estate. The long driveway reminded the girls of the houses in Jane Austin movies. They were grateful the college cards still had room on them because this wasn't the kind of place they could afford lunch, and they were hungry. They parked in the amble parking area[441] that was shaded by large, old trees and surrounded by lawns that were well manicured. They walked towards the entrance of a large, old white building. Inside, the front desk[442] was manned by a woman dressed professionally with her hair and nails done to impress. She welcomed the girls and invited them to purchase tickets for a tour that would start momentarily. They added souvenir glasses to their purchase as well as a gift packaged bottle of the very wine Napoleon himself drank.

When the tour began, the girls were led, along with a few strangers of various nationalities, behind the curtain, so to speak, but behind what was actually just a large glass wall, and then out on to catwalk-type pathways. They heard[443] long explanations of how the wine was made but, as they would always be Florida girls at heart, they mostly noticed the giant spider webs on the walls away from the catwalks and wondered what kind of spiders lived in South Africa. Could they be as venomous as Australian spiders?[444] Eventually, they were led out to a beautiful picnic area with an expansive view of the South African plains and a playground that was close enough for children to be in view but not close enough to be heard.[445] They sat at the table looking out over the view that was both welcoming and strange to them.

---

441. A parking lot worthy of a Dodge Challenger
442. Because all businesses have front desks
443. But did not listen to
444. The logic checks on this consideration
445. Genius placement

"Can I get you started?" asked a tall, lanky waiter dressed in black and holding a platter with glasses of water he started to put in front of the girls. "Maybe something to pair with the wine?"

"I think we picked the wine and chocolate pairing?"

"Oh, very good choice. Would you maybe like something harder to drink along with the wine?"

"Oh, no, we're not really big drinkers."

"Very well, I will have your first pairing out for you shortly," he said with an actual bow.

The girls sat and sipped their water and contemplated their life choices. As far as countries to land in go, this one didn't seem like a bad place to be, and despite the existence of Afrikaans as a language that was completely foreign to them, everyone seemed to speak English. Teaching in the K-12 world wouldn't be too bad. Charlie mentioned such to Tabby who suggested they start on applications when they get back to the house.

"Are you planning on staying in South Africa then?" asked the waiter who had silently appeared and started to set large glasses of wine in front of each of the girls.

"Well, we are looking for Jim Morrison. We think he moved here after he faked his death, but we might apply for jobs and stay."

"Very good. It's a good country to stay in," he said with a half bow and then he leaned over with a silently conspiratorial look on his aging face, "I've always thought Jim faked his death. Any man willing to stick it to the Ed Sullivan show by singing 'higher' even louder after being told the word wasn't allowed is the kind of guy willing to fight any system" he said with a laugh, showing himself to be a real fan. "What is your plan for finding him?" he whispered.

"Well, we have a list of men who immigrated from Europe around the time Jim died."

"Appeared to die."

"Yes."

"Can I see the list?" the waiter asked while looking around before taking a seat. Tabby pulled the list up on her phone and passed it to the waiter.

"Ah, so a few of these are local. I know this one name," he said tapping the screen. "He's not Jim. He's my uncle's long time live-in best friend," he said with a wink.[446] "Can you airdrop this to me?" he asked as he handed the phone back to Tabby and took his phone out. "For the guys in this area, since it's not a metropolitan area, possibly my uncle knew or knows some of them. I can ask in the back, too."

"That would be amazing," said Tabby as she sent the list and the waiter nodded, adding that the first glass of wine should be paired with the first chocolate.

"Ok, first, it would be great to have some local knowledge to knock a few more names off the list—"

"Or to find Jim"

"Or to find Jim. But also, uhm, the first glass goes with the first chocolate, there are five. Are we drinking five glasses?"

"Take it as it comes."

"I'm sure they don't give you *too* much. It's a wine tasting. And look, that table of South Africans seem to be drinking their full glasses," she said, pointing to the lone table of South Africans. The girls sat and sipped their glass of wine and slowly devoured the piece of chocolate it went with. While they weren't savvy enough to know if it did indeed pair with the chocolate, it was the best chocolate they'd had in their lives, so they didn't care.

---

446. South Africa is the only African nation where it is safe to be LGBTQ, but older generations haven't all relaxed enough to come out into the open

When they saw the waiter approaching, they quickly finished their glasses, wanting to enjoy every drop, and thanked him for the second glass. As they sat and watched children playing on the playground,[447] the time passed, and they repeated the pattern of indulging in chocolate and sipping wine, then gulping down the wine when the waiter replaced their glasses with fresh ones. By the time they were sipping the last glass, the winery was the funniest spot they'd visited so far on their trip. The last chocolate was the best (and least remembered), and soon they were being given a gift bag with a boxed bottle of wine[448] and two boxed wine glasses.

"Ladies," said the waiter, coming up behind them as they arose. "I've just airdropped the list back. My uncle knew a few names, or his partner did. I also asked around the kitchen and one man was related to one of the chefs. I think we've cut your list down a bit." The girls laughed in response, and Tabby nearly fell down the hillside, but the waiter caught her by the elbow.

"May I suggest some lunch," he said, pointing in the direction of another building uphill from the parking lot that they hadn't noticed on their way in.

"You know, I think I'm hungry," said Charlie with a laugh.

"Indeed," said the waiter as he helped the girls make their way towards the hill before waving them on while the South African table arose, gathered their children and drove home without a stumble.[449]

The girls laughed, walked, and fell their way up the hill and to the small restaurant.

"I've got to use the bathroom," said Charlie, patting Tabby on the arm while heading to the smaller building marked restrooms on

---

447. Because some parents like to bring their gaggle of small children with them while they drink five glasses of wine with a shot of something else on the side in a thirty-minute period
448. Because they needed more alcohol
449. As South Africans are raised with wine in the bottle, they are able to handle 68.5% more wine in a sitting than Americans, according to studies done by Cape Town College

the left while Tabby nodded and headed to the restaurant. Charlie entered the room designated for women and noted the sign about a view before heading into the stall. The stall was floor to ceiling windows and looked over the hill the girls had just climbed. The toilet provided a seat to sit and use the "Loo with a view," and Charlie, who was too tipsy to care, enjoyed the view before heading to find Tabby laughing with the waiter.

"Guess what."

"What?"

"We don't have to order," she said with a laugh.

"Yes, miss, it's a set menu. I will be right out with your first course. May I suggest a coffee for each of you?" The girls laughed and Charlie apologized profusely. "No worries, miss, we often have Americans visit," he said with a nod as he returned to the kitchen.

While the girls laughed and ate, the waitstaff brought them dish after dish, beginning with soup and scotch quail eggs and ending with a dessert that was more art than dessert. By the time they'd sipped their coffees and eaten dessert, life was less spinny and a bit more focused for Tabby. Charlie, who was living on motion sickness meds and really shouldn't have had wine to begin with, was still laughing. And so, as they sat and finished their second cups of coffee,[450] Tabby looked over the list and explained to Charlie that their list had gotten even smaller. They were left with only three names: two lived in Kalk Bay and one was in another spot that Tabby wasn't sure about.

"Well, three is more than one."

"That it is."

"And I'm not even the math professor."

"Clearly."

---

450. Given the amount of wine they'd consumed, the coffee tasted pretty good

"So, we do three," Charlie said, laughing at her own rhyming skills.

"That we do," said Tabby as she helped Charlie up from her chair and then down to their car in the parking lot, laughing all the way at their own ridiculousness as they went.

The drive home was quiet as Charlie passed out and Tabby was glad for the opportunity to sit and think. When they got home, they made their way inside, and Tabby deposited Charlie in her bed, grateful the alcohol and medicine mix hadn't led to vomit and then went to her own room and out on the balcony to think some more for a while. The list was significantly shorter, but while Charlie seemed optimistic, Tabby, who had a better understanding of statistics, knew their chances of finding Jim had gotten slimmer. Eventually, she went in and went to sleep, contemplating life working and teaching actual children in South Africa.[451]

---

451. The girls had considered their college students to be children, but with this job switch in front of her, Tabby knew the difference between college age students and the ones they would be stuck with in K-12

CHAPTER THIRTY-TWO

The Cars Hiss by My Window Like the Waves Down on the Beach[452]

Mornings in Misti Cliffs are always good. Life seemed shiny when the girls awoke to the sound of waves crashing on a beach in Africa and they got to sit on a balcony sipping tea and watching the waves for the first few moments of the day while they decided if they should wake up. The balcony ran the length of the house, but in the morning hours the girls respected each other's space by sitting only in the chairs in front of their own bedroom doors.

They sat in silence as the time ticked by, and they took turns refilling each other's teacups. Eventually, as lunchtime got closer and hunger kicked in, they decided to talk about what the day should look like.

"So, we head to another Jim door to knock on today."

"Yep."

"This is a bit discouraging."

"A bit."

"Maybe we should apply for jobs or something."

---

452. Morrison, Jim. "Cars Hiss by My Window." L.A. Woman. Elektra Records, 1971.

"We could apply for one or two and then go looking?"

"That would be very adult of us."

"I feel like we have to make plans for some kind of future before we're homeless."

"Which isn't too far off."

"Want to move down to the kitchen table and eat while working on applications?"

"Yes—I noticed last night that Indeed works here, so maybe we can fill out a few applications in the app."

"Sounds good," said Charlie as they packed up and headed downstairs.

Tabby sat down at the table with her iPad in front of her, and Charlie got them both more tea[453] and something to eat as they'd been so relaxed with the ocean view, neither of them had eaten.[454]

"Cookies? So, this is what we've sunk to?" said Tabby as she bit into a chocolate cookie.

"Hey, eggs, flour, dairy—what else could we need?" asked Charlie as she sat down with a cookie and the saltshaker.

"I still can't believe you do that," said Tabby with a shudder of her shoulders as she ate her cookie and tried not to see Charlie sprinkling salt on her chocolate cookie.

"I can't get enough of the salty and sweet combo," she said as she took a bite.

"Didn't your dad get you into that?"

"Yep. One of his many good influences," she said with a laugh.

"Well, salty cookies aside, I found a few applications. I sent some your way on Messenger."

The girls buckled down and sent in some resumes and cover letters with their fingers crossed for job possibilities and life with

---

453. Three-cup tea mornings are the very best of mornings
454. Tea, the one true need in the morning

a roof over their heads. What was left of the morning passed in tediousness as the girls filled in all the boxes on applications and uploaded documents in hopes of being hired.

"When do we stop?"

"Hmm . . . I filled in two so far."

"In an hour?"

"Math not English."

"I filled in five."

"Whatever. Quality not quantity."

"What do you say we get dressed and head out to the guys in Kalk Bay? I think we can see sea lions there."

"Sea lions are cool," said Tabby with her eyebrows raised as she shut off her iPad.

"The first two live close-ish to the harbor, and the third guy is right on the water."

"Lucky guy," said Tabby getting up to leave the view of the ocean.

The girls got dressed and headed out, and in what seemed like no time, they were parking near Harbour House, a restaurant Tabby'd read good reviews for. The parking lot was located in the harbor right next to the water, so the girls had a great view walking into the typical seaside establishment offering fried food and views.[455] The hostess sat them in the back, where they had a solid view of the parking lot, and the girls ordered fried prawns.[456] As they sipped their Diet Cokes and waited for their plates of fried amazement, they double checked the addresses they would need to visit after lunch. The waitress seemed less helpful than ones they'd had in the past, so they didn't ask Jim related questions.

---

455. The paradox of food made quickly so you can leave the view you don't want to leave

456. With much discussion over how English-speaking countries can't decide if the thing is a shrimp or a prawn, or are they actually different species?

When they were done with their fries and prawns, they paid the bill and went out to the harbor because at this point in their adventure, they felt better about their chance of success in finding sea lions than they did about finding Jim. And indeed, sea lions were basically a guarantee in Kalk Bay. As they left the restaurant and headed towards the water, they immediately saw enormously fat sea lions.

"Are they friendly? or will they try to eat me like baboons?"

"I mean, I don't think baboons actually eat people."

"No, but apparently you can't pet them."

"You shouldn't pet these guys either. I think we shouldn't pet any wild animals on the entire continent."

"Even the penguins?"

"Even the penguins," said Tabby as they approached the sea lions.[457]

Sea lions, once seen, are easily left, so the girls headed back to the car and put the first address into their GPS.

"At least these two are pretty close to each other."

"Not as close as that one and the salon."

"No, but still, we should be able to see both and then head to the grocery store for some dinner."

"Have we done McDonald's on this continent?"

"No, but do we have to?"

"We did in Dublin."

"You did, and we didn't in Istanbul."

"We didn't have time, so Istanbul doesn't count."

"You can get McDonald's, but I'm going to get some real food. Maybe some fish."

---

457. Sea lions are 97% easier to take selfies with than baboons, according to the South African tourism development board's Twitter feed

"It's always nice to eat fish when you're sitting along the ocean, and McDonald's does have fish sandwiches."

"But does it here?"

The girls continued to discuss the varieties of McDonald's as they drove towards the first neighborhood, which the GPS reported they would arrive at in seven minutes. The debate over the validity of fish being a part of fast-food fish sandwiches[458] was in full swing when the GPS led them into a small grouping of apartment complexes not far from the highway. The community appeared to be of the sort one would expect to find in a retirement community in the States.[459] Tabby parked the car in the space closest to the building listed on the address.

"So, is there going to be like a front desk or something?"

"What do we say if there is?"

"Could we be journalists from America doing a story on Jim?"

"I mean, people love Jim, but maybe we could go with immigration in South Africa in the '70s?"

"That is just specific and weird enough to be an academic focus. We're journalists from a university."

"Way more sense there. Ya, no one in the New York *Times* readership is interested in immigration patterns of people in Africa fifty years ago."

"But they would be if we find Jim in that group."

"True. You ready?"

The girls got out their pens, notebooks, and glasses, so as to look as scholarly as possible, and headed to the door of the old people's apartment building. In the entranceway, they found a front

---

458. Studies by Ichthyologist International have shown that one in five fast food chains have fish as a main ingredient in their fish sandwiches

459. Of the normal variety, not the STD capital of the nation variety

desk with flowers and a sign that said "Gone to lunch. See Mavis for any questions."

"Mavis? Who's Mavis?" asked Charlie.

"Uhm," said Tabby pointing to a fishbowl on the counter next to the flowers. The fishbowl had plants growing out of it and a large fish inside with a badge leaning against the bowl that read "MAVIS."

"So, it's a joke."

"Ya, I think it is."

"Who are you here to see?" asked a voice to their left. They turned and saw a little old man hunched over a walker and sitting on an old red chair, his glasses slipping down his nose. What was left of the hair on his head was wafting in an unseen breeze they hoped came from a hidden air-conditioning vent.

"Uhm, we're looking for Pierre DuPont," said Tabby.

"Well, come on in. There's no one working the desk. Never is. That's why we added Mavis. She watches over us," said the man waving them over. "My name is Sam. Have a seat," he said pointing at the chairs near him. The girls sat down with some hesitation lessened by the high cuteness level of the old man.[460] "Now, Pierre died last week, but maybe I can help you? I've been living here for longer than most."

"Oh," said Charlie "I'm sorry."

"Don't be. We all die, and most of us in here die sooner than those of you out there," he said with a laugh. "Here, have some candy. It's South African. My daughter brings it so people will sit and talk to me."

"So, you sit in the lobby a lot then?" asked Tabby as she reached for a candy, glad they were individually wrapped and thus had some hope of sanitation.

---

460. The movie Up did a lot to increase engagement with little old men.

"All day. Get to see a lot sitting in here. I feed Mavis every day, too."

"You knew Pierre?"

"As much as one can know anyone," he said with a laugh, "and I saw them wheel him out on one of those gurney things just last week. He was all bagged up," he said with an eerie laugh. The girls were unsure how to respond.

"So, you knew him," Charlie repeated.

"Indeed, I did," he said with a nod. "What can I help you with?" he said with a slightly toothless grin that still somehow beamed joy from all points of his face.

"We are academics from Florida State University researching immigration patterns from the 1970s."

"Really? Interesting," he said with a nod and a smile. "And Pierre immigrated."

"Yes, we were hoping to hear more of his story, where he came from, why here, did he move alone . . ."

"Oh, no. Pierre came with his wife and his two siblings."

"He did?"

"He loved to talk about his siblings. A brother and a sister, I think. The one was his twin. Not sure which. The siblings died a few years back. They were living on the third floor. The three of them were close. Really close."

"Interesting. And they were all able to get visas together," said Tabby, trying to add in some official sounding questions for legitimacy.

"Well, those sorts of questions you'd have to ask his wife."

"Does she still live here?"

"No, she had to move down the road. She needed more care than this building has, as you can see," he said with a wave of his left arm towards Mavis. "Once we reach that point, they move us over a few buildings to the full-service model."

"Oh, ok."

"Do you have a business card? I can get a card over to her if you want."

"No, the questions really were for Pierre, and we'll need to remove him from our study now."

"No females on that list? His wife immigrated with him, you know."

"No, it's a very focused group," said Charlie, "but I'm realizing the second man on our list may be in this same group of apartment buildings."

"What's his name, dear?" said the man, leaning forward on his walker.

"Gregor."

"Does he have a last name?"

"He does, but it's, well,"

"Yes,"

"Shitov."

"Gregor Shitov?"

"Yes."

"Shitov," he said with a laugh. "Well, I'd remember a name like that, and I don't, so I can't say I've met him," he said with a laugh.

"You've been very helpful," said Tabby rising, "but we better keep moving with our interviews."

"Good luck," he said with a laugh, "right, Mavis?"

His laugh continued as the girls waved and walked back out towards the rental car. The car was nothing special to look at, but Charlie found it comforting to drive because it was nothing special. They could park it in any space and not worry if someone might ding their car.[461] That peace made her almost[462] happy to be done with the Challenger. Once they got back into the car, Tabby pulled out her phone to set up the GPS directions.

"So, Gregor."

"Old shitty it is," she said with a sigh. "Hey," she said, looking at her phone. "I got an email from a school; they're looking for an interview. Said they'd be interested in me starting as soon as possible, depending on the interview."

"Really?" said Charlie.

"Really," said Tabby as Charlie got out her phone and found a similar email.[463] "So how do we respond?"

"Well, we have no other job prospects, we're almost out of money, and we committed fraud to get here."

"Yep."

"And we're in a country that's unlikely to extradite us over such a small amount of fraud."

"So, we have to take these interviews."

"We do."

"Mine has a link to schedule."

"Mine, too."

The girls clicked their individual links, glad that since they taught different subjects, they wouldn't be competing against each other. While they hadn't grown up hoping to move to South Africa, they were thankful for a country that seemed to be welcoming them in. Even if they didn't find Jim.

"Done, and I got a confirmation email with a list of documents to bring with."

---

461. A constant worry with Baby
462. Almost
463. Turns out schools on many continents are desperate for teachers as small children are terrifying to work with universally.

"This list suggests we might get hired immediately."

"That it does," said Tabby. "Well, the schools are near Misti Cliffs. Maybe the house has openings, and we could stay for a bit while we apartment shop."

"Hopefully we can find an apartment soon. The house is eating up what's left on our cards."

"That it is. Well, I paid for a second week last night, so we have it until a few days after the interview." The girls agreed that was a good start and headed out to find Shitov.

The drive was short, and Charlie was thankful because she'd decided both to eat a fried lunch and not to use motion sickness medicine.[464] They arrived at a building essentially a few doors down and got out, a bit more confident in the friendliness of older South Africans as they approached the front door of what they'd decided was truly a retirement home building. Behind the door they found the front desk staffed by a teenager who seemed a bit young to be at a front desk anywhere.

"Hi, we're looking for Gregor Shitov."

"Ah, old shitty. I think he's down by the hot tub," said the young boy nodding in the general direction of the hot tub room without looking up from his phone.

"More helpful than Mavis," said Charlie as they walked towards the door next to the "Hot Tub" sign.

"Barely," said Tabby as she held the door open for Charlie.

Behind the door they found a large hot tub full of elderly women laughing. There were at least eight of them crammed into the hot tub, which was large, but it was still a stretch for the amount of people in it at the moment.

"This is giving a bit of the Villages vibe."

---

464. A deadly combination

"It is," said Tabby nervously. "We can do this."

"Yes, but we can't do that," said Charlie, pointing at the sole man in the hot tub.

"Apparently, there's a line for that," said Tabby with a laugh as they walked towards the tub.

"Hello, we're looking for Gregor Shitov."

"I'm Gregor, what can I help you ladies with," he said with a wink, which was surprising given his advanced age and the level of wrinkling around his eyes. This was a man who clearly didn't believe in anti-aging cream, but judging by the group of ladies he had surrounding him, he wasn't in need of anti-aging anything.

"Hi, we're researchers from Florida State University, and we're conducting a research project on immigration from France to South Africa in the 1970s," said Tabby. Gregor laughed.

"And Florida State sent you all the way here to interview me," he said, raising one eyebrow and laughing again. "Come now, ladies. Don't try to con a conman," he said, sounding like he was quoting a movie as he got out of the hot tub and thankfully wrapped his large, hairy stomach up with a robe.

"Sir, we are both professors from Florida State."

"And you're here why?" he said, waving towards some chairs that were thankfully dry.[465]

"Listen," said Charlie, aware their lie wasn't going to be believed. "We are here trying to prove that Jim Morrison is alive."

"Didn't he die in the seventies?" said Gregor as he sat down. The older women in the hot tub had resorted to grouping together and whispering while watching the girls sitting and talking with Gregor, who appeared to be used to having a fan club.

"We don't think he did."

---

465. And thus no slightly naked elderly rear had recently sat on it

"Why not," he said as he grabbed a few peanuts from the bowl of nuts in the center of the table. His large ears nodded up and down while he chewed and his thick brown and grey eyebrows seemed furrowed in concentration as he listened to the girls. They saw why the older women liked him. He had an easy laugh, and when he listened, he really listened.

"Well, you know, he had a warrant out for his arrest when he died."

"Warrants. I get that. What was his for?"

"Public indecency in a concert."

"I imagine that wasn't hard to get charged with in that era in the United States," Gregor said as he leaned back in his chair.

"Well," said Tabby, "there were thousands of pictures at that concert and not one person had a picture of an actual exposure."

"Sounds questionable."

"The Florida courts erased the warrant a few years ago."

"A sort of come back Jim note," he said with a laugh. "Ok, I can see why a guy might run from a warrant, especially with the kind of money that he had. What else do you have?"

"He'd been asking to get out of the band for a while."

"The band was him and some musicians that couldn't make it without him," Gregor said as he ate a few more peanuts.

"Exactly. They didn't want him to go," said Tabby.

"And he had syphilis, so he was wanting out of the rock and roll lifestyle. He wanted to focus on his poetry."

"I see," he said nodding.

"And when he died, only his common-law wife was with him."

"And she would stand to inherit his fortune?"

"She was supposed to, yes," said Tabby.

"Ok, and what happened next," questioned Gregor.

"Well, he died and no one else who knew him saw the body except for his drug dealer."

"And then he was buried in a cemetery foreigners aren't allowed to be buried in."

"A decision I'm sure they regretted," Gregor said with a laugh. "What about his family?"

"Well, he was estranged from his family."

"All of them?"

"Yes, when he joined the band, he told them his parents were dead."

"That's harsh," nodded Gregor who seemed to be calculating over his bowl of nuts.

"And his sister said in an interview after his death that the rumors of his faked death were difficult for her because she thought he would fake his own death. That was something she could see him doing."

"I can see why someone, such as myself, would want to immigrate to South Africa in the seventies, but for Jim, why Africa?" Gregor asked, leaning in towards the girls, his elbows on the table, fully absorbed in the conversation.

"Well, he had this idol you see," said Charlie as she gave the explanation they'd given countless times on the trip, and Tabby interrupted to talk about lyrics she thought suggested Africa.

"I see," Gregor said with a nod. "This story makes more sense than a Florida university wanting to research why someone like me would want to move to South Africa," he said with his deep belly laugh.[466]

"Apparently."

---

466. According to Physiologyrus.com, big stomachs produce larger and louder laughter

"You thought maybe I was Jim," he laughed again, "and then my Russian accent, which still lingers after all these years, disappointed you." The girls nodded. "Well, I thought I saw disappointment in your eyes, and that's not something I'm used to seeing," he said with another wink. "I would like to say that I am Jim, but let me tell you my immigration story, since you've come here to ask it. In mother Russia there is a compulsory draft. Everyone serves. We are all ostensively eager to serve the mother country. Well, the Russian army was doing some shitty things, even for a Shitov. I was estranged from my family, and I couldn't support what my government was doing, so I left. There were some underground churches willing to help get me to France. Churches there supported me and offered name changes, but I knew what Jim knew, and maybe what you know, as well—South Africa had better things to focus on than exporting one little Shitov. So, I came on forged documents with my own name and you two ladies are the first ones to ever come looking for me based on my immigration," he said with a laugh.

"So, you aren't Jim."

"And you already knew that."

"Yes," they both said, heads hanging a bit.

"Smart of you to check with immigration. Although, I suppose he could have left France and immigrated from anywhere. He had the money."

"That's the thing; his money got tied up in a legal battle. His parents sued for the estate."

"So, difficult to get money, unless he'd been prepared with a large amount of cash."

"But how much would he need to relocate in Europe undetected?"

"So, coming from France makes sense."

"It does."

"How many are left on your list?"

"One."

"One?" he said with a laugh. "Well, I hope he's Jim, but if not, best of luck to you ladies either way," Gregor said as he rose, dropped his robe on his chair, and headed back to the group of ladies waiting for him in the hot tub.

And with that note, Tabby and Charlie headed back to the car, a bit discouraged. Curiosity and tiredness won out in the end, and they made plans to grab McDonald's before heading home, and then to knock on one last door tomorrow.

CHAPTER THIRTY-THREE

Looking for a New Ship[467]

McDonald's are like airports—they're basically all the same in every nation. Some are worse, some are better, but they're all McDonald's, just like all airports are airports. The girls brought their food home and sat and ate looking out in the dark at where they knew the waves they heard were crashing on the beach. They'd both scheduled interviews, and they'd sorted online what they would need to legally stay in South Africa. This wasn't where they thought their lives would take them, but they'd decided to take it as it comes, and this is where life brought them. They had one more man left on their list, so they went to bed hopeful, but mostly discouraged. After all the names they'd crossed off for death, the possibility that Jim had come here and his drug lifestyle hadn't led him to death a bit earlier than others seemed unlikely. But, they would get up in the morning and knock on one last door.

They went to bed with their balcony doors open so they could listen to the ocean and, as was their habit in this new beach lifestyle, they slept in fairly late and then sat and sipped tea on their balconies before getting ready to head to Boulder's Beach. Fortunately for the

---

467. Morrison, Jim. "Ship of Fools." Morrison Hotel/Hard Rock Cafe. Elektra Records, 1970.

girls, the last man lived right next to the best place to see penguins in Cape Town. Unfortunately for them, their stomachs weren't feeling well. By the time they'd both run from the balcony to the bathroom twice, they felt it was time to admit that something was wrong. While Tabby blamed McDonald's, Charlie reminded her of all the stress and fast food they'd had over the last few weeks, not to mention the travel. They stayed home and rested a while, and in the end they both took some medicine from Tabby's bag of pills and decided that they should be good for at least a few hours. With water bottles in hand, they made their way to the car, deciding not to eat out this time, but just to knock on the door and come back to rest. This would mean they would have time to know for sure before going into their job interviews if they'd found Jim. Not that it would matter, given their predicament, but it felt good to have some finality.

Boulder's Beach was easy to find and park at with their GPS, and once they'd parked, they found several local artisans selling goods on the path towards penguins.[468] Since they were card-only at this point, with no cash to their names, they passed all the little carvings and paintings but stood and watched a group of South Africans singing for a while. They were dressed in what the girls assumed were traditional clothing. The all-male group sang and danced, and the girls enjoyed the show for as long as their guilt over not tipping the group allowed them to. As they made their way down the sidewalk towards Boulder's Beach and the last house, they felt peace lessened by the stress of stomach cramps. The last house for them was on the right-hand side directly across from the

---

468. South Africans are aware of the draw of penguins for tourists.

entrance to penguin heaven. They opened the gate that led to some narrow steps up to a small cottage on the little hill. The front porch had a beautiful view of the ocean, though it was not as quiet as their Misti Cliffs rental.

The girls knocked on the door but heard no reply. Whoever lived here was not at home. They sat on the steps for a few minutes[469] before heading down to the beach. Boulder's Beach thankfully had a bathroom and beyond that, it had boardwalks weaving through the low trees and out to the ocean. All along the board walk and under the trees were little penguin families going about their days. They had holes and little shelters and many of them weren't phased by the steady stream of tourists. While the boardwalk gave a zoo-like feel, this was a refuge, and the birds had the ability to leave at any point. The girls were amazed at how stinkingly adorable[470] these birds were. They clearly had little families, which the girls had read, but seeing them cling to their partners and section off from the pack with their loved ones was really something else. Even in nature there is a need to have a good friend or a partner. They wove their way down the boardwalk, taking pictures as they went,[471] until the boardwalk ended out on the beach. Penguins were clearly visible playing in the sand and the waves. It really was a penguin paradise, and the girls stood and watched them play and let the time pass.

"Hey, is that a guy down there on a lawn chair next to the boardwalk?"

"Looks like there's a little path to get down there?" Tabby said in a questioning tone; the girls decided to go that way and see if they could get closer to the penguins. There wasn't a gate on the

---

469. Due to stomach cramps
470. And just plain smelly
471. While they generally took only a few pictures, penguins presented genuine cuteness that required photographing

boardwalk, but the man had clearly walked around the boardwalk and set his lawn chair out on the beach in plain view of the tourists. He sat in his chair with his button up shirt unbuttoned and his grey hair flapping in the wind, except for the portions tucked behind his enormous old man ears. His eyes were hidden behind dark sunglasses, but even from their vantage point, he looked hungover.

"Is he feeding the penguins?"

"Who would do that?" asked Charlie.

"Hey, the sign says not to feed the penguins," Tabby yelled out in her best teacher voice.[472]

"I don't read Afrikaans," the man yelled back without looking or stopping. Instead, he put his empty can of sardines back in a bag at his feet and opened a second can to continue feeding the birds who seemed to know him as they gathered around him and took the canned fish from his hands.[473]

"At least he isn't littering," said Tabby with a sigh.

"Oh, he's there every day," said a voice to their right. The girls turned to see an employee of the penguin refuge shaking her head.

"And I recycle to," he said, apparently hearing them but not turning to see them.

"So, he's local, and he can get away with it?"

"I don't know where he's from, but he's lived across the street for as long as I've been working here."

"How long have you been working here?"

"Six months."

"That's not all that helpful."

---

472. Teachers have the power to shut down all kinds of shenanigans in public with their teacher voice powers
473. According to Taylor Knickerbocker, Lead Aquarist at Aquamoon, penguins should not be fed canned sardines, even if the penguins tell you otherwise. Canned fish are not healthy for penguins.

"I suppose not, but there seems to be an agreement that we ignore him," she said as she went back to work.[474]

"Should we go talk to him?" asked Charlie, looking around and realizing that no one would be there to stop them.

"No, you shouldn't," said the man as he opened his third can of sardines.

"Let's go," said Tabby as she crawled between the fence boards and started walking towards the man who clearly didn't want to be bothered.

"Excuse me," said Charlie. "We're researchers from Florida State University, and we're looking to speak with men who moved to South Africa from France in the 1970s."

"And these men, they all want to speak with you?"

"Well, a lot of them have been dead."

"Dying to meet you I suppose."

"Something like that."

"You live across the street?" Charlie asked. The man nodded as he scooped more sardines out for the penguins now surrounding his chair. "And you moved from France in the '70s?"

"What is the point of this 'research' you're doing?"

Tabby saw the man would not be bullshitted. "We're looking for Jim Morrison. We think he faked his death and moved to Africa."

"Did he now. And you think he would want to be found?"

"No, I imagine he wouldn't want to be found."

"So, why are you looking for him?" he questioned and took off his glasses, revealing blue-grey eyes that still held a draw of attraction even in what must have been his early eighties.

"To know we're right."

---

474. Work with penguins is the very noblest of professions .

"It's important for you to know you're right then, is it?"[475] he asked as he packed up his empty cans and patted a few penguins on the head. While the girls were pretty certain the penguins would not be pet by them, or anyone else, they seemed to share a bond with this man.

"We're researchers, it's what we do."

"Some things are best left unknown," he said with a nod. "When the music's over, turn out the lights, don't go around with a flashlight looking for it," he said as he took up his chair and headed back up the hill and around the boardwalk back in the direction of the house that the girls had knocked on earlier.

"Ladies, you can't be in there," said the woman they'd spoken with earlier.

"So, it really is a privilege just for one," Tabby mumbled under her breathe as they made their way back on to the boardwalk, offered apologies, and decided to listen to their stomachs and head back to the car. It was time for them to go home and rest.

"Do you think that was Jim?"

"I mean, the eyes were right."

"And the attitude," said Tabby with a laugh as she sat down in the driver's seat.

"So, what do we do now?"

"Nothing. We won't know if that was him. He could be an ornery old man messing with us."

"He did seem the type."

"Or he could be Jim."

"His accent wasn't placeable."

"No, but a European who moved here decades ago would have a weird accent."

---

475. Academics have to know they're right at all times

"As would an American."

"True."

"Well, we have our first maybe. We may have to let it rest at that."

While the girls wouldn't normally be able to leave a stone unturned, their stomachs led them more than any kind of lack of determination. After all, they were apparently going to be living in South Africa, and this man frequented the same beach enough to have made friends with a colony of birds. Surely, they could find him again. But as they drove off, they wondered if they should. He seemed the sort to mislead. If he wasn't Jim, he might keep going with misdirects. If he was Jim, he might keep going with misdirects. And if he was Jim, didn't he deserve to rest and live out his days on the beach, giving junk food to birds? They pushed the decision on down the road and went straight home to rest and take more stomach medicine, which they had left at home in Misti Cliffs.

CHAPTER THIRTY-FOUR

My Knees Got Weak[476]

In the morning, the girls sat on the enclosed porch looking over the endless line of waves coming and going on the beach. Jim's voice played over the bluetooth speaker, and they sipped their tea. They'd made it to South Africa and not found what they'd wanted to find, or not conclusively, but they'd had a great trip. They had interviews lined up to teach in South Africa. They'd read that retirement visas weren't hard for Americans to get for South Africa, but with the little they had left on the college cards, they wouldn't be ready to retire. They'd scheduled appointments with the consul in Cape Town to get visas, assuming they were offered employment, and they were glad they took the advice of Tabby's tattoo artist to see about teaching full-time at the K-12 level, something they had sworn off entirely, but well, hunger and fear of homelessness makes one open for all kinds of work.[477] They weren't eager for it, though, and the ocean was so calming, they sat a while longer. As they sat, a soft drizzle started to come down, bringing more peace and reason for sitting and watching the waves over hot tea.

---

476. Krieger, Robby. "Love Me Two Times." Strange Days. Elektra Records, 1967.
477. Thus the entire prostitution industry is explained

"Tabby."

"Yep."

"It's raining."

"Yep. I see that."

"And we're in Africa."

"Very observative of you."

"I blessed the rains down in Africa,"[478] Charlie started to sing in a loud voice as she got up and danced. "Come on, let's go," she yelled as she moved out the sliding door onto the porch.

"Of course," said Tabby with a sigh.

As the girls ran on the thick sand of South Africa, their feet barely touching the cold waves just starting to warm as the nation moved into their backwards summer, the drizzle came down on them, and they sang. They didn't know what would come next, but they had each other, and they had music. With that and the hope that their degrees could finally lead to some kind of full-time employment, even if it wasn't the employment that they wanted, they felt peace in knowing there was a possible path forward. Jim had at least led them to a nation that would let them stay, and it was one that they could afford to stay in with the income they could possibly earn, which is better than they had living in Florida.

"Tabby."

"Ya," said Tabby as they stopped dancing and moved back towards the house.

"Is that a person up there on the driveway? Between our house and the one over there?"

"Shit. I think that is someone. Do you have your phone?"

"No, but who would I even call? I mean, do you know the South African version of 911?"

---

478. Paich, David. "Africa." Toto IV. Columbia Records, 1982.

"No, but that's a guy up there, and he seems like he's coming down here."

"I could call the Airbnb host."

"If you had your phone on you."

"Right."

"He's waving."

"Well, we've had polite thievery already, we couldn't possibly have polite murder on the same trip, right?"

"I mean, the way this trip's been going," said Tabby with a shrug.

Charlie waved back, and the figure started walking towards them. As he got closer, she heard Tabby breathe in quickly, and in that second Charlie realized she knew that tall outline, and if there were any doubts, the messy brown hair tied up at the back of his head took those doubts away.

"Is it?"

"I think it is."

"How?"

"I said we weren't feeling well last night. He asked if he could send soup."

"You've been texting him?"

"Well," and so the girls continued walking up the beach as their favorite Irishman came walking down.

"Ladies," he said, but he stepped forward towards Tabby only.

"You came."

"I did. Is that ok?"

"I mean, it's not bad," said Tabby in response.

"Listen, I know you two have options, what with your education and all, but I came to make a pitch. I can't move here. My life is in Ireland. My baby is in Ireland."

"You came without her?"

"Well, she doesn't like to travel, and she's a bit large for the plane, so she's with Rob."

"Ah," said the girls in unison.

"I understand you can't move back to Florida."

"Not without having to pay back nearly twenty thousand between us," said Charlie.

"So, not sure if you remember this, or if he told you, but Rob's sister teaches at Dublin City University."

"Can't say he mentioned that," said Tabby.

"His sister's girlfriend is the Consul General in Miami. Rob and I talked to his sister, who got her girlfriend on the phone. Turns out there's work at DCU. If you want it."

"Can we do that?" asked Charlie, realizing one of them needed to be practical.

"The Consul General says yes, and the university is a bit desperate as one of their history professors quit without warning, so the visa and the interim position could be sorted rather quickly."

"One job?" asked Charlie.

"One job," he said, looking at Tabby

"In the history department?"

"History, yes," said Cathal, his eyes locking with Tabby's. "There's only one way for you to come," he said to Tabby as he got on one knee in front of her. "I've been alone since my accident. It's been a long year. I'm awkward, I know it. My life moving forward isn't what it was behind me, and I want to make the best of it. I can do that with you. I finally found the most beautiful woman, and she's like me. I can't pass you up. I can't let you go. You are my wild love, and if you will say yes, I will love you until the heavens stop the rain," he said as the rain drizzled on around him.

"How will we live? Do you work?" said Tabby, holding his hands, wanting to say yes, but her practical nature always holding her back.

"I don't work anymore."

"Oh."

"My dad owned those buildings we were in."

"Buildings," said Charlie, an emphasis on the plural.

"The ones that have the tattoo parlor?" asked Tabby

"And Faction next door."

"Oh."

"And the tea shop."

"Now that makes some sense," said Charlie with a laugh as Cathal hung his head as if the money he was revealing he had was somehow embarrassing.

"So, you don't work?"

"Not now, but sometimes I help at the tattoo shop or the music shop."

"Or the tea shop."

"Or the ice cream shop?"

"No, I don't own that building."

"Bummer."

"So, we could come with you? Both of us?"

"Yes, and we could be married and live in my apartment in Temple Bar. Charlie, I think the one above Faction is open or will be soon." Charlie smiled, glad to see her friend happy, glad they could be together, and overjoyed at the thought of returning to Ireland and working at a college level institution. No more K-12 hellish employment for her.

"Yes."

"Yes—you mean, yes?"

"I mean yes," said Tabby, looking down at Cathal and holding his arms a bit tighter.

"Fantastic," he said as he rose to his feet and pulled Tabby into his arms. While they didn't know the ins and outs of their trip back, or what life would look like moving forward, they knew it would be grand, and they would be together. They had a few more nights in their South African Airbnb to revisit their penguin feeding friend[479] and then they would head to Ireland. Tom would come to visit, and they'd all be in Dublin. Could it really be that simple? Well, according to Mr. Holly, it's so easy[480] to fall in love.[481]

---

479. The girls will stay true to their determination to tell no one if they found Jim.
480. So dog gone easy
481. Holly, Buddy and Norman Petty. "It's So Easy." Brunswick, 1958.

End Note

Thank you for making it this far into my rambling madness. First, I want to address the possibility that Jim himself may have somehow stumbled on this book and read it. Jim, if you are out there, send me a note, and I will keep your secret.

For every one else who has made it this far and yet is not the one and only Jim Morrison, please do this author a huge favor, and leave a review on Amazon or Goodreads. If you feel so inclined, mention in your review what your favorite part of Charlie and Tabby's journey was.

Thank you again for your support. See you on the next road trip . . .

Two Friends on a Worldwide Search for the Lizard King

www.ingramcontent.com/pod-product-compliance
Lightning Source LLC
Chambersburg PA
CBHW022145010726
47493CB00002B/340